A BO
IN TH
LAK

BOOKS BY GRAHAM SMITH

Death in the Lakes

A BODY
IN THE
LAKES

bookouture

Published by Bookouture in 2019

An imprint of StoryFire Ltd.

Carmelite House
50 Victoria Embankment
London EC4Y 0DZ

www.bookouture.com

ISBN: 978-1-78681-839-3
eBook ISBN: 978-1-78681-838-6

For Daniel. A young man who is a constant source of pride.

CHAPTER ONE

DC Beth Young's drive to Lake Ullswater would have been enjoyable had she not been travelling to a grisly task at the location where a body had been dumped.

Copper beeches stood out from other trees, their leaves turned a deep burgundy by the morning sun, and there were hydrangeas, lilacs and azaleas in bloom in the gardens she passed, which provided a colourful alternative to the uniform green of the grasses and trees lining the road. Even the roadside hedgerows had patches of colour as the hawthorn hedges sprouted a myriad of small white flowers.

The drive was uneventful with only a minor delay behind a tractor that turned off the road after a mile. It was only as she neared the crime scene that Beth started to get what her mother would describe as a 'fey feeling'.

A scatter of emergency service vehicles lined the lake side of the A592. At each end of the procession a uniformed constable was directing traffic along the narrow road. Worst of all was the line of press vehicles that had formed. Beth counted three different news crews as she drove past them, before parking behind the last emergency vehicle.

A series of forensic stepping plates led to a low wall that was missing sections where neglect and bad driving had taken effect. Beth's boss, DI Zoe O'Dowd, was standing with a uniformed sergeant; when she saw Beth approach, she pointed at the stepping plates.

'Go see what Hewson's got.'

Once she was clad in a paper forensic suit Beth stepped over the remnants of the wall and onto a new stepping plate. Instead of tarmac, there was long grass here. The lakeside trees and bushes sent branches out meaning she had to press through them on her way to the screens that had been erected to prevent the press telephoto lenses getting shots of the body.

Beth skirted one of the screens and announced her arrival to the pathologist.

'I'll be done in five minutes, DC Protégé, I'd appreciate it if you stood there and waited for me to finish before you try and get the information Dowdy O'Dowd wants. While you're waiting, you may examine that which you can see.'

Despite the sombreness of the situation, Beth could feel a smile forming on her lips. Dr Hewson and O'Dowd had a long-running battle that masked the fact their working relationship was based on mutual respect.

She was glad of the chance to take in the scene as she always liked to draw her own conclusions rather than read the reports of other officers.

The naked body Hewson was crouched over belonged to an elderly lady. The legs were riddled with varicose veins that were a deep blue and what she could see of the woman's bald head was covered with liver spots. In repose her face had smoothed out a lot of the finer wrinkles, but the crow's feet radiating out from her eyes spoke of a long life.

Hewson moved to one side, allowing Beth to get a clearer look at the woman's puckered mouth and yellow-brown teeth.

Beth guessed the woman had been a heavy smoker and that she'd had a hard life. The signs of hardship were etched into her face. Even in death she looked forlorn, as if the daily struggle was too much to bear.

The woman's limbs were thin to the point that Beth wondered if she'd been malnourished. The skin on her arms seemed to hang off bones rather than sheath muscle, and when Beth looked at the skin a little closer it appeared to have the same translucence as tracing paper.

Hewson rose to his feet and stood on a footpad beside the body.

Now she could see all of the woman, Beth took in more of the same: a flaccid chest and stomach topped a pubic mound devoid of so much as a whisper of hair. As Beth's eyes traversed the body, she was looking for signs of injury: a knife wound, or bruising. There was no sign of any blood, although Beth could see a darkening of flesh on the parts of the woman's body where it was in contact with the ground. That was normal; a body's blood sank to the lowest point in death, and this lividity told Beth the woman had lain as she was since being dumped here.

There was always a possibility the woman had wandered out from her home and ended up here, but even as frail as she looked, the night had been warm and Beth didn't believe she'd died from exposure.

The clincher to this theory was the light bruising around the woman's throat. In one so frail, it might be expected there would be significant bruising, but if, as Beth suspected, the marks on the woman's throat were from her killer strangling her, the skin would stop bruising as soon as her heart stopped beating.

Beth lifted her eyes and took in the surrounding area. Tranquil was the best word she could think of to describe it. The morning sun glittered across the dappled surface of Lake Ullswater, and on the fells at the opposite side of the lake a flock of sheep was grazing, completely unaware of the terrible scene unfolding around Beth.

Hewson touched her elbow. 'Your thoughts?'

'It doesn't look good. From what I can judge, it looks to be murder. Would I be right in saying that cause of death is strangulation?'

'It would appear so, but until I get her onto my table, I can't be sure.'

Beth grimaced in distaste at what her next question must be. Whenever a woman's body was found naked, one of the first things to cross an investigator's mind was the possibility the woman had been raped before being murdered.

'I'm guessing you'll say the same if I ask you if she's been raped.'

'My first conclusions are that she hasn't been raped, as there are no signs of blood around her vagina; however that doesn't mean it didn't happen. As she was naked when she was found...' Hewson trailed off and gave his head a sideways tilt.

He didn't need to say anything more. Beth knew where his sentence was going.

'Speaking of post-mortems, please tell me that you'll be on with hers this morning, or at least this afternoon.'

'As luck would have it, I have nothing scheduled in for today, so as soon as the photographer is finished his job and the CSI boys have done their bit, we can get her back to Carlisle and I can take a proper look at her.' Hewson took a draw on his e-cigarette and blew out a thick cloud of vapour that smelled of melon. 'You're a smart lass, but you've overlooked something. Take another look at our victim and tell me what you see that's wrong. Describe what you see if it helps.'

Beth didn't know what she'd missed so she gave the elderly lady another slow scan.

'She's thin, frail to the point of being malnourished. The way the skin is hanging off her bones, I'd guess that she's been ill recently and the fact she's got no hair makes me wonder if she had cancer and had received chemotherapy.'

'Now you're getting there.' Hewson let the twinkle in his eye creep into his voice. 'Judging by the extent of her rigor mortis, I'd say she's only been dead a few hours. However, when I tucked a thermometer into her armpit, her core temperature was higher than it should be. I know last night was a warm night, but even so, her temperature should have been several degrees lower.'

'What are you getting at?'

Beth knew from her training the usual method of taking a body's temperature was rectal thermometer, but Hewson had foregone that to use the victim's armpit. Knowing how meticulous the pathologist was, she worked out that he wasn't taking any chances that he might contaminate any evidence. *Does he really think she'd been raped?*

'I'd say she was running a fever when she was strangled, and not just a cold or flu, but something more serious. The way her skin has thinned to become almost translucent backs up your suggestion of cancer. There are bruises on her arms that are synonymous with intravenous drips that also support this theory. Whether the chemo was successful or not, I cannot say, but my guess would be that it wasn't.'

'Wow. The poor woman.'

'Indeed.' Hewson nodded towards the road. 'You might want to speak to the CSI team. When I got here, they were doing their bit, and I have to say, they seemed to have an awful lot of evidence bags.'

'Thanks for the tip. Please let us know when you're doing the post-mortem; I want to be there.'

Beth turned and made her way back to the road, the forensic oversuit rustling with every step she took. She could see O'Dowd was talking with a group of officers and from the expression on the DI's face, she could tell she wasn't in one of her sunnier moods. Rather than risk bearing the brunt of the DI's ire, she went to speak with the lead CSI technician.

CHAPTER TWO

The CSI boss was a taciturn man who never spoke unless spoken to first. Even then he was monosyllabic with most of his answers. In lighter moments, Beth had joked with the rest of the team that the guy's heroes were probably Clint Eastwood and Charlie Chaplin.

Beth knew that being businesslike never worked with him as he just told them he'd email the results from the lab. The man, however, did think he was something of a stud and he was vain enough to fall for a little flattery and charm.

She walked over to him with a wide smile on her face. 'Dr Hewson tells me you found a lot of things you thought worthy of collecting. I know you'll probably have to discard half of it, but is there anything I should be getting excited about?'

'One or two bits.'

This was a good start. He was receptive to her and although non-committal so far, he'd given her a way she could prise some information from him.

'Excellent. Would you care to tell me about them?' Beth hated herself for doing it, but she wound a strand of hair that had come loose from her ponytail around one of her fingers. She'd never liked playing on her looks, as doing so was false, but she'd caught the glances the guy had given her and knew he was a receptive audience. 'My DI is on the warpath and I could use any help you can give me.'

'We got a few bits and pieces. Two of which should give you a suspect.'

'Really? What are they?'

'An invitation to a party and a credit card.' The CSI man reached into the evidence box at the back of the van and pulled out two bags, which he held out to Beth. 'Here, have a look for yourself.'

Beth took the two bags and examined them with great care. The first held the invitation. It wasn't named but it invited the bearer to attend the mayor of Carlisle's annual Christmas ball. The date of the ball was the 17th December, but there was no year.

When Beth turned her attention to the credit card she heard herself gasp. This wasn't an ordinary credit card, it was a platinum American Express card. A signifier of extreme wealth. The name on the card was 'Derek Forster'. Beth knew from news reports that the charismatic mayor of Carlisle was a former businessman called Derek Forster.

'This is fantastic; what else did you get?'

'We got a swab of something from her vagina. Might be semen.'

'You're wonderful.' Until the CSI man smiled at her Beth thought she'd overdone the flattery. 'How soon until you can get the DNA results back to us?'

'Twenty-four hours minimum. Maybe more, you know how it is.'

Beth got what he meant at once. Any DNA samples found in Cumbria were sent to a privately owned lab in Lancashire. As the lab dealt with all the DNA samples from the whole of the north of England, there was every possibility that their samples wouldn't get tested for a few days.

As always, with this kind of thing, queues could be jumped if there was sufficient coercion from the brass, or a financial incentive to prioritise their sample ahead of others. It all boiled down to how busy they were and how much pressure could be exerted on them. Beth was sure O'Dowd would get whoever was available from the senior brass to speak to the lab, but it galled her that they wouldn't get the results as quickly as she wanted them.

She left the CSI man and went to see O'Dowd as the DI was pocketing her phone.

'Well, what did you get then?'

Beth recounted what she'd learned from Hewson and the CSI. To plant a seed in O'Dowd's mind, she mentioned her hopes that one of the senior officers would speak to the lab.

'I'm not a bloody imbecile, Beth. I'll remember to speak to the chief super without your half-arsed amateur psychology.'

'Ma'am.' Beth waited until she could see O'Dowd had calmed a little. 'Dr Hewson says he'll be doing the post-mortem as soon as the body is returned to Cumberland Infirmary. I think I should be there, to see what he finds.'

'I agree. While you're at it, get that lateral brain of yours to do its stuff. We need to catch this guy before he kills again.'

Beth nodded at O'Dowd and wandered off to collect her thoughts. The DI's comment about her lateral brain was testament to Beth's love of puzzles. She liked nothing better than a riddle or conundrum to solve and found that her position in Cumbria's police force, working in the Force Major Investigation Team – or FMIT – gave her plenty of fodder.

A paramedic was loitering at the side of a stationary ambulance. With the victim deceased there was nothing for him or his partner to do, but they couldn't be released until O'Dowd gave the order.

She'd met him a few times before. He was good at his job and had a calm manner that radiated to all around him.

'Hey, Beth.' He waved her over.

'What is it?' Beth let her eyes dart to his name badge. 'Ethan' was his name. 'I'm not being rude, but I'm kind of busy here.'

'Yeah, I know. It's just that I may be able to help you out.'

'How?'

Ethan didn't speak. He just looked at her with a disarming smile. When his eyes settled on the scar decorating her left cheek they held a hint of pity tinged with anger.

'Come on, Ethan. Spill it.'

'Couple of years ago I was called out to a similar thing. A young lass was dumped on Rockcliffe Marsh. She'd been murdered and was left naked. I'm not sure, but I don't think her killer was ever found. I certainly never heard about anyone getting done for it.'

'Thanks.' Beth's mind whirled as she wondered if the two women were connected in any way. 'Do you remember her name?'

'Harriet something.' Ethan's face creased in thought. 'I think her surname began with a "Q" but I can't remember what it was.'

Beth knew it'd be easy to identify the unfortunate Harriet and learn all the details. There weren't that many murders in Cumbria, but if the cases were linked, it could mean there was a serial killer operating in the county.

She looked at Ethan and returned his smile. 'Thanks again. That may turn out to be really important.'

'No problem. There's something else you should also know.'

Beth couldn't keep the eagerness from her voice; Ethan had already given her one great lead. 'What is it?'

His smile widened. 'When you're pretending to flirt with the CSI guy, don't keep looking over his shoulder. It makes you seem false.'

'What do you know about flirting?' Even as the words left her mouth, Beth could feel her face reddening. 'That was me showing him a professional courtesy while maintaining an observation of the surrounding area.'

'I'd believe the last part of your statement if your cheeks weren't scarlet. And with regards to your question on what I know about flirting, well, meet me for dinner tonight and I'll show you what I know.'

'Dinner?' Normally Beth would have laughed at Ethan's cheeky approach, but she was conscious of the body not thirty feet away. 'I've just picked up a murder case. Dinner will be a sandwich at my desk if I'm lucky.'

'Fair enough, some other time maybe.'

Ethan's casual acceptance of her excuse for not having dinner stirred something in Beth. 'I should be able to make it to the Crown for a drink around nine.'

'See you there.'

As she swapped numbers with him then bade her goodbyes, Beth tried to work out why she'd agreed to meet Ethan. Sure he was good-looking, and she had a gut feeling that he was decent, but agreeing to a date while investigating a murder was something she'd never thought she would do.

CHAPTER THREE

The FMIT office wasn't the biggest room in Carleton Hall, but at least there was enough space for all four members to have a desk of their own.

Beth rubbed her forehead and broke from the case to think about Ethan for a moment. She knew she should be focussed, but the look he'd given her earlier had stayed with her.

She knew a lot of people considered her to be attractive, and she'd even modelled in her teenage years until she was old enough to join the police. As such, Beth was used to admiring glances, yet it was only on rare occasions she felt herself being assessed with such scrutiny.

The scar on her left cheek slowed a lot of men, but Ethan had glossed over it and had let his desire for her show in his eyes.

She'd been an innocent bystander when a fight had broken out in a Carlisle pub. One of the fighters had thrust a broken bottle at his opponent and the bottle had been deflected away from its intended target. Her cheek had stopped the jagged base of the bottle and, despite a surgeon's best efforts, her left cheek was a mess of scar tissue.

Beth pushed Ethan out of her mind. She might not even turn up tonight: the case was everything; it had to be. If that elderly lady had been killed, she deserved to have her murderer jailed.

The office was quiet as Beth went over what she knew. The two pieces of evidence linked to the mayor of Carlisle were incriminating, to say the least, but there was still work to be done. The invitation and credit card that had been found pointed a finger of blame at the mayor, but Beth knew a good lawyer would explain them away without even breaking a sweat. They'd both be taken away for analysis, including fingerprinting, and, with luck, they'd get a solid lead from them. The mayor would make a good suspect if it could be believed that a rich and charismatic man would be responsible for murdering an elderly and cancer-stricken lady.

If they could ascertain the woman's identity, they'd be able to take a huge step forward. They'd be able to look for links between her and the mayor to back up what may be viewed as circumstantial evidence.

As a precaution against making an incorrect assumption, Beth accessed HOLMES, the Home Office Large Major Enquiry System and ran the details of the case to see if there were any similar cases in the area. This would be the surest way to find out the details of Harriet Q.

Murders always had happened and always would happen, but the age and health of the victim had Beth wondering if there was something else afoot. The victim didn't fit into any of the high-risk categories, and if she'd been euthanised by a family member, it was unlikely they'd have dumped her naked body beside a lake.

She bent forward as her computer screen flashed up its results.

The lady who'd been found this morning wasn't the first naked woman's body to be found in the Lake District. Three other women had been found in the same way and none of their killers had been identified.

Christine Peterson had been holidaying in the Lakes five years ago when she'd disappeared, only for her naked body to turn up a day later. The same had happened with Joanne Armstrong eighteen months after. The final known victim was Harriet Quantrell who'd not returned home from a night out with friends in Carlisle and had been found near the Solway Firth four days later. This last murder was a month short of two years ago.

All three women had shown signs of vaginal and anal rape, and they had all died via strangulation.

That they'd all been killed by the same person was a logical conclusion, but what concerned Beth most of all was that each investigation had been more or less dropped due to a lack of evidence.

What amazed her, was that no one had connected the murders. Yes, they might be spaced over a period spanning almost five years, but to her mind it was obvious that there was a serial rapist and murderer at work.

As she examined each case in more detail, Beth found small reasons why the connection hadn't been made, but collectively the reasons spoke of a failure rather than negligence.

Christine Peterson's body had been found on a beach near Barrow, whereas Joanne Armstrong had turned up in a wood on the banks of Lake Buttermere. Harriet Quantrell's body was dumped on Rockcliffe Marsh, which lies near the border of Scotland and between the points where the mouths of the rivers Eden and Esk join the Solway Firth.

In terms of geography, the three deposition sites were at the south, middle and north of Cumbria. Each location was isolated and serviced by a different police station. It was possible that the investigating officers never looked for other victims, but to Beth's mind, the seriousness of the respective deaths should have compelled them to check HOLMES and other police databases for similar crimes as a matter of course.

The Barrow cops deserved a free pass as their victim was the first, or at least the first in Cumbria, but the teams from Workington and Carlisle should have picked up that there was a serial rapist and murderer operating in the area.

All three victims had shown signs of having been sluiced down before being abandoned. Where there was a distinction between them was in their ages.

Christine Peterson had been a sixty-two-year-old woman with grandchildren; Joanne Armstrong was a mid-thirties singleton, and Harriet Quantrell was in her early twenties and was engaged, with a daughter who was six weeks old at the time of her death.

The pictures attached to their files showed three vastly different women. Without being judgemental, Beth saw that Harriet was pretty, but obese, Joanne was stick thin and not blessed by the gods of beauty. Christine's face was lined with age, but it was clear that she was a handsome woman.

Together they were thin, fat, old, young, pretty and ugly. Which meant the rapist either had no preference, or was an opportunist who seized whichever female he could to satisfy his twisted desires.

The toxicology reports on the three victims showed them clear of illegal substances, but Harriet's blood had had sufficient alcohol content for her to have been three times the drink-drive limit. To Beth's mind, that tallied with Harriet having been taken after a night out. She may have been drunk enough to make a bad judgement call which would have made it easier for her killer to abduct her. Both Christine's and Joanne's blood had tested negative for alcohol, but that didn't mean a lot. A gun or knife could have been used, and if the victims had been fed a date-rape drug such as Rohypnol or GHB, there was a chance the small amount they'd been given to make them compliant had dissipated from the body before they'd died.

Beth realised that she was thinking of the women by their Christian names and knew that was because she was getting drawn into their lives and was caring for them.

The more she thought about it, the more she grew angry about the system failure which had allowed the rapes and murders to go unconnected until she'd stumbled across them thanks to Ethan's tip. It was bad enough that two different teams had failed to connect their cases to a previous one, but at a regional level, the chief superintendent, deputy chief constable or even the chief constable himself should have picked up on the connection between the three unsolved rapes and murders.

As ridiculous as the idea seemed to Beth, she couldn't help but wonder if there was an element of collusion going on. If the mayor was involved, he was a wealthy and powerful man who travelled in the same social circles as the top brass. They might well be members of the same golf club or masonic lodge.

Beth scrubbed the train of thought from her mind. Senior cops didn't cover up murders for anyone, regardless of their status in life. If they were guilty of anything, it was a negligence of duty or incompetence rather than subterfuge.

The point still remained that they'd missed it though.

Whichever way she looked at it, the case was likely to explode in the face of everyone involved in it.

Beth was rising from her seat to go and share her discovery when O'Dowd burst into the room trailed by DS Thompson. Their demeanour was enough to inform Beth that something else in the case had broken.

'Ma'am, you're not going to believe what I've found.'

'Wait your turn.' O'Dowd flapped a piece of paper towards Beth. 'Here, read this and tell me what you think. It arrived this morning.'

Beth took the paper from O'Dowd and looked at it. It was a photocopy of an anonymous letter. Like ransom notes from old films about kidnappings, the letter was made up of newspaper clippings. It had one simple line of text:

Mayor Forster has killed and raped before and will do so again.

'Well, what do you think?' It was Thompson who spoke. His tone gruff and insistent as was his way. His wife had early-onset Alzheimer's and was extremely frail. He might think he was coping with her illness and the conclusion it would bring, but he wasn't.

He was snappier than usual and there were times he'd adopt a vacant look as his thoughts drifted to his wife. 'Come on, Young Beth, what do you think?'

'Coincidence. Foreknowledge. Scared.'

'Do you want to elaborate?' O'Dowd lifted an eyebrow.

Beth flushed as she was again betrayed by her habit of blurting out random words while her thoughts kaleidoscoped.

'This letter arrived today, which means it must have been posted on Friday or Saturday. Therefore it's a huge coincidence that a letter implicating the mayor arrives here on the same day a body is found and there are two pieces of evidence beside it pointing at the mayor. That also speaks of foreknowledge to me. Did the person who sent the letter know about the murder before it happened? If the mayor is a killer, the person who sent the letter must be scared of him. He's a rich and powerful man. It'll be tough to pin a charge on him without hard evidence. They'll be terrified that if they are identified as his accuser they'll be killed.' Beth gave O'Dowd a look. 'I have a few questions, ma'am.'

'I thought you might. Ask away.'

'The envelope the letter came in, did it have a postmark, and if so what was the date it was sent and where was it sent from? Also, has the letter been sent to the lab for fingerprinting? Can they get a DNA sample of saliva from the stamp? Who was the letter addressed to?'

'It has a Carlisle postmark and it was actually posted a fortnight ago. The original letter and the envelope are on their way to the lab now.' O'Dowd pulled a face. 'The envelope had a printed label with the chief constable's name on and it was marked "private and confidential".'

That the letter was addressed to the chief constable explained why it had lain unopened for almost a fortnight. He'd been on annual leave, and had only returned to duty today. Had the letter been opened the day it arrived, they might have started looking into the mayor and the allegations against him. If the mayor was a killer, he might have been identified as one and charged, or at the very least, he would have been aware of the police interest in him, and would not have dared risk killing another woman. Either way, the lady found at the side of Lake Ullswater may have still been alive.

Once Professional Standards learned of how the letter had lain unopened on the chief constable's desk for at least ten days, there would be an investigation into the reasons and blame would be allocated.

Thompson rubbed at his chin with more force than was necessary to scratch an itch. 'You wanted to tell us something when we came into the office. What was it?'

'When I was attending the scene at Lake Ullswater this morning, I spoke to a paramedic. He told me he'd attended a similar deposition site, even gave me a name for the victim.'

'And?' O'Dowd planted her hands on the desk and leaned towards Beth. 'What have you found?'

Beth explained to Thompson and O'Dowd about Harriet Quantrell, Christine Peterson and Joanne Armstrong.

'Shit.' O'Dowd looked back and forth between Beth and Thompson. 'I hope one of you two has a bright idea.'

'Actually, ma'am, there's more—'

'More victims? Please tell me there aren't any more victims. Four is more than enough.'

Beth didn't bother to hide her irritation at O'Dowd's interruption. 'Not victims, connections to the mayor. Harriet Quantrell had done a short internship for him three years ago when he was deputy mayor, and when I checked out the other two victims, I saw a newspaper report that placed the mayor in Barrow at the time Christine Peterson was killed.'

'What about the other woman? Was he anywhere near her when she disappeared?'

Beth shook her head. 'I couldn't find anything online, but it's only an hour away from where he lives in Carlisle to the place her car was abandoned, so I don't think we need to worry about whether or not he was in the area.'

'We're going to have to arrest him.' O'Dowd huffed out a long breath and looked at Thompson. 'I'll let the DCI know what we're doing; you get a few uniforms organised and we'll get on the road to Carlisle in ten minutes.'

Thompson gave his chin another vigorous scrubbing. 'You sure that's wise?'

'What? Arresting the mayor? No I don't think it's wise, but I do think it's necessary.'

'No. I meant freezing Young Beth out of the pickup. She's done all the legwork here and it's only fair that she's there to make the collar.'

O'Dowd gave Beth a stern look. 'You up for this? Two women arresting a possible serial rapist and murderer.'

'Definitely, ma'am.'

As she waited for O'Dowd to return from the DCI's office, Beth tried to work out if Thompson was acting out of generosity or self-preservation. If they were wrong about the mayor's involvement in the killings, there could be the kind of fallout that stalled careers.

CHAPTER FOUR

When Beth started out her police career, she never imagined that she'd have to arrest a mayor. Yet there she was, standing on the step of a Georgian house on Stanwix Bank in Carlisle. She was glad O'Dowd was with her, although the DI looked to be as reluctant as she was. While duty had to be done, this case was as toxic as they came. They'd had a lecture from both the chief super and their DCI before leaving their office at Carleton Hall.

O'Dowd had tried without success to wriggle out of the case. The mayor was a handsome, charismatic man who claimed his word was his bond, and he'd fought to deliver on every one of his election promises. Where some mayors donned the robes for ceremonial duties only, Derek Forster strove to improve the lives of others. A self-made man, he'd built up a tech business which he'd sold so he could concentrate on his mayoral duties.

If the evidence against Mayor Forster was substantiated, proving his guilt would shock the county's residents, and if they were false, the team investigating him would become hated for maligning the reputation of a popular and benevolent man.

Beth knew she should feel reassured that O'Dowd was with her, but the DI's blunt manner didn't fill her with confidence. If words were weapons, O'Dowd would always choose a broadsword over a scalpel.

When O'Dowd's finger pressed on the doorbell, Beth felt her mouth dry up even more than it already was. Her tongue felt like a burst pillow and she could feel beads of sweat trickling down her back that had nothing to do with the morning sun.

As befitted his status and personal wealth, Mayor Forster's house was imposing without being flash. From where she was standing, Beth could see both Rickerby and Bitts Parks and the River Eden. As views went, it was among the best in the city.

The door creaked open to reveal a handsome man in his fifties. Beth hadn't expected the mayor to answer his own door, but she knew she shouldn't have been surprised that he had showed the ordinary touch, which he capitalised on at all times.

'Good morning, ladies, how may I help you?'

The mayor's voice was layered with Carlisle's relaxed drawl, but his mannerly greeting and gentle smile added a level of class that was absent from the local accent.

O'Dowd lifted her warrant card so the mayor could see it. 'DI O'Dowd and DC Young. We're here because we need to talk to you about a number of cases we're investigating.'

Forster's smile slipped from his face, and the way he took a half step back made Beth think he was going to slam the door in their faces and dash through the house so he could escape via a rear exit.

She was wrong. Instead of slamming the door he pulled it wide open and stood to one side.

'Then I think it's only right that I invite you in.'

Beth followed O'Dowd as the mayor led them to his kitchen. The house had been decorated with taste, and while original features such as picture rails and decorative cornices remained, the house had an element of contemporary styling to it.

When they entered the kitchen there was the same mix of traditional and modern. A red Aga was surrounded by granite worktops laden with a variety of cooking gadgets.

Either Forster was a keen cook, or he was a gadget freak. When researching him before leaving Carleton Hall, Beth had learned that the mayor was unmarried and he wasn't currently in a public relationship.

'Can I offer either of you a coffee?'

Maybe it was the man's manners, or his relaxed attitude to the fact he had two detectives turn up at his door to question him that jangled Beth's internal alarms, but she could tell that they were either on the wildest of goose chases, or they were about to take down a serial rapist and murderer.

'Mr Mayor.' O'Dowd waited until Forster looked her way before continuing. 'In the course of our investigations, we have received intelligence and have evidence that leads us to believe that you may have raped and murdered three women over a five-year period and that you have recently killed a fourth woman. At this time it isn't known if this fourth victim was also raped. Out of respect for your position in the community, we've not come mob-handed, but there are several officers stationed around your house who're listening to us on an open channel.' O'Dowd tapped the radio in her hand to emphasise her point.

Beth knew O'Dowd was uneasy about the risk they were taking if Forster was the killer, and she applauded the way she'd warned him against taking any aggressive action.

'This is preposterous. I have done no such thing.' Forster's head gave violent shakes as he denied the allegations. 'I wouldn't. I'm not a rapist, nor a killer. It's not me you're looking for. Look, you must know I didn't do it. I understand you have to go through the motions, but believe me, I'll do whatever it takes to prove my innocence.'

'It's not as simple as that, Mr Mayor. I have to arrest you and we will have to impound all of your computers, phones and tablets as part of our investigation. Derek Forster, I am arresting you on suspicion of…'

Beth tuned out as O'Dowd read the shocked mayor his rights. Her focus was on the second part of his denial. The mayor was under the assumption that he'd be allowed to assist in the proving of his innocence. That he'd be able to sit and explain what they found and his whereabouts at the time of the assaults. He was only half right. He'd be able to answer their questions, but not in a comfortable office or his showroom kitchen: he'd be sitting across a table from them in an interview room.

O'Dowd lifted her radio and gave the instruction to proceed.

Beth went to greet the team who'd take Forster to Durranhill Station. Once the mayor was gone, another team would collect his phone, computer and any other communication devices he possessed. Another team would enter his chambers at the council offices and remove any hardware he had there. Digital Forensics would analyse everything and find anything which might implicate or exonerate the mayor.

As Beth returned to the kitchen, O'Dowd was pulling out her handcuffs. 'Would you like to leave via the back door, Mr Mayor?'

'Absolutely not. I have nothing to hide and will not skulk around like a common criminal. I shall leave via the front door so the world can judge me and find me innocent. Do not worry, Inspector, I know you are doing your job; and for the thoughtful consideration you've shown me, I bear you no malice.' Beth felt the mayor's eyes bore into hers. 'Nor you, my dear.'

Those last four words and the look in his eyes chilled Beth. In that one exchange she'd witnessed another side to the genial bon-homie the mayor presented to the world. His look had been that of a predator assessing its next meal. She had no idea how things would play out from here, but she was confident the connections she'd found between the mayor and the four victims would help them secure a conviction.

'Right, Beth. Off you go to the hospital.'

Before leaving Carleton Hall, O'Dowd had suggested Beth bring her own car as Forster's house was only a mile from Cumberland Infirmary, and she wanted Beth to attend the post-mortem of the unknown victim.

As she walked to her car, Beth tried to brace herself for the grisly task ahead of her.

CHAPTER FIVE

Beth marched along the hospital corridor. As she eased to a walk, seeing Hewson emerge from his office, she still had some last traces of music rattling her brain.

Pop music and the latest dance tunes weren't something she listened to much any more, not since she discovered eighties hair metal. Bands like Poison, Def Leppard and Bon Jovi were what she listened to now when she wanted to relax her brain and give it a chance to run free. Their music was fast and upbeat, it gave her an energising buzz that left her invigorated.

When she wanted something more enduring, she'd listen to heavier rock music like AC/DC, Guns N' Roses or Metallica. Her journey from Carleton Hall to Forster's house then the hop to Cumberland Infirmary had seen her select *Appetite for Destruction* on her iPod.

Guns N' Roses' anger-fuelled debut album not only matched her mood, it was ideal music to crank loud and drive fast to. She'd sung alongside Axl Rose and had rejoiced in the way Slash could always make the hairs on her arms stand up with the opening riff from 'Sweet Child O' Mine'.

Now she was out of the car and the world was silent by comparison, she was trawling her brain to see what, if anything, had been shaken loose.

There was the kernel of an idea, but it wasn't developed yet, and she didn't want to pursue it until she had more facts.

Hewson threw a side nod her way. 'C'mon then. Let's do what we have to do.'

As they walked to the pathology suite, Beth put a smear of VapoRub onto her top lip to combat the nauseous smells she knew were coming.

'I'm going to start by giving this lady a non-invasive examination. If I'm right with my thinking, you want two key questions answered: Has she been raped? And was she strangled?'

'As always, you're on the same page as I am.'

Hewson gave a curt nod as he reached up and took hold of an X-ray machine on a mechanical arm that reminded Beth of the anglepoise lamp her mother used for reading. Now that the pathologist was beside the stainless steel table he was all business.

Beth watched as he directed the nozzle of the machine to the woman's throat, placed an X-ray plate underneath her neck and then waved at Beth to join him behind a glass screen. He took images from three different positions, changing the plates after each one.

Once he'd taken the images, he peeled the metallic film from the plates and fed them into a lightbox attached to one wall.

'Hmmm.' Hewson pursed his lips and walked back to the table. 'The hyoid bone is intact, but the bruising on the throat indicates asphyxiation as do her bloodshot eyes.' He flicked his eyes towards Beth. 'Don't worry. I'll be able to establish from testing her muscle tissue if she died of strangulation; although considering how the cancer has ravaged her body, it's possible her heart gave out before she died from lack of oxygen.'

When Hewson opened a cabinet drawer and pulled out a speculum, Beth retreated to the head end of the table.

As much as she wanted to know whether or not the victim had been raped, she felt the woman was due some respect and consideration. She wouldn't learn anything more by gawping over Hewson's shoulder than she would from standing by the woman's head.

Hewson bent to his task and Beth tried not think of what he was doing.

In this room, he was the solver of medical mysteries and the cracker of cases. His findings would implicate criminals and point the finger of blame at misdiagnoses. How the man kept a spring in his step and a general air of affable bonhomie had been beyond her until she realised that, like her, Hewson was driven to solve puzzles. For him the mystery would be everything, and as long as he had one to solve, he'd be able to disassociate himself from the horrific nature of his work.

'DC Protégé, I think we have a problem.'

'What do you mean?'

'This woman wasn't raped, as such. From what I can tell, she has been penetrated both vaginally and anally, but not by a human being.'

Beth didn't follow what the doctor was getting at, so she raised an eyebrow and rolled her hand so he'd continue.

'She has internal injuries that go deep inside her. She also has significant tearing which is synonymous with violent, forced intercourse, but it's one of the worst I've ever seen. And I'm afraid it happened post-mortem.'

Beth nodded rather than spoke in case the anger that was washing over her was given a voice. All thoughts of the earlier jests she'd shared with Hewson had been driven away by the knowledge of what had happened to the woman on the table.

She had been strangled and had then had something pushed into her orifices to give the impression she had been raped. The object in question didn't matter, but Hewson shared his opinion that it was most likely a sex toy of some description. If that wasn't a terrible enough fate, she'd been dumped by the side of the lake as if her life had meant nothing.

Her life as she'd known it may have been over the moment the doctor had given her the news about her cancer, yet some cruel, vindictive pervert had stolen her last hours and then defiled her corpse.

A knock snapped Beth's head towards the door as a man in a checked shirt and cords walked in and headed straight towards the table. 'Morning. This your victim?' The man stood at the side of the table and looked down at the woman. His eyes closed and his jaw set as he dealt with the death in front of him. 'That is Felicia Evans. She was a patient of mine. If you need me to sign anything to verify her identification, you know where my office is.'

Felicia's doctor strode to the door. Beth dashed after him. He'd known Felicia, dealt with her and seen her at what would have been her lowest moments.

'Wait up, Doctor. I have a couple of questions for you.'

'You'd better be quick. I have the parents of a six-year-old girl waiting for me to give them her biopsy results.'

Something in the doctor's eyes told Beth the parents weren't going to hear the news they'd surely have been praying for.

She understood what he was going through. As the bearer of bad news, you found yourself torn between wanting to procrastinate so you never had to say the words that don't want to be heard, and wanting to get the horrible experience over with as soon as possible so that you can pass the terrible burden on to someone else.

'You obviously knew Felicia Evans to some degree, what was she like as a person?'

The doctor pulled a face. 'She was tough. She faced her diagnosis without shedding a tear.'

'I sense there's a "but" missing from what you've just said.'

'Is it that obvious?' He splayed his fingers as he spread his arms wide. 'I don't want to speak ill of the dead and all that. She was a difficult woman to deal with. Very forthright with her opinions, and her opinions were generally that there was only her way to do anything. She gave the nurses a rough time and when the hospital chaplain visited her she sent him away with a flea in his ear.'

'Sounds like she was quite a character. Do you know if she had any visitors? Family members, or friends perhaps?'

'Not a soul. I suggested she bring someone to accompany her when she had her chemo, but she told me she neither needed nor wanted anyone to hold her hand.'

Beth thanked the doctor and left him to his unenviable task of passing on the biopsy results to the girl's family. Now that she had this information, the idea she'd had earlier was starting to develop into a more recognisable shape and it wasn't pleasant whichever way she looked at it.

Beth bade Hewson goodbye and set off for Durranhill Station. Not only would O'Dowd want an update, but the mayor would need to be interviewed.

CHAPTER SIX

The interview room at Carlisle's Durranhill police station wasn't in the best of conditions, but at least it was fit for purpose and had the necessary audio and visual recording equipment.

It was a nuisance for the FMIT to have to travel to a different building every time they wanted to conduct an interview, but they were a roving team and, as such, tended to conduct their interviews in the nearest station to wherever their suspects lived. Their base in Carleton Hall was purely because the top brass wanted FMIT in the same building as them.

Carleton Hall was a former manor house on the outskirts of Penrith and had been used as the police headquarters since being purchased in the 1950s. More an administration centre than an operational station, apart from the FMIT, the Roads Policing Unit had their garages in the outbuildings at the rear of the south-facing building. The frontage of the building was dominated by two semi-octagonal bay windows and the rooms they belonged to had been claimed by those furthest up the ranks.

To Beth, Carleton Hall was an ugly building as she only ever saw the functional rear, rather than the decorative front. She knew it was a mistake on her part, but as much as she loved the prestige which accompanied those who worked out of Carleton Hall, she also despised the fact that the building was unattractive and its systems were all make-do-and-mend.

Where other teams around the county had purpose-built offices, with all the relevant communications systems installed as a matter of course, Carleton Hall had been adapted on a regular basis for the best part of seventy years. Every new technological advance, such as the intranet and Internet, saw a different bunch of cables and sockets being added to a house that was first wired for electricity more than a century ago.

It had been decreed by O'Dowd that she and Beth would have the first contact with Forster and their interview would be followed up by one featuring DS Thompson and the final member of FMIT, DC Paul Unthank. O'Dowd had explained her reasoning and it had made sense to Beth. Lots of rapes were about the rapist's power over the victim and by having the two women go first, it would unbalance the mayor by not having the power in the room.

The biggest issue Beth had with the plan was whether the tactic was subtle enough to trip up someone who'd thrown themselves into political life. It was an open secret that when Forster's two years as mayor were over, he intended to run for MP.

She expected the man to be difficult to pin down and that he'd try and charm his way out of the situation. He maybe wouldn't lie, but Beth was expecting a war of words that would be a series of thrusts and parries from both sides.

As she pulled into the car park, she prepared her mind for an interview that she expected to be fascinating and frustrating in equal measure.

CHAPTER SEVEN

When Beth followed O'Dowd into the interview room the first thing she noticed was Forster's lawyer.

Someone in Forster's position in life didn't settle for the duty solicitor, they used their phone call to summon their lawyer. Forster's lawyer was a Mancunian who'd moved to Carlisle and established his own practice in record time.

Neville Vaughan was the kind of lawyer the police dreaded going up against: he knew every trick in the book and while he may have a cultured air about him, he was quite happy to get down and dirty when the need arose. His practice specialised in criminal law and she knew she should have expected that Forster would use him.

O'Dowd recited the names of those present and the reason for the interview for the benefit of the recording equipment and then fixed Forster with an enquiring stare.

'Before we begin, Inspector, my client would like to state for the record that he is an innocent man and that he will do everything in his power to prove that to you.'

'Thank you, Mr Vaughan. Your client's cooperation will ensure this process is carried out as smoothly and quickly as possible. I should, though, like to point something out in return.' O'Dowd pointed her pen in Forster's general direction. 'Almost everybody who sits in that seat says they're not guilty and that they'll do anything to prove it.'

'Touché, Inspector. Let's cut to the chase, shall we?' If Vaughan's smile had been any oilier, Greenpeace would be protesting about the pollution he was causing. 'You have made an as yet unfounded allegation against Mayor Forster. The burden of proof lies with you, and as my client is innocent, you will not find the necessary evidence to charge him, let alone proceed with a prosecution.'

'That's the whole point of this interview. To establish your client's innocence. Or guilt, whichever is appropriate.' O'Dowd turned to look at Forster. 'The evidence we've uncovered tells us that you raped and murdered four women. In order they are: Christine Peterson who was murdered and raped five years ago; Joanne Armstrong, three and a half years ago, Harriet Quantrell, almost two years past, and finally, Felicia Evans.'

Forster's face scrunched in concentration. 'You think I'm responsible for poor Harriet's death? You presumably know she interned for me for a fortnight as part of her college course when I was deputy mayor? I didn't kill or rape her, I went to her funeral for God's sake.'

Beth hadn't expected Forster to be so open. She'd thought he be guarded with his answers and that there would be a lot more verbal fencing before they got to this point.

As O'Dowd hadn't answered, Beth decided to enter the conversation. 'You're right, we do know she was your intern. She was twenty-two years old and three weeks away from being married when she was abducted, raped and then murdered. Her daughter was six weeks old at the time.' Beth slid a piece of paper across the table, on it were three dates. 'We need to know your exact whereabouts for each of those dates. We also need to know where you were last night. You said you wanted to cooperate, this would be an ideal time to start.'

'You cannot expect my client to remember his whereabouts on specific dates that go back five years.'

'It's fine, Neville.' Beth felt the full power of Forster's charisma. 'I'm sure the young lady doesn't expect me to rely on my memory alone. I remember her saying earlier that they would be taking my phone and computers. Because I have a busy life, I use my phone as my diary and I have done so for the last ten years or so. It's synced with my computer, so you'll get ten years' worth of my diary.'

'Our tech guys are going through them as we speak.' Beth knew her counter was weak but she was willing to try anything that might rattle Forster.

'That's good, they'll prove my innocence to you. As for last night, I was at a dinner at the golf club. Your chief superintendent was at my table. He'll verify that I was there and that, while I wasn't drunk, I was in no shape to drive around killing people.'

Vaughan raised his pen, so Beth nodded permission for him to ask his question.

'Out of interest. Where were the first three women found, and which dates apply to which women?'

Beth recited the facts without looking at her notes. Every relevant detail of the case was already imprinted onto her brain.

Vaughan jotted down the information on his pad and adjusted his pince-nez once he was done.

O'Dowd reached for the file she'd brought in with her. 'You seem very confident, Mr Forster. Perhaps a look at these pictures will remove some of your bluster.'

'My goodness, Inspector, you really are using every cliché in the book, showing my client pictures of his alleged victims in the hope he'll break down and confess, or say something that you can pounce on.'

'Clichés are clichés for a reason. This is Christine Peterson, she was sixty-two years old with three grandchildren.' A second photo was pulled from the file. 'Joanne Armstrong, thirty-six and single.' A third and fourth photo were slid across the table. 'Harriet Quantrell. Felicia Evans, she is the latest victim. A walker found her on the bank of Lake Ullswater this morning.'

As the four pictures were presented to Forster his face registered shock. Beth was looking for any hint of recognition in his eyes, but there was only a flash when Harriet's picture was shown and it had already been established that he knew her.

'We get it, Inspector, four women and we've already discussed the unfortunate Miss Quantrell.'

Beth wanted to smash the lawyer's stupid little spectacles into his face for his callous dismissal of Harriet, but she managed to keep her temper in check. Beside her she could feel O'Dowd bristle in the same way. This was all wrong: they were supposed to be making the lawyer and his client squirm, not the other way around.

Beth tried changing tack. 'Mr Mayor, can you explain why we found a credit card with your name on it near where Felicia Evans's body was found?

'Was it my Amex card?'

'It was, yes.'

'I wondered where that had got to.' Forster gave a non-committal shrug. 'I lost it last week. If you check with Amex themselves, they'll tell you I called up to cancel it the day I realised I'd lost it.'

All Beth wanted to do was grimace at their best piece of evidence being thrown back in their faces so easily.

O'Dowd reached for the folder again. 'Perhaps if your client saw the pictures of the first three women that were taken at the crime scenes, rather than the ones given to us by the victims' families you would treat these women with a little more respect.'

Forster again put his hand on the lawyer's forearm. 'There's no need to show me any more pictures. You have eyes in your head and you've been using them to watch my reactions to your questions. At the risk of sounding conceited, I know I'm not an unattractive man. I'm wealthy and because of my position as mayor, I have a certain power and influence. For the last five years, I've been named as one of the top five of Cumbria's most eligible bachelors. I will even confess that the *News and Star* calling me Foxy Forster on some occasions is a little tacky.' Forster gave what Beth was sure was his best campaign smile. 'I'm sorry to burst any bubble you may have, but I don't need to rape anyone, much less kill them. I have sufficient offers of companionship to keep my libido more than satisfied.'

Beth knew that what Forster was saying was all true, yet there were the old maxims that power was an aphrodisiac and that power corrupts. As much as Forster may have plenty of women showing their interest in him, perhaps he didn't find their acquiescence gave him the buzz that he wanted. He may well prefer to get his kicks from dominating reluctant women and bending them to his will.

'If I may add something to what my client has just said?' When O'Dowd nodded, Vaughan continued to speak. 'My client is a handsome man; that fact is well documented and evident for all to see. At the risk of speaking ill of the dead, the women he normally dates are far more successful and, dare I say it, more attractive than the women who have fallen prey to a heinous killer. I am certainly no expert on the subject, but aren't rapes usually committed against women who are out of the rapist's league? You really should be asking yourselves why a man as good-looking as my client would rape and murder four women who are, with all due respect, nowhere near as attractive as the women he has his pick of.'

Vaughan opened his own file and slid out four pictures. They were screenshots from the *Cumberland News*'s website and each one had a picture of Forster in his ceremonial robes with a stunning woman on his arm.

The lawyer had made his point, and as much as she wanted to bend his point back and use it as a fishhook to gouge out his eyes for the disrespect he'd shown the victims, Beth found it hard to argue with his logic.

That didn't mean she wasn't going to try.

'Perhaps what you say is true, and perhaps your client raped these women so he could get something from them he wasn't getting from the women he was dating. However, you couldn't be more wrong about rapists targeting victims who are out of their league. Rape isn't just about sexual gratification, it's about power, exerting control over them, dominating the victim until they surrender. The only reason I can think of for you being so wrong, is that you're naive to the mind of a rapist and, considering your profession, that doesn't reflect well on you.'

'Please, Constable, explain what you think he was getting from the women he's alleged to have raped that he wasn't able to get elsewhere.'

'The women were all raped anally as well as vaginally. For a man such as your client, I don't suppose there is a shortage of offers for normal sexual intercourse, but as for anal, well that could be a different matter altogether.'

'I'm sorry to burst your bubble, but I have no interest in anal sex.' Forster's face backed up his words. 'The very idea is abhorrent to me. Please, you have to believe me, it's not something that appeals to me.'

O'Dowd arced an eyebrow. 'If you were female I'd say you doth protest too much.'

'It's bad enough that you're accusing me of rape and murder, to also suggest that I'd kill just so I could have something I don't want is twisted.'

'Really? You think it's twisted, do you?' Beth kept her tone level, but made sure she got her message across with the questions she asked. 'What about the fact that four women were raped? What about them being murdered? What about the fact that they were all strangled? Can you imagine their last hours? I've been thinking of little else since we got this case. Let me tell you what I imagine their last hours being like: they'd be terrified, confused probably. Everything they feared happening to them, would happen. They'd be violated against their wishes.

'You're a man, so the odds of you being raped are a lot smaller than they are for a woman. You've probably never worried about a situation, never walked home with your keys in your hand in case you're attacked. Just about every woman I know takes these kind of precautions all the time. We don't live in constant fear of rape, but for women it's an ever-present threat that we have to be aware of. You maybe don't ever think about it, but the thought of someone forcing themselves onto me terrifies me.'

The horrified look on Forster's face wasn't enough to stop Beth continuing. 'I can see you're starting to understand; well, when you've got your head round the rape, try imagining what it must be like to be strangled to death. It'd be a slow process; you'd feel your throat being constricted until it was impossible to breathe. Your vision would blur at the edges as your brain was deprived of oxygen. You'd feel your limbs weakening. Maybe you'd be begging for your life, or trying to escape. It wouldn't work. Perhaps the last thing you'd see would be the face of the man who killed you. Tell me, Mr Mayor, how scared do you think those women were? And you, Mr Vaughan, the next time you open your mouth, you should show a little respect for the dead.'

'I said, that's enough, Beth.'

Beth felt a hand on her arm. O'Dowd was pulling her back into her seat but she had no recollection of rising to her feet.

'That's okay, Inspector. Your colleague is right: as a man I have no idea how women fear rape. As I've stated all along, I'm innocent and will be proven so. When investigating crimes of this magnitude, it's right that the investigating officers are fired up and passionate.' Beth felt the power of Forster's charisma being directed her way. 'When this is over, I'd like to do more to help victims of violent sexual crime. Maybe set up a local charity or something like that. I know you see me as the enemy right now, but once it's proven I'm not, I'd love someone with your passion to be involved to help women, in particular, feel that their attackers have been made to pay for their crimes. That scar on your face would instantly give you credibility when speaking to victims.'

Beth kept her mouth shut.

She had to.

If she said another word, she'd wind herself up further and would end up either being taken off the case or possibly facing a formal disciplinary hearing.

Forster had made light of her rant and had done the rich-man thing of identifying a problem, and finding the solution in his wallet. In doing so, he'd also managed to appear gracious when attacked by her vehemence. Beside Forster, Vaughan was failing to keep the smugness off his face.

That last line about her scar rankled her more than anything else. So far as she was concerned her scar didn't give her victim status, it showed that she was a survivor, that she could face adversity and triumph against it.

O'Dowd suspended the interview, and as Beth was trudging out of the room after her, she was cursing herself. She'd known before beginning the interview that it would be a battle and she'd failed to keep a lid on her temper. Worse, she'd lost the plot and had been on the point of insulting the solicitor. She knew that she'd been lucky O'Dowd had interrupted her before she said something that damaged their case beyond repair.

CHAPTER EIGHT

25 JANUARY

Dear Diary

Today was my first day working for the deputy mayor. I'd heard about how good-looking and suave he was and everything I'd heard was true.

Everything poor Harriet told me about this job was true and I'm so lucky to have it.

Until tomorrow.

CHAPTER NINE

As he went about his day, he felt that old familiar urge begin to grow again. Today had been no different than any other day, the same boring routine that he had the other 364 days of the year.

His daily grind had once been everything to him. What was it they said, 'choose a job you love, and you will never have to work a day in your life'? This had been true for him.

Work had been his life, sixteen, eighteen, even twenty hours he'd worked some days, and what for? The money in his bank? The prestige of having a Jaguar in the drive and a big house in the country? Wealth and its trappings meant nothing without someone to share it with.

His was a family business. It had started off as his great-grandfather's and had been handed down to each eldest son in the traditionally sexist way. When it had passed to him, he'd put in twice the hours his father had. Reinvested the profits instead of squandering them. The business had grown exponentially due to his effort.

Timing had been on his side when he'd looked over the fence and seen greener grass. The neighbour had accepted his offer after an evening spent surrounding a bottle of whisky as they haggled.

Twice more he'd visited a neighbour with a bottle of whisky and dreams of expansion. Twice he'd been successful.

Now though, the business victories were hollow ones.

Nobody greeted him with a cuppa in the morning. There wasn't anyone to ask how his day was when he returned from work.

Worst of all, there was nobody to cuddle into when he pulled the duvet up to his chin and switched off the light. Loneliness was a constant companion who was only displaced when sexual frustration came to visit.

The pattern was a recognisable one. First there would be the tingles, then the sense of despair followed by the burning desire. It wasn't something he could explain any further; he just knew that the more he tried to ignore the urges, tried to deny them, the stronger they'd become.

Yesterday had been the despair day. Now all he could think about was the urge and his need to sate it.

He knew it was wrong to pursue it, that he shouldn't give in to his desires again.

He also knew that however much he tried to talk himself out of it, he was going to find a way to deal with the urges.

It was something that he had to accept. It was time to go hunting again.

CHAPTER TEN

Beth kept her mouth shut and listened as O'Dowd started talking to the woman who'd arrived at Durranhill police station to see them. The DI had given Beth a short dressing-down over the way she'd lost her composure earlier, and to be fair to O'Dowd, Beth knew she'd gone too far and that losing her cool was unprofessional.

She had passed her probationary period in FMIT, but she was still the newest member of the team and felt as though she had to prove herself every day.

As much as she knew she was wrong to have behaved the way she had, Beth had felt an emotional pull to the case as soon as she'd learned of the victims' fate. Of all the crimes one human can perpetrate against another, in Beth's opinion, rape had to be one of the worst. Beth had heard rape described as a stealing of the soul and she understood why it was called that. She was aware that in the eyes of the law, murder, infanticide and a whole host of other offences such as paedophilia were all more serious crimes, and she knew why, but rape was an invasion of the body. For the victims, there would be terror that they'd be killed once their rapist was done with them. Plus there would be the humiliation of being powerless to prevent themselves being used without permission and last of all, the actual physical pain.

Like most women she knew, she had experienced sexual harassment, and received unwanted attention. Unlike one of her closest friends though, she had never experienced anything worse.

Beth had been the one Steph had turned to the morning after her drunken boyfriend had forced himself on her against her wishes. When the boyfriend had gone to the pub to watch the football with his mates, Beth had helped her friend load all her belongings into their cars and had put a roof over Steph's head until she found herself a new place to live.

It had been Beth who'd nursed her friend through the trauma. Steph's tears had stained her shoulders on a nightly basis as she wept for herself, for the ruined relationship and the knowledge that someone she loved had violated her. Steph had, by turn, ranted, cried and made vows never again to allow a man to hurt her.

Beth had listened, cajoled and nursed her friend back to the point where she'd regained enough of her original self to start the next chapter of her life.

Since moving out, Steph had been resolute in her resolve to remain single. Beth had tried, without success, to persuade Steph to report the rape, but her friend had refused. As much as she hated her ex for what he'd done to her, she told Beth she couldn't face putting herself through the ordeal of testifying against him should the case go to court.

Like all cops, Beth knew the statistics regarding rape convictions were tragic. Few of the reported cases would get as far as a courtroom and many of those which did would take a frightful toll on the victim. Defence lawyers would blacken the victim's character as a matter of course as they did everything they could to discredit their account of the event, by saying the intercourse was consensual or the victim and her abuser had both been drinking. Then the CPS would have to make its judgements on the argument of consent and alcohol intake with regard to the Sexual Offences act. All of this had to be balanced against the likelihood of a successful prosecution before a decision about whether or not to proceed was made.

Nobody knew how many rapes went unreported due to the failings of the system, but as flawed as the system was, Beth believed it was better than nothing.

Of course the system had a duty also to protect accused rapists from false allegations, but the net result was cases going unreported and low conviction rates, meaning rapists potentially walking free.

Beth couldn't miss the parallels between her own thoughts and the situation with Forster, yet she was still aggrieved at the injustice of everything. Steph's experiences had shown her first-hand the damage that a rapist can do to a person.

Steph had laid herself bare to Beth and it had been heartbreaking to hear how her friend had felt violated, not just physically, but mentally. That the boyfriend had disregarded her protestations, and had held her down just to satisfy his own drunken needs, had scarred her as much as the forced penetration. Steph had loved him; she'd previously confided to Beth that if he'd proposed to her she'd have said yes in a flash.

That had all been blown away by a gutful of lager and a refusal to take no for an answer.

What had infuriated Beth most of all was the way the boyfriend had moved on without being punished for his actions. A week after the rape, Beth had been driving home after a late shift and had seen him leaving one of Penrith's livelier pubs with his arm round another girl.

With Steph unwilling to put herself through the ordeal of pressing charges, and the subsequent interviews and possible court case, there was nothing Beth could do to make the boyfriend pay for his crime without resorting to vigilante action. As much as she believed the boyfriend deserved to be punished, she had a greater belief that it was her duty to uphold laws rather than break them.

Beth had been strong for her friend and had kept her own emotions private as she listened to the horrors of Steph's ordeal.

The one time she'd cried in front of Steph was when her friend had told her that she might have forgiven her boyfriend, had he not blackened one of her eyes and broken her nose when punching her into submission.

Steph's rationalisations betrayed all Beth held dear, as, to her mind, Steph had given the punch greater importance than the rape. Beth was convinced that had Steph's boyfriend not punched her, she would have forgiven him.

To Beth, neither action was forgivable, but the scars from the beating would always fade quicker than the ones from the rape.

CHAPTER ELEVEN

Beth followed the woman who O'Dowd was leading towards the room where witness statements were taken. This room wasn't as sterile as the interview rooms and had once been decorated in a way that suggested it was intended to offer calmness and reassurance to witnesses.

The decor had faded with time. Lies and mistruths had polluted the room along with tears of despair and shock.

Unlike the interview rooms, the door to this room had no lock and there was a small table with dog-eared magazines that were flicked through without ever being read.

'Thank you for coming in to see us, Miss Dereham.'

'Please, call me Eleanor.'

Beth had only been half-listening when Eleanor had been introduced to them, but she paid the woman proper attention now.

Eleanor Dereham was a good-looking woman who had poise and style – evident in her clothes and the traces of make-up on her face. The perfume she wore wasn't one Beth was familiar with, although if Eleanor's clothes were anything to go by, the perfume wouldn't be one a DC could afford on a regular basis.

'So, Eleanor.' To Beth, O'Dowd's smile was obviously false. 'You say you have come in to attest to the innocence of someone we arrested this morning. I'd be very interested to hear what you have to say.'

'Shall I start the story at the beginning or would you like me to jump to the key point?'

'The key point works for me. We can hear the whole thing afterwards if necessary.'

'Fair enough. I know Derek Forster didn't rape and murder those women because I used to date him and can tell you that sexually the man is as vanilla as they come. He wasn't remotely interested in anything kinky, and specifically he wouldn't have anal sex with me.'

Of all the things Beth had heard during her police career, none had flabbergasted her the way Eleanor's statement had. She planted her elbows on the table and rested her chin on her fists. The action as much to ensure her mouth didn't hang open as to give her time to think. From the corner of her eye, she could see O'Dowd having the same struggle she was.

Eleanor's well-to-do appearance and the obvious class she exuded was at odds with her bold statement. Beth tried not to make predisposed opinions of people based on their appearance, but she'd experienced contact with people from all walks of life and had found that in a majority of cases, her first impressions were rarely far wrong.

Still, she'd had Eleanor down as the kind of woman who'd keep her business private and probably wouldn't discuss sex with anyone. She'd been wrong; the brazen admission proved that, as did the amused look in Eleanor's eyes.

'You both seem a little shocked by what I've said.' A twist of her lips added a wryness to Eleanor's smile. 'Well you don't need to be. I'm a grown woman and I have needs. I like sex and from time to time, I like to have anal sex, among other… things. Derek wouldn't hear of any of it, so eventually I finished with him. It wasn't an acrimonious split; we just had different tastes.' She gave a shrug. 'I think I disgusted him a little.'

Beth lifted her chin off her fists and hoped her voice wouldn't betray her amazement at Eleanor's frankness. 'How did you know he was here? We only arrested him this morning and the only person we are aware he's spoken to is his lawyer.'

'His lawyer is my cousin. He knows we used to date so he called me an hour ago.' Eleanor scratched at her shoulder causing the fine material of her blouse to rustle at her touch. 'I told him the truth about me and Derek, and when he asked if I'd come down and make a statement to you, I agreed.'

With that last sentence, Beth realised how the lawyer had played them. Everything that was said in the formal interview was nothing more than a stalling tactic until his star witness came forward. Forster must have told him about the anal aspect to the rapes when calling to hire him.

What Beth had to find out now would waste her time as well as delaying the investigation into the mayor.

First of all, they would have to establish if Eleanor really was Vaughan's cousin and whether or not she was lying to help out Forster's case.

Second, they'd need to see how eager to help Eleanor really was. Telling her tale to two women in the privacy of the witness suite was one thing. Testifying in court was another.

'Your revelation is very damning to our case. I'm sure that when it goes to court your testimony may well swing the jury's opinion. However, just because he didn't want anal sex with you doesn't mean he didn't desire it with other women.'

'We both know that's not true. Vanilla is vanilla. The case won't go to court. You'll not get enough evidence for that to happen.' Eleanor shifted her eyes from Beth to O'Dowd. 'Your DC seems to think I'm afraid of testifying in court. That I'm ashamed of my appetites. I can follow her logic, but I have to tell you, I'm not worried about my reputation.'

Beth kept her mouth closed as Eleanor rooted in her handbag and produced her phone. After unlocking it and scrolling through the apps for a few seconds, she slid the phone across the table until it was sitting between Beth and O'Dowd.

'What's this?' O'Dowd made no effort to keep the anger from her tone.

'It's the first in a series of pictures that were taken at a wedding. Specifically, my niece's wedding. You'll see the bride being given away by her father. You'll also see a family photo where Neville and I are with my mother and his father. He looks like his father and I'm like my mother. His father and my mother are twins.' A smugness crept into Eleanor's tone. 'I'm sure you're wondering if I'm really Neville's cousin or someone who's been hired to lie Derek's way out of jail. I am his cousin, and yes I did have a relationship with the mayor. If you keep scrolling through the pictures, you'll see several of me and the mayor at civic functions back in May. There are also some selfies of the two of us.'

O'Dowd lifted the mobile and swiped her way through the hundreds of pictures on the phone. Her eyes narrowed further with each swipe and when she passed the phone back to Eleanor, she almost threw it at her.

Beth got why her boss was that way. She felt the same emotions. Not only had they been outmanoeuvred by the lawyer, his cousin's testimony was destroying their case.

The mayor may well be innocent of the charges against him, but the way he'd looked at Beth at his house had revealed his truer nature. Whether or not he'd killed and raped the four women, he was still a predator. Worse than that, he was a predator with funds at his disposal, powerful friends and enough charisma, influence and popularity to make any allegation against him seem like a witch hunt.

As Beth watched Eleanor walk out of the building all confident air and pocking heels, she heard O'Dowd's mobile ring.

She turned to watch her boss. Maybe she'd be able to interpret what the conversation was about from the side that she heard.

O'Dowd was listening rather than talking and from what Beth could see of her face, the DI wasn't liking what she was hearing.

CHAPTER TWELVE

Beth watched as Forster climbed into the passenger seat of his lawyer's Jaguar, and cursed the world in general.

Digital Forensics had checked Forster's diary and found that he was engaged in a series of civic events around the county when two of the women had been raped and murdered. There was no way he could have attended all the various events and still have found enough time to identify, abduct and then rape and kill his victims. Yes, he may have been at the nature reserve around the same time as Christine Peterson was suspected of being taken, and he was in the vicinity of Keswick when Joanne Armstrong was abducted, but unless his support staff were in on the rapes and murders, it just couldn't have been him. Plus he was at the same function as the chief super last night – a quick word with the chief super had not just verified this, but backed up the mayor's claim he was too tipsy to drive – which meant that he couldn't have killed Felicia Evans either. The final clincher was the call she'd put in to American Express. It had taken a bit of wrangling, but she'd managed to speak to someone who'd confirmed the mayor had reported his card as stolen last week.

The good news was that this meant that FMIT had proven beyond doubt that the mayor was innocent and, as such, they were freed from the toxic aspects of the case.

The bad news was now that they'd established the mayor's innocence, they had no clues as to who was behind the murders. A dozen and one questions burned in Beth: Was the mayor's presence at two sites a coincidence or was it something that linked the killer as well? Was the killer part of the mayor's entourage? Now that the mayor was off the suspect list, who should be on it? The invitation and the mayor's credit card being found at the site where Felicia's body was dumped, along with the anonymous letter that was sent to the chief constable, made Beth think that someone was trying to frame the mayor.

The thing which troubled Beth the most was that she couldn't work out if the mayor was being framed as part of a vendetta or as a way to deflect attention from the real killer.

She planned to pore over the reports of those who'd investigated each murder, memorise the details and compile her spreadsheets until she had every fact and detail at her disposal for cross-referencing. There had been no other credible suspects and after the fiasco in the interview rooms, she realised just how tenuous the mayor's involvement now looked.

Beth couldn't help but feel frustrated and aggrieved at the way they'd wasted their time investigating the mayor when they should have been following normal procedure for the murder of Felicia Evans.

As much as Beth was sure the mayor was a major player in the dating field, she couldn't stop herself admiring his drive. Even as he'd been leaving, he'd repeated his request that she get involved when he managed to set up his charity.

As much as she'd wanted to tell him where to get off, she'd stayed her tongue and had accepted the card he'd given her. If he was true to his word, he might well do some good and, if she did get involved, she would make sure the charity also focussed on helping to bring rapists to justice.

Beth joined O'Dowd once she had finished her phone call and set off back towards Carleton Hall. The DI was silent and Beth could feel the waves of fury emanating from her boss. It was an anger she shared, but Beth could also feel a pulse of excitement acting as a breakwater.

The FMIT had four murder cases to investigate and, because of this, she'd be given a chance to deliver some closure to the victims and their families. Above anything else, it was the desire to see wrongs righted that had compelled Beth to join the police. Now that she had a chance to tackle three unsolved cases plus the murder of Felicia Evans, she knew that she'd do whatever it took to find the killer and stop him before he killed again.

'See when we get back to Carleton, Beth, you and I need to have a not-so-little chat about how to conduct yourself in a professional manner.'

CHAPTER THIRTEEN

Beth kept her mouth shut and her eyes on the floor as O'Dowd raged at her. On a deeper level, she knew that half of the DI's anger was directed at the hopelessness of the case they'd been landed with, the fact that they had to deal with the political hot potato of the evidence against the mayor, and that they'd picked up three incredibly cold cases.

'Answer me, Beth. Tell me what made you think it was appropriate to give the mayor such a hard time when the evidence against him was so circumstantial?' O'Dowd flumped herself into her seat and scowled at the world in general. 'Well?'

'Maybe I could have chosen my words with more care, but come off it, ma'am.' Beth knew she may be digging herself deeper into O'Dowd's bad books, but she couldn't help but speak her mind. 'Just because he's got a fancy title that comes with a red shawl and a blingy chain, it doesn't mean he shouldn't be questioned with the same thoroughness that any other suspect gets. I was trying to get under his skin. Okay, I failed, but I don't think I was harder on him than other suspects I've interviewed.'

'That's enough. In a perfect world, all people would be created equal. Tell me, do you think we'd have jobs if we lived in a perfect world? Like it or not, some people are more equal than others.' O'Dowd stood and flashed a hand at the papers strewn across Beth's desk. 'You're on the cold cases. Get your head down and find me a lead to pursue on who *did* rape and murder those poor women. I'm going to go update the DCI, and forewarn him of the complaint that may very well come from the mayor's lawyer.'

As O'Dowd stomped her way out of the office, Beth reached for the files on her desk. So far she'd made some notes, but she hadn't yet found the time to create one of her spreadsheets. She knew that different things worked for different people and her preference was to see all the relevant information in one place. For her, neat columns and ordered rows were the key to aligning similarities and matching known facts across different elements of a case.

DI O'Dowd had an artist's pad on her desk that she filled with haphazard scribbles as thoughts and ideas came to her. The two other members of FMIT – Thomson and Unthank – both tended to rely on memory and, while Beth knew it was sexist of her to do so, a part of her wondered if the reason they leafed through the files and trusted their brains had more to do with male arrogance than anything else.

They'd be leading on the murder of Felicia Evans and, if the truth was told, Beth would rather be investigating a current case than a bunch of cold ones, but she supposed this was O'Dowd's way of rapping her knuckles.

As she bent to her task, she was spurred on by the desire to not just solve the cases, but to beat Thompson and Unthank to the result.

Another thing that was bothering Beth was O'Dowd's deference to Forster. The mayor had a certain standing among the community as befit his station, but to her, he was just another person who'd come into their sights and been dismissed when the evidence had backed up protestations of innocence. Whatever political office Forster held, or might go on to hold in the future, had no place in their reckoning: he must be judged as all other suspects were, and that's what she'd done.

Rather than give in to her frustrations and rant or rage, Beth turned back to the reports and the notes she had on the three cold cases.

As with any investigation, the starting point was the first thing to happen to the victim. While there may have been previous unknown events such as stalking or even surveillance, they could be backtracked to, once the first point of contact between victim and attacker had been established. In the cases of the three murdered women, that point was the one where they'd been abducted.

Christine Peterson had left her husband to look after the grandchildren they'd taken on holiday while she'd headed off to Sandscale Haws National Nature Reserve with her camera. Beth didn't know the area well, and what she found online showed her an isolated beach, with a myriad of sand dunes festooned with the tough grass synonymous with much of Cumbria's coastline.

Christine's Mazda had been parked in the reserve's car park and the CCTV footage from the lone camera fixed to the wall of the gift-shop-cum-tearoom had shown Christine leaving her car and wandering off into the dunes with her camera slung around her neck.

To Beth it looked as if Christine was serious about her photography, as when she'd googled the make and model of Christine's camera, she'd learned that it was a larger professional one and that Christine had also carried the kind of equipment bag professional wedding photographers use.

That was the last time anyone had seen her alive. To be fair to the investigating officers, they'd tracked down everyone else who'd used the car park and spoken to them. All had been holidaying families, apart from a group of students from Lancaster University who'd been there to study the newts which could be found in the dunes.

Joanne Armstrong had been staying in Keswick. Her purpose in the Lakes was hillwalking, as it was for so many visitors to the area. Rather than following the normal protocol of walking in a group, Joanne had travelled to the Lakes by herself and she walked alone.

On the day she was taken, she'd been tackling the Coledale Horseshoe, which was one of the toughest walks the Lakes had to offer. She'd set off at eight thirty in the morning and hadn't been seen again. Like Christine's Mazda, her little VW sat in a car park until the police traced it.

Appeals had gone out for anyone who might have seen what happened to Joanne, but until her body turned up two days after her sister had reported her missing, it was presumed that she'd had an accident during her walk. The mountain rescue team had scoured the hillside looking for Joanne, as a matter of course, but naturally they'd found no sign of her. Beth knew it was too much to expect that they'd identified the place from where she was taken, but she wished that the investigating officers had at least asked the question.

Harriet Quantrell was a different proposition. She'd last been seen walking home from the bars and clubs of Botchergate in Carlisle.

Like Joanne she'd been alone. The last of her friends had said goodbye before Harriet had embarked on the last quarter of a mile.

Maybe the young women should have got a taxi, but the fact it had been a balmy summer's night and they all lived within a mile of the city centre suggested that the girls had chosen to walk.

It was a decision which had more than likely cost Harriet her life.

All the files gave details of the victims' families and notes on any behaviour which had struck a chord with the investigating officers. There was the usual outpouring of grief and anger from all families. What stood out was Harriet's uncle, a Howard Stanton. According to the reports from the Family Liaison Officer who'd sat with the Quantrell family, he was a hothead whose rants about getting revenge on the person who'd killed his niece had suggested a serious intent rather than anger finding an outlet in empty words. The FLO had kept an eye on him, but as there had been no progress with apprehending Harriet's murderer, his anger had turned on the police. In the end, Harriet's mother had dealt with Stanton by unloading her own anger at him in a tear-filled rant.

Beth's next thoughts were about how the victims had each been transported from where they'd been snatched to where they were dumped. As much as it might be a cliché for abductors to use a van, they were the perfect vehicle for the job. With no rear windows and plenty of space for the victim, vans ticked every box. Their presence on the roads is as unremarkable as the average car and as such they are ignored.

That two of the three women had been taken at a beauty spot made it even less likely that the abductions were observed. Faced with a panoramic view, very few people would pay attention to a van and its occupants.

The question Beth was struggling with was: How had the killer got the women into the van? A ruse about seeing some puppies wouldn't work on grown women and if he cracked them over the head with something, he'd still have had to lug their bodies to the vehicle. While bystanders may have their attention on the scenery, they wouldn't fail to notice a woman being bundled into the back of a van. Plus, none of the victims' PM reports had noted any head trauma.

Christine was from Bolton and Joanne from Newcastle, so the nearest and most logical person to investigate first was the third victim, Harriet.

Beth got the address for Harriet's fiancé from the file and reached for her jacket. As much as she wanted to continue with her spreadsheet, she also needed to get out of the office and speak to someone connected to a victim. The fire in her belly that compelled her to work as hard as was necessary to catch a killer was building nicely, but she knew from experience that a single conversation with a victim or one of their family members would fan its flames enough to keep her at her desk long after everyone else had gone home.

CHAPTER FOURTEEN

Denton Holme in Carlisle is known as a village within a city and the red-brick terrace houses that line its streets are bland in their uniformity. Once home to the workers employed by the city's textile mills and manufacturing plants, the area is devoid of individuality beyond the colours of woodwork and the cars sandwiched nose to tail along the cobbled streets.

As much as Beth despised having to cut her lawn, she knew she'd rather spend an hour a week doing that, than live in a place where a hanging basket or a window box constituted a garden.

She knew this area well enough from her days in uniform. There was a community spirit like few other areas in the 'Great Border City'. Despite the fact that everyone's house was laid out the same way, or a mirror image, right down to the positioning of doors and plug sockets, they seemed to rub along with more grace than could be expected.

The street felt claustrophobic to Beth as she knocked on the door of Harriet's last-known address. There was something about its narrowness and the way the sun was streaming between the chimney pots that made her feel like she was trapped.

For those who'd returned here after a long day working in the mills it would have been even worse. They would live and work with the same people all their lives. By day they'd stand beside a noisy, dangerous loom or some other piece of machinery, and at night they'd be cooped up in their tiny identikit homes with three or more generations living in each other's pockets.

Beth closed her eyes momentarily and pictured the street as it would have been a hundred and fifty years ago. Boys in short trousers playing games on the cobbles while girls jumped along a hopscotch grid or helped their mothers. The rooftops would be wreathed in the smoke from a hundred coal fires.

The men in her vision wore flat caps and grim expressions, while the women wore looks of acceptance for their lot as they went about their daily routine. Above them all, Dixon's Chimney would tower like a guard post, its presence a reminder of where they belonged and where they must remain.

When it was completed, Shaddon Mill – which was the reason for Dixon's Chimney – was the largest cotton mill in England and its accompanying chimney was the eighth tallest in the world.

Beth couldn't begin to imagine the workers' fury if they knew their place of employment had been converted into flats, or their sense of containment living in the shadows of their workplace, but it made her feel happier about her own circumstances. Her job let her travel around the county on a daily basis; her home might be a subsidised police house, but she had it to herself and because of this she benefitted from all the freedoms which came from living alone.

The door creaked open and a young man with a toddler on his hip opened the door. The man had the kind of mussy hair that took effort and the girl snuggling against him was clean and well clothed, if bleary eyed.

'Alreet.' His voice was as broad a Carlisle accent as Beth had ever heard.

Beth introduced herself and checked the man's identity. When he confirmed that he was Rory Newham she explained why she was there.

As soon as she mentioned Harriet's name his eyes flashed in hope. It was a primitive reaction borne of a longing for news of an arrest and the closure it brought. Regardless of anything she may learn from Newham, that split-second glimpse into his pain had made the visit worthwhile in Beth's view, as the memory of his grief would drive her on through what was bound to be a long and difficult investigation.

'I'm sure this is all very painful for you and I certainly don't want to reopen old wounds, but I'd like to ask you a few questions about Harriet.'

Newham opened the door and stepped back so she could enter. As with all houses on the street, the front door opened right into the living room and there was a staircase directly in front of them. It was the kind of arrangement that was once common for working-class homes, although it was as impractical an arrangement as Beth had ever known. On winter days, the open door would flood the house's main room with cold air and back in the days of coal fires, the doors would have been a constant source of draughts.

As Beth let Newham direct her to a seat, she took in the room. It was tidy without being a show home. The furniture was an eclectic mishmash of styles that spoke of Newham picking up second-hand bargains. The decor was simple but tasteful, and a wicker basket tucked beside a chair held a variety of children's toys and books.

The most striking thing about the room wasn't the 40-inch TV dominating one corner but the picture gallery hanging on the chimney breast. In pride of place was the same picture of Harriet that had been stapled to their file, and surrounding it was a medley of pictures featuring Harriet and Newham, or of the two of them with their infant daughter. Below the central picture was an image of a tired, but ecstatic Harriet holding a newborn baby wrapped in a pink blanket.

If ever Newham had been questioned in relation to Harriet's murder, this spoke of his innocence. The man had become a single parent the day his fiancée had been murdered, and here he was, nearly two years later, still seemingly carrying a torch. The pictures on the chimney breast said as much, but they also said a lot more.

Until Beth had seen them, she'd subtly looked around for a pair of woman's shoes or a cup with a smear of lipstick. It had been instinctive to her to check for signs that Newham had moved on.

All those ideas had been refuted by the presence of the pictures, and there was nothing to suggest that his affections lay anywhere other than with his daughter.

'I hope you have more success in finding the charver who killed our Harriet than them other coppers. Right bunch of radgees them lot.'

There was no hostility in Newham's tone, and Beth had spent enough time working in Carlisle to translate 'charver' into man and 'radgees' into idiots without having to think about it.

Like so many other parts of the country, Cumbria has its own speech patterns and while a lot of the terms have influences from neighbouring counties, many have origins in the traditional Cumbrian dialect. This dialect has been traced back to the fifth century when Cumbria was central to the kingdom known as Rheged – which covered Northern England and southern Scotland – when a form of the Brythonic language spoken by the tribes at the time had evolved into Cumbric. Norse influences crossed the Irish Sea in the tenth century and its effect was best found in place names, although it had many subtle effects on the slang which lay between proper English and the traditional dialect.

'I get what you're saying, Rory.' Beth used his first name to try and establish a bond. Newham was skeletally thin, and other than his carefully mussed hair, he had nothing going for him looks-wise. 'But I'm not here to criticise my colleagues; I'm here because my team has been tasked with bringing a new focus to the investigation into Harriet's death.'

'Mummy.' The girl peeled her way out from under Newham's arm and pointed at the picture on the chimney breast.

Newham lifted the child up so she was level with the picture. 'That's right, Kerrie. That's your mummy.'

Beth fell silent as Newham dealt with his daughter. Her mind was on the little girl; the girl who would grow up knowing only a photograph as a mother.

For the child to not have a mother to lean on would be incredibly hard. Beth had always enjoyed a close relationship with her own mum – even during her teenage years – and she couldn't imagine what it would be like for a girl to navigate her way through adolescence and puberty without a mother's support. Grandparents and family would, of course, step up, and Newham seemed to be a very caring, loving father. But the girl would still miss out on an awful lot of natural support.

As Beth half-listened to Newham's answers to her questions, she tried to find a new angle, a question that had yet to be asked, but she couldn't think of anything that hadn't been covered.

When Newham mentioned that Harriet had disappeared on her first night out after Kerrie had been born, it had been all Beth could do not to take the child from Newham's arms and give her a huge cuddle for the misfortune which had befallen her young life.

Kerrie would become Beth's poster girl for her determination to solve this case.

CHAPTER FIFTEEN

When Beth walked into the Crown that evening, her eyes flitted round the room in the same practised way they did whenever she entered a busy area. Always at the back of her mind was her desire to spot the man with the two kisses tattooed on his neck, as he was the one who'd deflected the bottle into her face on that fateful night.

She didn't spot him, but she did see Ethan. He was standing by the bar facing the door.

Beth liked that he'd picked a vantage point where he could see her arrive. She also appreciated that he wasn't engaged in a deep conversation with anyone as she entered.

She gave him a quick assessment as she crossed the bar to meet him. He was dressed in a smart shirt and a fashionable pair of jeans. His body language was relaxed and the pint on the bar with a mouthful out of the top was his first if the clarity of his eyes meant anything.

'Hi. Good to see you.' His tone was easy and he gave her the space she needed without being stand-offish. 'What would you like to drink?'

Beth caught the unspoken message. He'd had doubts as to whether she'd come. That was fair enough, she'd had the same doubts herself.

'Good to see you too. A glass of white wine, please. Chardonnay if they have it.' Beth gestured at her clothes. 'Sorry, I haven't had the chance to go home and change. You'll have to take me as you find me.'

As soon as the words were out, Beth gave an inward wince. Had she just given him the wrong signal?

'You look fine.' Ethan's shrug was accompanied by a mischievous smirk. 'Well, a little rumpled if I'm honest, but I'd sooner you turn up rumpled than not show at all.'

'Why thank you, kind sir, you really know how to flatter a lady.' Beth lifted her glass and toasted him. 'Shall we get a table?'

'Yeah, sure.'

As she trailed Ethan to a vacant table, Beth felt a pulse of excitement. Ethan seemed like he was good company and, best of all, there was something about him that put a smile on her face. Whether it was his good looks, easy charm or his jokey nature, she felt that she was going to have a pleasant evening.

When the barman called last orders, Beth saw her own surprise at how quickly the time had passed reflected on Ethan's face. They'd only had two drinks and yet almost two hours had gone by.

Beth was glad that Ethan sipped at his pints rather than glugged them down as if it was a race to drunkenness. As a general rule she could take or leave alcohol, and she didn't want to date someone who liked to get drunk four nights a week.

The conversation had flowed back and forth between them. They'd discussed their jobs, and although he had the good manners not to ask, which was something she appreciated, Beth had filled Ethan in on the fact his tip-off had given the police a solid lead.

'Do you want another drink?'

'I do, but I'm going to have to say no. I have an early start what with the investigation.'

'I understand. I'm on shift at seven tomorrow morning myself.'

Beth returned Ethan's rueful grin. 'The joys of shift work. I don't miss it one bit, but even now I'm with FMIT, I still can't predict what time I'll get home.'

Ethan held the door open for Beth as she exited into the street. 'I'm free on Wednesday night if you'd like to meet up again.'

Beth leaned in and gave him a quick kiss. 'Here at nine again works for me.'

'Sweet.'

As Beth was climbing into a taxi, she got a text from him.

'*Goodnight, beautiful. I really enjoyed chatting with you tonight and I'm looking forward to Wednesday.*'

CHAPTER SIXTEEN

The dog whistle went to Willow's mouth for perhaps the hundredth time since her springer spaniel had run off. As a rule of thumb, Spike was a good and obedient dog, but the move back to Maryport had unsettled him.

Spike going missing was an end to her day that she could well do without. As part of her role at the bank she had to visit customers at their home or office. The first visit was with a customer called Andrew Cooper, which had been bad enough as he'd flirted with her awkwardly, despite her not giving him any kind of encouragement, but when she'd arrived to meet her next client, Oliver Morrison, the experience with Cooper had paled into insignificance by comparison.

Cooper had been polite and respectful in his awkwardness whereas Morrison had been plain lecherous. It wasn't so much that he was undressing her with his eyes, more that he was re-dressing her in whatever outfits fuelled his fantasies. As she'd left she'd felt the need for a long shower and she was already dreading her next visit to his business.

Willow put the whistle to her lips again. Spike had lost the battle for supremacy with her mother's black Lab and as such he was struggling to find his place in the new environment. But Willow had had to return to the family home – it had become necessary when she'd caught her husband in bed with the next-door neighbour.

If it had been their neighbour's pretty wife she may have been able to understand, but what attraction he'd found in a balding man with a paunch was beyond her.

Willow had thought a long walk along the banks of the River Ellen would tire out Spike while simultaneously giving him a treat. He'd gone wandering off a half hour ago just as the light was beginning to fade and she had been thinking about turning for home.

She'd walked this route often enough in the days before she left home to not worry about navigating it in the dark, but until she found Spike, there was no way she was returning to her parents' house.

As he'd run off, she was left in a quandary, should she head up or downstream looking for him, or should she remain where she was?

Perhaps he'd crossed the river and was gadding about on the far bank. Letting him off the lead the first time she'd brought him on this walk had been a mistake. He'd wandered off at once, his nose following a thousand and one smells, but he'd done his usual trick of coming back every few minutes and checking where she was.

Until he'd sauntered off and hadn't returned.

Willow took the whistle from her mouth and tried shouting Spike's name along with a few of the usual entreaties she used to attract him.

Still he didn't come, so she tried again. Even as she was shouting his name she was trying to keep her irritation at him from showing in her voice. If he was lost he'd be worried, and she didn't want him thinking he'd be in trouble.

When she stopped yelling for him she fell silent and strained her ears. She was listening for splashing as he padded in the river, or rustling as he bounded back to her through the tall grass.

A bark would have been music to her ears, but she knew Spike only barked when he heard a doorbell or a knock at the door.

Most of all, she was listening for a whimper, a sign that her beloved dog was hurt.

She heard nothing.

Willow forced her way through a clump of nettles that bordered the river and gritted her teeth against the expected pain. She looked left and right as her eyes sought out Spike's white coat in the fading light.

Not finding him up or downstream she turned her eyes to the far bank and scanned as far as she could see. Twice her eyes picked out white shapes, but when she focussed on them she identified them as clumps of wool snagged from a sheep's back.

The sky had turned a dark purple as the sun sank below the horizon and shadows cast by the trees and bushes lined both banks. Willow couldn't help but feel that this place she had known all her life had taken on a spooky, malevolent presence. Instead of warm and fuzzy memories, all she was getting was menace and the stuff of nightmares.

By the time the last of the light was fading, and Willow was on the point of tears, Spike came bumbling along with a live rabbit in his mouth.

He dropped the rabbit at her feet and looked up at her with that irresistible doggy grin of his that always melted her heart.

Willow reached down and slipped her fingers round Spike's collar lest he pursue the escaping rabbit.

With his lead clipped in place she chatted away to him, asking where he'd been and why he hadn't answered her call.

She didn't expect an answer from him, it was just her way of dealing with the fear she'd had that some ill had befallen Spike.

As she set off for home, she was unaware of the man who'd been watching her, or that he planned to bring a sedative for the dog the next time he followed her along this secluded path.

Most of all, she knew nothing of the fate he had planned for her.

CHAPTER SEVENTEEN

The spreadsheet in front of Beth was growing at an exponential rate. Columns were filling and extra rows were being added as she fed the key points from the various reports into their respective places.

As always she'd run her daily circuit around Penrith before coming into work, had a quick shower and by 7 a.m. she'd got to her desk. Her damp hair may have left a dark patch on the back of her jacket, but if today's weather was anything like yesterday's it would be damp patches under her arms that would be the bigger problem.

The office assigned to FMIT possessed only one window and no air-conditioning. The window faced south, which meant that the sun heated the room from ten in the morning until the middle of the evening. A couple of desk fans moved warm air around without actually changing the temperature.

O'Dowd had been on to Maintenance a dozen times about getting them a portable air-con unit, but none had yet materialised. Carleton Hall being an old building with thick walls helped to keep a steady temperature, but with four computers pushing out heat, the room didn't take long to get stuffy. Even in the winter months, the window was kept open a crack to ensure there was some fresh air in the room.

O'Dowd rapped her pen against a cup to get everyone's attention. 'Right my little band of intrepid investigators. Here're your tasks for today. Frank, I want you to personally speak to the officers who investigated each of the three murders; I want their every thought, especially the ones they didn't put into the reports.

Go see them face to face. If their superiors block you or tell you they're busy, refer them back to the chief super. Ambush them in their gardens if you have to, but speak to them.'

That O'Dowd had given this task to Frank Thompson made sense to Beth; as a long serving copper he'd be treated with a certain amount of respect, as would his rank of DS. He was senior enough to suggest they were taking the investigators' testimonies seriously, yet not so senior as to make them fearful of saying the wrong thing.

'Paul, I want you to collate all the information you can get about the snatch sites. I'm talking about ANPR records, CCTV footage that was examined, witnesses who were spoken to and any other avenues that were explored and can be cross-referenced.'

The task that Unthank had been given was an onerous one. His would be a day of drudgery trapped in an office that had ambitions of becoming an oven.

As O'Dowd turned her gaze upon her, Beth gave her fingers a mental crossing that the tasks given to her would at least get her out of the office.

'Due to your conduct yesterday, DC Young, and a development that you're not yet aware of, I have a special task for you.' O'Dowd's smile was viperous in every way.

'Ma'am?' Beth could hear the dread in her voice, and she saw O'Dowd's smile widen.

'Two things: first off, I've heard back from the CSI team. The invitation and credit card were devoid of any prints. Not even a partial was recovered, which suggests they were wiped down before being left. Second, I've had an email from Digital Forensics. They found over a thousand images of child abuse on Forster's computer.'

Beth's pulse throbbed and she could feel horror coursing through her entire body. This new evidence would allow her to nail Forster good and proper.

'What the?… I thought he was Mister Squeaky Clean. We going to arrest him again?'

'Wrong.' O'Dowd's smile never faltered. 'Forensics cross-referenced all the times the images were downloaded against the mayor's diary. Literally all of them were downloaded when he was away from home. And none of them have ever been opened.'

'So he hasn't had chance to look at them since he downloaded them. They're still on his computer. Unless he wasn't the person who downloaded them.'

'You're underestimating Forensics. In case what you're saying is true, they dug a little deeper. Well, much deeper if I'm honest. They found that someone had hacked into the computer and placed the images in the records.' O'Dowd raised a hand in a halt gesture. 'And before you ask, no they haven't been able to trace the person who put it there, and yes, they're trying everything they can think of, but so far, they've drawn a blank.' The raised hand flapped in a dismissive gesture. 'I didn't understand half of what they told me, but apparently the trail leads to servers in the Cayman Islands, Beirut, Iceland and about a dozen other countries. They also mentioned dynamic IPs, whatever the hell they are, and suggested it was done via Tor and the Dark Web.'

Beth knew what a dynamic IP was and about the Tor Browser. Computers all have an Internet Protocol, or IP, address. These can be static, which means the number is fixed at all times, or they can be dynamic, which means the number changes every time you go online. The Tor Browser cloaks its users's searches, so it was the default browser people used to search the Dark Web, which is where the Internet is at its worst. Things like terrorism cells, hitmen for hire, and all the worst kinds of pornography can be found there among a multitude of other illegal and immoral things.

Beth couldn't help but pull a face. 'If the person who put that porn on the mayor's computer used Tor to cloak his movements, it'll be incredibly hard to trace them.'

O'Dowd pulled much the same distasteful grimace as Beth. 'That's pretty much the impression I got from Forensics.'

'So what is it you want me to do, ma'am?'

'Go see the mayor, find out the names of everyone he figures may hold a grudge against him. Then speak to his mayoral staff and one or two of his opponents, see who they point the finger at. Be discreet with them and hint that some unfounded and scurrilous allegations have been made without telling them the full truth.' O'Dowd raised a hand again to forestall any objection Beth wanted to make. 'It's come down from on high that we're to look into who put those images on the mayor's computer, so whatever you've got to say about the subject is going to be a waste of breath.'

'Ma'am.' Beth could hear the resignation in her tone but she didn't care. O'Dowd had given her this task as a punishment and if she didn't complain a little then the DI may find a further way to make her life miserable.

'When you've done that, I want you to go and see Dr Hewson to get his take on the post-mortems of the first three victims. He only performed one but I want his opinions on the other two as well.'

Beth grabbed the post-mortem files and tucked them under her arm. She might have got the stick from O'Dowd with regards to having to go and play nice with the mayor, but she'd also been given the carrot of speaking to the twinkle-eyed pathologist.

Dr Hewson was a ball of contradictions and his mind was sharper than any scalpel he'd ever lifted. She enjoyed the verbal jousts he initiated and she'd never left his company without learning something.

Beth had a suspicion that she needed to share. 'I've been thinking, and you're not going to like what I've come up with.'

'I don't like the sound of this.' O'Dowd ran a hand though her unruly hair. 'Is this your sideways-thinking brain again?'

'If you want to call it that you can. I've been thinking about the timeline and how someone is obviously framing the mayor. That letter that came, it was sent before Felicia Evans was killed, then when she's found there's evidence left at the deposition site that points the finger of suspicion at the mayor. We know the letter sat on the chief constable's desk for ten days before being opened. We also know that Felicia Evans was raped with a sex toy or some such thing rather than actually being penetrated by a man. What if, and this is something of a stretch, the person who sent the letter was the same person who planted the images on the mayor's computer? Did Digital Forensics say when the images were planted?'

'A fortnight past yesterday.'

Beth twiddled a pen between her fingers as she connected the timings. 'That's the day before the letter was posted. Now that we've established that timeline, let's move forward a few days. The mayor's accuser is waiting, watching the news and reading the papers. Because the letter hasn't been opened, nothing happens. The mayor isn't arrested. He doesn't get done for the images on his computer. So he escalates. Somehow he steals the mayor's credit card. This would be a minor inconvenience until it turns up near Felicia Evans's body.'

'Jesus, Beth. Are you about to suggest that Felicia Evans was killed just to frame the mayor?'

'I am. Think about it. She wasn't raped the same way as the other victims, and while someone in the police should have connected the three previous murders, there's nothing to stop a member of the public hearing about the murders and rapes and using them as background to implicate the mayor. I'm also thinking about the choice of victim. Felicia Evans was dying of cancer. Perhaps the person who killed her and used her deposition site as a place to frame the mayor, chose her because they knew she was dying.'

'What? You mean he was trying to lessen the impact of what he'd done?'

'I think so, ma'am. I think that he may have convinced himself that he was euthanising her rather than killing her. I spoke to her doctor; she only had a few weeks left. In terms of what he did, she was the perfect victim.'

'Dammit, Beth. Why does that brain of yours keep coming up with ideas like this? Why can't you dream up a scenario where kittens and Easter bunnies look cute?' O'Dowd used one hand to scrub hair from her eyes. 'I think you're wrong about that and Felicia was murdered to satisfy his killing lust, and the framing of the mayor is a sideline. Four women killed and sexually violated can't be a coincidence, so it stands to reason that is the killer's prime objective. However, as Felicia is the most recent victim, she's our best lead. Before you see the mayor and Dr Hewson, I want you to find out everything you can about Felicia Evans. Who her friends and family were. Who knew she was ill and anything else you can think of.'

'Yes, ma'am.' Beth got out of her seat and made for the door.

As she opened the door of the office she was met with a man wearing the smartest inspector's uniform she'd ever seen.

She knew who he was by reputation before he even spoke. Martin 'Mannequin' Moore was the face of the Professional Standards Department and the scourge of many a good copper.

Beth had no issue with the man rooting out bent cops and making sure that rules were only bent not broken, but Mannequin was as fastidious with his job as he was with his uniform. No speck of fluff was allowed to tarnish his appearance in the same way that no minor transgression of the rules was permitted.

'DI O'Dowd and… DC Young, is it? I'm glad you're both here.'

CHAPTER EIGHTEEN

Moore shooed Beth back into the FMIT by holding his hand palm downwards and flapping his fingers towards her. It was a gesture that spoke of domineering command and told her that he knew how his reputation preceded him and wasn't afraid to play on it.

That one unspoken gesture was enough for Beth to decide she didn't like the man for his personality let alone his fastidiousness. When you added in his parade-ground posture and the condescending manner, it was small wonder that he was hated by almost every officer in the county.

Mannequin shut the office door in a way that caused the latch to give a deliberate click. With the door shut, he positioned himself in front of it and held his body in a rigid stance. The aftershave that he wore was a traditional one which Beth couldn't identify. Her best guess was that it was something like Old Spice or Brut. The aroma fitted him and his personality every bit as well as his uniform.

'DI O'Dowd, DC Unthank and DC Young I can see. However, there are four members of the Force Major Investigation Team. Where, pray tell, is DS Thompson?'

That he knew their names wasn't a surprise to Beth. A PSD inspector would be sure to do their homework before entering any situation.

'He's gone to get me a low-fat mochaccino with extra cream and six sugars. Either that, or he's out doing his job and investigating the murder and rape of four women. Which incidentally, is what the rest of us would be doing if you hadn't arrived to hold us back.'

Beth wanted to applaud O'Dowd for the way she got under Mannequin's skin. There wasn't a part of her target's body that wasn't quivering with suppressed anger. O'Dowd had scored her points, but until they learned why the PSD inspector was here, it might have been wiser to play along rather than antagonise the man.

'I see you have not changed since our last little meeting, Inspector. Still the same confrontational nature. You may not believe it, but I am not here to persecute you, nor do I take any delight in reprimanding any of my colleagues. I am merely the upholder of the high standards that her Majesty expects of those paid to keep the streets of her mighty kingdom safe.'

'Spare us the holier-than-thou rhetoric and say what you have to say and then beggar off so me and my team can get on with our jobs.' There wasn't a sneer on O'Dowd's face, but Beth couldn't miss the one in her voice. 'If you're here to bollock us, do it and be on your way. If, as you say, you have another purpose for being here, state it and be on your way. When I said we have four rape and murder cases to investigate I wasn't kidding.'

'It is those very crimes that I am here to discuss with you.'

Beth felt her pulse throb that little bit harder. *Did Mannequin have a vested interest in the cases?*

O'Dowd twirled a pen around her fingers. 'I'm curious as to why a PSD inspector wants to discuss an ongoing case when the investigating team haven't had any time for impropriety. Unless that is, a complaint has already been made against us.'

'There have not been any complaints, Inspector. It does interest me, though, that you suggested that one may have been made. That tells me you are sailing as close to the wind as you usually do. On that point, I think it is only fair to warn you that I will be paying very close attention to this case. I shall be reviewing the tapes from the interview room, reading all statements. To all intents and purposes, I will be a silent partner to your team. However, that is not why I came to see you on this occasion.

You mentioned a moment ago that you have only had this case a short time. That is correct. Your team, however, is not the first to investigate three of the rapes and murders. Three other teams worked on them. They failed to get a result. Neither the second or third teams, nor their superiors, managed to identify that Cumbria has what appears to be a serial rapist and murderer at large. That speaks to me of failings. Whether it is the system that has failed or individual officers is something I have to identify. The three unsolved murders which your team has been tasked with investigating are as good as cold cases. Should you solve them, it will be because your team is better than the others. You have the highest-rated team in the county, and I think that if anyone can catch this killer, it is FMIT. However, you must see that if you do solve the murders as cold cases, the original investigating teams are sure to have their deficiencies highlighted.'

Beth wanted to rage at Mannequin, to tell him what an odious creep he was. Explain to him how his proper enunciation and clothes-horse appearance was nothing more than someone applying polish to a steaming pile of excrement. Not only had he warned them they'd be under his direct scrutiny for the duration of this case, he'd as good as intimated that he'd use any success they had as a stick to beat other officers with. That wasn't just wrong, it was demoralising and little more than bullying. There was no justice to be had in what the PSD man was saying, just persecution.

'We understand your concerns, Inspector, and we will, of course, bear them in mind at all times during this investigation.' O'Dowd pointed at the door behind Mannequin. 'If you'll excuse us, we have work to do.'

CHAPTER NINETEEN

As she drove from Penrith's Carleton Hall to Caldbeck, Beth had to fight her instinctive anger at Mannequin's little speech. Had she given in to her baser instincts, she'd have mashed her foot on the throttle and pushed her little car to its limits. To calm herself, she repeatedly went over the details she knew about Felicia Evans. She'd thought it would have been too much to hope for that the woman had already been reported as missing, but sure enough, a report had been made.

Felicia Evans was eighty-three and six weeks ago she had been given two months to live. She'd opted to die at her home in Caldbeck, so the hospital had arranged for carers to visit her four times a day.

The file showed her as having no next of kin. Whether Felicia was estranged from her family, or just the last of her line was something she could find out later; for now, all she could think of was an old woman dying alone. Maybe she'd got some comfort from the carers and maybe they'd been strangers who she only tolerated because she had no one else.

Beth closed her eyes and thought about what it must be like to make that decision. To go home and be alone, or to stay in hospital as she waited for the inevitable. It wasn't one she ever wanted to have to face, and the idea of not having a loved one to grieve her passing terrified Beth.

While the information she had on Felicia – after seeing the woman's corpse, Beth already felt she knew her well enough to think of her in Christian-name terms only – fitted with her theory about the woman being selected as a victim for the sole purpose of framing the mayor, she knew she had to be careful not to fit the facts to her theory and keep an open mind.

A carer had made a visit to the home of Felicia Evans and had found her missing. The broken timber around the back-door's lock and the fact that Felicia had terminal lung cancer was enough to have the carer dialling treble nine.

If it was the case that Felicia Evans had been chosen because of some unknown vendetta against the mayor – and it looked very much like she had been – she was the perfect victim. An old woman who lived alone and was in the final days of her life would be missed by fewer people.

What stood out more than anything else in Beth's mind was that *if* Felicia hadn't been killed by the same person as the other three women, the FMIT had *two* killers to apprehend.

The carer who opened Felicia's door to Beth was a middle-aged woman with a kindly face and a body that was a perfect cylinder. Her eyes held a mixture of sorrow and wisdom.

As she followed the carer into the low cottage, Beth felt like she was stepping back in time. Nothing in the cottage looked as if was built, decorated or made after 1980. The wallpaper looked old enough to have come back into fashion at least twice since it had been hung.

'Bare. Dated. Spotless.'

While dated, the house was clean. Cleaner than it should be for someone suffering with end-stage cancer. The areas behind ornaments were clean, which indicated the surface had been wiped by someone who was house-proud, rather than a carer giving surfaces a quick once-over to help out their charge.

Instead of a 40-inch TV, the small lounge was dominated by a wall of bookshelves. When Beth took a look at one or two of them, she saw they were crime novels. The books were in varying conditions, with some worn from multiple reads, whereas others looked pristine. The covers showed an eclectic mix of old and new titles. One or two, like *Shutter Island,* she recognised as having been made into movies.

The carer took a seat. 'I don't know how much I can help you. I spoke to a constable yesterday, nice young man he was, and told him everything.'

'I know.' Beth gave a tight grin. 'I just have a few follow-up questions. You said that Mrs Evans never had any visitors. Did she talk about her family or mention friends to you at all?'

'Never. She talked about her books and criticised the other carers.'

'Other carers?'

'Yeah. When people are terminal and want to pass at home, we come and look after them. We pop in four times a day. There's three of us been visiting Felicia. I'll be honest, when I heard the complaints she made about my colleagues, I ignored them. The other girls are professionals. We all are. People in Felicia's position often feel angry and scared. We come in, disturb them when they're poorly and they often take out their anger on us.' A shrug. 'It's crap, but it's a part of the job, so we deal with it.'

Beth couldn't help but feel for the carer. The woman dealt with death on a daily basis. If not actual death, imminent death. Now she'd met her, Beth had seen that she was a carer in a lot more ways than just her job description. She could even picture her sitting by a bedside, holding a withered hand long after her shift had finished.

As a detective Beth had grown used to deaths, but she'd really only ever dealt with the aftermath of when people had died. While she might learn about their lives in this way, she'd never achieve the closeness the carer and her colleagues did.

She put a few more questions to the woman without learning much at all. Felicia Evans was a solitary person who was happiest sitting in her chair with a good book. Her one self-pitying comment to the carer had been that she'd never get the chance to read all the books she'd collected.

To Beth the books were the key to Felicia's soul. Whatever had happened to the woman in her younger days, the impact had shaped her life. Whether she'd been shunned by a lover or victimised by someone wasn't the real point. Felicia's books were her escape route. She'd avoid her own dark thoughts and live the characters' lives in her mind.

With the woman's library made up of little but crime fiction, Beth wondered if Felicia was looking for a fictional resolution that she'd never been given in real life.

It was possible that Felicia just liked the puzzles, but if that was the case, wouldn't it stand to reason she might also have a TV so she could watch crime dramas and quiz shows? While not a novel reader herself, Beth knew that when her mother read, she became immersed in the fictional world to the point where she'd lose track of time and wouldn't hear her name being spoken.

Beth tried questioning the carer one last time, but she knew her questions were neither new nor insightful. From the way the carer kept looking at her watch, Beth guessed the woman had another charge she needed to visit, so she finished up and let the woman go.

Beth stood in the cottage and drank in everything she could. Every room had been pored over by a CSI team, yet she didn't expect them to have found anything of note. If this was the rapist's work, he'd not left a decent clue yet. If he was clever enough to hack into computers and leave fake evidence to frame the mayor, it wouldn't be too much of a stretch to expect him to have taken precautions against giving them clues that would lead them to his door.

There was a smell in the cottage that filled every space and she didn't know whether it was due to Felicia's personal decay or the years of scents that had gathered in the furniture. Beth took a few minutes to peer into some of the cupboards and poke about in the writing desk. What she found gave her a profound sense of sadness.

The food in Felicia's cupboards was all supermarket own-brands, while the fridge held tins of corned beef, tongue and spam, a few vegetables, a small block of cheese that was going mouldy and milk that was three days past its sell-by date.

To Beth it spoke of a frugal existence, but the bank statements in the writing desk showed that Felicia was spending only a fraction of her pension. With no known relatives to leave anything to, Felicia was either being overly cautious with her money or perhaps she was punishing herself for something.

For the killer, the taking of such a life would be easier to rationalise. With Felicia being friendless, unloved and near-death from a painful disease, her killer would be able to convince himself that by killing her, he was actually saving her pain.

The question that was now bugging Beth was, if this theory was right, how did Felicia's killer know she was already close to death? Supposedly she was a person who drove others away, didn't tell anyone what was going on in her life. Therefore her killer must have some connection to her, unless she was chosen entirely randomly.

The more Beth thought about it, the more she wondered what had gone on in Felicia's past, as other than her books, everything in Felicia's life was from another time.

With as much insight collected into Felicia's life as she was likely to get from the house, Beth snipped the lock over and pulled the front door closed behind her. She needed to get to the local shop before it closed.

CHAPTER TWENTY

The village shop was just a hundred yards up the road, so Beth set off walking. In villages the shop was the hub at the centre of the gossip wheel. If the shopkeeper didn't have the answers to her questions, nobody would.

Caldbeck was one of those idyllic villages which had been around for ever. The stone houses aged, yet chocolate-box beautiful. Most had window boxes and hanging baskets providing a riot of colour, and the gardens she walked past were all manicured to within an inch of their lives.

As she walked to the shop, she tried to establish a timeline for the night before last in her mind.

Felicia's carer had left the cottage at ten thirty and another had arrived at eight o'clock the next morning. At 6.45 a.m. the walker who'd spotted her body had called it in. Therefore Felicia had to have been taken between 10.30 p.m. and 6.00 a.m. at the latest.

The forty-five-minute window Beth had allowed for someone to kill, defile and then transport Felicia to the deposition site on the banks of Lake Ullswater was tight, but she knew that she had to work to the maximum parameters.

Beth rapped her knuckles on the shop's window a second time but she knew it was a forlorn hope. The shop's lights were off and the A4 piece of paper sellotaped to the window stating its opening hours told her it closed an hour ago. It was only noon, but in a village this size there probably wasn't enough trade to warrant longer opening. The locals would all know the shop's opening times and use it accordingly.

She knew what most of these little village shops were like. They sold newspapers, cigarettes and essentials like bread, milk and cheese. There would be a selection of tinned goods and a limited supply of soft drinks and chocolate bars. The prices would be higher than supermarkets, but the locals would pay them without complaint because the shop was handy for emergency supplies.

Frustrated that she'd missed the chance to speak to the shop-keeper, Beth trudged back towards her car.

When she was halfway back she saw tendrils of smoke rising from the back of a cottage and heard music. It wasn't loud or offensive, just someone playing a radio in the back garden.

Beth went to the house and knocked on the door in the hope the occupants would know where the shop owner lived.

A teenage boy answered, his face a riot of acne, but he was pleasant and Beth could see that once he grew out of the spots, he'd be handsome.

Two minutes later she was in the back garden waiting to speak to the lad's parents. A large barbecue was being tended to by the father while the mother was arranging half a dozen chairs around a wooden table on the lawn.

Beth put her questions to the mother first and then the father. Neither admitted to knowing much about Felicia. Their contact with the woman was limited to greetings or short conversations about the weather. They said they used to invite her to barbecues and the odd dinner party but she always declined their hospitality.

As she'd talked to the father, Beth's stomach had growled at the smell of the burger he was cooking. He'd smiled and served her a burger in a sesame seed bun without even asking if she wanted it. By the time she'd finished the burger, more of Caldbeck's residents had arrived. The father, being the good citizen he was, directed each of his guests Beth's way so she could speak to them in turn.

Beth had been at the house for an hour or so when she realised that other than paying a jobbing builder to rebuild her garden wall, Felicia had kept contact with her fellow villagers to an absolute minimum.

A neighbour Beth had chatted to said that when Felicia was in her garden, she'd either be gardening or reading. The neighbour had tried chatting to her over the wall but it had become clear that the woman just wanted to be left alone.

The burger in her stomach felt good as Beth drove out of Caldbeck. She'd not had the chance to eat today and as she navigated the narrow road south to the point where it joined the A66, she was wishing that she'd been offered a second one.

While her body was mostly content, her brain wasn't. She'd put a call in to O'Dowd and had related her lack of findings. The DI had been crotchety, but not too bad.

To Beth's way of thinking, Felicia Evans's lifestyle spoke of either self-flagellation for some reason known only to Felicia or a desire to hide away and delight in solitude. Beth knew that she would have to investigate the victim to catch her killer. What she had to find out was the reason Felicia had chosen to shut herself away from the world. She'd meant to run Felicia's name through the PND and HOLMES to see if it came up with anything relevant, but after Mannequin's arrival into the office, the idea had been forgotten.

It would be the first thing she did upon her return to the office.

CHAPTER TWENTY-ONE

Beth's desk was as tidy as her mind. Everything had its place and while she didn't have any OCD tendencies, she liked to have everything in its rightful home so she knew where things were without even having to look for them. The pile of notes and folders she kept to the left of her keyboard looked haphazard to anyone else, but Beth knew what was in each folder and what each note was relevant to.

Sitting at her desk, reading the files on her screen, she found herself understanding the old lady's need for isolation.

Felicia Evans had been gang-raped in the early 1970s. She'd reported it and her rapists had not only stood trial, but they'd been convicted.

That Felicia had been the victim of a sexual assault in death, as in life, somehow made it all the more horrific. Before death, she'd been a lonely woman, cloistered away and friendless. The way she'd hidden herself away spoke of a lasting trauma.

Reporting a rape and seeing it followed through right to conviction was an emotional and sapping ordeal in today's world, even with measures such as video testimony to lessen the impact of giving evidence. Beth couldn't begin to think how horrific it would have been over forty years ago, when attitudes were different.

The fact that Felicia had endured the challenges of reporting her rape, and the subsequent trial, spoke of a massive inner strength. Whether she'd been fuelled by a desire for revenge or retribution wasn't important, what mattered was that justice had been served and that Felicia would have had a crumb of comfort to help her manage any nightmares she had.

On the off-chance that Felicia had been murdered by one of the four rapists who'd assaulted her, Beth ran their names to see where they were now. Three of the four had passed away as they'd been a minimum of ten years older than Felicia and the fourth was back in prison for another sexual assault he'd committed.

Regardless of the fact she had few clues to follow, Felicia's plight made Beth even more determined to solve her murder.

Another thing that was playing on her mind was the rapist's change of tack. Instead of penetrating Felicia himself he'd used a sex toy or some other object. It didn't make sense to Beth, but she couldn't think of a credible reason for the change.

Whatever else broke with the case, no matter how many hours she had to work, Beth made a silent promise to Felicia that she'd catch her killer, and another to young Kerrie Newham that she'd make sure the person who robbed her of her mother would pay.

Even as she began to pack up her things for the day, an idea of how to identify the rapist came to her. It was too late in the day to pursue it now, but she planned to put the suggestion to O'Dowd the next morning so she could pursue the idea.

CHAPTER TWENTY-TWO

Beth parked her car in The Lanes car park and sat where she was for a moment collecting her thoughts one final time. She'd put the idea she'd had about tracing Felicia's killer to O'Dowd and, while the DI had agreed with her line of thinking, O'Dowd had told her that she'd had instructions from on high and that Beth was to spend her time trying to identify who was framing the mayor, as the DCI and chief super both believed that was the best way to catch Felicia's killer.

The playlist she put on for the journey had been stocked with power ballads. It was her 'calm down' music, as she wanted to chase away the anger at what she felt was unnecessary interference from the higher-ranking officers.

She accepted that the case had generated a lot of media attention. The killer had been dubbed 'the Lakeland Ripper' by the ITV news. As was typical, once someone had christened the killer, the name had stuck and other members of the press were sure to use it.

Once she got to the outskirts of Carlisle she managed to refocus her mind from its wandering across all aspects of the case and concentrate on how she would handle the mayor.

O'Dowd had made it clear that she must be respectful and that she had to apologise for the ways she'd pressured him on Monday. That wasn't something she was looking forward to, but she was aware it had to happen whether she liked it or not.

The greater concern to her was how she should act around the mayor. There was no doubt in her mind that behind his public image he was a different character. That he wasn't as squeaky clean as he made himself out to be. The fact someone was trying to frame him as a rapist and a murderer was a big red flag as far as she was concerned.

Sending an anonymous letter was one thing, but that the killer had escalated his campaign – by planting evidence at the scene which implicated the mayor and also secreting child abuse images on his computer – spoke of a deeply personal vendetta.

Maybe the DCI and chief super were right: maybe her best chance of catching Felicia's killer was to trace him through his campaign against the mayor rather than following the trail from Felicia's murder.

Beth felt a compelling urge to wonder if the vendetta was an indication there was a darker side to Forster's nature, but she knew that while it wouldn't be an easy thing to prove, it would be even harder to have her proof believed. When she factored in to the equation the mayor's status and Mannequin's scrutiny, she knew that any evidence she uncovered which showed the mayor had wronged someone who was a rapist and murderer would have to convince the DCI and chief super long before it got anywhere near a courtroom.

None of these reasons were enough to convince Beth that she was wrong. The internal voice telling her the mayor had played some witting or unwitting part in the chain of events spoke with too much conviction to be ignored. Besides, she'd never backed down from a challenge before and the series of obstacles in front of her only meant she'd have to rise higher than normal to deal with this particular challenge.

Beth's fingers groped around the glove box until they found the small bag in which she kept a limited supply of make-up and a tiny bottle of perfume.

The last thing she wanted to do was make Forster think she was trying to entrap him, so she pulled only a thin smear of lipstick across her mouth and added a dribble of perfume to her finger which she then dabbed once behind each ear.

With her lippy applied, Beth climbed out of her car and headed for the stairs down to the shopping centre.

The Lanes was built in the eighties and its brick facades have stood up to the intervening years well. Its streets throng with people of varying statuses and there is a good mix of high-street shops.

On her days off work, Beth would often come here for a browse, or to source an outfit for a special occasion. Today though, she didn't so much as glance at the window displays as she made her way through the covered alleyways of The Lanes and exited onto Lowther Street.

Derek Forster had set up an office for his mayoral staff at Broadacre House amid other such public services as Jobcentre Plus and the Chamber of Commerce.

During the short walk from the shopping-centre car park to Broadacre House, Beth did what she always did when walking the streets; she looked at every man she passed. Her eyes seeking a pair of lipstick kisses tattooed onto the side of a neck. Neither Neck Kisses nor the man who'd been holding the bottle that had ruined her cheek had been apprehended, but that didn't mean she wouldn't stop looking until she found them.

As she entered the building, the cynical part of Beth's nature told her that the mayor's door would be considerably more open for those who were members of the Chamber than those who frequented the job centre.

CHAPTER TWENTY-THREE

The mayor's office wasn't anything like Beth had expected it to be. Instead of the country-house study she'd somehow imagined, it was like every other office she'd been in. Filing cabinets and desks laden with files took up most of the floor space. The walls were adorned with shelves lined by folders with handwritten labels and general office supplies like paper, envelopes and ink cartridges for printers.

Inside the office, three women were sitting at desks. All were busy typing or speaking into their telephone headsets, although one did look up and indicated she'd be with Beth in a moment.

The wait didn't worry Beth. It gave her a chance to look at the women with more care. Each of them fitted the same criteria: thirty-five to forty-five years of age, good-looking and well-turned-out. None of the women carried more than a stone above what their doctor would advise, and only one of them wore a ring on their left hand.

To Beth it was as if the mayor was surrounding himself with pretty women. She couldn't help but wonder if he'd turn his charm on to any of the women when the mood struck him.

Beth had read the reports of the officers who'd interviewed all of Forster's mayoral staff. None of them had raised any suspicions, and all had been aghast at the idea that the mayor had been implicated in such a way.

The woman who'd acknowledged her a moment ago was ending her call, when the mayor came into the office. Beth saw the flash of recognition in his eyes when she turned. As was so often the way with strangers, his gaze fixed on the scar on her cheek before moving away.

Beth held out her hand. 'Mr Mayor, it's very good of you to spare me some of your precious time.'

Forster gave her the full election-winning smile as he took her hand. 'It's no trouble at all. I'm eager to help.' He released her grip and gestured to a doorway at the back of the office. 'If you'd like to follow me.'

The mayor's handshake had been firm, although the skin of his hands had been soft. Like so much about him, his handshake was a statement. Firm to provide confidence, but not so hard as to be a challenge or inflict pain. It spoke of reassurance, of power and of consideration. It told her that he was giving the impression of a man who could be trusted.

After shaking his hand, Beth trusted him even less than she had before.

The mayor closed the door of his mini office behind her and offered her a seat. His office was a smaller version of the main one, although she could see he had a few photos of himself at various events on the spare wall space.

Beth found it interesting that he had an ego wall. It told her even more about the real him than his handshake.

Businessmen had ego walls to provide confidence to other businessmen who came to their office, to show off their successes, and on the bad days, remind themselves of the good times.

The mayor had no need of an ego wall in this office. Any non-mayoral business he conducted wouldn't happen here, it would take place on a golf course or a flash restaurant. This office was a place of work, functional rather than decorative, which meant there was nobody to impress beyond himself.

The pictures on the wall were nothing more than a back rub for his ego. Derek Forster was at the peak of his achievements: he was mayor of Carlisle and on an upward trajectory. He'd made a fortune selling his business and was always being named as an eligible bachelor. That he needed to massage his ego in this way gave Beth an insight into the man's psyche. To some, the collection of photos might suggest that regardless of his achievements and successes, he could be insecure and used the wall as a way to bolster himself against the rigours of the office, but Beth didn't think he was insecure.

When arrested for rape and murder on Monday Forster had been calm, assured, and even in the face of everything she'd thrown at him, he'd never lost his cool. He'd retained enough surety to overcome their accusations and never once had his confidence wavered. If anything, the more she pressed him, the stronger he got.

Beth took the seat she was offered, and a deep breath, before opening her mouth.

'First of all, I'd like to apologise to you if you thought I was overly harsh the other day. Rape and murder cases are very serious and I'm afraid I let my emotions get the better of me. It was unprofessional for me to do that.'

Forster leaned back in his chair and laced his fingers together across his chest. 'Well, I have to say I wasn't expecting that. I'm sorry, but I don't accept your apology because I feel there's no need to apologise. I knew I was innocent, just as you knew you were doing your best to prove me guilty. Circumstances made us adversaries and the truth ended the war. As a citizen of Cumbria, let alone the mayor of Carlisle, I support a determined, impassioned police force, who're doing everything in their power to apprehend criminals.'

'That's very gracious of you.' Beth meant it. There was something about Forster's manner and the way he spoke that exuded charm and engendered belief. She recognised that she was being charmed by him, so she pressed on with the reason O'Dowd had sent her. 'I'm afraid you're not going to like what I say next.'

'Try me.' There was a quiet confidence in Forster's tone.

'When the guys from Digital Forensics were looking at your home computer, they found over a thousand illegal images of child abuse.'

'That's absurd.' All the colour had drained from the mayor's face. 'Utterly ridiculous. I would never do such a thing. I never look at any porn, let alone kiddie porn.'

'I know.' Beth spread her hands wide. 'I'm here on my own; there's no arrest team with me today. The times and dates that the files were added to your computer matched with times you were at civic functions. What you said about not looking at any porn is also backed up by your search history. We don't think you looked at those images and videos, but we do think that someone wants us to believe you did.'

'You mean you're not here to arrest me again?'

'Not at all. I'm here to try to find out who planted those images on your computer and who left your credit card beside the body that was found yesterday morning.'

'That poor woman.' The mayor's face lost some of its colour. 'How did my card end up so close to her? I've checked, and since I lost it, nobody has tried to use it. Why steal a card only to toss it away?'

Beth kept her tone soft and her eyes on the mayor. 'We're actually working on the theory that the card was deliberately placed near Felicia Evans's body to implicate you in her murder.'

'What? How did the person who stole my card know where a murder victim had been dumped?' A hand flapped. 'Sorry, that was crass of me. I didn't mean it the way it came out.'

Beth didn't say anything; she left the mayor to draw his own conclusions. A hand shot up to his mouth as if trying to catch the last of the colour as it drained from his face.

'No. Please tell me that you're not thinking that lady was killed just to frame me. Please?'

The mayor's hands shook as he reached for the glass of water on his desk. His eyes never left Beth's as they sent out a silent plea for absolution of blame.

'That's not what we're thinking. We think that a rapist and murderer is trying to frame you.' As much as she might have some doubts about the mayor, Beth felt sympathy for him. While the fact the killer had murdered and raped more than one victim may offer some reassurance to Forster that Felicia hadn't died for the sole purpose of framing him, there would always be that nagging doubt at the back of his mind. 'I know this probably won't help you come to terms with what's happened, but Mrs Evans was dying from cancer.'

Forster washed both hands over his face a few times. 'To be quite honest, right now I don't know if it helps or not. Who would do such a thing? Why would they do it to me?'

'That's what I'm hoping you can tell me. I need a list of who has previously had access to your computer. And I want to know about anyone who may harbour a grudge against you.'

'I… I… I can't think of anyone who'd do this to me. I'm the mayor for goodness' sake. I'm respected for the good works I do and the charities I've supported.'

'Take a minute and think about who would want to damage you and your reputation so badly they'd try and frame you for rape and murder.'

The way that Forster was blustering and the shocked expression he wore told Beth that her news had left his brain reeling.

She had to look at the facts: the mayor had been a successful businessman before dedicating his life to local politics. Neither field was one where you could succeed without picking up a few enemies along the way; a partner bought out before the business really took off, a rival put out of business because Forster had undercut him or sold a better product. Maybe it was a political opponent who'd tired of losing against the mayor and had taken to smearing Forster in this underhand way.

While any of these scenarios would present boundless options for grudges to get out of hand, a part of Beth was still wondering what the mayor had done to attract the hatred of someone who was a multiple murderer. The taking of a life, even one as close to death as Felicia had been, was a huge thing and to her mind it seemed unlikely that the killer was a political rival. While she didn't trust politicians, she didn't believe one was a serial rapist and murderer.

The way Forster had mentioned that he was the mayor and that he supported charities grated on Beth. It was as if those qualities overrode any other deeds he may or may not have done. Not for the first time since she'd entered his private office, Beth was being shown the size of the man's ego.

She decided to press him a little while he was still off balance; it was a bit malicious of her, but just as in the interview room, witnesses sometimes needed to be prodded to provide their answers.

'Have you any ideas as to who may bear a grudge against you?'

'Nobody I can think of.'

'Right, shall we start with who had access to the computer at your home?'

'No one did. It's passworded and nobody but me knows the password.' Forster tilted his head to the side. 'I was in IT, trust me, nobody could guess my password and I never wrote it down.'

'Okay then, perhaps if I prompt you a little. Tell me about the business you used to have.'

'It was a tech start-up I created when the Internet began to really take off. You know the booking engines like Booking.com and Ticketmaster?'

Beth nodded; she'd used both on several occasions. 'You mean like hotels and so on? How does that work?'

'Exactly.' Forster's natural confidence returned as he talked about himself. 'Hotels, sports stadiums, and a multitude of other venues were suddenly finding that people wanted to book online. To use Booking.com as an example; when someone searches for a hotel in Carlisle, Booking.com will trawl its database and the person doing the search gets presented with the results.'

'I'm with you so far. I've used Booking.com.'

'Most people have these days. Anyway, when a hotel wants to sell its rooms on Booking.com, they have to upload their availability and what prices they're charging for each room on each particular date. To do this manually for a large hotel would be a full-time job when you consider how many sites like Booking.com there are. As technology changed and more hotels began to get computerised diaries, or property-management systems to give them their correct name, there became a need for the OTAs like Booking.com to speak directly to the individual hotels' PMSs.'

'Excuse me, but what do you mean by OTAs?'

'Sorry, acronyms were part of our daily lives. OTAs stands for online travel agents such as Booking.com, LateRooms and Expedia. Along with my team, I developed software that sat in the middle ground between the OTAs and the PMSs. Our software was called SimpleBooker and it would integrate over three hundred different OTAs with more than four hundred PMSs.'

'Wow, I never knew there was a need for such a thing. It must have been terribly complicated working out all the kinks.' Even as she said the words, Beth winced inwards at how simpering they sounded. While she didn't want Forster thinking she was too smart, her pride prevented her from wanting to be taken for an idiot. 'Why did you sell the company? It sounds to me like you'd have a business for life.'

'I got an offer from a competitor that I really couldn't turn down.'

'What about your employees? Were any of them upset at losing their jobs?'

'They were all a bit sad that the company was being taken over, but in the terms of the sale contract I put in a clause stating that my employees all had to be retained by the new company for a minimum of two years, working out of our old office. I also made all four of them directors of the company and gave them each a

1 per cent share. After tax, they'd all have cleared something in the region of a quarter of a million.'

Beth took a minute to consider this act of generosity. While it was a wonderful gesture from an employer to look after his staff in this way, the fact that he'd mentioned the staff each got around £250,000 after tax gave her an idea of the figures involved. Allowing for a 50 per cent tax rate meant that the 1 per cent share was worth £500,000 and the company £50 million.

Those kinds of numbers boggled Beth's mind, but when you factored in office politics, they also gave a possible motive for the campaign that was being conducted against the mayor. If one of the former employees believed that Forster had made millions from their hard work, and had passed out just a paltry 1 per cent to each of the people whose hard work had earned him the payday, then there was a breeding ground for resentment. Especially when you factored in the sums of money involved. The problem was, if that theory was correct, it meant that one of his former employees was the murderer.

'That's very generous of you. As you're out of that industry, I'd like to speak to your former employees to see if someone from that industry bears a grudge against you. For all you know, another competitor may have been wanting to sell their business to the same company you did, only for the deal to fall through because your sale happened first.'

Forster removed a piece of paper from the printer behind him and wrote down four names and addresses.

Beth was surprised he could remember his ex-employees' addresses so readily until she thought about her own memory. While she was rubbish at remembering things like family birthdays, she could bring to mind the names of every suspect she'd ever interviewed, where they'd been picked up and how they'd looked and dressed.

She knew that recollection had a lot to do with interest, French lessons at school had taught her little more than *oui*, *non* and *je suis*, but she could sing every word to the songs she'd listened to at the time. If something was important to her, even if only for a fleeting time, it lodged itself into her brain for eternity, whereas the details she found irrelevant tumbled straight from her mind.

'What about any employees you had to dismiss? Were there many of those?'

'None actually.' A proud look overtook Forster. 'My hiring process was extremely rigorous and the people I hired were all good workers.'

'What about people who left your company to go and work elsewhere? Is it possible they felt they were forced out?'

'I only had one such employee and she only left because she wanted to start up her own company. She calls me from time to time to pick my brain, and where I can, I help her out. She was always more interested in the workings of the PMS systems than the integration, so that's what her company does. As her business and mine were complementary, we'd recommend each other to our customers. Check them out if you have time; EdenData is growing nicely and she's won awards for her entrepreneurship.'

'What's her name?'

'Donna Waddington.' Forster checked his phone then reeled off her number.

Beth added the details to the list Forster had provided as she thought about how best to deal with the elephant in the room. Not finding a subtle way, she opted for being direct.

'These five people, they're all programmers, are they?'

'Yes, that's right. What of it?'

'Forgive my terminology, they're all programmers, computer geeks if you like. To my mind, that means they'd all have the skills or abilities to hack into your computer and leave some incriminating evidence. Say, a thousand images of child pornography.' Beth gave a self-deprecating shrug. 'I'm fairly tech savvy when it comes to using systems others have built, but I wouldn't know where to start with regards to hacking into your computer. To my mind, they would be able to do it with ease. I'm sure the same thought has already crossed your mind. I mean, according to Digital Forensics, your computer was loaded with the best malware and antivirus software available. That means whomever put those images on your computer was no ordinary person who was a bit tech savvy; in my book it means they were a major computer geek. And lo and behold, you used to employ five such people.'

When Beth looked into Forster's eyes she could see that he was battling the news. From his point of view he'd been betrayed by someone he trusted. Knifed in the back by someone he probably counted as a friend.

There was little doubt in her mind that's how he thought of his ex-employees: gifting them a share of his windfall had proved that he thought highly of them. That one of them may be a serial rapist and murderer would make their betrayal even worse for him.

Forster shook his head as he tried to get his brain round the idea. To Beth it had been an obvious leap, but he'd been unable to see the possibility because of his closeness to the employees.

There was also the fact that a lot of people who were as clever as Forster, had a deficit of common sense. They might be super-smart when it came to writing reams of computer code, but they'd be unaware of what was going on around them; they'd be the last person to spot danger, recognise a charged atmosphere or understand the frailties of human nature, and comprehend all the duplicity that came with it. To have succeeded in political office, Forster must have had good instincts and awareness, but that didn't mean that he hadn't given someone trust when they didn't deserve it.

'I can see what you're getting at, but you're wrong; none of them would try and frame me like this. They wouldn't do it. I might not have been close friends with them, but we got on as well as any tight-knit team could be expected to. Besides, if what you're saying is true, one of them is a serial killer. You're wrong, wrong I tell you. Wrong.'

Beth didn't respond; she just let Forster carry on thinking. It wasn't her he was trying to convince, it was himself.

The colour hadn't yet returned to his face, and there was a tremble to his voice that hadn't been there earlier. As far as Beth was concerned, she was seeing another hidden part of Forster: she was seeing him weakened and distraught as he came to terms with thoughts he found unthinkable.

Throughout her life, Beth had encountered the usual mix of people that everyone does. Some she'd liked and some she hadn't, and she couldn't get away from the feeling that she really did not trust Derek Forster. Surely anyone who'd hurt someone enough for them to frame him in this way couldn't be a wholly good person?

'Mr Mayor.' Beth only used his title to remind him of how far from grace he could fall. 'If what you say is true and it's not one of your former employees, who do you think it could be?'

'It's not them, I tell you, they wouldn't do that to me. By all means, check them out, but I'm telling you, you'll be wasting your time.'

Beth lifted a hand from her knee. 'Please, Mr Mayor, calm down. It wasn't my intention to upset you. I'm just a police officer who's been trained to think a certain way.'

'I'm sorry.' Forster dragged a hand down his face as he tried to pull himself together. 'I just find the accusations against me reprehensible and the thought that it might have been one of the SimpleBooker guys has sickened me.'

'I know this can't be easy for you.' Beth didn't intend to make it easy. What she intended to do was ally herself to him by making it hard and then presenting a solution by solving the case. 'But if we're to identify your persecutor, then all of this will go away. Please, think about who could have enough of a grudge to do this to you. Have you had any threats made against you? Any damage to your property?'

Forster's face crumpled a little then twisted in anger. 'My car had a tyre slashed a few weeks ago. Before that it was scratched while in a car park.' A shrug. 'I put it down to someone who didn't agree with my politics or someone damaging a nice car just because they could.'

'I see. Did you report either of these incidents?'

'I didn't bother. Like I said, I thought it was someone jealous of my success or someone who held a different political stance. The acts were small and petty and I didn't want to waste the police's time, as I know how stretched you all are.'

'Were there any other incidents?'

'None that I can recall.'

'So, there weren't any altercations? Nobody gave you a piece of their mind, shouted abuse at you for something they thought you'd done?'

Forster shook his head.

'Okay.' Beth used the blunt end of her pen to scratch an itch at the back of her neck. 'That's that part of your life dealt with. Still a long way to go though.'

Forster slumped back into his seat. 'What else do you want to know?'

'We've covered the business side of your life, so we need to look at the political side, and that will leave just one part of your life to discuss.'

'What's that? I'm a businessman turned politician. What else is there to discuss?'

Beth managed to not smile at Forster's unwitting naivety. 'The personal side. By your own admission you're one of Cumbria's most eligible bachelors and it's no secret that you enjoy, shall we say, female companionship?'

Forster gave a terse nod to say that he was up for the discussion, but to Beth he looked weakened and vulnerable.

CHAPTER TWENTY-FOUR

Forster's political life had yielded no obvious suspects as to who might want to frame him. He claimed to have good relationships with his opponents and that there was no deep-seated animosity despite opposing political opinions.

That left his love life to discuss.

It was clear that Forster was reluctant to speak about his sex life, and it wasn't a subject Beth wanted to get too far into, but she knew that it was a credible line of enquiry and, as such, it would have to be pursued regardless of how uncomfortable either party may feel.

'Okay. Now you need to tell me about your relationships. I'm talking about the women you've dated, courted or even had a one-night stand with. I suggest you start at the present day and work backwards.'

'I thought a gentleman should never tell.' The wan smile that accompanied Forster's words never got close to his eyes.

Beth couldn't stop herself adding a harder edge to her voice. Even as he was being questioned about his persecutor, there was a charm to the mayor's words. 'That applies to locker rooms and bars, not police investigations. Who are you currently seeing?'

'Do you really need to do this?'

'Yes, we do. If you want us to find the person who's framing you. Someone who, I might remind you, in addition to being a rapist and murderer, would have paid child abusers for images of children, just to incriminate you. There are reasons for doing this.

So, if we can just focus for a moment on your love life that would be good. I guess it could also be someone who was rejected in favour of you, or a boyfriend or husband of someone you've dated?'

'Come on now, I'm not in the habit of dating people who're in relationships. I make a point of only seeing people who're single.'

'And how do you know they're single? Wedding rings can be taken off, the existence of partners can be denied.' Beth looked up from her notes at him. 'Take me for example, say we met at a civic function and there's no obvious man on my arm, do you think I'm single, married or in a relationship?'

Forster gazed at her. Let his eyes jump to her left hand and then back to her face. Beth could tell he was focussing on the scar adorning her left cheek.

He hesitated a moment before answering and scratched at his chin. 'Based on what I've seen of you, both today and back on Monday when you arrested and interviewed me, I'd say you're too driven to be in a relationship, that you put your work above everything else. It's not that you don't want to have someone in your life, it's more that at this moment, you don't have the time or mental energy to cope with everything a serious relationship entails. Having said that, you're a very attractive woman and you'll probably have plenty of offers. I think you'll see someone for a short period of time and then break it off once it starts to get serious. Where you are in that cycle just now is anyone's guess.'

'Okay, so you've got me pegged. For the record I'm currently single. But you had previously met me. If I had met you at a party you wouldn't have had that experience to draw on. You would have had to have trusted me, or researched me through mutual acquaintances. Do you research the women you date or take them at face value?'

'Face value.'

Beth was pleased with his admission, although disappointed with the answer. If Forster had done his research, it would have meant that there would be a lot less chance of him attracting the ire of a husband or boyfriend, thereby cutting down the amount of work she'd have to do.

While the mayor's assessment of her had been rather damning and had made her come across as a commitment-phobe, she was pleased her current dating status had remained mysterious. Her mind drifted to Ethan. She'd only been on one date with him so far, but she enjoyed his company and it was obvious he enjoyed hers. The fact he wanted to see her again two days after their first date boded well. She knew that one date didn't make for a relationship, but as far as she was concerned, until she or Ethan suggested they no longer liked each other, she wasn't interested in anyone else. Beth's moral code didn't allow her to see more than one person at a time, regardless of how often or how long they'd dated.

Although the date with Ethan had come about by little more than chance, she was looking forward to seeing him again. He was good company, funny and best of all, he'd accepted her for the person she was. He'd looked at her face and had had the decency not to mention her scarred cheek. Other men she'd dated had asked about it, had wanted to know its origins and had continually looked at the scar or referred to it to the point where she'd cut the date short.

She couldn't begin to imagine Ethan being so crass; conversely, she now found herself wanting to tell him about it.

'Okay, Mr Mayor. So who are you seeing just now?'

'Nobody. I split with my last lady friend around two months ago.' He gave a rueful gesture. 'We saw each other a couple of times a week for about three months. After a while it became obvious that we had little in common beyond physical attraction. When she ended the relationship, she told me that she wanted a husband not a boyfriend.' A shrug. 'I wasn't looking for a wife, so we said our goodbyes and moved on with our lives. There were no tears or shouting, just an acceptance that we wanted different things.'

Beth heard the same kind of story from Forster three more times, before she'd covered the past two years.

It seemed to her that Forster was content with his life. He'd date for a while, tire of that person and then move on to someone else. What he'd guessed about her love life was actually a reflection of his own. Beth figured that he didn't want to settle down; he was happy to always have the early days of a relationship when everything was about exploring each other's bodies at every given opportunity. He'd forsaken real love for the artificial infatuation that is driven by hormones.

His life wouldn't be lonely as his ego was large enough to keep him company. He'd know that he could have his pick of women if he put his mind to it, his looks, charm and money would ensure that he'd always be able to find a companion when he wanted one.

To Beth, this seemed like an empty and soulless existence. She had no idea where things would go between her and Ethan, but she'd known when she'd agreed to have a drink with him, that she would let the relationship run its natural course. Whether that one day led to two point four kids and a people carrier in the drive, or two months of unbridled passion wasn't the issue, she liked Ethan, and while Forster had been right that she was driven with regards to her career, she didn't envisage spending her whole life as a singleton. One of the best things about Ethan was that he worked as a paramedic; therefore he got the shift work and understood the vagaries of the job in a way that lots of others didn't. His easy smile and bluest of blue eyes drew her to him along with his jocular nature and the way he made her feel like the only person he could see.

'Thanks.' Beth laid down her pen. 'We've covered your relation-ships. Did you have any one-night stands during the last two years?'

Forster let his gaze dance around the room before he brought it back to her. 'I had three.' He gave a half scowl, half smile. 'Two were with ladies I know. From time to time, one or other of us will call the other for some company. If we're single at the time, we meet up.'

'Lots of people have fuck buddies. It's nothing to be ashamed of.' Beth wasn't trying to be kind. She was aiming for the shock value of using the term. 'What about the other one, who was she?'

A look of distaste overtook the mayor's face. 'I'm afraid that wasn't my finest moment. I met a lady at a civic function over at Workington. We chatted and, as I was leaving, she asked me if I'd like to join her for a drink. It was just before Christmas and I thought sharing a drink with a beautiful lady was a better way to spend the rest of the evening than sitting in front of the telly.'

'What was her name?'

'Lorraine.' A pause to grimace. 'I think that on reflection it might not have been her real name.'

'Why do you say that?'

'When I used her name she didn't always answer first time. It was like she was using a false name and then remembering that she had to answer to it.'

Beth gave a rueful smile. 'It's all part of the games people play. So, you had a drink with Lorraine, what happened then?'

'We had the drink in the bar of the Wall Park and then we went up to her room. I left a few hours later and I haven't seen her since.'

Rather than give a trite reply, Beth maintained a silence. For two people to hook up in this way wasn't unusual. Both would have their needs satisfied and so long as nobody expected more from the encounter, no feelings would be hurt.

A one-night stand wasn't something she'd ever done herself, but there had been times when she had definitely fancied a no-strings night of passion. More than anything else, the main reason she'd never done it was the fact that whenever the desire was strong in her, the only available candidates were either drunk or married, and she thought too much of herself to hook up with a drunken stranger or a cheater.

That the woman had potentially used a false name spoke of a desire for anonymity. This, in turn, suggested that she was maybe married or in a long-term relationship, which also suggested there could be an aggrieved party.

Beth questioned Forster about the event for a while and then, with her hand aching from all the notes she'd taken, she got up to leave.

'Before you go, there's something I'd like to ask you.'

Beth stopped moving for the door and rested a hand on the back of the chair she'd just risen from. 'What is it?'

'When I spoke about setting up a charity for rape victims I was serious. It's something I want to do and I'd like to have you on board in an advisory capacity. Together we could potentially help hundreds of women. As a man I admittedly don't know a lot about how women might feel talking to counsellors, how many women bury the experience and never talk about it. That it's happening is bad enough, but I'm sure that many cases go unreported and, as a police officer, you'll have a better handle on that than me.'

'Why me? You're a well-connected and influential man, you can probably pick up the phone and speak to any councillor or the chief constable. The force has rape counsellors who're way more qualified than I am to help you.'

'You may well be right, but all those counsellors are tainted by the existing system. What I plan to create is something different. Something that puts the victim first and the rapist in jail. I'm talking about getting these women justice as well as help. It won't be easy, and I'm aware that a lot of the women will be terrified of appearing in court, but one of the things I plan to do is negotiate a rate with a specialist lawyer which means the victims can have a representative who's smart enough to not let the defence lawyer blacken their character. It'll take money to set it up, but I have money and I have a team of people who can get this kind of stuff done. I want you on board because you're passionate, honest and, if I may be frank without causing offence, the scar on your cheek lends you an air of toughness. That's what I want to have fronting my campaign: a passionate woman who looks tough enough to handle anything. That's the dream I want to sell these women. That times may be hard for them just now, but that there is a bright future out there if they can only find the strength to grasp it.'

'Hang on a minute. It's not as cut and dried as you think. That business about the victims having their character blackened, that'll only happen if the victims waive their right to anonymity. They're afraid of that, but most people don't know that's an option which is why they never make the report. Plus, you forget that even with anonymity, the rapists who're guilty often know their victims, which means that if an accusation is made and no charges are brought against the accused, the victims are at risk of violent retribution from the people they've named.'

Despite herself, Beth found that she was being swept along by Forster's words. The ideas he was pitching at her covered everything she wanted to achieve in terms of helping rape victims get through their ordeal, and of equal importance to her, he was going to help her expose the foul men who forced themselves onto women.

'I tell you what, DC Young, how about you and I sit down to discuss this properly sometime?'

'We could do that. When should we meet?'

'How does tomorrow night sound? I'm free after seven. This place is closed up at that time of night and as it wouldn't be appropriate for us to visit each other's homes, why don't we talk over dinner? You can choose the restaurant.'

Beth suggested a place and time, but it was as she was walking down the stairs that she realised what had just happened. She'd visited the mayor for answers, not just to the case she was investigating, but to try and work out what he'd done to attract the killer's ire, and here she was, effectively going on a date with him. Except she didn't think of it as a date and there was no way that she was going to let him think it was anything other than a business meeting.

In light of the fact someone was targeting him with a hate campaign that seemed to be trying to have him locked up, she didn't think the mayor would be interested in trying to seduce her or anyone else. As it was, she was amazed that he was even thinking about establishing his charity with everything else that was going on.

Things had worked out better than she'd hoped they might, yet there was a little doubt in her mind that Forster had an agenda of his own and that she'd have to guard against it.

CHAPTER TWENTY-FIVE

The door to Dr Hewson's office was open when Beth arrived at the mortuary and pathology lab beneath Cumberland Infirmary.

She'd been here more times than she cared for, and each time she'd visited she'd been filled with sadness for the people whose last journey started here. It was a sterile environment filled with drab colours and the ever-present whiff of industrial-strength cleaning products.

For Beth, visits here were a necessary evil but for the pathologists and lab workers who spent their days in these basement rooms it would be just another day at work.

Beth stepped into Hewson's office as she knocked on the door, but the room was unoccupied. A sandwich with one bite missing lay on top of the desk with a piece of cling film spread beneath it to act as a plate. Steam rose from a mug and there was a background sound of muted organ music adding an even greater sombreness to the air.

As she looked at the sandwich Beth's stomach growled. She hadn't eaten since the bowl of cereal she'd wolfed down after her shower, and even though she now felt the first pangs of hunger cramping her belly, she was more interested in the doctor's whereabouts.

The half-eaten sandwich and abandoned cuppa spoke of an emergency, but she couldn't imagine what situation required the urgent response of a pathologist.

She backed out of the office and looked up and down the corridor. An orderly was pushing a trolley laden with containers, but apart from him, there was nobody else to be seen.

The door to the gents bathroom opened and Hewson came scurrying out, a pained look on his face. As always his shock of curly hair was unruly, but his usual smile was missing as he greeted Beth.

'Ah, DC Protégé, I'm sorry to have kept you. Mrs H tried a new recipe last night and I'm pretty sure that, like your boss, it didn't agree with me. How is Dowdy anyway? Still too uptight for her own good?'

'She's fine.' Beth gave a tight smile and did her best to ignore Hewson's bout of oversharing. As much as she respected the doctor, she didn't want to know about his bowel movements.

As they took seats in Hewson's office, the doctor cleared away his sandwich and took a sip of his tea.

'You said you wanted to consult with me on a cold case. How about you tell me the details.'

Beth spent a few minutes bringing Hewson up to speed on the murders of Christine Peterson, Joanne Armstrong and Harriet Quantrell. When she mentioned Harriet's name she saw the doctor give a sharp nod. He'd performed the post-mortem and it was no surprise that he remembered Harriet's name.

'This is all very fascinating, but you haven't explained how I'm supposed to help.'

Beth passed three folders across the desk. 'These are the post-mortem reports on all three ladies. I'd like you to take a look at them and give me your opinion. Tell me of the commonalities you find as well as the inconsistencies.'

As Hewson picked his way through the reports, Beth thought about what she'd been able to glean from them herself. It wasn't a lot if she was honest. Her understanding of medical terminology was her weak spot, and while the reports had been written in plain enough English, her lack of knowledge prevented her from getting any decent insights.

'Jesus. Thank God the old fool has retired.'

'What is it? What have you found?'

'The first victim, Christine Peterson. The man who did this report was an imbecile. He's left out what may be a key detail.'

Beth was on the verge of telling Hewson to get to the point when he dropped the report on the desk and scowled. She knew the scowl wasn't aimed at her, but she was burning with impatience.

Hewson's finger jabbed at the report. 'Do you see here, where he's noted down the vaginal and anal tearing?'

'Yes, what of it?'

'The damn fool has noted that the vaginal tearing showed signs of fresh bleeding. He makes no such comment of the anal tearing. When you read the transcript of the post-mortem commentary, there's again no mention of the anal tears bleeding. He also mentions that the tears are minor and do not indicate vigorous penetration.' Hewson looked up at her with expectation on his face, but Beth didn't know what she was supposed to be surmising.

Beth splayed her hands in a helpless gesture. 'I'm sorry but you're going to have to spell it out to me.'

'Whoever raped this woman was a pervert, that much is a given. However, what the report doesn't spell out, and bloody well should, is that the damage to the victim's vagina and anus is minimal and doesn't go very deep.'

'What, you're saying he had a small?…'

'I'd say his penis was smaller than average, yes.'

This news cast a whole new light onto the rapist. Not only was he in possession of a twisted set of desires, he wasn't well endowed.

The possible implications of this on the rapist's psyche were numerous. If he'd been mocked by women it could have made him bitter. Had he not been able to ever satisfy a lover, maybe he'd felt diminished as a man and that had bred resentment against women and fostered his desire for superiority. Both of these traits – failure to conduct normal relationships, and a desire for superiority – were often found in rapists, and more than anything else, they'd make the man more likely to continue forcibly sating his desires.

Beth's mind whirled and then locked onto something else the doctor had mentioned.

'You said the tears to Christine's vagina had bled but not the ones to her anus. Would I be right in saying that he raped her, killed her and then raped her anally?'

'That's what the evidence suggests to me. Why that idiot didn't spell this out for the investigating team I'll never know, but that's what I think happened.'

'I don't understand why the rapist would do the final rape after she'd died.'

Hewson's face adopted the world-weary understanding of a kindly grandfather. 'You're young, both in name and years. As women age, and particularly after they have children, their pelvic floor muscles weaken. It's where incontinence troubles stem from. With his undersized penis, a woman of the victim's years may not have been a good, er… fit. The tearing is minimal and the report mentions traces of lubricant synonymous with condoms. If there wasn't enough friction to bring him to orgasm, it was a failed attempt. He'd be angry and probably that's why he strangled her.'

Beth picked up the narrative. 'Once she was dead, he was still aroused, so rather than try vaginal sex again, he tried anal in the hope that he'd be able to orgasm.'

'Correct. That just makes him even more despicable, doesn't it?'

Beth nodded her agreement. That the killer had been compelled to add necrophilia to his crime went a long way past despicable. It was bad enough that he'd violated Christine in life before killing her. To continue with his debasing actions in death made him worse than filth. Beyond even an animal.

To Beth the rapist was a monster, preying on the vulnerable and taking his sick pleasures from them. She imagined the rapist leaning over his victim, her clothes strewn around them. His hands fastening on her throat and squeezing her airways closed.

For the victims it would have been all their nightmares come true at once. Their bodies invaded. Then the steady inexorable pressure on their throats.

Had he looked into their eyes as he'd killed them?
Had he drunk in their fear?

Perhaps he'd spoken to them, insulted them or told them he was in love with them.

However the women's final moments had passed, they would have been filled with abject terror.

'Interesting.' Hewson looked up from the report he was reading. 'Joanne Armstrong would appear to have had a quite different end.'

Beth looked at Hewson and rolled a hand for him to continue.

'I'm not an expert on the subject, but I would suggest that Miss Armstrong was raped on more than one occasion. I think that her attacker was the same small-appendaged beast who defiled Mrs Peterson. Not only are the internal wounds very similar, but so was the depth of wounding. However there was considerable tearing to both Miss Armstrong's anus and vagina; therefore in my opinion the rapist had attacked her on more than one occasion.'

Beth ran a hand over her face. 'Shit. This just keeps on getting worse, doesn't it?'

'It does. The final victim is someone I remember meeting on my table. I recall all the details as if the post-mortem was yesterday. Her injuries were more extreme than either of these earlier attacks. Now that all three women have been connected, it's not hard to see how our rapist is warming to his theme.'

'It's all too clear.'

Every word Beth spoke was pushed out through gritted teeth. Catching this rapist and murderer before he struck again was far more important than protecting the mayor from any potential future harassment. Even her own private plan to work out what Forster was hiding was insignificant when viewed in big-picture terms.

'All three were strangled. Is there a way to determine if they were all strangled by the same person? And could it be the same person who attacked Felicia Evans?'

'DC Protégé, you really do think up the most interesting, and hard to answer, questions.'

Hewson leafed through the folders until he found the relevant pages and the accompanying photographs.

'Right, pay attention. All three women had their hyoid bone broken, which is synonymous with 30 to 50 per cent of strangulations depending on which set of statistics you believe.' Hewson pressed a hand against his stomach making Beth worry his wife's cooking was about to affect him again, but he removed it after a few seconds. 'So the statistics tell me that at least one of them shouldn't have had their hyoid broken, but all three did. However, the bruising on their necks is technically higher than the optimum position which is why the strangulations all resulted in broken hyoid bones. To my mind, the person who killed them was probably kneeling on their chest or lying along their body. The victims will have craned their heads back as they tried to escape. It was the wrong thing to do as they exposed their throats to the man who killed them. From his position on their body, his hands would have slid up their throats and lodged under their chin, right where the hyoid bone is.'

When Hewson pointed at his own neck to show where the hyoid bone was, Beth lifted a hand and traced her fingertips over the same part of her throat. She couldn't feel anything she hadn't felt before and after talking about strangulation, there was no way that she was going to squeeze her throat hard while trying to locate her hyoid bone.

'What else can you see in the reports?'

Hewson flicked through a few pages and then shook his head. 'There's nothing else that you won't have picked up yourself. I take it that you've noticed the traces of adhesive on their wrists?'

'Yeah I spotted that. Duct tape, the abductors favourite tool along with zip ties. Tell me, Doctor, I saw in Harriet's report that there was slight tearing to the sides of her mouth and two of her front teeth were described as loose, what could have caused that?'

'A gag of some kind would be my first guess, quite possibly a ball gag. It would stop her screaming as she was raped. If he was rough putting it in place there's every chance her mouth would have torn and that some of her teeth were loosened.'

'You never answered my question about whether it could be the same person who killed Felicia Evans.'

'I didn't. I'm a pathologist, you're the detective, and I've told you everything I know.'

As much as Hewson's words were a brush-off, the spark in his eye told Beth that he was again challenging her to think for herself.

'Okay. So Felicia Evans wasn't penetrated by a human being and her hyoid bone wasn't broken. She was, however, left naked after being murdered and sexually assaulted post-mortem.' Beth fell silent for a moment as her thoughts took a firmer shape. 'Perhaps the killer didn't have penetrative sex with her himself because doing so with the other women hadn't stimulated him in the way he wanted. Maybe he got himself off in some other way, hence the use of a sex toy.'

'Interesting. Now, can you explain the intact hyoid?'

'If he'd planned to use the sex toy in that way, he'd have no need to keep her alive. Therefore he could kill her in her bed while she was lying prone. This would mean she'd be easy to get out of the house and into his van or car. Would I be right in saying that if he'd been standing by her bed when strangling her that his hands would be in a different position?'

'You would indeed. I wasn't sure myself, but everything you've said makes sense.'

As Beth stood to leave she could feel herself growing even more determined to catch the heinous killer.

It was only when she was back out in the sun that she had an idea. It would need to be checked out against the information Unthank and Thompson were still gathering, but it may lead them towards the killer.

CHAPTER TWENTY-SIX

When Beth strode back into the FMIT office she could feel a charge in the atmosphere. The air seemed to pulse back and forth with an unseen energy.

The problem was, there was nothing positive about it. Every wave was filled with negativity, as were the faces of her three colleagues. Thompson, in particular, looked abject and defeated.

She didn't need to be Sherlock Holmes to work out why. He'd spent the best part of his day finishing up his interviews with the other detectives about the cases they'd failed to solve. No detective likes to have another question their work, and for Thompson to bring to light the fact that two of the teams had missed a serial killer wouldn't have gone down well. No matter how he had reported it, the news would have been seen as an accusation of incompetence. In a lot of respects his questioning them and their work would make him feel like one of Mannequin's Professional Standards Department minions. That's certainly how the detectives he spoke to would view it.

All officers knew the necessity for professionalism, but the Professional Standards Department always seemed to be persecuting good officers for one careless comment or a mistake borne out of too big a caseload. Because of this, the PSD was roundly hated and the subject of many unkind nicknames. Rubber-heelers was Beth's preferred term as it described the way they crept up on people.

'What's the score, Beth?'

The eagerness in O'Dowd's voice told Beth everything she needed to know about how the others had fared. If one of them had picked up a good lead then the information she had wouldn't be deemed so important.

'I have four maybe five potential suspects who have the skills to have put the images on the mayor's computer, and a possible aggrieved husband. That's not the best bit though.'

'Spill it then. This isn't a fucking reality show where you're supposed to build tension.' Thompson's face had twisted into a gurn as he snapped at her.

It was another indication of the bad day he'd had, and Beth didn't mind letting it slide. His wife hadn't recognised him or his daughters for months now due to her Alzheimer's and as well as having a shell for a wife, Thompson was raising their girls by himself while carrying out a demanding job. If this wasn't bad enough in itself, there was also the fact that his wife's physical health was dwindling. She didn't have a lot of time left.

Since learning of Thompson's wife's condition, Beth had taken the time to do some research and while the name early-onset Alzheimer's implied the early stages of the disease in general, it was actually used to describe the 5 per cent of Alzheimer's sufferers who contracted the disease at a young age. It not only affected the sufferer's mind, but would progress until the body could no longer fight a disease or an infection like pneumonia.

There were times Thompson's frustrations boiled over, but it was understandable, and he was a decent enough man to apologise for his outbursts once he'd calmed down.

Beth filled them in on what she'd learned from Dr Hewson and sketched out what she'd learned from Forster as well. She could see her own disgust at the killer reflected on each of their faces. O'Dowd in particular looked repulsed.

Thompson stood and walked to the whiteboard they used to collate the pertinent details. He wiped off the press's moniker of 'the Lakeland Ripper' from where suspects would be listed and wrote 'Justin'. When he returned to his seat, most of his anger seemed to have been replaced with a schoolboy smirk.

O'Dowd pointed at the whiteboard. 'Would you care to explain?'

'What do you call a man with a one-inch cock?' Thompson nodded at the whiteboard. 'Justin.'

Unthank giggled like a child despite O'Dowd's scowl. Beth knew the 'what do you call a man' jokes well. Her father had told them to her for years. This hadn't been one he'd shared, but then, he'd never told anything which even approached being a dirty joke in her presence.

Unthank stood to address the room. 'What do you call a man with a car on his head?'

'Jack.' The answer was out of Beth's mouth before O'Dowd could launch her stapler at Unthank.

'I give up.' The stapler was put back down and a folder lifted which O'Dowd used to point at Thompson. 'I'm off to see if I can persuade Mannequin to do his own dirty work instead of getting you to do it. Make sure that name isn't on the whiteboard when I get back or I'll personally dob you in, do you understand me?'

'Yes, boss.' Thompson's reply was automatic, but there was no contrition in his voice.

It was typical in their line of work that black humour would be present. Not only did they work in a tight-knit group, they had to deal with subjects and sights which the general public couldn't begin to imagine. The Justin moniker was tame compared to a lot of things that had been said, and had O'Dowd not been so frustrated at their lack of progress, she would have been the first to laugh at Thompson's joke.

So far as Beth was concerned though, calling and thinking of the killer as Justin showed disrespect to his victims and belittled what they suffered before they were strangled. She couldn't bring herself to say the name out loud, and to counter any tendency to go with the name Thompson had bestowed on the killer, she made a mental effort to only think of the killer as 'the Lakeland Ripper'.

Beth listened as first Unthank then Thompson shared what little they'd learned.

Unthank had concentrated his attentions on each of the snatch sites. The Lakeland Ripper had chosen well: none of the areas was properly covered by a CCTV camera and all were secluded enough to afford him the opportunity to grab his victims.

By far the boldest of the abductions had been Harriet's, but she'd been taken in the early hours of the morning when the streets would have been all but deserted.

Where the Lakeland Ripper's first three victims differed from Felicia Evans was the fact they were all in good health and had all been snatched from a public place seemingly at random, whereas it seemed Felicia had been abducted from the sanctity of her own home. To Beth's mind this showed that the Lakeland Ripper was refining his methods and getting bolder.

How he'd enticed each of the women to him was a mystery. None of their blood samples had shown traces of any drugs, although Beth knew that date rape drugs such as Rohypnol and GHB were absorbed by the body within a few hours.

Nor had the women shown any signs of head trauma synonymous with them being knocked out.

If they weren't knocked out or drugged they must have been overpowered in some way.

Christine Peterson was a frail-looking woman, but while Joanne Armstrong was slim, she was a dedicated hillwalker, therefore she'd have muscles honed by hours of trekking up slopes. It was unlikely that she'd been snatched easily.

Harriet Quantrell was a different matter altogether; she was two stones past voluptuous. She wouldn't have been easy to manhandle. Even if she'd been drugged or knocked out, she would have been an awkward and heavy load to move.

With these options ruled out, that left only two more: trickery or coercion. While it was possible that a drunk Harriet had been tricked somehow, she didn't believe the other two women would have fallen for a ruse, so Beth's money was on coercion.

Unthank had pored over the statements taken from those in the vicinity of the abductions, but he'd found nothing of note. Nobody had seen anything untoward or heard any screams.

Thompson's conversations with the investigating officers had yielded the same lack of results. When he'd heard about the details not highlighted in Christine Peterson's post-mortem his face had twisted into an anguished grimace. Those were often the type of details which could make all the difference during an investigation. As good as the investigating officers may have been, they couldn't do their job with half the facts and due to the time that had passed, it was unrealistic to expect them to recall every detail of their case.

All of the people he'd spoken to had given him a fair response without ever providing a good answer, the truth lost by either backside covering, or the sands of time.

The idea Beth had had at the hospital now seemed like a waste of time, but she voiced it anyway.

'Don't laugh at me, but you know how women have boob jobs, what if the Lakeland Ripper has looked into having a penis extension?'

'Don't you mean Justin?'

'I mean the Lakeland Ripper.' Beth fixed Thompson with a stern look. 'You can maybe make jokes about someone who kills and rapes women, but I can't. You call him what you like, but until I learn his real name, he'll be the Lakeland Ripper to me.'

Thompson raised a hand in her direction. Beth wasn't sure whether he was shutting her up or apologising, until she saw the contrition in his eyes.

'A penis extension, can they even do that?'

'Shut up, Paul. Young Beth may well be onto something here.'

There had been a time when Thompson had re-ordered her name as a way to goad her, but Beth knew it was now meant as a term of endearment. That he supported her theory gave her hope that it wasn't a daft idea.

The problem was in identifying those who'd had such an operation. When you factored in the shame and embarrassment the men would likely feel about the size of their penises, there was little chance they would broadcast the fact that they'd undergone enhancement surgery. They'd be more likely to do the opposite and keep their surgery a secret.

Perhaps a wife or lover would know, but Beth didn't think that the Lakeland Ripper had anyone in that role. To her way of thinking, he was single, a loner, but not by choice. He would be friendless or perhaps have one close friend who was as weird as he was.

The Lakeland Ripper would be awkward around women, obsessed with sex, yet afraid to get intimate with a woman because they'd learn his shameful secret.

He may have tried visiting a prostitute, but that wouldn't have given him what he wanted. His physical needs may have been dealt with, but his psychological ones would remain. He'd have wanted to feel that he had a level of sexual prowess, that he could please a woman in bed. He'd have known that the prostitute was only acting as if she was aroused, and that would have eaten at him, burned at his psyche with a series of self-mocking thoughts of worthlessness.

It wouldn't surprise Beth if the Lakeland Ripper suffered from depression, that his black dog was walked on a very short lead.

Beth went online and looked for the names of the leading cosmetic surgeons in the country, and she had to wade through a few different sites before she established that the nearest place to Cumbria that offered what they called augmentation surgery was in the Sunderland area.

She didn't know if the surgery would be funded by the NHS or whether the Lakeland Ripper would have had to pay for it from his own money. That was something else she needed to find out.

'See, what you're thinking about him getting one of the penis extension operations…' Unthank looked at Thompson then Beth. 'I think you're going straight for the nuclear option. I don't know much about such things, but I've been around enough to know there are lots of gadgets and pills that are touted as giving you a boost. If I was in the killer's position, and believe me, *I'm not*, I'd try absolutely everything else before I let anyone near me with a scalpel.'

Beth had to smother the smile Unthank's final sentence put to her lips. How typical of a man to insist that his penis wasn't tiny. His point made sense though, and she agreed with his suggestion that the Lakeland Ripper would try all the other gadgets and drugs before going under the knife.

O'Dowd could make the decision regarding contacting the surgeons. Rather than waste time on a probable dead end, Beth went back to her spreadsheet and began to feed in the new information she had.

CHAPTER TWENTY-SEVEN

Willow put down her bag and bent to greet Spike. As ever when she returned from work, he was scampering around her and jumping up so she could pet him. It was something he'd done since puppyhood and his claws had ruined many a pair of tights, but she didn't mind.

Her day at the bank had been more of the same. Since coming back to Cumbria she'd landed a position as financial advisor to a number of small businesses and she was still getting to know her customers and their foibles.

Some had little idea of how to manage the money their business was making and these were the customers she liked dealing with. They were compliant and would listen to what she was suggesting and take her advice. She knew that she could make a little more commission by steering the customers towards certain aspects of the bank's offerings, but she'd never been so greedy as to give what she felt was wrong advice just so she could line her own pockets.

The customers she liked the least were those who thought they were cleverer than they were. They'd want to gamble on certain stocks or would be asking her about some scheme they'd heard about and wanted to sign up to. They'd be insistent and wouldn't listen when she explained that the bank didn't offer that service or their money would be better used in a different way. These customers were the ones who'd lay blame at her door for investments that went wrong. Despite not heeding her advice, they'd point the finger at her, complain about the money they'd lost. Even when they did heed what she advised them, they'd complain their investment wasn't growing as fast as they wanted it to.

Willow had dealt with two of these customers today and she was worn out from the mental acrobatics she'd had to perform just to keep them calm. Oliver Morrison was another prime example of this kind of customer, but thankfully she'd not had to see him or the less aggressively flirtatious Andrew Cooper today, and wouldn't for at least another month. All she wanted to do tonight was soak in the bath and then curl up with a good book.

One benefit of moving back in with her parents was that her mother would always have dinner cooked. The drawback to this was that her parents were creatures of habit. They had a routine and they stuck to it with a religious fervour. Meals were prepared on a rota system that saw mince on a Monday and fish on a Friday. Their menu was traditional hearty food which gave no concession to the weather.

On a day as warm as today, a nice salad would have suited Willow, but she could smell the sausage casserole her mother always made on a Wednesday. So far as her parents were concerned spaghetti Bolognese was a walk on the wild side. Even on the rare occasions when they dined out they would have the same thing. Soup, steak and a cheeseboard for her father and steak pie followed by a slice of cheesecake for her mother.

She knew how the conversation at dinner would go tonight. Her mother would twitter about how her day had gone, and her father would keep his silence. He was still raw about the details of Willow's break-up. He'd done the possessive father thing and had threatened to beat up her husband. A part of her had wanted him to do it, but she didn't want her father to get into trouble. Her plan was to hurt her ex financially.

Her mother was already suggesting men she might want to date, but she had no interest in that side of things. For the time being, she was content to live a single life while her broken heart healed. Her mother would argue that she was a beautiful woman, and that she shouldn't be shut away. The subject of prospective grandchildren had hung like a Damoclean sword since she'd first announced her engagement. Willow had wanted kids, but despite a battery of tests that had found nothing amiss with either her or her husband, they'd never managed to conceive.

After dining with her parents, Willow changed from her work clothes into sweats and picked up Spike's lead. He'd stay on it tonight that was for sure. There was no way she wanted a repeat of the other night's palaver.

Her pace was fast as she tried to invigorate her limbs with exercise and burn off the huge plateful of food her mother had put in front of her. Rather than walk along the river again, she took a route that took her down to the harbour.

Maryport had a long history as a fishing village, but the Senhouse family had turned it into a coal port during the eighteenth century. The town's original cottages were laid out on a grid system and its main industries were coal mining and ship building. It now had a maritime museum and another museum which focussed on the Roman artefacts that had been uncovered in the area.

When she'd married and moved south, Willow had been delighted to escape Maryport and its small-town mentality. Like all places of its size, the locals had fierce rivalries with the other towns in the area and it was normal for the young men to end up battling with their counterparts from Aspatria, Cockermouth or Workington.

Back then she'd hated the familiarity, the way everyone knew your business. A night out would entail going to the same few pubs and talking to the same faces. Life here had been about routine rather than change, yet she now wanted that routine. She'd kept in touch with friends from the town and was looking forward to joining three of her old schoolmates for a drink on Friday.

She knew that a part of her was trying to regress, to go back to the days when everything was familiar and safe. Willow could handle that: she knew it would be a transitional phase.

As she pounded the streets, she thought about the dresses she'd bought at lunchtime. They were impulse purchases, made to bolster up a shattered confidence. Both were a little shorter than she would normally buy, but what her husband had done had made her feel unloved and unattractive. She'd told herself, and heard her mother say it, that she was a good-looking woman and that she could turn heads when she wanted to, but she hadn't felt her usual confidence. Instead she'd felt worthless, rejected.

Friday night was about a lot more than a night out with the girls. It was about her feeling attractive and desired.

She strode back along the street that led to her parents' home with a joyful Spike at her heel. He liked the fast walks almost as much as he enjoyed being let off the lead and left to his own devices.

Willow unlocked the door and called out a greeting to her parents.

The whole time she'd been out, she'd been oblivious to the man who'd been following her; waiting for the one chance he needed to snatch her.

With Willow back in her family home, he gave up and walked back to his pickup. As keen as he was to grab Willow, he knew he had to wait for the right opportunity.

Unlike the other women he'd spent time with, he knew Willow. Rather than abduct another woman at random, Willow had been selected on purpose.

She was bright, beautiful and wonderfully sexy. It was a bigger risk taking a woman to order, but he was sure that Willow would satisfy his urges far better than any of the previous women.

He was looking forward to enjoying the release her company would bring, but he knew he'd have to be patient and wait for the right chance to take her.

CHAPTER TWENTY-EIGHT

The spreadsheet in front of Beth was growing ever larger. She'd got all the relevant details into place and she was now studying the rows and columns looking for the commonalities.

The pen in her right hand was drumming a furious beat against a cup as her eyes flickered back and forth without finding what she was looking for.

She was alone in the office. Thompson had gone home to his daughters, and O'Dowd had taken Unthank away on an errand. It was just as well the others were out as she wasn't in the mood for chit-chat or the interruptions which always happened in a busy office. O'Dowd had listened to her theory about penis enlargements, and while she'd agreed it may be something they could pursue, the DI had decided that it was a long shot and their time would be better spent following other leads.

Each one of the little boxes on her screen mocked her. They just sat there, every one an unmatched piece of the jigsaw. No one thing aligned with another in a way that could be classed as making sense.

The victims were old, young, tall, short, fat and thin. They were from different backgrounds, and while they were all working class.

The only thing they had in common was their fate.

That the Lakeland Ripper had escalated his methodology was a worry. He was learning what gave him pleasure and had discovered a way to take it. In Beth's mind, raping the women would be his revenge for all the slights he'd endured, for all the times he'd felt inadequate and for the thrill he got from the experience.

Beth's greatest fear was that because the Lakeland Ripper was escalating the way he'd taken his desires, he would also escalate the other parts of his process, that he'd refine his methods. The women he'd attacked so far had been missed by loved ones and they seemed randomly selected. But there was a chance he could escalate by fixating on a single target and increasing his levels of violence after the abduction, or by targeting an increased number of victims such as those who were vulnerable. If he'd moved on to targets who were less likely to be reported missing, there was every chance that he may have killed again without the FMIT's knowledge.

And if he was sticking to his cycle, he was overdue to strike again, if he hadn't already.

As a matter of course, she'd checked HOLMES again to look for similar cases in Cumbria and its neighbouring counties. None had been listed, but that didn't mean a lot. Christine Peterson's case hadn't been considered major by the inspector who'd led the investigation, and therefore it hadn't been added. It was possible there were other cases out there which also hadn't been added.

That was one for Mannequin and his PSD team to pursue. Their focus was on finding police errors and they'd be all over this case as there had been clear failings of the system. While he may be viewed as an officious prig by many, nobody had ever denied Mannequin's intelligence, therefore he'd make it a priority to look for anything else connected to the case that may have slipped under the radar.

If the Lakeland Ripper was going down the route of selection in favour of opportunity, then he'd be far more dangerous as he'd be engineering the abduction to occur at an optimum time. The way he'd already taken four women without leaving a trace showed he was clever and resourceful.

Beth guessed that he'd also be forensically aware. That wasn't such a surprise any more considering the proliferation of police TV dramas. There was barely a week that went by without one show or other depicting a crew of white-clad Scenes of Crime Officers going about their job. The fictionalised versions got a lot of the details wrong, but they still made the public aware of how the police could find the tiniest piece of fabric, a hair or a flake of skin that would tie the criminal to the scene and solve the case. This meant that those of a criminal persuasion knew to take measures to prevent leaving trace evidence of any kind.

That was the one thing which had shone through about each of the women. None of them had carried any evidence underneath their fingernails, no hairs or obvious skin particles found anywhere on their bodies. In the absence of definitive abduction sites, there were no specific locations to search for the tiny clues which may have identified the Lakeland Ripper. The deposition sites had all had a thorough forensic examination, but none of them had yielded a piece of evidence that had produced a solid lead.

Regardless of this, Beth went over the crime-scene pictures again. Christine Peterson's naked body lay on the sandy dunes of the Barrow beach in the south-west of the county. Sand was a notoriously tough medium to gather evidence from as it could drift in the wind or shift with footsteps.

The tree-covered bank at the side of Lake Buttermere where Joanne Armstrong had been discovered was central to Cumbria and it was layered with pine needles and there were myriad rabbit holes in the surrounding area. Like the sand at Barrow beach, the pine needles weren't the best medium for finding evidence and the fact there was so much wildlife in the area meant that a vital clue may have been carried off or trampled under the rabbits' feet.

Harriet Quantrell's body had been found on the northern reaches of Cumbria. The tough grasses of Rockcliffe Marsh were good at catching evidence, but like Joanne's and Christine's deposition sites, the location where Harriet was found yielded no secrets.

A thought struck Beth and she knew it had merit. That it should be checked out. The first step was to check the police database: that yielded six options, but the database would only cover the instances that were reported.

Beth ran a couple of searches on Google and found the phone numbers she was looking for.

CHAPTER TWENTY-NINE

Beth poured herself a glass of water and slumped down on her couch. She'd worked at her spreadsheet until eight. The rape charities and counsellors she'd spoken to had been guarded, but she'd managed to get what she needed from them.

Her thinking had been that the Lakeland Ripper may not have killed every woman he'd raped. All of the people she'd spoken to had denied having anyone in their care who'd been raped by a stranger who'd abducted them. They'd promised that they'd contact her if they heard anything, but Beth had gleaned from their tone that they didn't think it likely.

As good as it was that no women had told of having been snatched for use as a rapist's plaything, it was also terrible that the majority of the women who had reached out for help must have known their attacker. Beth had spent hours trying to decide which would be worse: being taken by some unknown person and used to sate their desires, or having someone she knew and liked break her trust and destroy her faith in them. She pushed the idea out of her head: both were utterly abhorrent.

When she was speaking to the women from the charities, she had also tried to learn as much information as she could from them about how they worked. The more she knew the better she'd be able to contribute to Forster's vision. If she was going to get involved in his charity, she wanted to have her say about how it was set up, and to do that, she had to understand how the existing ones could be improved upon.

Of the sixteen rape victims she'd found on the police database who'd suffered their assault in the two years since Harriet's death, there were thirteen cases where there was an accusation but not enough evidence, while two had been advanced to the point where the CPS had taken over and the court case was impending.

That left one possible option. Beth had taken down the woman's details and she planned to contact the investigating officer tomorrow morning, to see if her theory panned out.

Beth supposed that if the Lakeland Ripper did stop killing it could only be a good thing. His not killing all of his victims would give them someone to interview. They'd be able to get an idea of what he was like.

She didn't expect that he'd be foolish enough to show his face to his victims, but they'd at least be able to describe his general build, if he spoke with an accent. Whether he was muscular, fat or thin.

It was as she pondered on what the Lakeland Ripper was like, that she realised something about his victims. None of the women were any taller than five foot seven and Harriet Quantrell had only been five one.

Joanne's and Harriet's diminutive heights would make them easier than a taller, stronger person for the Lakeland Ripper to manage. It'd be easy for him to slip an arm over their shoulder and around their throat. A knife pressed into their backs would make them compliant until he could bind them with his tape.

Their height was a definite thread, but it could have been nothing more than a coincidence. Still, at this moment in time, it was one additional factor that linked the cases together.

She cast her mind back to the spreadsheet as she twiddled a lock of hair round her finger.

None of the women's clothes had ever been found, but Beth figured they'd been disposed of in random bins, or burned to remove the possibility of trace evidence. Even their shoes, or hiking boots in Joanne's case, had gone missing.

The more she thought about it, the more she was struggling to make sense of anything. She knew her mind was overloaded with details and that she needed to move away from the subject otherwise she'd never be able to let her subconscious loose on the puzzle.

Beth rose from the sofa and went up the stairs. She had a half hour to grab a shower, put on some clean clothes and get across town to meet Ethan.

When her phone beeped her first thought was that it was Ethan cancelling on her.

The message wasn't from Ethan, though, it was a terse message from O'Dowd giving her a list of tasks for the next day. The DI had a court appearance in the morning so she wouldn't be on hand to deliver the briefing she normally gave.

O'Dowd's instructions weren't the ones she was hoping for. Rather than work the murder cases direct, the DI had reiterated that Beth's task was to identify whomever was persecuting the mayor.

The timing of this plot against the mayor was also something she questioned. Forster was coming to the end of his tenure as mayor. The elections were being held in the next few weeks and while Forster might have greater political ambitions than mayor, he was yet to announce his candidacy for the forthcoming local elections.

Forster had been arrested because of an allegation made by letter and because his card had been found beside Felicia's body. Had Digital Forensics not been so diligent, it was entirely possible they would be looking at the mayor in a different light.

Beth's fingers were curling into a fist and then straightening as she worked things out in her head. It still felt most likely that one of Forster's former employees was the Lakeland Ripper. Though, if the mysterious Lorraine had been married, it wasn't beyond the bounds of possibility her husband had learned of her infidelity and followed up on this, but that felt more tenuous. After all, all he'd need to do to humiliate the mayor would be to cite him in divorce proceedings. Plus, if Lorraine's husband was the killer, he'd only be drawing attention to himself by targeting Forster.

As Beth thought her idea through, she pictured Lorraine pleading with her husband for another chance. Maybe she even told him that the mayor had taken advantage of her when she was drunk.

What she had to do was find a way to identify Lorraine and then work back from there. If she could at least eliminate the woman from the investigation, she could focus on Forster's former colleagues.

Even as she drove across town to meet Ethan, the details of the case were still kaleidoscoping around her brain, looking for the pattern that offered clarity of thought.

CHAPTER THIRTY

Before she set off for Carlisle, Beth was at her desk running the names of Forster's former employees through the Police National Database.

One of the four had once been arrested for drink driving but they'd only been a fraction over the limit and, as the laws were more lenient in the eighties, had only lost their licence for six months.

None of the others had so much as a parking ticket against their name, but that wasn't unexpected. A high proportion of criminal offences were committed by a small portion of the community. Therefore, beyond the odd driving offence, the majority of people had no police record.

Their names suggested that rather than pimply youths, Forster's team had been made up of responsible adults. What surprised Beth as much as anything was that there were two women on the team of four, plus Donna Waddington who'd left to found EdenData.

She knew it was wrong of her to assume that the programmers would all be male. There was no reason whatsoever why there shouldn't be females working in that industry. It was just that any time she'd encountered anyone who knew a lot about computers, especially in the Cumbria police force, they'd been male.

When Beth took a look at EdenData's website she found a slick and professional-looking business which offered reservations systems, EPOS software, front-office management software and a whole host of other services that meant little to her.

An online demo that she watched showed what she assumed to be their reservation system. It linked to the EPOS – electronic point of sale – software which ran bar and restaurant tills. Event management software could be added, as could a channel manager to integrate with online travel agents. The demo even showed a series of reports before concluding with a sales slogan.

Beth's next move was to check out EdenData through Companies House. The business was showing year-on-year growth of 40 per cent most recently, and it had been between 30 and 50 per cent for the last six years.

To Beth this showed a steady hand on the business's tiller. Donna Waddington's company had grown at a more or less steady rate for years. That spoke of diligence and good management. People who had these qualities rarely laid traps for people out of spite. This felt like a woman who had enough brains to know which battles to choose and how to conduct them. She would go and speak to Donna Waddington at some point, but Beth knew before she made a note of the business address that it would almost certainly be a waste of time unless Donna Waddington was somehow in cahoots with the Lakeland Ripper.

With as much information as she could gather on the people the mayor had employed at SimpleBooker, Beth turned her attention to the mysterious 'Lorraine'. She began her investigation by calling Forster and asking if there was a guest list for the party where he and Lorraine had met and the details of the person who'd thrown the party.

By the time the call had ended, she had the name of the photographer who'd been hired to take a few publicity shots and the mayor's reassurance that he'd visit the photographer and get a reprint of any pictures which Lorraine featured in.

It might take a bit of exhaustive legwork, but the challenge of something like tracking down Lorraine was one of the things Beth loved most about police work. As much as the desire to deliver justice drove her on, Beth loved nothing more than a good puzzle she could test her brain with. Not so much Sudoku or crosswords; she liked logic problems and riddles. The less sense a puzzle initially made to her, the more she was compelled to try and solve it.

She had one more call to make before she left to visit the offices of Forster's old company.

It was clear the officer she spoke to remembered the case well, as Beth could hear her struggle to manage her emotions as she answered Beth's questions.

When Beth thanked the officer and put down the phone, she closed her eyes and rested her forehead on the desk until she was sure that no tears would escape.

The rape victim had been walking her dog through a wood on the outskirts of Keswick when she was grabbed from behind. A hood had been placed over her head and she'd felt a knifepoint press against her ribs.

She'd done as her abductor had instructed and had walked deeper into the woods. A hand had been placed at the side of her head and her head thrust into what she guessed was a tree.

The woman had been dazed and had drifted between unconsciousness and agonised moments of semi-lucidity until she came fully to. She'd been left where the man had raped her. Her clothes ripped and cut off, blood leaking from her vagina. The final insult was her little terrier lying by her feet, the lead tethering it to a tree not quite long enough to allow the dog to give her comfort as she lay there.

In a lot of ways, Beth wanted this to be the Lakeland Ripper's work, but the examination carried out by the police doctor had found severe internal tearing that went far deeper than they believed the Lakeland Ripper was capable of.

The Lakeland Ripper not being responsible for this rape was a bad thing for two reasons. Because it meant there was another rapist out there. And because there was still no evidence the Lakeland Ripper was letting any of his victims get away alive.

With this idea now disproven, Beth grabbed her jacket and made for the door. The warm sun that was streaming down would mean the jacket would get cast aside soon, but its pockets held her keys, handcuffs and myriad other bits and pieces that she would normally keep in a handbag.

It was important to her that she presented the right image when dealing with the public. She knew that many members of the public she met thought that she was too young to be a detective. When their eyes lit on the scarred cheek, she could almost see them wondering if she'd been given a pity posting due to her injury. So far as Beth was concerned, the best way to dispel negative opinions was to show herself in a good light. Being smartly turned out was part of her armoury against negative assumptions her youth may create; the other part being her brain. She'd often seen people revise their opinions of her when she started questioning them, or they heard her responses to their statements.

The mayor's former employees would be the next group of people she'd have to encounter. As computer programmers, they'd all have above-average intelligence and she suspected that, to them, she'd be little more than a nuisance. A young, low-ranked officer who'd been sent to interrupt their day with silly questions.

She'd have to prove each of them wrong.

As she strode to her car, she felt her determination growing. One way or another, she had to catch a murderous rapist and find a way of identifying why they were targeting the mayor.

CHAPTER THIRTY-ONE

The offices of the mayor's former company were sited in a converted farm on the outskirts of Carlisle. The whitewash of the buildings had lost its initial lustre and was peeling off to reveal pink sandstone beneath.

Around the courtyard there were several other small businesses operating out of the former farm buildings. A man was using a barrow to haul a washing machine into one of the units, the neighbouring unit was signed as a fruiterer that Beth had seen supplying hotels and pubs, and a third was a small accountancy firm.

Outside the offices of SimpleBooker, four cars were parked in neat regimen. All of them were less than three years old, but none were unnecessarily ostentatious. There was a BMW, but it was a small hatchback rather than a fire-breathing racer or a grand tourer. Two of the other cars were everyday saloons and the fourth was a Volvo SUV.

While these cars may have been nothing more than runabouts to the owners, Beth didn't think they were. Rather she was thinking that instead of being flash and using their windfall from the sale of SimpleBooker to buy an expensive new car, the employees had merely got a decent but sensible one. Therefore they'd used their shares in a responsible way.

This made her think that none of them would have frittered away the money. In addition to the windfall, it was likely they were all on a very good wage. The company they now worked for had valued SimpleBooker as being worth tens of millions; therefore it stood to reason that the people who wrote the software would be well compensated to ward off rival companies poaching them. If that was the case, then any possible motive to bring down Forster would lie in another area than financial.

Beth walked through the door of the office and took in the scene before her. Everything she'd expected to find was missing. There were no dynamic youngsters with traces of acne and superhero T-shirts, nor were there cluttered desks laden with files. In the background she could hear a DJ introduce the next song on his playlist.

Each desk was spartan in its appearance. Beyond two computer screens per desk, a wireless mouse and keyboard, there was only a mug or a glass of water resting on each polished surface. While she liked to work in a clean environment herself, this was just too sterile for her taste.

The four people in the office all confounded her expectations as well. In the absence of young comic-book nerds, she'd thought that there would at least be a man with a ponytail. Instead there were two men old enough to be her father. Both wore smart trousers with a crisp shirt.

The two women in the room were mid-forties and, like the three manning Forster's mayoral office, they were both good-looking and dressed in the same sort of smart casual clothing the men had chosen.

To find four people so smartly dressed working in a place that had once held livestock sat at odds with Beth's perceptions of how computer programmers would dress and act. Beth knew that she was wrong to have come here with preconceived ideas. She also knew that the way these people dressed and kept their office was a probable reflection on their ages, the last vestiges of Forster's influence and their individual professionalism.

As one of the women came to greet her, Beth threw a glance at the pictures on the walls. There was a framed photograph of the four people in the room all popping the cork on bottles of champagne, with Forster in the centre of the picture. To Beth's eye, every one of their expressions looked to be filled with joy. A newspaper clipping in the corner of the frame had a headline that told of the sale of SimpleBooker. The other two pictures were of coastal scenery and could have been from anywhere, although Beth thought she recognised the location of one of them.

Beth introduced herself and explained why she was there.

'I know why you're here. Derek called us and asked that we answer your questions.' The woman's smile was as soft as her voice.

The fact the woman was on first-name terms with the mayor was understandable. They'd all worked together in this office, and with there only being five of them including Forster, they'd be a tight-knit group. While they might not have been overfamiliar with Forster, they'd have discussed holidays, meals out and all the other minor events and occasions that made for small talk.

Forster having called ahead was something of a concern to Beth. If he'd done as the woman had suggested and asked them to cooperate, it wasn't the end of the world, but it also made her think their cooperation could be manipulated. It wasn't that they'd lie at his request, more that they might try and cover up something if they thought it was in their best interests. If one of them was the Lakeland Ripper or was working with him, they'd now been forewarned.

The picture on the wall gave the outward appearance of them all being one happy family, but she knew that any one of them could be putting up a façade of togetherness while plotting to bring Forster down.

The one thing she *was* sure of, was that the four people in the room were all more than capable of hacking into the mayor's computer and leaving the incriminating pictures that Digital Forensics had found.

Beth gave a gentle smile to the woman with the soft voice and watched as her eyes locked onto the scar. Women tended to react in a different way to men. They'd see the scar and horror would fill their eyes as they imagined what it must be like to carry such a wound; they'd think of their own looks and how they'd hate to lose them in the way Beth had.

Men, on the other hand, would often see it and try to act as if they hadn't. Their eye contact would be too forced or they'd revert to type and avoid looking at her face at all.

'I'm Inga and they're George, Pete and that's Claire in the far corner.' Inga's hand pointed out each of the others as she spoke.

George and Pete looked round and nodded a hello, but Claire remained focussed on her screens.

'Thanks.' Beth looked around the room. There were two doors in one wall and she hoped that one of them would be a second office where she could talk to each of the four in turn. 'Is there somewhere we can talk in private?'

Inga's face creased in apology. 'Sorry, those doors you were looking at lead to the bathroom and the kitchen. We could use the kitchen I suppose.'

'The kitchen will be fine.'

Beth would have used a broom cupboard if necessary. The last thing she wanted to do was conduct interviews in a place where the next people she would speak to could overhear everything that was said. She didn't want to give any of them too much time to prepare their answers, and she wanted them all to feel they could speak privately without the others knowing what they were saying.

The kitchen was big enough for them both to fit in and leave a two-foot gap between them if they pressed their backs against the worktops. Like most office kitchens it had a microwave, fridge, kettle and toaster. A collection of blue mugs sat upside down on the small draining board.

Inga gave Beth another of her soft smiles. 'Before you start asking me your questions, I'd just like to say that I have no idea who'd want to harm Derek in any way. He's a good man who does a lot for charity and he's the only politician I've ever known who actually does what he says he will.'

'I've met him. He seems like a lovely man to me. So genuine.' The lie nearly choked Beth, but she wasn't averse to white lies if they uncovered black truths. 'You say that you have no idea who'd try and ruin his reputation. I take it that you've discussed this as a group?'

Beth listened to the answers Inga gave to her questions and rephrased them to see if she could catch the older woman from a different angle. Nothing she tried got a different perspective, let alone story, from Inga. Despite the woman having obvious intelligence, Inga seemed too nice, twee almost, to Beth to have an understanding of the darker side of people's nature. Inga's intellect and class shielded her in a way that bred naivety.

When she'd finished with Inga she talked with both the men. Neither gave her any great clues as to who might be behind the defamation, but something Pete said about Claire pricked her attention. It wasn't an accusation of any kind, but there was enough in his scoffed comment to suggest that the SimpleBooker family wasn't as happy as outward appearances suggested.

Pete's overall demeanour intrigued her. While he was open with his answers, he came across as something of a cold person. Maybe he was the kind of man who didn't suffer fools or had a superiority complex, or perhaps he was just having a bad day. His hair was short and while his shirt was tight on his body, he was in good shape for a man in his fifties. And for all he came across as cold, nothing else about him jangled a warning bell for Beth. She recalled that his police record was non-existent.

George was a different character. He was meek, polite and apologised with every answer that stuttered from his lips. Unlike

Pete, his shirt hung loose on an obese body. His every mannerism belied his discomfort at being questioned and while it was obvious he wanted to help, he didn't know anything.

Claire's attitude was different to that of the others. Where they'd been respectful of her status as a detective, Claire seemed to be indifferent. If the SimpleBooker employees were a family, Claire was the sullen teenager.

'So, you don't know of anyone with a grudge against Derek Forster? Can't think of someone who'd like to bring him down a peg or two?' Beth hardened her questions in response to the challenge of Claire's attitude. 'Are you going to be like the others and tell me that he's basically a saint that someone is trying to martyr?'

'I'm going to tell you the truth. I don't know of anyone who's got it in for him. He was very generous when he sold the business and easy to get on with when he was my boss. There's nothing more to tell.'

Beth was convinced that Claire had a lot of story to tell. The way she'd dressed was novel in itself. Her skirt was mid-thigh and the blouse she wore showed a generous amount of cleavage. A thin necklace hung down her chest with an engagement ring hanging at its lowest point.

To Beth the outfit was overkill for the job she had. Claire's clothing was chosen for a reason other than practicality. Both George and Pete had worn wedding rings; therefore unless she was trying to seduce one of them, she must be meeting someone else straight after work.

Even so, the length of her skirt and the amount of cleavage she was showing was more suitable to a night on the town than eight hours in a former barn.

Whatever the reason, Beth wished that Claire hadn't been the last person she spoke to. If one of the others had followed her, she'd have been able to ask if this was how she usually turned up for work.

Regardless of what she thought of the woman and her choice of workwear, Beth had questions she needed answered.

'How did you get on with Derek on a personal level? You've said he was generous and good to work for, but did you get on with him?'

'You've met him right? You know what it feels like to have him turn on the charm for your benefit. He's suave, charismatic and handsome as hell. I got on with him as well as I've got on with anyone in the workplace. He was my boss and that's how it was between us. Him the employer, me the employee. We'd chat about shit that didn't matter and then go our separate ways.'

Beth couldn't help but notice the wistfulness that crept into Claire's tone when she mentioned Forster's looks. 'Sounds like he was decent enough to you.'

'Oh he was. To a point. He held the power and while he never abused it or even mentioned it, he'd just assert his authority with a quiet word or a look.'

'Really? I've never seen that side of him.'

'You won't have. He'll see a pretty young thing like you as a potential conquest; me, I was paid to do a job.' Claire looked at her watch. 'And on that note, the new owners aren't as forgiving as Derek was in terms of missed deadlines; I'm afraid I need to get back to my desk soon.'

Beth put a few quick questions to Claire, but it was clear the older woman thought she'd crossed a line and had clammed up in case she said anything that might cause trouble for Forster.

As Beth laid her jacket on the passenger seat of her car, her entire focus was on what Claire had told her. She was sure the programmer had intimated something and then drawn back from it on purpose. She'd been given a riddle that she had to solve.

CHAPTER THIRTY-TWO

7 JUNE

Dear Diary

Derek has only gone and been elected as mayor of Carlisle!!!

He was on his best form and insisted we join him for a celebratory dinner. I've told you how charming he is as a person, well tonight he just oozed charisma, and if I'm honest with you, more than a little sex appeal.

Don't worry, Diary. Derek pays my wages and there will never be anything between us.

I'm nobody in comparison.

A girl can dream though.

Until tomorrow.

CHAPTER THIRTY-THREE

The Wall Park Hotel was an old building. Its sandstone walls shone bright in the noon sunshine and its tree-filled garden gave it the air of a country house hotel despite it being in the centre of Workington.

When Beth entered the reception there was a huge wooden desk behind which a young woman sat. She wore the kind of uniform that was standard to hotels the world over and her greeting was warm and friendly.

Beth explained who she was and why she was there.

The girl's smile never slipped as she invited Beth to have a seat while she located the hotel owner.

As she waited, Beth took a quick look around the reception. A set of carpeted stairs led to what she assumed would be the guest rooms and off to one side a bar-cum-restaurant housed a dozen tables. Only two of the tables were empty, the rest were surrounded by what her mother described as 'ladies who lunch' or businessmen tapping away at laptops. In the far corner a fat bald man in jeans was reading a battered paperback with an intense concentration.

It was the scene she'd expected to see. Wall Park Hotel wasn't the kind of place that welcomed those of a working-class disposition. It was aimed at the higher end of the market and this was reflected in the prices she'd seen when looking at the hotel's website.

The receptionist returned with the owner: a tall man with a stoop and thinning hair.

'Good day, Detective. My name is Ketteringham.' The man's accent was local to Workington, but refined, as if he'd sanded its rougher edges to better impress his guests. 'If you'd be so kind as to follow me, I think my office is the best place for us to talk.'

While the man was cordial, Beth couldn't help but pick up on his snooty condescension. The fact he'd introduced himself by surname only spoke of an inbuilt snobbery that was decades out of date. There was no welcoming handshake and he'd taken control of the situation in the way he had requested she come to his office.

As she followed him she had to bite down on her temper. Tempting as it was to play hardball with him, he could easily clam up and refuse to give her the information she needed from him. It'd be easy enough for her to get a warrant, but that would take time and she knew that the case was being closely monitored by not just the brass, but also the PSD. Therefore any errors of judgement she made would have greater repercussions than usual.

His stoop made him look as if he was scouring the ground for lost change, and as spic and span as he might be, the image that stuck with Beth was that of a drunk person bumbling their way home.

Ketteringham took a seat in the leather chair behind his desk and waved a hand towards a plastic chair by Beth.

She didn't know the man, but she'd already taken a dislike to him. His having a hard uncomfortable chair for visitors would be his way of exercising his superiority and making sure visitors to his office were keen to leave at the earliest opportunity.

'I'll stand if you don't mind, I've been in the car for an hour so it's good to stretch my legs a bit.'

Beth would have taken the seat in other circumstances, but she didn't want to yield any ground, and by standing she retained some dominance.

'Of course.' Ketteringham twiddled with his cravat. 'Now, if you could be specific about the information you require, I'll see what I can do about it.'

Beth told him the date the mayor had met with Lorraine, her room number, and requested that he share what information he had about the booking and the person who'd made it.

'I see. Shouldn't you have a warrant to justify me breaching a customer's confidentiality?'

'That depends on you, Mr Ketteringham. I can come back with a warrant. But I'm investigating four rapes and murders so your cooperation will save me a lot of time.'

'I see. And do you think the killer may have stayed here, at the Wall Park?'

'Not that I know of, but I think the person who did stay in that room on those dates may be connected to the killer.' Beth put a hard look into her eyes. 'Now, are you going to give me what I need, or do I have to come back with a warrant?' The way Ketteringham held her stare was infuriating to Beth, so she decided to add a little extra pressure. 'You have a bar in the Wall Park, therefore you must have a licence to sell alcohol. I'm sure I don't need to tell you that licences and their renewals are granted by the licensing board, and that they take into account the opinion of the police when they're assessing individual applications or renewals. I'm sure that you don't want a black mark going against you.'

'You wouldn't.' Ketteringham's face had blanched with shock and fury. 'You're blackmailing me to give you information without a warrant. That's immoral and despicable.'

'I'm doing no such thing.' Beth feigned an air of innocence. 'All I'm doing is pointing out how the decision you're about to make may come back to haunt you. If my DI or DS was here with me, they would suggest there may be surprise visits from Customs and Excise to check your measures and the provenance of your alcohol supplies. I'm sure you have invoices from breweries for every drop of alcohol on the premises and that you don't buy it from a supermarket, because you know fine well that it's illegal for a licensed premises to purchase liquor from a public retailer and then resell it. Something else they might do if they wanted to force you to answer their questions is threaten you with anonymous complaints to the likes of Trading Standards and Environmental Health. They aren't here though, and all I'm doing is asking you to save me a few hours and a bit of paperwork, because, let's face it, one way or another, we'll have the information from you before the day's out. So it's up to you, Mr Ketteringham. When I leave here, will I be calling my DI to share information, or will I be asking her to sort out a warrant?'

Beth didn't hear what Ketteringham muttered under his breath as he opened the laptop on his desk and she didn't care. She'd get what she wanted and that was all that mattered.

She didn't speak as the hotelier looked up the details of the booking.

After five minutes of awkward silence the printer whirred into life and spat out a sheet of paper. It contained the details of the booking and the name and address of the person who'd made it: 'L. Jones'.

So Lorraine's surname was Jones and the listed address was in Keswick.

Best of all, though, was the mobile phone number.

As she scanned further down the page, Beth saw that the room had been booked through the Booking.com website. As delicious as the irony was that there was a chance Forster's software had unknowingly been used by the woman he'd slept with, Beth was pleased that she'd used the system. The name may well be false, the surname of Jones suggested it may be, as might the address and even the phone number, but Beth remembered signing up for Booking.com herself. She'd had to feed in her card details, and therefore Lorraine would have had to do the same. That meant she could still be traced if the other details turned out to be false.

'One last thing, Mr Ketteringham, if this number and address don't check out, I may need details of the card used to secure this booking.' Beth lifted a hand to silence the man's protests. 'I'm not asking for them now, but I may call for them later. I would appreciate it if you could have the details to hand should I call.'

Beth got a terse nod as his answer.

When Ketteringham left her to find her own way back to reception, she had to resist the urge to nip into the bar and scream 'mouse' while pointing at the far side of the room. It would be a petty action and one beneath her, but it might prick Ketteringham's pretentious bubble.

Rather than making mischief, she had a higher priority. Now she had Lorraine's full name and address plus a number for her, she could arrange to speak to the woman.

CHAPTER THIRTY-FOUR

Rather than go straight back to Carleton Hall, Beth put in a call to the office and connected with Unthank. Within a couple of minutes, he'd run the address for Lorraine Jones and found that a Louise Jones lived there.

If Lorraine was a false name, and it seemed like it was, it made sense to Beth that Louise Jones would keep the initial the same as her real name. The nearer to the truth a lie was, the easier it was to maintain.

She asked Unthank to arrange a meeting with Louise/Lorraine Jones and set off towards Buttermere. She wanted to go and visit the area where Joanne Armstrong had been found.

As she drove the narrow roads to Buttermere, she was held up by a car towing a caravan. This was a regular occurrence in the Lake District. Caravanners would navigate the smaller roads at a snail's pace as they made their way to a campsite. Time after time the driver in front of her slowed to a crawl as they met an oncoming vehicle. As much as she wanted to blast her way past the caravan, the driver in front showed no consideration for the cars whose progress he was impeding. As soon as the oncoming vehicle had edged its way past they'd continue with their trundling journey.

Beth could imagine the scene in the car as the caravanners consulted their satnav and pointed at the beautiful scenery. For them, their holiday had begun when they'd hitched the caravan to their car and set off for Cumbria. As they were on holiday, they were relaxed, unpressured and keen to take a leisurely approach to their progress along the road.

As keen as Beth was to get to her destination, she could handle the delay without impatience today. The sun was high in the sky and sending a torrent of glints across the dappled surface of Crummock Water, the fells had that scorching effect created by prolonged good weather and, most important of all to Beth, she had a puzzle to solve.

Claire's words had been pointed, if cryptic. As a programmer, she'd be used to writing in code. What Beth had to do was decipher Claire's unspoken insinuation.

The caravan indicated right, slowed to a stop and crept its way into a campsite with a fair number of failed attempts at getting through the gate unscathed. The multiple times it reversed, and then tried again before achieving success, suggested that the driver was new to towing a caravan or that the site owner needed a wider gateway.

With the slow vehicle out of her way, Beth put her right foot nearer the floor and covered the last few miles to her destination at a far more respectable pace.

Buttermere looked as magical as ever and there were a number of small boats with fishermen in them and a couple of people windsurfing. Like a lot of the smaller lakes, Buttermere was one where motorised boats of any kind were prohibited and due to its size there weren't any yachts, or even facilities to launch or moor one.

Beth parked in the car park of a café and bought herself a bottle of water and a packet of crisps. She munched on the crisps as she travelled along the bridleway which started between the café and a hotel that had tourists occupying every one of the tables outside.

She passed through three gates as she walked along the bridleway. Holidaymakers smiled and nodded at her as she strode along. To either side of her sheep grazed in the small fields.

As she made the five-minute walk, her mind was focussed on the question of how the Lakeland Ripper had transported Joanne Armstrong along the bridleway. The first answer she came up with was that he'd waited until nightfall and had simply walked her to the place where her body had been found; Joanne's compliance provided by a healthy dose of GHB or Rohypnol. Except that wouldn't work. There had been no evidence found at the site and no traces of drugs in Joanne's blood. The access to the bridleway was between the café and a hotel, which meant the Lakeland Ripper couldn't have carried or dragged Joanne without risking being seen.

Therefore she must have been alive when she was brought here. Like the carrying or dragging, she couldn't have been led along the bridleway at knife or gunpoint in case someone staying at the hotel had looked out of their bedroom window and seen what was happening.

Beth dredged every detail in her mind about Joanne Armstrong's deposition site. She thought about the crime-scene photos, the CSI reports and the statements of the original investigating officers.

It was only when she recalled the date Joanne was found that she had an epiphany. Joanne was one of those hardy fell-walkers who paid scant attention to the seasons. Her body had been found on the thirteenth of January. A time of year when the nights were long and the tourists few and far between. Places like the two hotels in Buttermere tended to shut down in January due to a lack of trade and to allow the staff and proprietors to take their own holidays. Therefore there was every chance the hotel beside the bridleway had been deserted. If the Lakeland Ripper had known this, he'd have been confident enough to lead Joanne down the bridleway at knife or gunpoint in the middle of the night.

All these things went through Beth's mind as she followed the bridleway. After cutting right, and running parallel to the lake, the gravel track gave way to a pathway which followed the banks of the lake until it was swallowed up by the wooded slopes of High Stile. A small bridge was in place to allow people to cross the river which connected Buttermere to Crummock Water.

It was in this wood that the naked and defiled body of Joanne Armstrong had been found by people hiking towards High Stile. At over two and a half thousand feet High Stile was one of the higher peaks in the Lake District.

As she stood at the edge of the wood, Beth took in what she could see and thought about what she couldn't.

A family was sitting under the shade of an oak tree having a picnic, while another family was paddling in the shallow waters at the edge of the lake. Further along the bank, a fisherman was casting back and forth, but Beth never saw him allow the line to settle.

On glorious summer days like this, the area was populated in frequent regularity by hikers, fishers and ramblers, and the fields at the back would be visited by farmers checking their stock. Even on the days where the weather turned nastier, the farmer would still come by, and there were many fishermen who'd turn out regardless of rain and wind.

All in all, this area would have a certain amount of daytime traffic. That much was a given. But once the sun went down, especially in winter, it would be deserted, derelict of life.

As she turned and set back towards her car, Beth had a sheen of perspiration on her forehead and her shoes were coated in a film of dust from the bridleway. She was halfway back to her car when her phone beeped. She checked her messages and saw that Louise Jones had been contacted and an appointment to speak to her had been set up. DS Thompson was also on his way there to sit in on the interview.

Although decent enough, Thompson was an impatient man who hated to be kept waiting.

Tough. Before she headed back, Beth ducked into the hotel and spent a few minutes questioning the proprietor.

Her suspicions were right, the hotel shut down every January and had done for the last ten years.

Beth returned to her car, gunned its engine and sent a spray of gravel from her tyres as she rushed to get to Keswick before the DS had a good reason to grumble at her.

Her little car grunted and strained as she navigated her way along Newland's Pass. The narrow road wasn't designed for fast driving and after the first time she entered a corner that little bit too fast, Beth eased off the throttle and accepted that being late was better than not getting to her destination.

Newlands Pass ran from Buttermere to Braithwaite and its route saw it winding its way between Robinson and Grassmoor Fells. The scenery was breathtaking as Beth travelled along the mountain pass. At one point there was only a foot-high mound of earth running alongside the road between the tarmac and a steep slope than fell hundreds of feet to the valley floor, and there was a hairpin bend beside a farm where the road steepened to a gradient that was almost three in one.

The route was both desolate and beautiful, although Beth was glad she was making the journey under a blazing summer sun rather than during a downpour. Winter frosts would make the road impassable to those without four-wheel drive, and considering some of the steep drops, Beth knew she'd always take the long way round rather than try and navigate Newlands Pass in treacherous conditions.

CHAPTER THIRTY-FIVE

The appearance of the woman who opened the door didn't surprise Beth in the slightest. Like Eleanor Dereham, she was stylish and well bred. This much Beth could tell by the clothes she wore, the way she carried her head and the quiet confidence she exuded. That she lived in a house with panoramic views over Derwentwater didn't do anything to alter Beth's opinion.

Not one thing about Louise Jones suggested concern at being questioned by a couple of detectives. Rather than worry, there was a wry amusement on her face.

Beth introduced herself and Thompson then explained to Louise they wanted to ask her a few questions.

'Fine, come on in.' As they were led to the kitchen, Beth couldn't help but notice that the house was furnished in the same tasteful way the woman had dressed herself.

Once they were seated and the offer of a cuppa declined, Louise sat opposite them.

'Would you care to tell me what this is all about, please?' A heavily be-ringed hand tucked a stray wisp of mahogany hair behind her ear. 'The officer who arranged this meeting was rather vague as to why you wanted to speak to me.'

'It's about something that happened last year.'

Compared to Louise's soft voice, Thompson's tone was gruff and unfriendly. He'd nipped Beth's ear about having to wait ten minutes for her, and when she'd explained where she'd been he'd complained about her going off on her own.

Rather than have Louise drag the information from Thompson, Beth followed up from the DS's statement quickly.

'You attended a function last year. You stayed at the Wall Park Hotel in Workington.'

'That's right.' A sly look crossed Louise's face. 'Nice hotel. Manager was a bit up himself though. I'm guessing it's not him you're asking about. Would you care to explain what you want to know?'

'Of course, silly of me.' This wasn't the first time Beth had played the airhead to fool someone, and she wasn't averse to using the tactic if it gave her an advantage. 'We have a few questions we'd like to ask you about events that took place that evening.'

Louise interlocked her fingers and rested them on her stomach. The gesture was one body-language experts would interpret as being closed, but the way Louise carried herself suggested otherwise. 'Ask away. I have nothing to hide.'

'Would I be right in stating that you had a one-night stand with Derek Forster after a function in Workington last December?'

'You would.'

Beth heard Thompson clear his throat to speak, but she didn't want him interrupting her flow. So far Louise was talking without any issue and she wanted to keep things that way.

'Mr Forster was under the assumption that your name was Lorraine rather than Louise. Can you explain why he thought that?'

'He thought that because I told him my name was Lorraine.' A wry look passed across Louise's face. 'And before you ask, I lied about my name because sometimes you don't want to be yourself. It's not often that I go to bed with a stranger, but as soon as I saw him, I knew I had to have him.' She shrugged casually in response to Thompson's raised eyebrow. '*You* might think it's not terribly ladylike or something, but women have needs the same way men do. That night I was feeling, shall we say… needy, so I took him to bed.'

'Let me get this clear.' Beth leaned forward a little. 'You pursued and seduced him?'

'In laymen's terms, yes.' Beth caught the knowing look Louise tossed her way. 'In reality, I turned things around so he thought he was pursuing and seducing me.'

Beth understood Louise's point and tactics even as the woman was speaking. Men like Forster could often have their pick of women, yet when faced with enough of something that's easy to obtain, it's human nature to desire the thing you can't easily have. Be it an expensive sports car, a house with a bigger garden or the person who is unaffected by your best efforts to charm them.

These are relationships of inverse proportions: the less obtainable the item is, the more you want it. The most bedevilling aspirations are those which are fractions beyond the fingertip. Close enough to visualise and communicate with, but just out of reach.

If Louise had piqued Forster's desire and then intimated that she was unobtainable, he'd have been in her thrall. A man as powerful and successful as Forster would have enjoyed the challenge of seducing someone. His ego would never have allowed brain space to the idea that he'd been played by his conquest.

'So, you lured him into your bed. You say you used a false name to add a layer of spice to the experience.' Beth leaned back and mirrored Louise's relaxed slump. 'I'm sorry if it sounds like I'm doubting you, but your reasoning for using a false name doesn't ring true to me. I think you used a false name because you didn't want your husband or boyfriend to find out.'

'I have neither a husband nor boyfriend and haven't had for quite some time. It's why I get needy from time to time.' Louise pointed at her handbag. 'May I?' When Beth nodded she reached inside and brought out her mobile and pressed its screen a couple of times. 'Here, this is my Facebook feed. Have a look through it. Scroll back to the dates in question if you like. You may want to pay particular attention to the relationship status.'

Beth placed Louise's mobile on the table where she and Thompson could both see it. As she scrolled through the feed she saw a myriad of nondescript posts and plenty of ones about her being free, single and ready to mingle. The relationship status was marked as 'single' and the overall theme Beth got was that of a single woman enjoying life. None of the pictures on Louise's Facebook wall showed her with a man in anything other than a group photo and there was no mention of romantic dinners out or dates with anybody.

'Okay, I think we've established that you're single and have been for some time.' Thompson passed Louise's mobile back to her. 'What about your exes, did you have any nasty break-ups? Did you put anyone out on their arse? Break their hearts?'

'No to all of your questions. My marriage fizzled out five years ago, and once I'd got used to living a single life again, I dated here and there for a few weeks, but never serious. I may have needs, but they're not so strong that I'll settle for second best rather than be alone.'

Beth kept her face implacable, but inside she was giving Louise a mental high five. Her life was in order and she appeared to be happy with her lot. When she had needs she dealt with them and went on with her routine. It wasn't the life Beth wanted for herself but she admired Louise for living a life she enjoyed.

Louise's face crumpled in thought. 'So you're not so much asking about me, as any partner I may have. You're also asking about the night I spent with Derek Forster. That makes me think something has happened to Derek. Am I right? Is he okay?'

Beth tossed a look at Thompson and caught the tiny nod he gave.

'We think someone is trying to frame the mayor for a crime he didn't commit, but we don't know the person's motivation.'

Louise pulled a face. 'I get it. You think my partner may be that someone. The problem with that line of thinking is that I don't have a partner or anyone who cares enough about me to set up someone I had a one-night stand with.'

Thompson rose to his feet. 'We're sorry to have troubled you.'

Beth wanted to reflect on what little they'd learned from Louise, but before she'd passed through Louise's garden gate, her mobile went off.

A minute later she was running back to her car. O'Dowd's insistence that she be at Carleton Hall by 4.45 p.m. was a worrying development, especially as the DI hadn't given a reason for the summons.

CHAPTER THIRTY-SIX

Beth made it back to Carleton Hall with two minutes to spare thanks to getting a clear run along the A66 from Keswick. For once there had been no slothful caravans or tractors to impede progress on the parts of the road which weren't dual carriageway.

As she entered the office, she took in the scene. Unthank was at his desk, phone pressed against his ear as he scribbled notes or peered at his screen. O'Dowd was fiddling with an ink cartridge for the ancient printer that refused to die despite giving a death rattle every time it was asked to print more than a full stop. She looked up at Beth as the younger woman put her jacket over the back of her chair.

'What is it, ma'am?' As fearful as she was of getting a bollocking from O'Dowd, Beth had learned that the best way to deal with the DI's capricious moods was to front up and face the music.

'Press conference at five.' O'Dowd reached into the printer. 'The brass are running scared so I have to take it and, quite frankly, I'm not of a mind to face that pack of wolves alone.'

Beth couldn't believe what she was hearing; she'd never attended a press conference before, and to have to go into her first unprepared, and while investigating a crime with so few leads, couldn't end well. If the brass were throwing O'Dowd to the wolves, the DI was doing the same to her.

'Surely DS Thompson would be a more suitable companion? He's more senior than I am, both in age and rank.'

'Bugger.' O'Dowd withdrew her hand from the printer. It was covered in black ink and she scowled at the printer as if it would apologise to her. 'He is. But look at him, he's exhausted, literally running on empty. Both physically and emotionally. One wrong word from a reporter and he's likely to give them a piece of his mind. That can't happen when the cameras are rolling.'

'Cameras rolling?' Beth shot a look at O'Dowd. 'So we're going to be filmed telling the world we haven't got a clue who killed those four women. That's just marvellous, bloody marvellous.'

'Aye well, some things are what they are. It was either you or Unthank, and the way he's been lately, I can't trust him not to try and shag that new reporter from the *News and Star*.'

Beth got what O'Dowd meant. The new reporter wasn't above batting her eyelashes to get what she wanted, and Unthank had reacted to breaking up with his fiancée by trying to jump into the bed of any woman who spoke more than four words to him. If the two of them were left alone in each other's presence for any length of time, it was a racing certainty he'd end up being teased into feeding her titbits about the investigation.

'With due respect, ma'am, a wee heads-up a bit sooner would have been nice. You know, a chance to run a brush through my hair or at least put some lippy on.'

'That's precisely why I didn't tell you sooner. I want you going in there with a sheen of sweat on your brow and a knot in your hair. Catching a killer is hard work and I want you looking like you've been working hard, not preparing for a bloody date.'

Beth pulled a face at the DI's back as the printer rattled and clacked into life. The first sheet it spat out was handed to her by O'Dowd. 'Here, that's from the press officer. It's a list of non-committal phrases he deems acceptable. Have a deeks at them and memorise as many as you can.'

'Isn't he going to be there?' Beth took the sheet of paper and started looking at it as instructed.

'He's on a course.'

'A golf course, do you think? It's ridiculous. This is his job, not mine.'

'That's enough, Beth.' O'Dowd's tone was as hard as Beth had ever heard it. 'I don't like it either, but we have to do the press conference. Me as the detective inspector, and you as the bright young thing working her backside off to get a result. Your past results have earned you a certain amount of credit with the press and today's the day we're going to spend it. You're to stick to the stock phrases, keep your temper and trust me to field any nasty criticism that comes our way.'

'So, basically all you need is for me to sit there doing nothing?'

'No. I want them to see the fire in your eyes, to get a sense of your determination to get a result. I want them to realise how smart that sideways-thinking brain of yours is when you put it to good use. Whether you like it or not, you're on a career trajectory. Sometimes you'll get handed the shitty end of the stick and the way you either grasp it or let it fall to the ground will define your career.'

Rather than answer, Beth turned her back on O'Dowd and started to scan the trite, meaningless phrases issued by the press officer.

As much as she was angry with O'Dowd for the way the DI had forced her into attending this press conference, she knew that O'Dowd's reasoning made logical sense. She also recognised that a layer of flattery had crept into the argument.

This was the reason she'd turned away from the older woman. Whenever the slightest blush fed onto her face, the scar on her left cheek appeared to whiten and give away her emotions.

When she'd read the stock phrases twice she balled the paper and tossed it into a bin. To hell with the press officer and his non-statements. If she was asked a direct question, she'd give the straightest answer she could without giving away any details of the case.

CHAPTER THIRTY-SEVEN

Derek Forster tied his laces and sat back in his seat to think for a few moments about the forthcoming evening. As well as all the details that would need to be ironed out about the charity he intended to establish, he also wanted to make a good impression on DC Young. She was the perfect wounded puppy to front the publicity he wanted to generate for the charity. Coupled with the defining scar on her face, she had passion by the bucketload and if he could find a way to harness that and her inbuilt drive, then this new charity may well be the thing which got him a seat in parliament, or even the House of Lords.

It didn't matter to him how she'd picked up the scar, it just mattered that she wore it like a badge of honour. Most of the women he knew would have vainly tried to disguise the remains of the wound. A few strands of hair hanging down the face or a layer of thick make-up were the obvious solutions, but DC Young did neither. The scar changed colour with her mood, and when she was fired up, the scar would flare white.

Her being an otherwise beautiful woman made the scarring seem even more tragic to him. The amount of inner strength she'd presumably used to come to terms with the injury and its lasting effects was unknown to him, but he marvelled at her fortitude.

He knew he'd stared at her scar when he'd first met her, but she'd ignored the lapse in manners and kept her focus on the matter at hand.

Forster knew that he'd only scratched the surface with her, but from what he'd seen, he'd learned that she was very smart, determined and imbued with a passion for justice that he'd rarely witnessed in anyone before. The word 'driven' was bandied about a lot, but in the case of DC Young, it was the best word he could think of to describe her.

As he climbed to his feet and patted his pockets to check for his car keys, Forster was trying to work out what attracted him to her the most. Her brain, her strength or the way she looked.

It was only as he gunned the engine of his Range Rover that he realised what was really driving his feelings. It was the simple fact that she wasn't one of the women that thrust themselves upon him. DC Young carried the indifferent air of the disinterested. She'd admitted that she was single, and while there was a considerable age gap between them, he'd dated younger women than her before.

DC Young not showing attraction to him was the key to his feelings. She was a challenge. If he could bed her, it would be an experience far better than sleeping with the women who offered themselves to him without any qualms.

Seducing her wouldn't be easy. It would take tact, charm and more than the odd nice dinner.

He could play the long game. After all, the longer the chase, the sweeter the kill.

CHAPTER THIRTY-EIGHT

Beth walked into the Stoneybrook Inn and cast her eyes around the room. Forster was sitting at the bar and Tattoo Neck was nowhere to be seen, not that she expected him to be here. The mayor was engaged in conversation with the barman, but his body was half turned so he could survey the room and keep an eye on the door.

His hand raised in a wave when he saw her.

As she'd expected he was well turned out. The shirt he wore was a designer one and it was crisp with a sharp collar, his tan chinos a good match for his shirt, and the cologne he wore was strong and manly.

He'd made an effort.

So had she, after a fashion. By the time she'd got home after the press conference and a short yet blistering reprimand from O'Dowd, she'd had forty-five minutes to shower, dry her hair and throw on some clothes.

Beth had spent little time deciding what she should wear and had gone for practicality over fashion. The weather had turned humid and as she'd spent most of the day perspiring, she'd grabbed a long skirt and a fitted T-shirt. Normally she would have preferred to have worn a shorter, knee-length skirt but she didn't want Forster getting the wrong idea, so she'd picked a floral one that hung to her ankles. The one concession she made to fashion over comfort was a pair of wedged sandals.

When she saw the way Forster instinctively slid his eyes down her body, she was glad she'd went for demure rather than cool.

He was a predator and she knew that she'd have to keep her wits about her if she was to avoid becoming his prey.

'I see you've come prepared.' Forster pointed at the folder which hung from her left hand, then at the briefcase perched against the leg of his barstool. 'Me too.'

As one of the waiting staff showed them to a table, Beth glanced round the room. A former coaching inn, Stoneybrook Inn had morphed into a bar and restaurant. Sited a mile north of Penrith, it survived by serving up good food at reasonable prices. It might never win a Michelin star, but it was homely and had a friendly atmosphere which enticed customers to return on a regular basis.

Forster took the menu offered to him by a young waitress wearing a branded T-shirt and skinny jeans. 'Shall we order first and then talk business while the chef does his stuff?'

'Sounds good to me.' Beth ordered herself a glass of iced tap water from the waitress, along with a glass of house wine. 'Is that the voice of experience speaking?'

Forster gave an easy smile and a self-deprecating shrug. 'You got me. I've had many a dinner meeting and I've found it best to order first then talk shop. We can also get a bit of thinking space as we eat each course.'

'That makes sense.'

Beth fell silent and looked at the menu. It wasn't that she was deciding what to have: she had no intention of having anything more than one course, and it was too hot for anything more than a salad anyway.

Now that she was here with Forster she was torn by differing emotions. If he was serious about setting up the charity, then he deserved plaudits, but what if he was using it as a smokescreen to get close to her so he could learn about the investigation, or indeed to mask his own guilt for whatever he'd done to instigate the framer's campaign against him?

She couldn't quell her suspicions about the mayor being a player, largely because of Forster's propensity to surround himself with good-looking women. The three secretaries in his mayoral office were all attractive, as were Claire and Inga. And the picture she'd seen of Donna Waddington, who'd left SimpleBooker to found EdenData, had shown her to be quite beautiful.

Then there were his girlfriends. The women he'd dated and those he associated with. Louise Jones too. All of them were attractive.

It made her wonder at his interest in her. Objectively Beth knew that she had once had a pretty face, although the disfiguring scar on her cheek had changed that.

After her thoughts were interrupted by the waitress taking their order, Beth wondered how Forster saw her. As a pretty trinket to be seen at his side during fundraisers and recruitment drives for the charity, or was the scar on her cheek actually the real reason he wanted her involved?

So far as she was concerned, the scar portrayed her as a survivor, but to a politician like Forster, she assumed it would be seen as a badge of victimhood. If she became the public face of a victims' charity, many, if not all who saw her might assume she was a victim of rape.

She knew this would be a burden she'd have to carry alone, but it would be worth it if Forster was serious about making it easier for women to report their rapists and feel confident that their attackers would face imprisonment, while also providing shelter and counselling to help them through their ordeal.

'I'm sure that you can't talk to me about your investigation into the person who's behind the murders and planted what I'm sure are disgusting images on my computer, and I'm not going to put you in an awkward position by asking you about them, but I will say that I saw you on the news.' Forster gave an approving nod. 'You certainly made quite an impression when you called out that reporter for his stupid question.'

'What did he expect? I mean, who puts a deadline on an investigation?' Beth shrugged and thought back to the swearing O'Dowd had given her for the way she'd lambasted the man who'd asked if the killer would be caught the next day while ignoring his more troubling question about why none of the first three murders had been connected before Felicia Evans's body had been found.

After fielding the majority of questions put to her during the press conference with ease, a piercing question had caught Beth off guard and as she was recovering her poise the foolish reporter had made his move. Despite the nudges then kicks O'Dowd had delivered to her ankle under the table, Beth hadn't been minded to stop unloading her frustrations at the lack of real progress with the case onto the hapless reporter. She'd pointed out the effort they were all putting in, the way there were no restrictions on resources or budget and that despite all their hard work, there were very few leads to pursue.

O'Dowd had ended the press conference once Beth fell silent and as soon as they were alone she'd had a rant of her own. The only way Beth had been able to defend herself was to point out that her rant had saved them from having to answer the one question they'd been dreading would be put to them: why didn't a senior officer with a countywide overview pick up on the similarities between the murders sooner?

Nobody ever wants to make public criticisms of a superior's failings in a hierarchical system, but the question had been asked, and neither Beth nor O'Dowd had been able to offer either a convincing answer or a reasonable deflection.

Beth hadn't lied to O'Dowd by claiming the rant was a deliberate tactic to get them off the hook they were on, but she had pointed out that it had been a handy side effect. Another future benefit was that it was unlikely she'd be invited to speak at another press conference anytime soon.

'I have to say, I thought you were very impressive. The way you conducted yourself when you were quite clearly furious was nothing short of brilliant. You put that man in his place and let the world see your determination to solve the case. But more than that, you showed how fired up you are, how the case is personal to you. As a member of the public, it was uplifting to see that kind of zeal in a police officer. Too often these days we hear about coppers spending half their time on diversity courses or filling in forms. You showed them a stressed but determined frontline copper who's intent on solving a case.'

'Really? I was worried I came across as someone who'd lost the plot.'

'Quite the opposite. I saw that same zeal when you rounded on me the other day. That's why I want you involved in the charity we're here to discuss.'

He fell silent as the waitress appeared with their meals.

'Thank you.' Beth cast her eyes across the room, afraid to look directly at him. She could feel the blush on her cheeks as the waitress put Forster's starter in front of him.

As he ate, Beth composed herself as best she could. Forster was a slippery manipulator and she knew the flattery he'd laid on her was designed to lower her defences and bring her onside. She also had to consider the way he'd said he wouldn't ask about the investigation; that was reverse psychology if ever she'd met it. He'd stated his position in the hope she'd throw him a few crumbs out of respect for his understanding.

As she watched him spear his food, she knew she'd have to keep her guard up against his wily manipulations. He appeared as if he was acting without thought, that everything he said was genuine, yet there was no denying that he was pressing the right buttons at every point in the conversation.

When he'd arranged his knife and fork on the plate and dabbed his mouth with a napkin, she threw him a bone to make him think his ploys were working. 'I spoke with the team at SimpleBooker today; they didn't know who might want to target you and I didn't get the impression any of them would want to.'

'I didn't think they would either.'

'I also managed to track down the lady who called herself Lorraine, and I'm confident it's not her or anyone who might be connected to her either.'

'I see.' Forster scratched at his forearm and revealed an expensive-looking watch. 'Is that good or bad news?'

'Both. Good for her that we've eliminated her as a suspect and bad because it's the last half-decent lead we had.'

'So what next?'

'Next we talk about the charity. I've told you all I can, Mr Mayor.'

'That's fair enough. I appreciate that you've told me anything at all. Please though, call me Derek. If we're going to be working together, we don't need to be so formal, do we?'

'No, we don't.' It was there again: asking her permission to be less formal was just another of his ways to inveigle himself into her good books. 'I'm Beth.'

Beth spent the next twenty minutes listening to Forster's vision for the charity. She knew nothing about how charities were set up or run, but he seemed to have a clear idea about the administration side of things. She liked the majority of his ideas and the desire to do good that was fuelling them, but there were some areas where she felt his thoughts were off base.

'Can I just stop you there? What you're saying about creating an environment where women can feel confident about reporting their sexual assaults is great in theory, in practice it's not that simple. The police have trained officers for that as well as counsellors. Not only would you be duplicating what's already in place and working as well as it can, you'd be asking the victims to go through everything with the charity as well as the police. I think that may be too much for a lot of women. I'm the first to admit I'm no expert on the subject, but I do know a lot of rape victims blame themselves, that they're sure the defence lawyers will paint them as some kind of slut for wearing a short skirt or a low-cut top. Many rapes also happen in a domestic setting over a period of time. The women are afraid to escape because they have no money or because they love, or have loved, their rapist. Again, these women, wrongly, often blame themselves for not having a libido that matched their partner's.'

'Wow. I didn't realise there were quite so many facets to it.'

'That's the problem. A handful of rapes, like the ones we are investigating, are horrific individuals attacking random victims, but the majority of rapes are committed by people the victims know. Rape is also part of the domestic-abuse spectrum. Many domestic abusers escalate to rape and because they have power over their partners; these situations can go on for years.' Beth paused to sip at her wine. A crisp Chardonnay with undertones of citrus fruits. It was delicious, and while she wanted more than just one glass to wash the sour taste of their conversation's subject matter from her mouth, she'd made a point of driving the two miles from her home to Stoneybrook Inn so she could only have one alcoholic drink. The last thing she wanted was to make it easy for Forster to ply her with wine. 'Then you have the false accusations.'

'The what?' Forster's puzzlement was spread across his face and layered in his tone.

'False accusations. Some people cry rape to take revenge on someone for something the claimant believes the accused has done to them. Let's face it, someone's making false allegations against you. All the false allegations have to be dealt with in the same way as the genuine ones, which adds to the workload created by the genuine victims. Yes, the official statistics on false rapes are less than one per cent, but those figures only include the claimants who were prosecuted for wasting police time or perverting the course of justice, which means the real figure is probably higher as not every false allegation will end in prosecution for either party. I think your idea about encouraging people to report their rapes is fantastic, and if you hadn't mentioned it, I would have. However, that may well create a deluge of claims if it proves to work. Have you taken into account the fact that once your charity is up and running with a few successes under its belt, it may well become the go-to place for all claimants and perhaps those reporting historical rapes? That would be fantastic, but we'll have to make sure the police infrastructure is in place to deal with all the calls in the right way and to make sure each is investigated properly.'

'Agreed. There is one thing that I'm wondering though. What do we do when victims come to us and refuse to report the rape to the police?'

'We try gentle persuasion. We do everything we can to encourage them to report their sexual assault, but we always respect their decision. It is them who'll have to stand in the dock and explain their actions and decisions to a court, not us. And that's before you factor in the horror of having to tell a room full of strangers every detail of what might have been the worst experience of their life. If they can't do it, then we have to respect that and offer them counselling instead.'

'Is that all? Couldn't you lock the guys up, or at least put a scare into them?'

'You're joking me, right?' Beth was annoyed at herself for letting the scoff creep into her voice. 'What do you think would happen once we released the guy? I'll tell you what would happen in most cases, the woman would be taught a lesson. One of the biggest reasons women pull out of reporting the fact they've been raped is that they're afraid of repercussions.'

Forster held up a hand in contrition. 'Sorry, I didn't think of that. You know best.'

Beth ignored the comment about her knowing best and reached into her folder to retrieve the pages of statistics she'd printed from the Rape Crisis website. 'I don't know how much research you've done yourself, but have a look at these figures and you'll see the scale of what you're dealing with. I got these from a national charity, which begs another question, do you plan to stay regional, or will you go national?'

Forster took the papers and laid them down as he pulled a pair of reading glasses from his jacket pocket. 'I think we should set up as regional first and then once we've got ourselves established and have the kinks ironed out, we should roll it out nationally on a county by county basis.'

Beth was starting to think of this charity as a partnership between the two of them, but she also needed to make her level of involvement clear. 'I like how you're including me in everything, but I have to warn you, I'm not a charity worker. I'm a detective and that's what I want to be. I'm happy to be an advisor as you set the charity up, and I'll even help you with some publicity, but there's no way I'll ever be able to commit to more than that. I shouldn't even be your police liaison; there are other officers who're way more qualified to fill that role than I am.'

'I see. We'll I'm glad we've got that out of the way at the start. I find it's always better to know these things at the outset, don't you?'

Beth nodded her agreement as the waitress returned to clear their empty plates. Forster had gone for a steak with home cut chips and she'd ordered the Caesar salad. His steak was cooked the way she liked hers: still pink inside with the merest hint of blood running from it.

Forster leafed through the pages of statistics she'd printed off for him. She saw his eyebrows raise when he got to the page which detailed the number of men who'd fallen victim to sexual assaults and rape.

As with domestic abuse, there were also always a number of male victims, but in most cases the men were reluctant to report the crimes that had been committed against them. Many people didn't stop to think that a man could suffer rape the way a woman could, but it was a fact of life that they did.

Beth watched Forster closely as he got to the last page. This was the one where she'd written out what she intended to say should their discussions ever bring the charity to life.

Forster nodded as he read. When he got further down the page, his expression changed as he took in her words.

She knew it was a powerful statement: one which laid her bare and exposed her secrets for the world to see.

'You'd say this to the press? You'd let me use it on advertising that I used to create awareness of the charity?'

'Absolutely. The women who have the guts to report their rapes will go through far worse than I will making that statement. If it helps give them courage, then I'd be honoured to say it.' Beth gave a humble shrug as Forster nodded in thought. 'It's still a bit rough round the edges and needs a little adjusting here and there once we know names and dates, but its core points will stay the same.'

'You really are a remarkable young woman. I'm lucky to have you on my side, even if the circumstances we met in were not exactly ideal.'

Beth waved away his compliment as an elderly lady approached the table, the man behind her wearing the expression of the permanently beleaguered.

When the woman opened her mouth, her voice was large enough to carry across the whole room. 'Excuse me, young lady. I saw you on the telly, didn't I? You were saying how you'd stop at nothing to catch the man who raped and killed those women. Well, talk to you is quite obviously cheap. Not two hours later you're sitting here having dinner with your father. You're nothing but a hypocrite.'

The lady looked at Beth with defiance as she waited for a response.

'I did indeed say that. But I'm not dining with my father, I'm consulting with a generous man who's looking to establish a charity to help victims of sexual abuse. For your information, I have been working fourteen-hour days on my current case and I intend to continue to do so until it's solved. In the meantime, though, I still have to eat.'

The woman strode away, her face blanching as she flapped a hand at the husband to follow.

'Bravo. You really knocked her down a peg or two there.'

'She was right though.'

'Nonsense. Tell me, what do you plan to do when you leave here? Go home and watch something on the TV? Or will you be poring over your notes on the case until you're exhausted? For what it's worth, my money is on the latter.'

Beth pulled a face. 'You'd win your money.'

'And look at what we're discussing; this is a working dinner. You even told her as much yourself. You shouldn't let what she said get to you. You have to eat, and your involvement in my project is you going over and above the call of duty. Anyway, you think you were insulted, she thought I was your blooming *father*!'

'All I'm going to say about that is: no comment.'

'Very funny. Don't let her get to you. She's a bitter old woman who doesn't know what she's talking about.'

As kind as his words were, Beth knew she'd made a mistake dining out after making such a public statement. The elderly lady had voiced her opinion, but she wasn't the only person in the room that may have seen the news. If she had thought that Beth was a hypocrite, others would too.

The way Derek had reassured her about the woman's comments felt good to Beth. When she added in his impeccable manners, the unmistakable charisma and the fact that he was a classically handsome man, Beth knew that her opinion of him was changing and that her first impressions of him had been wrong.

Forster returned the subject back to the charity and they chatted about the need for male counsellor, counsellors who were multilingual, and the fact that only 40 per cent of rape trials ended in a conviction.

As a copper, Beth knew that the reasons for this were myriad. The victim could have fallen apart under the defence lawyer's questioning and given poor answers, there may have been a lack of evidence, or a mistake by the investigating officers. Sometimes, the verdict just didn't go the right way though. It was always one person's word against another's, and if the question of consent couldn't be properly answered, for example, if the victim was too drunk to remember all the details, then a guilty verdict would rarely be found.

When it came to paying the bill, Beth insisted on going Dutch despite Forster's protests. All she wanted to do was get home and go through her notes. An idea had come to her about the murder case and she wanted to see if it checked out.

CHAPTER THIRTY-NINE

Beth settled down on to her couch and thought about her evening. Despite herself, she had to admit that she was warming to Forster. His drive to establish the charity was something that had to be admired, and there was no doubt that he could lay on the charm when he wanted to.

He'd been suave all evening and had been courteous to all those he encountered, but on one or two occasions she'd caught him checking her out. The odd comment of his had crossed the line between polite and flirty. She'd replied to the flirtier comments with directness, but had allowed a faint smile to creep across her face. Beth didn't want him to be sure if she was attracted to him, but at the same time, she wanted him to hope that she was. She'd been flattered by his attention and now she was thinking about it, she had to admit to herself that if she hadn't had the two dates with Ethan, she may have been tempted.

The idea she'd had at the Stoneybrook Inn about the murder case checked out to a degree, but she'd need to look at it again in the morning with her spreadsheet in front of her, as the notes she'd brought home with her didn't have the relevant data. She was sure the information on the birdwatcher had made it to her spreadsheet, but if it hadn't, it would be on the original investigators' reports. If she was right, it would need to be made a priority as they would have a suspect for the murders. The first thing she'd do in the morning would be to run the person she suspected through the PND to check out his background.

Beth was so convinced in her idea that she found herself torn between waiting for morning and going into Carleton Hall at once. She was tired but knew that it would take at least an hour before her brain shut down enough for her to sleep. The more she thought about going into the office the more she was inclined to follow the lead.

In the end she decided to stay put, as even if she confirmed her theory, nothing would happen until morning. The link was too tenuous to get a warrant in the middle of the night, and the back shift would have their hands full with the day-to-day stuff. Nobody would thank her for bringing in extra work that could wait until she was back on shift.

To salve her conscience, Beth decided to get an early start to allow her to check out her idea. If she was right and the guy in question had any kind of record, she'd be able to present her findings to O'Dowd as soon as the DI arrived.

Even as she thought about the next day, her mind drifted to Ethan. She wanted to send him a message, but didn't want to come across as needy.

Like the police, paramedics had good days where lives were saved and children born, but they also had the bad days where things went wrong; they might lose a patient or attend an incident where they saw horrific sights.

Their relationship wasn't yet developed enough that they supported each other through the bad stuff, but Beth knew that it had a better chance of getting to that stage because of the fact they both worked in the emergency services, which would ultimately mean they'd each understand the other's pain and frustrations on the bad days.

For those who worked in the front line of the emergency services, finding lasting love was often tough. Inconsiderate shift patterns, along with regular delays in getting away from work, meant meals went uneaten, dates got cancelled at the last minute and partners were let down on a regular basis. That she was dating someone who was in the same figurative boat was a plus. No resentment could build up over ruined plans as they'd both be guilty of last-minute call-offs at times.

The one negative to their relationship developing was that matching their shift patterns would be nigh on impossible some weeks. Still, if things worked out long-term, it'd be a small price to pay.

Ethan's next night off was on Sunday and they'd made tentative plans to go for a meal then a few drinks. Whether she actually *could* go would depend on how the case was going. She hoped she could, even if it meant catching up with him later in the night.

She hadn't worried too much about telling him she would be having dinner with Forster, but she had wondered how he might react. His reaction had been everything she could have hoped for though. Instead of worrying about her dining with a rich and attractive man, he'd been supportive of the fact that she could do some good by helping with the charity.

Beth channel-hopped until she found a wildlife documentary and then settled down to let her brain empty itself. Five minutes into the programme she began to wonder if the reason Ethan had been supportive of her meeting Forster was really because he didn't care that much about her. It was far too early for the conversation about where things were going, and neither had they made any firm commitment to the other.

They'd had a couple of dates: drinks in a bar where they chatted and got to know one another, but other than goodbye kisses, things hadn't exactly got physical. Beth had assumed that Ethan had respected that she wasn't the kind of person who would be rushed and so had behaved like a gentleman. But she couldn't stop herself worrying that he was losing interest in her.

The cushion beside her received two solid slaps. Was it the same old tired story? Women held off from sleeping with someone too soon in the relationship in case they were thought of as sluts, thus denying their own libido, all the while wondering whether the man in question would tire of waiting and dump them for a girl who wouldn't make them wait so long.

Ethan wasn't like that though. Was he? He was the first person she'd found herself attracted to for quite some time, and from where she was standing, he was everything she wanted in a boyfriend. Besides, there really should be no stigma in this day and age.

She was about to pour herself a glass of wine when her phone beeped. She lifted it wondering if the message was Ethan telling her he didn't like the idea of her having dinner with the mayor.

All at once she realised the contradiction to her thinking: she didn't want to be with someone who didn't trust her. If she did stop working on the charity at Ethan's request, maybe she'd be giving him control over her life, subjugating herself instead sharing an equal role?

The smile she gave to the phone was instinctive.

Ethan had asked about her date with Forster. Hoped that she was home safe and that she'd had a nice meal.

Beth got all the subtext that lay behind the message. He was asking because he cared, and maybe was a little worried she was dining out with another man so soon into their relationship.

She liked that. It was why she was still smiling to herself as she tapped out a reply. It was good that he cared; she would have cared if he'd been having dinner with another woman. Even if it was a platonic meeting like hers had been.

Except the meeting *hadn't* been entirely platonic. It had been a game that both parties were playing. As well as involving her in the charity, Forster was trying to seduce her, and Beth knew, deep down, if Ethan wasn't on the scene, she might have let Forster succeed.

Beth was putting clothes out ready for the next day when her phone started to ring. Her first thought was that it was Ethan, but when she saw 'Dad' on the screen her first instinct was to worry something had happened to one of the family.

'Dad, is everyone okay?'

'Of course they are.' Her father's voice was filled with calmness and tinged with something else. 'Why would you think owt else?'

'Oh right. You don't usually call me at this time of night.'

'Yes, well, I have a good reason for calling tonight. I've just seen the late *Border News* and *Lookaround*.'

Beth felt her heart sink. Her father was a quiet man who believed in causing neither offence nor spectacle. Now that he'd seen her ranting on *Border Craic* and *Deeksabout*, as the news show was often called by locals, he'd be sure to have a few words of admonishment for her.

'I can explain, Dad.'

'You have nothing to explain. The reason I'm calling is to let you know that your mother and I are very proud of you. Our little girl has grown up to become a force to be reckoned with. You're a warrior in the war against injustice, and your brains as well as your tenacity will see you catch this killer. Like I said, we just wanted to say we're very proud of you.' He paused. 'Well, that was all. I'll say good night now. Let you get some rest.'

'Good night, Dad.' Beth had to cut the call before her father heard the catch in her throat.

She knew her parents loved her; they just didn't express it very often. For her father to call her like this was unprecedented, although very welcome.

As Beth laid her head on the pillow she wore a big goofy grin. The combination of Ethan's texts, her parents' pride in her, the idea of helping Forster establish the charity for rape victims, as well as her potential breakthrough in the case, had made this day – which had started off so badly – a lot better than she'd ever imagined it could be.

CHAPTER FORTY

Both O'Dowd and Thompson arrived in the office ten minutes after Unthank. To Beth, Unthank was the only one who looked as though he'd slept. Thompson's lack of sleep was no mystery due to what was going on with his wife, but she wasn't sure about O'Dowd.

The DI's teenage daughter, Neve, was filled with an independent spirit and Beth knew that O'Dowd was increasingly concerned about her daughter's behaviour, worrying about her on a daily basis. Even when she was having a few calm days, the DI was always wondering about what was to come when the girl had her next adventure. She knew O'Dowd also feared that the way her daughter was going, it wouldn't be long before she would be dabbling in one kind of drug or another.

The scowl O'Dowd tossed at Beth told her that she still hadn't been forgiven for the scene she'd made during the press conference.

'Ma'am, I've something to tell you.'

'It had better be good. You needn't think coming in early will get you off my shit list.'

'Would the name of a solid suspect be classed as good?'

Beth knew she'd been a little too glib, but the news she had to share ought to be more than good enough to get her off O'Dowd's list, therefore she didn't worry about it as much as she might usually.

'If you have found our killer, I'll have your babies and pay your mortgage for a year.' O'Dowd joined Thompson and Unthank in staring at her. 'Come on then, out with it. Who're you pointing the finger at, and why?'

'His name is Tom Gracie. He's a birdwatcher who was interviewed by the team investigating the murder of Christine Peterson. He was at the wildlife reserve the day she went missing. One of the investigating officers had a father-in-law who was showing an interest in the hobby, so he got a list of good places to watch birds. Lacking another piece of paper, he wrote the list in his notebook. On that list were Buttermere for ospreys and the Solway marshes for oystercatchers.'

Unthank pulled a face as he bent an arm behind his back and began scratching. 'It's a bit of a stretch.'

'Oh ye of little faith. You should know that she'll have something better than that otherwise she'd have warned us it was tenuous.'

'Ahh that's better.'

'Shush you sad sack. I'm trying to listen to Beth.'

Beth ignored the commotion as Unthank bickered with O'Dowd. 'Naturally I checked him out on the PND. He has had three warnings for being a peeping tom; he was also assaulted two years ago. The guy who beat him up said he'd been following his wife, hence the fact he got a kicking.'

'Good work, Beth. I take it you've got an address for him.'

Beth handed over a request for an arrest warrant. 'More than that, ma'am. I've got this filled out ready for you to get approved.'

'Consider yourself moved from the shit list to top of the want-to-buy-a-drink-for list.' O'Dowd tossed a look at Thompson. 'See, girls are better than boys.'

'Very funny.' Thompson didn't share O'Dowd's change of mood. He pointed upwards. 'Aren't you forgetting something?'

The smile left O'Dowd's face as she faced Beth. 'The chief super wants to see you at nine sharp.'

'Ma'am.' Beth didn't need to be clairvoyant to know what the summons was about. It was sure to be a dressing-down over the press conference. 'Exactly how mad was he?'

The chief super was famed for his ability to give the most thorough bollockings of all the senior officers in Cumbria. He wasn't a shouter or a ranter. He never raised his voice; in fact the angrier he got, the quieter he spoke. There were tales of officers failing to hear his admonishments which prompted another round of whispered accusations. His favourite weapon was the asking of unanswerable questions that damned you whichever way you answered them.

'I'd say it's fair to expect a few of his deep-shit questions coming your way.'

A check of her watch told Beth that the meeting was a half hour off, so she tried her best to prepare some kind of defence, although she knew it would probably be a waste of her time. At the very least, it stopped her brooding about the impending interrogation.

It was typical that just when everything was going right for her, something would go wrong. Try as she might, she couldn't help but speculate as to the outcome of her meeting with the chief super. At best she'd get reprimanded and made to feel like she was five years old. The worst-case scenario would be a suspension and a black mark on her record. The black mark would be the worst thing as it would prevent her from climbing the ranks the way she intended to.

CHAPTER FORTY-ONE

Beth had never learned what Chief Superintendent Hilton's first name was and this wasn't the time to ask. She was standing at attention in front of his desk. Off to one side, Mannequin of the PSD was also in a parade-ground stance, but that was his norm.

Hilton surveyed her with a detached expression. He had one of those faces that never gave anything away. Whether he was walking his daughter down the aisle or witnessing the death of his parents, his face would presumably adopt the same form.

'Do I need to explain why you're here, Detective?'

'No, sir.'

O'Dowd had warned her to keep her answers short, and it was advice Beth planned to stick to.

'So you're aware of the furore your little outburst at yesterday's press conference has caused?'

Beth didn't know anything about a furore. The way Hilton had said the word, he'd made it sound like he was talking about an Italian sports car. Still, she didn't want to admit that she wasn't any the wiser. Rather than speak and admit her ignorance, she kept her mouth shut.

'I asked you a question. Would you like me to repeat it, or did you hear it the first time?'

Beth had had enough of playing nice; it wasn't going to get her anywhere. It was time the truth was told. All the same, she kept her tone respectful.

'I heard you, sir. I'm just not sure I follow you. I know I shouldn't have lost my temper the way I did, but the truth is that if I hadn't, we'd probably have had to explain why no senior officers had picked up on the fact there was a serial rapist and murderer at large in Cumbria.'

'I know about that. I read the transcript of the press conference. Your rant saved you having to criticise senior officers, myself included. All in all, it was very timely, if ill-advised.' Hilton's voice lowered a little. 'I'm talking about something different. You either know what I'm talking about, and you're playing dumb, or you're covering for the fact you don't know. I'd like to know which it is.'

'I'm sorry, sir, I don't know what you're talking about.'

Hilton lifted a sheet of paper from his desk. 'Five thousand shares on Facebook, one hundred and eight thousand retweets. It would seem that your little rant has gone viral.' The emphasis Hilton put onto the last two words made it sound as if going viral was on a par with war crimes. 'Thankfully, the public seem to like your spirited rant and there are calls for, and I quote, "more coppers like you".'

'Sir.' Beth didn't know what else to say, but she could tell the chief super was expecting a response from her.

'I'm not one to pander to public opinion and neither is the chief constable. However, your little outburst has drawn a lot more attention to your case than anyone wanted. From now on, you will lead all press conferences related to your case. I must warn you though, now the press know that they can get a reaction from you, they'll all be doing their best to provoke you into saying something untoward. I'm glad you kept your wits about you the last time and didn't give away any sensitive details. But I'm sure I don't need to tell you that if you had, there would be a formal disciplinary hearing instead of this friendly word.'

'Sir.'

'That is all.'

As Beth made her way back to the office she tried to work out what had just happened. Instead of the industrial-strength bollocking she was expecting, she'd been almost praised.

She supposed Hilton's comments about the press conferences were her punishment for speaking out the way she had. The way he'd dangled the threat of disciplinary proceedings was him exerting control over her in the future.

This would only be a real issue if Tom Gracie turned out not to be the Lakeland Ripper. If he was the Lakeland Ripper, there would be a short press conference to announce they'd caught the killer and then she'd go back to her normal life, away from the glare of the public. If Gracie wasn't the killer, she'd have to admit to the assembled press that they'd wasted their time on a dead end. She expected that if she did so, the press would turn on her and criticise not just her work but that of the entire FMIT.

CHAPTER FORTY-TWO

Tom Gracie lived in Penrith which made things simpler in terms of getting to his house. Working all around the county often meant long drives on narrow rural roads with all the hindrances they held, but at least they didn't have to do that today.

Before they left the office, Beth had run the suspect's name and address through a couple of databases and got his national insurance number and the licence number for his van. Gracie was employed as a maintenance man at the Whinfell Forest holiday camp on the outskirts of the town.

Beth and O'Dowd had established that Gracie wasn't at home, so they were now at the security gate of the holiday camp. A guard checked their warrant cards and directed them to the maintenance sheds. If Gracie wasn't there, his manager would be able to let them know where he was.

The maintenance sheds were in a small clearing in the towering pine trees. They were low buildings clad in panelling which matched the bark of the surrounding pines. A small forklift was parked to one side of the sheds and there was a long greenhouse like those found at plant nurseries beyond them. As they rounded the sheds, they saw a man loading a four-wheeled barrow with pointed posts and some timber rails. A large hammer lay on the barrow and there was the smell of fresh-cut timber in the air.

The man stopped what he was doing and looked their way. His eyes danced past O'Dowd and settled on Beth. The examination he gave her made her skin crawl as he ran his eyes over her body.

Every instinct and piece of intuition she possessed told her that the man giving her a lecherous look was Tom Gracie. He was mid-fifties, thin and had shoulder-length grey hair that looked as if he'd dipped it in chip fat.

O'Dowd strode forward. 'Are you Tom Gracie?'

'Yeah. What of it?'

As soon as the DI flapped her warrant card open and introduced herself, Gracie's whole manner changed. Instead of looking at them with affability, he took on a look of panic.

The barrow was shoved at them as Gracie wheeled away and sprinted towards the door at the back of the maintenance shed.

While O'Dowd grabbed the barrow before it crashed into her, Beth was off and running; she skirted a pile of timber and navigated her way past a row of lawnmowers and strimmers. When she got to the door at the back of the maintenance shed, she saw Gracie disappear into the greenhouse. Beth surmised he knew of another door out of it and plunged after him.

CHAPTER FORTY-THREE

The computer on Forster's desk was logged into Facebook, and while he didn't use the social-media site much himself, he knew of its power. He had a second window open and that showed his Twitter account. He'd been alerted to the fact Beth's rant at the press conference had gone viral by the member of staff who managed his social-media profile. Since he'd found out, he'd checked the stats every hour and was pleased to see they were still rising at a consistent rate.

It had been a no-brainer for him to use the clip for his own agenda and he'd written a short message praising Beth and calling for more police officers to share her zeal. He couldn't wait to see her deliver the speech she'd handed to him last night. In terms of impact, it would make this already viral clip seem like a bland after-dinner speech delivered by an adenoidal trainspotter.

For perhaps the tenth time since she'd handed it to him, he read the statement again. He didn't need to look at the paper as he'd memorised every word, but he found that when he looked at the page, he could picture her delivering the words to camera.

The statement was handwritten in a neat cursive script that was easy to read.

My name is Beth Young. I'm a detective constable and I would like you to listen to what I have to say.

As I'm involved in (insert name of charity) you're no doubt thinking that I have been raped. That I have suffered the soul-stealing indignity that so many women, and yes, some men, have endured. I haven't; I'm one of the lucky ones, and yes, not only do I know how lucky I am, I give thanks for that good fortune on a daily basis.

You have probably noticed the scar on my face by now though. My story is this: I was in a bar four years ago when two guys started to throw punches at one another. One of them picked up a bottle. The man he thrust it at deflected the bottle and it smashed into my cheek.

I had five different operations and skin grafts to repair the damage that bottle did to my face.

The men who were fighting were never identified or punished for what they did to me. I was in the wrong place at the wrong time. That doesn't matter, I got no justice.

Until I could join the police, I was a model. My looks were taken from me. I got no justice.

I had the love and support of my family. That helped more than I'll ever be able to tell them.

I had offers of counselling. I said no. Looking back, I know that it might have been better for me if I'd said yes.

That's why I'm urging you to contact one of (insert name of charity)'s advisors. They are here to help. They'll give you emotional support and legal advice. Please, I implore you, don't feel that you're alone, don't think there's no one to help you. That's what (insert name of charity) is here for. To help you.

Contact (insert name of charity) and talk to one of our advisors.

You will receive confidential counselling.

You'll be advised on how best to proceed if you want to report your attack and get justice.

We will help you find a lawyer who's experienced in dealing with sexual assault cases.

We will support you emotionally.
We will be there for you.

I'm not going to lie to you, it will be tough. But we're here to make it easier for you.

I didn't get justice, but you can. Contact (insert name of charity and phone number, website etc) and you can get the counselling I refused, and the justice I was denied.

The person who sexually assaulted you chose to do it. Now it's your choice as to whether or not they face justice. Take the power back, let your rapist rot in prison while you embark on an exciting new chapter of your life.

As soon as he'd read Beth's statement, Forster had recognised its power, how it laid Beth wide open. Now that her rant had gone viral, he had to harness her popularity and cash in on the goodwill that was flowing her way as soon as possible.

He lifted the phone and called a friend who ran a small charity for the homeless. To fully maximise the 'Beth effect', as he thought of it, he'd have to move quickly before the world became fixated on something else.

CHAPTER FORTY-FOUR

Beth dashed into the greenhouse after Gracie and was hit by a wave of sweltering heat. It was filled with the heady aroma of peat and the chemical smell of a less-natural fertiliser. Gracie was twenty yards ahead of her and pulling plants off the timber benches that filled the greenhouse as he tried to escape. Beth couldn't reach anything like her top speed as she had to hurdle the plants as she went.

Her work shoes were sensible flats, but they had smooth soles which didn't offer a fraction of the grip the trainers she wore for her morning runs did. Try as she might to increase her pace, she could feel her feet slipping a little whenever she had to make the slightest turn, or when she planted a foot to leap over one of the obstacles Gracie was scattering in her path.

She exited the greenhouse and saw Gracie ahead of her. He was heading for the treeline and his back was straight as his arms pumped at his sides. On this gravel area Beth could get more traction and by the time she got to the treeline she'd gained five yards on Gracie. Rather than waste her breath shouting after him, Beth concentrated on getting her breathing right as she lengthened her stride.

Beth's morning runs were about building stamina and staying fit. Her competitive nature had her trying to improve her times for the various routes she ran, but she was a distance runner rather than a sprinter. If she was to catch Gracie, then she'd have to get him soon before she blew herself out.

She ducked under low branches as she wound her way between the trees. The soft carpeting of pine needles felt greasy beneath her feet, but she powered on.

The gap between them was less than ten yards when Beth's foot slipped on a tree root. She didn't fall, but it took her several paces to recover from the stumble.

Gracie wasn't looking back at her; his entire focus was on getting away. Beth watched as he emerged from the trees and crossed one of the pathways. A family cycling along the path stopped to watch the man who'd dashed in front of them; their presence creating a ten-foot-wide barrier of bicycles and Lycra.

Beth cut behind them lest they set off to continue their journey. Her breaths might have been coming in pained gasps, but she could feel her stubbornness kicking in and knew that there was no way she could let Gracie escape. She pumped her legs and arms in a steady rhythm as she chased after him. Every time he altered course to skirt an obstacle she was able to gain a few inches on him by taking a straighter line.

He burst out of the treeline into an area where there were picnic tables. At this hour the tables were empty, but beyond the picnic tables, children were playing in a woodland adventure fort, while their parents sat on benches and watched over them.

Gracie rounded a picnic table and went to dash past the woodland fort. Beth was only two yards behind him now and closing.

Ahead of them was a cycle shack where the visiting families could hire bikes to carry them around the holiday park. Beth knew that if Gracie got on a cycle he'd get away. She was almost close enough to grab the back of his overalls when he glanced over his shoulder.

Beth saw the surprise in his eyes that she was so close. He put on an extra burst of speed which opened the gap.

As much as her lungs were burning from the sprint, Beth matched his burst and once again closed in. A slope led down to where rows of bikes were arranged ready for hire, and with Gracie almost in reach of them, Beth threw herself down the gradient after him.

Her legs couldn't keep up with her upper body's momentum so Beth allowed herself to topple forward. She wrapped her arms around Gracie's waist and let the weight of her body slow his pace.

As he slowed, she let her grip loosen and slid down his body until her arms were at his knees. She tensed her muscles and squeezed his legs into her body. As rugby tackles go, it wasn't the greatest ever performed, but it brought Gracie down, which was all that mattered.

He writhed and flailed at her as he squirmed round so he was facing her, his arms throwing punches towards her head as he kicked to be free. Her ear rang as he landed a blow on it and a punch split her eyebrow causing blood to trickle down her face. She hung tight until one of his blows hit her shoulder. She didn't know whether it pinched a nerve or landed on a pressure point, but a bolt of fire seemed to explode down her arm.

With her grip on him loosened a little, Gracie's writhing started to bear fruit and he was managing to wriggle free. She couldn't allow this to happen, so she reared over him and then slumped her body forward as her good arm bent back so she could retrieve the collapsible baton from her pocket.

Beth could feel the gasps of air from Gracie's mouth on her face, could smell his rank smoky breath and hear his curses. As she struggled to free the collapsible baton from her pocket, she felt his arms move between them. She butted her head forward and burst his nose, but Gracie didn't react to the blow. Between them she could feel his hands press against her body as he tried to lift her away so he could get free.

Beth was in the throes of flicking the baton so it would extend when one hand grabbed at her breast. Gracie didn't try and push her off, instead he dug his fingers into her and squeezed her flesh, twisting his hand as he fought her off.

'You like that, don't you, bitch?'

O'Dowd's voice roared across the morning air. 'Hoy, you flaming pervert.'

Beth reared back with Gracie's hand still clutching her breast. The collapsible baton in her hand swung towards his forearm. A dull crack and her breast was released. A second swing, harder this time, landed on the inside of his right elbow. He yelped and released his grip of her entirely.

With her left arm now working better, Beth fished out her handcuffs and slipped them over Gracie's wrists. She wasn't sure if she'd broken his arm with her first blow and she wasn't particularly bothered. So far as she was concerned, Gracie deserved everything he got.

O'Dowd arrived and bent over them, hands on knees as she fought to get her breath back and a sheen of sweat covering her forehead. When she spoke it was between huffed breaths.

'You must be one of the stupidest men I've ever met. I have just witnessed you physically and sexually assaulting a police officer while resisting arrest. I suggest that you be a good boy from now on, otherwise I'm going to give in to the temptation to revisit the days when police brutality was an everyday occurrence.'

O'Dowd turned her gaze to Beth. 'Read him his rights and make sure that you include every possible offence that you can think of, and if you can think of a way to do him for being a vile and smelly bastard who's such a perverted loser that the only way he can get physical contact with a woman is to molest his arresting officer, well, do him for that an' all.'

Beth did as she was told and named all the offences Gracie had committed along with the suspicion of four counts of rape and murder.

Her breast stung from where he'd grabbed it and as much as she wanted to pass his groping off as part of the job, she knew that she would have to report the assault in full. The thought of having the police doctor examine her, and if there was bruising, take pictures for evidence, chilled her, but not only was it part of the due process, there was no way her conscience would allow her to lie and say she was unhurt and didn't need any attention. She'd been sexually assaulted and while it wasn't anything like as bad as it could have been, she would be a fraud if she didn't report a sexual assault against her while planning to front a rape charity that urged victims to report their own experiences.

There was also the question of how she'd discuss this all with O'Dowd. The DI had been adamant that they didn't need Thompson and Unthank or some uniforms to help them arrest Gracie, yet because of O'Dowd's insistence on grabbing the glory, the suspect had nearly got away and the whole mess of the assault had happened.

It was poor decision-making at best and incompetence at worst. This case was too important to mess around and try to score points with the top brass.

CHAPTER FORTY-FIVE

O'Dowd went through the names of those present and the litany of charges against Gracie while the man in question sat mute. Beside him was a duty solicitor. Bob Lewis was an affable person but a poor solicitor. A capable man, he gave what advice he could and did no more. He was a realist, and if his client was playing silly beggars, he'd tell them as much and then do the bare minimum necessary to protect them.

If given the choice, every detective in the county would want him sitting beside their suspects as he rarely went out of his way to put up a strong defence. On the other hand, if he had a genuine belief that his client was innocent, or the victim of unfounded allegations, then he'd be tenacious and would argue every point, however minor.

'First let me say, that my client denies the sexual assault on DC Young. He was merely resisting arrest at the time. This he will plead guilty to.'

The bored tone in the solicitor's voice pleased Beth. It meant he wasn't interested in this case and therefore wouldn't put up too much of a fight.

'Of course he's pleading guilty to that, it'd be impossible for him to wriggle off that hook. For the record, DC Young has been examined by a police doctor and the injuries to her chest have been recorded. I've also given a written statement about what I witnessed. Mr Gracie will be in court for that assault one day soon. It's a dab on and you know it. As we're involved in that crime, we won't be the ones to investigate it; that'll be done by another team. Fortunately, we have experts in such matters.' O'Dowd licked her lips as she stared at Lewis. 'I know you're using today's events as a stalling tactic, that you're trying to deflect from the reason we had an arrest warrant for Gracie.'

'Really, Inspector, do you think I consider you so foolish as to fall for such an obvious tactic?'

Beth cut in before O'Dowd and Lewis could develop the bickering into a spat. 'It doesn't matter what we think your opinion of us is. Mr Gracie was in the vicinity of an abduction which resulted in a violent rape and murder. He gave a statement to the police investigating the original abduction.'

'There's nothing wrong with that. He was being a good citizen.'

'Indeed he was. His statement was that he didn't see anything. However, he did chat about birdwatching with the officer who took his statement.'

'So he shared a common interest with someone. I see no reason to accuse him of multiple rapes and murders.'

Beth wanted to massage the pain in her breast away but there was no way she was going to do so in front of Gracie. To prevent her subconscious from stepping in she laid her hands on the table.

'Mr Gracie may or may not remember the conversation, but the officer he spoke to recorded it.' Beth shifted her focus from Lewis to Gracie. 'You recommended some good birdwatching sites to him. I still have his notes. The bodies of Christine Peterson, Joanne Armstrong and Harriet Quantrell were dumped at Barrow beach, Buttermere and Rockcliffe Marsh respectively. During Sunday night, Felicia Evans's body was dumped at the side of Lake Ullswater. Every one of those locations was on the list of places you recommended.'

'So I happen to know Cumbria, that's not a crime. I have never killed or raped anyone. This is a coincidence and nothing more. Tell me, how many places were on that list?'

'Nine.' Beth didn't like the conviction in Gracie's voice. He didn't sound defensive or afraid, to her he had the tone of someone who believed their innocence would be proven.

'You mentioned four names. That's slightly more than one third of the places my client suggested to one of your colleagues. I'd hardly call that conclusive, would you?'

'Perhaps indicative would be a better word than conclusive.' Beth folded her right arm over her chest and pressed inwards as she scratched an imaginary itch on her neck. The action relieving a spike of pain in her chest. 'And your maths is off if you think four places out of nine is only slightly more than a third, because I make it almost a half.'

'These places that were mentioned. Were they out of the way locations or had you heard of them yourself?'

Beth didn't like the way that Lewis was perking up. He was paying more interest to the case and it was only a matter of time before he'd be giving his best efforts to protect Gracie. His question was a good one that needed to be answered with care.

'I'd heard of most of them, although if I'm honest with you, I've only been to about half the locations mentioned.'

'I see. Had you heard of the deposition sites before investigating this case?'

This question was even tougher to answer than the previous one. The lawyer would be proud of this question, because if Beth said no, it would make it seem as if she didn't know the area she was paid to police, whereas if she said yes, Lewis would undoubtedly pounce and claim the deposition sites were well known to locals and that they would have to produce evidence tying Gracie to the crimes or release him.

'Mr Lewis, I think you're rather forgetting how this works.' O'Dowd's voice was soft, but there was no mistaking the steel in her tone. 'We ask the questions, not you.'

'Then ask a question, but you better have evidence to back up your claims because this is seeming more and more like a fishing trip than a proper interview.'

O'Dowd was right back, asking Gracie to account for his whereabouts on the dates the first three women were abducted.

Gracie's tone was apologetic with a hint of condescension. 'I'm sorry, but I can't remember where I was on any of those dates. They were years ago.'

'Fair enough. What about Sunday night? Can you remember where you were then?'

'I was at home. Watched a bit of telly and then went to bed.' A cocky grin. 'Wanted to get a good night's kip ready for work.'

'Okay. Was there anyone with you to verify what you're telling us?'

'Nah. Just me.'

'Perhaps you can tell us about the time you were beaten up. If my memory serves me right, the man who beat you up alleged that you were stalking his wife.' Beth was trying to get the interview back on track, but the way it was going suggested that Lewis was digging in on Gracie's side. 'We also have to consider the occasions you were arrested for spying on ladies as they undressed and the warnings you received.'

'I fail to see what relevance that bears to this investigation. Any previous offences my client may have committed should not be considered as they were dealt with at the times in question.'

Beth gave the solicitor a tight smile. 'Nice try, Mr Lewis. We're investigating four instances of a sexual crime that escalated to murder. Your client has a history of voyeurism. That's one red flag. Your client was accused of stalking. That's another red flag. The way he assaulted me when I arrested him is another red flag. Mr Gracie has shown a progression in his deviations, and because of this, any first-year psychology student would be worried about what he may do next. As a police officer, it's my job to know about such things and, quite frankly, your client fits the profile of the person we're looking for. Yes, he may pretend to use his binoculars to watch wagtails and terns, but I reckon it's a different kind of bird altogether that he prefers to watch.'

'You're mistaken, but I can understand your thinking. I haven't murdered anyone and I have never raped anyone. I'm innocent of those crimes and, as such, you're wasting your time accusing me of them. I hope that you catch the person who's really behind the rapes and murders, before he strikes again.'

O'Dowd leaned across the table and glared at Gracie. 'Maybe we've already got him. Maybe I'm looking at him now.'

When O'Dowd reached for the switches that controlled the recording equipment, Beth stopped her before she could suspend the interview.

'There's something that's puzzling me, Mr Gracie. Why did you run when you found out who we were? For all you knew, we could have been there to inform you of a family member's death. Yet you ran away before you knew what we wanted to speak to you about. That speaks of guilt to me and now I'm wondering what you've done that made you run away. Would you care to tell us?'

'No comment.'

CHAPTER FORTY-SIX

The terraced cottage where Gracie lived was even worse than Beth had anticipated it would be. Every room stunk of cigarette smoke and had a yellowed ceiling. While not massively untidy, there was a thick layer of dust on all of the unused surfaces and the kitchen sink was loaded with unwashed dishes. There were no books on the lounge's bookshelf and most of the DVDs she found were X-rated. Unthank had braved the bathroom and bedroom, but had lasted only a few seconds in each before he ran through the cottage opening all the windows.

'See anything, Paul?'

'He's got an industrial-quantity of wank mags by his bed, and when I leafed through one or two, I found that they were all proper hardcore images.'

'Dirty old perv.'

'You don't know the half of it, Beth. There were a lot of images of anal sex.'

Beth couldn't help but give a fist pump. The content of the magazines may well be nothing more than circumstantial, but it was still damning enough to help them build their case.

'What do you call a man with a slow cooker?'

Beth knew the answer right away. 'Stu.'

Unthank returned her smile. 'What have you found?'

'His basic household paperwork.' Beth lifted a paper folder from a drawer. 'His insurance documents, driving licence and bank statements.' She flicked through a few more envelopes. 'Oh, and his passport.'

'Have you looked at this?' Unthank pointed to a laptop that was on the coffee table.

'Not yet. It'll probably be password protected. I was gonna bag it and let Digital Forensics have it.'

'I think I'll take a look first. Maybe let some of the smell out of the bedroom before I give it a proper search.'

'Suit yourself.'

Beth left Unthank to deal with the laptop while she worked her way through Gracie's paperwork. It was all standard and seemed to be in order. The fact Gracie drove a van piqued her interests as well as her suspicions. She'd thought all along that the Lakeland Ripper may well use a van to transport his victims around unseen and here was their prime suspect, a van owner.

It seemed too good to be true. It was as she was leafing through Gracie's passport, that she found out it was.

'Get in. Got you, you sick fucking bastard.'

Unthank wasn't one to swear and the vehemence in the way he'd hissed the profanities told Beth that he'd unearthed something of significance.

'What have you found?'

'Rape porn. The sick bastard has viewed hundreds of videos. I looked at a couple and some of the women don't look anything like they're eighteen. The cocky sod never even passworded his computer or bothered to delete his browsing history. It goes back a couple of years. We've got him, Beth, we can nail his arse to the wall with what's on here. We've got the killer.'

'No, we haven't.'

'What? What do you mean, we haven't got him?'

Beth held up Gracie's passport and gave Unthank a look at the page she'd bookmarked with her finger.

'Fuck.'

'Agreed.'

Tom Gracie may have been guilty of lots of sex offences, but he wasn't the Lakeland Ripper. His passport showed him as having been in Thailand during the time when Joanne Armstrong had been abducted and then found dead in the woods near Buttermere.

That he'd chosen Thailand as a holiday destination spoke volumes to Beth. While many travelled there for a beach holiday or to see the sites, it was also well known that cities such as Pattaya and Bangkok were hotbeds of sexual activity and that sad, desperate men like Gracie often flocked to them. For a couple of weeks maybe he'd felt like a prince as one Thai hooker after another tried to entice him to their beds.

It was distasteful to think that Gracie was likely a sex tourist, but regardless, the real sickener was that they were back to square one on the murder case. What O'Dowd would make of it was anyone's guess.

'Here.' Unthank handed her a large evidence bag containing the laptop. 'You head back with this; I'll stay and oversee a proper search by a search team. You can get the ball rolling.'

As she put the evidence bag onto the passenger seat of her car, Beth couldn't work out whether Unthank was doing her a favour by letting her escape the foul cottage or if he was making sure he wasn't the one who had to deliver the bad news to O'Dowd.

CHAPTER FORTY-SEVEN

When Beth returned to the office O'Dowd was sitting at her desk going through reports and Thompson was nowhere to be seen.

'How'd you get on?'

Beth relayed what she and Unthank had found and waited for the inevitable explosion at the way their best, and only, suspect had been proven as being out of the country when one of the crimes they'd accused him of was committed.

The explosion didn't come. O'Dowd's only reaction was a hissed exhalation that lasted a full ten seconds.

'Buggeration and other such words. It was a good idea and all that, but it didn't pan out. What you found on his laptop will still put him away, and explains why he did a runner, so all in all, it's a decent job, well done.' O'Dowd looked at Beth. 'Take the laptop to Digital Forensics, write up your report and pass the whole lot over to DI Yates; he and his team will take it from here.'

Beth nodded at O'Dowd. She wanted nothing more to do with Gracie after what he'd done to her, and as his victim, there was no way that she could work on his case. Interviewing him with O'Dowd had been a big enough risk without her presence further tainting the case against him.

'It's not just you that's off the Gracie case: I'll be getting the whole team off it. So far as we're concerned, it's solved. Yes all the legwork is still to do, but if what you've told me is true, and I have no reason to doubt you, you've got more than enough to secure a conviction.' O'Dowd wiped a hand across her face. 'All that's left to do is collate the evidence, let Yates and his team deal with that. They can spend their days looking at the filth on his laptop. I want you where you should be, in FMIT. That brain of yours is too good to waste on a job that any idiot can do.

'Plus, I don't want you getting fucked up by having to deal with looking at rape or kiddie porn for days on end. I have a killer to catch, and don't want to lose you to a different investigation. Doubly so if your involvement in that investigation may compromise the trial. I'm sorry, Beth, I know what you're like and that you'll want to follow it through, but right now, the murder case is our priority.'

'Ma'am.' As disappointed as she was with O'Dowd's decision, Beth was also pleased that she'd not have to deal with Gracie again. 'What do you want me to do now?'

'Go over what's known until you can come up with another idea. That's all I can think of unless you have any suggestions.'

'There has been one thing that's been on my mind. The spacing of the kills is pretty much eighteen months, yet it was twenty-two months between Harriet and Felicia. Normally you'd expect the dates between incidents to get shorter instead of longer as the killer escalated, yet the Lakeland Ripper ended up overdue. His lusts and desires will have been at breaking point.'

O'Dowd laid her pen on the desk. 'What are you getting at?'

'Maybe we should be watching the misper reports. When a woman is reported missing we should start looking into their disappearance as soon as it's reported rather than waiting the usual twenty-four hours. He didn't penetrate Felicia himself and there's no way of knowing whether doing what he did to her satisfied his desires.'

'Do it, but keep me in the loop; I don't want you out looking for every Cinderella who doesn't get home by midnight.'

As Beth reached for the phone to contact Control she avoided O'Dowd's eyes. Her request for the misper reports to be monitored had another reason she wasn't yet ready to share with the DI. She'd spied a couple of anomalies in her spreadsheet, and the thoughts they were prompting were too horrifying to voice until she could back up her suspicions with hard evidence.

CHAPTER FORTY-EIGHT

The streets of Maryport were quiet as Willow made her way towards the river. Rather than have Spike miss his usual walk because of her having a night out, she'd elected to take him along the riverbank beforehand. Tonight's walk wouldn't be a long one, though, she intended to only go half the usual distance, and instead of her normal saunter, she was walking at pace to make sure the walk was completed in the least time possible.

The riverbank was alive with insects and Willow had to slap at a few as she went. It would be typical for her to get a bite on her face or arms tonight of all nights.

She was looking forward to meeting up with her old friends, but most of all she was looking forward to getting herself glammed up for a night out. It had been a long time since she'd felt the need to make the kind of effort that would get her noticed.

When she let Spike off his lead he immediately disappeared into a clump of nettles that edged their way right down to the water. A second later she heard splashing and knew he'd found his way into the river.

She called him back, knowing he wouldn't come at once.

Willow crossed her fingers that he wouldn't do another of his disappearing acts. She didn't have the time for him to play his games tonight.

*

The man in the woods put the binoculars to his eyes. The woman he was watching as she walked her dog was gorgeous. Not like those others. They hadn't been to his taste at all.

He planned to keep Willow as long as possible. Use her until he was spent and tired of her. Only then would he crush her throat and dump her somewhere far away.

CHAPTER FORTY-NINE

14 June

Dear Diary

Now that Derek has become mayor, things are even busier.

But today has been the best day since the election results came in.

Remember how I told you I would have to attend a function with the mayor as a kind of +1 / PA? I confess that when we got back to Carlisle, I kissed him.

He kissed me back. Tender at first and then with a ferocity that told me of his desire. Despite the many reasons why I shouldn't, I damn near shagged him there and then. Why oh why do I fancy him so much? Is it because I know it can never happen?

I should know better, I do know better.

All the same, I want to, even knowing all the hurt it will cause.

What's wrong with me, Dear Diary? Maybe since Harriet died (and they still haven't caught her killer, you know), I just know how short life is. But maybe that's just my excuse.

Until tomorrow.

CHAPTER FIFTY

Beth couldn't help but feel that the spreadsheet she'd constructed was mocking her. All of its rows and columns were silent, apart from her secret theory that still felt too horrific to contemplate. None of them spoke to her in a way that offered clarity. It was as if the document was a suspect who refused to comment on anything.

What had started out as a good day had taken several bad turns. The business with Gracie's case being handed over to DI Yates's team was a godsend in a lot of ways, but she still felt it was a job half done.

She still ached from where Gracie had manhandled her. His grip had been so strong he'd left bruises on her skin and had bent the underwires of her bra. She'd tried to straighten the wire back, but judging by the way it dug into her flesh, she'd not got it right and would have to throw away the bra.

The examination by the police doctor had been perfunctory, and while she'd been glad it had been a female doctor, she hadn't liked the fact photographic evidence was taken. If the case progressed to court, which she knew was the likely scenario, both defence and prosecution lawyers would see those pictures. She'd done her best to cover her nipples with either the wooden ruler the doctor used to give the photographs scale, or her fingers, but she knew she hadn't been successful every time.

The best that she could hope for was that Gracie would plead guilty to assaulting her, thereby saving his energies to fight the more serious case involving the images of minors. That way nobody would have to see the picture the doctor had taken of her injuries. Yes, the pictures were cold, hard evidence and as such would have no titillation value, but she still didn't like the idea of lawyers from both sides looking at pictures of her breasts.

Even now, a few hours after the event, she could still feel the grip of Gracie's hand and see the lust in his face as he'd groped her. Now that she'd seen the dirt in his cottage and had learned where his tastes lay, she was even more repulsed by the idea of him having touched her at all. As great as her desire for a long, hot shower might be, there was too much work to be done with the case for her to think about her own needs.

She eased herself out of her chair and went to the door of the FMIT office. It wasn't that she wanted to be anywhere else, or had somewhere other than home to go to, more that she needed to remove her eyes from the spreadsheet. Twice she paced the length of the short corridor before she returned to her seat.

Time and time again, she looked at her spreadsheet without finding anything else that would back up her theory. With the spreadsheet refusing to give her the answers she needed, Beth turned to the reports on her desk. They too yielded nothing so she checked her emails. So far there had been no reports of anyone going missing, although she didn't think enough time had passed for anyone to have gone missing since they requested for new misper reports to be monitored.

It was a long shot to hope that they could work from a missing-person report, and O'Dowd's point about them not getting involved in every misper case made logical sense, but she still had enough doubts to compel her to take on the extra workload.

What made Beth's frustration grow more than anything else, was the way that the Lakeland Ripper seemed to have covered his tracks so well. That fact coupled with the failure of senior officers to connect the first three murders meant their investigations were well and truly hampered.

As she wasn't making any progress staring at the reports, she decided to go out and visit Harriet Quantrell's deposition site. It was a forlorn hope to think that she'd spot something that nobody else had but she was at a loss as to what else she should do.

CHAPTER FIFTY-ONE

Beth followed the country lanes until they got her as close as they could to the place where Harriet Quantrell's body had been found.

At the end of a lane, a derelict cottage stood by a small yard with an open-sided farm shed. Two gates led from the compound into the neighbouring fields. Neither of the fields were too big and the boundary fence of one was pinned flat in places by huge logs which must have been deposited by a high tide. It was a desolate, isolated area that was filled with silence and the smell of grass scorched by a sun that had blazed for days.

In the near distance Beth could see the mudflats of the twin estuaries formed by the River Eden to her left and the Esk to her right as they converged to form the Solway Firth. Across the mudflats she could see the roofs of Gretna's houses. When she cast her eyes along the Solway Firth, she could see the northern fells shimmering in the evening air. On the Scottish side, Criffel was wreathed in a heat haze that gave it an ethereal quality.

A bird chirruped as it passed over her, but she paid it no heed as she passed through a gate and set off towards the Rockcliffe Marshes. Beneath her feet the grass was tight and coarse; Solway turf was well known for its durability. Strong as it was, it still cushioned each footstep before springing back to its original shape.

Beth remembered the weather report which accompanied Harriet's file, it had told of a four-week dry spell prior to her murder. The current good weather had lasted for three weeks, so it was fair to say that the conditions were much the same.

Beth tried to dig her heel into an area where the grass was short. Her foot didn't mark the ground, which gave credence to the theory put forward by the investigating officers that the killer had driven a vehicle part of the way here when dumping Harriet's body.

She passed over the stricken fence and walked for five minutes until she was at the point where someone had left a rudimentary cross. It had been buffeted from the vertical by the Solway's ferocious high tides. Across its transom someone had carved Harriet's name along with the date of her death. It was a simple memorial, made by loving hands, and as she looked at it, Beth could see mental images of both Harriet and her daughter.

Twice she made a slow rotation, taking in all she could see, both the near and the far. As isolated as this place may be, with its clumps of grassland interspersed by narrow rivulets that had been riven open by raging tides, it still retained an element of peacefulness. Here and there a small pond would stand, their waters low in the absence of high tides and rainfall.

Beth remembered childhood Sundays on the similar Burgh Marsh, her mother fussing with a picnic and her father watching over her as she tried to catch tadpoles with a colourful net on the end of a bamboo cane.

It had been idyllic then, but now she was standing here, Beth's thoughts were on another little girl. If her father ever brought her here, would she want to explore the ditches and ponds the way Beth had? Or would she join her father in mourning the mother she never knew?

With nothing more learned than that the assumptions of the original investigators were likely to be right, Beth ran her fingers along the top of the cross and turned to go back to her car.

As she trudged across the tough grass, she was hoping that something on the case would break and give them a decent lead, or at least a suspect they could focus their attentions on.

CHAPTER FIFTY-TWO

The night on the town was turning out to be everything Willow had dared to hope it would be and more. The way she'd picked up with her old friends made her feel as if she stepped into a time warp and transported herself back ten years.

They'd started off by having dinner in the Lifeboat Inn, before progressing to the busier bars. There had been laughter, gossip and enough Prosecco to wash away all the years since she'd last done this.

Compared to the other girls – Willow knew they were too old to be classed as girls any more, but that's how she thought of them – she was overdressed, but she didn't care. Tonight was all about having fun. She wasn't looking for any serious male attention, as the last thing she wanted in her life right now was another man, but she did want to feel noticed, desired.

Since the day she'd caught her husband in bed with another man, she'd felt unattractive. On an intellectual level she knew that his desires lay in a different direction, and the fact he'd chosen a man rather than a woman to cheat on her exonerated her from feeling any level of blame for his indiscretion. However, the fact he'd cheated at all had dented her confidence more than she'd realised. What had made the pill so bitter to swallow was that she'd made love to him the day before she caught him in bed with their neighbour.

For too long she'd felt worthless, undesirable; and now tonight, when she was out with the girls, she knew she was drawing admiring glances. The dress was shorter than any she'd worn in the last five years and it clung to her backside and body in a way that showed off her trim figure. So far she'd caught three men ogling her and had had one guy wander over to chance his arm.

In the normal course of events, she'd have felt seedy at being ogled, and would have sent the guy who'd tried to chat her up back to his mates with a stinging put-down. Tonight was different though; tonight was about her having fun and rebirthing herself. Whether she liked it or not, she was single now, and while she planned to stay that way for some considerable time, she knew the first steps back on the road to happiness involved redeveloping her sense of worth. It didn't matter how many men fancied her, or chanced their arm with her tonight, one already had and that was enough for Willow. If more guys showed their interest, so be it, she'd already had more attention than she'd expected to get, so any more that came her way would be a bonus.

CHAPTER FIFTY-THREE

Beth lay back on her sofa and stared at the ceiling. Her mind was awash with thoughts about her day. She'd looked at the evidence and her spreadsheet until all the details were burned into her brain. Nothing had come of it.

With all the evidence they had, there had to be a clue of some kind that had been overlooked, but no matter which way she examined the known facts, she couldn't identify that one detail she knew would break the case wide open.

After such a good end to yesterday, she should have known that today wouldn't go so well. The summons to Hilton's office had been the first sign, but she'd thought it would be the only negative as she'd been swept up in the thought of Gracie being the Lakeland Ripper. Not only had their suspect almost escaped, she'd had his hands pawing at her to contend with.

In terms of being molested it could have been a lot worse: the way he'd gripped and twisted her chest spoke of anger rather than lust. It was his words that disgusted her more than anything. There had been malevolence in his tone as he'd snarled at her. She knew that the question, 'you like that, don't you, bitch?' would stay in her mind long after the bruises on her chest faded.

Ethan had called, and while it had been good to hear his voice, he'd also had a rough day at work, so they hadn't chatted long. She'd told him about having to chase down Gracie and the subsequent struggle, but had omitted the molestation from her story. She didn't know Ethan well enough to predict how he'd react to such news and she didn't want to give him reasons to worry about her.

Her left arm still twinged when she moved it in certain ways, but it was bearable. The pain in her ear had dissipated after an hour or so, and the police doctor had glued her split eyebrow closed.

There was also the business with Forster to resolve, not just the charity but the fact he'd wronged the Lakeland Ripper enough for the killer to try and frame him.

Beth remembered Forster's ex-colleague Claire and her coded message. The computer programmer had referred to herself as someone who was 'paid to do a job', and she'd described Beth as a 'pretty young thing' and a 'potential conquest'. Beth's current train of thought solved the riddle with ease. Claire had made it known how she felt about Forster; but had her advances been rebuffed, or worse, had he slept with her once and then returned her to the status of employee?

Claire had also intimated to Beth that Forster would make a move on her as the mayor would see Beth as a challenge. When she thought back to Forster's behaviour over dinner, Beth knew he'd held back the flirting, but instead given her a full enough blast of his charm and charisma for her to change her opinion of him.

If nothing progressed with the case by noon tomorrow, she'd speak to Claire again, pull at that thread until it unravelled a little. Perhaps speaking to the woman at her home on a Saturday would be better; she might talk more freely away from work.

Beth levered herself off the couch and made her way upstairs. Perhaps tomorrow would be an improvement on today. It couldn't be much worse. Maybe that's the way things would be: one good day, one bad one.

CHAPTER FIFTY-FOUR

Willow cackled with laughter as she dumped the polystyrene tray into a bin. She'd forgotten how good chips with cheese and gravy tasted after a night on the town. With a cheery wave to her friends, and promises to repeat the night soon, she turned and looked for a taxi to take her home.

There was only one in sight and it was loading up people, but she spoke to the driver and he promised to come back for her in ten minutes. Waiting wasn't a problem: the night air was warm and there was that once-familiar teenage feeling that as long as she didn't go home, the party was still happening.

A guy was walking along the street with an open pizza box. He shut the lid and licked his fingers as he tossed the pizza box into the same bin Willow had used. Willow recognised him. He'd chatted her up about an hour ago; he'd even bought her a couple of shooters, something she hadn't had in years. He was nice with a friendly face and decent manners. Not handsome in the traditional sense, but nor was he ugly. He was well fit though; his shirt was tailored to be snug against his body and she could image the six-pack beneath it.

She gave him a little wave; he'd maybe keep her company until the taxi returned. 'Hello again.'

'Hi there, gorgeous.'

'Give over.' Willow gave a playful swipe with her hand. 'You're drunk if you think I'm gorgeous.'

'Assh not dwunk.' It was a mock slur that widened Willow's smile. 'Seriously, I'm not drunk, you are gorgeous; in fact, I'd go so far as to say you're the best-looking woman I've seen all night.'

'We're in Maryport, that means you've probably only seen a couple of dozen women.'

'It would apply if we were in Carlisle, or even London.'

'You're such a charmer.'

The guy looked into her eyes. 'I do my best when I meet someone as gorgeous as you—'

Willow silenced him with a kiss that was returned with lust.

Her hands found the small of his back and pulled him forward. His body was as hard as she'd imagined it would be.

She knew it was against her principles to behave this way: she'd never had a one-night stand and had never envisaged herself having one, but ever since she'd caught her husband in the wrong bed, she'd fantasised about rebound sex.

There was a narrow alleyway a few doors along the street. She knew it led towards a path that ran along the riverbank.

Willow took the guy by the hand. 'C'mon. This way.'

They got to the riverbank and sat on a bench, Willow astride the guy so they could keep their mouths pressed together. For Willow it was the perfect rebound scenario, fast, anonymous sex with a stranger. Her estranged husband would never know, but she would and that's all that mattered to her.

The guy's hands caressed her backside as her fingers grappled with the buttons of his shirt, but he was too rough for her liking. While tonight was about sating animal needs, rather than tender or gentle sex, she didn't want to feel any pain. She moved a hand behind her back and squeezed the guy's hand so his fingers couldn't grip her backside as tight as they were.

Willow broke their kiss. 'Not so rough.'

'Whatever you say.'

When he pulled her dress down enough that he could put her breast to his mouth, Willow felt the first tinge of uncertainty.

'Please. Not that hard.'

'You want it, you teasing cow. Don't think you're changing your mind now.'

'I am changing my mind. Please, stop.'

'You can't do this to me.' The guy used the arm he had behind her back to pull her forward to his waiting mouth.

'I think you'll find the lady asked you to stop.'

Willow jumped at the voice. She hadn't noticed anyone coming along the path as she was so wrapped in the moment. As she climbed off the guy, she was covering herself with one arm while trying to pull her dress up with the other.

Even as Willow grappled with her dress, she looked to see who her saviour was. His face was in half shadow, but she could see enough to recognise the man was one of her clients. A man she'd met while doling out financial advice.

Willow watched as her supposed beau squared up to the client.

'She's with me. Now, fuck off, or else I'll be forced to fuck you off myself.'

The client's arm flashed out and Willow's erstwhile attacker went down in a heap.

'Come on, Willow, isn't it? I'll take you home.' The client offered her his arm. 'If you turn around, I can do your zip up for you.'

'Thank you, thank you so much.' Willow turned around so the client could see what he was doing.

Of all the people she'd thought might appear to rescue her from the supposed beau, Andrew Cooper was pretty much at the bottom of the list. But as much as she might dislike the man, she was grateful he was riding to her rescue. The way he was averting his gaze from her semi-exposed body compelled her to trust him. He might be a flirt, but right now, he was behaving with nothing but decency, and had just saved her from potentially being raped.

'The zip's bust. Here, have my coat.'

As she walked to where Cooper had parked his car, Willow never questioned why he was miles away from home, walking along the riverbank so late at night, or why he was wearing a long coat when it was so warm.

CHAPTER FIFTY-FIVE

Thompson was the only person in the office. He looked to Beth as if he'd had maybe two hours sleep in the last week. His wife's deterioration was exacting a terrible price from him and, as much as she felt for the man, it was only a matter of time before his exhaustion caused him to make a serious mistake.

'Where's O'Dowd and Unthank?'

Thompson lifted his hand from the pile of paperwork he was sorting through. 'She's upstairs speaking to the DCI, and he's gone to the loo.'

'Has anything broke with the case?'

'Nothing. You'll have to wait for O'Dowd.' Thompson huffed out a long sigh. 'Paul's due in court on Monday. The Felcham case. His testimony is key and it's come down from on high that he's to spend the weekend swotting up all of his notes so the prosecutor can't trip him up.' Thompson flicked his eyes at Beth and then turned them to the far wall. 'I have to go to the care home. My Julie has caught pneumonia, the doctor says she can't fight it and that she's only got a few days left.'

Beth felt as though she'd been gut-punched by Thompson's words. As disturbing as she found the news, it was utterly heart-wrenching to hear the pain in Thompson's voice.

The sergeant had his back to her which Beth was grateful for. She didn't know what to do or say. No words or gestures could make things better for him, but that didn't mean she wasn't going to offer him her support.

She took three steps across the office, laid a hand on his shoulder and gave a gentle squeeze. 'I'm so sorry, Frank. Get yourself off home. We'll cope here.'

'I know you will.' Thompson's attempt to sniff developed into a snivel. 'O'Dowd tried to chase me home as well. I know I should be with my girls, or at the care home.' Thompson's head dropped forward. 'When I'm there it's real. When I'm here…' He paused to give a muffled sob. 'Here, I can kid myself it isn't.'

Beth gave Thompson's shoulder another squeeze. 'It is real though, isn't it?'

'I know. It's real, and I have to face up to it. Have to go and say goodbye to Julie. Have to be strong and look after my daughters.'

'That's not what I said.'

'Not in so many words.' Thompson turned, gave her a wan smile and a nod. His eyes filled with unshed tears and immeasurable pain. 'You may have only intimated it, but you're right.' Thompson stood and made for the door. 'Tell O'Dowd I've gone and that I'll… I'll—'

'I'll tell her.' Beth felt she had to interrupt him. To prevent him from having to say he'd let O'Dowd know when his wife passed.

Thompson left the office in the slow shuffle of someone who knew that what they were about to face might well break them.

Beth sat at her desk to give him a chance to leave on his own terms. Her thoughts conflicted between the impossibility of the case and the terrible situation Thompson had to deal with.

As there was nothing she could do for Thompson, Beth forced herself to concentrate on the case.

The biggest issue they had was the way the team had been halved. As important as it may be to have the case Unthank was testifying about fresh in his mind, it was also vital they continue trying to catch the Lakeland Ripper and the person framing the mayor.

If Unthank and Thompson were replaced, their replacements, however good they may be, would take at least half a day to catch up on the details of this case and that was time they didn't have to lose.

It was typical of the brass that they'd insist on the maximum effort to solve a case and then hamstring the investigating team. Beth knew she was being cynical, but it wouldn't surprise her if they didn't get replacements for Unthank and Thompson until Monday at the soonest. Every team in the county was stretched by the double whammies of their workload and the budgetary cuts imposed on them. When you factored in leave and stress-related sickness, it was nothing short of a miracle that so many crimes actually ended up with convictions.

Unthank walked into the office. 'What do you call a man in a pile of leaves?'

'Russell.' Beth had the answer in a flash. If Unthank was going to catch her out, he'd have to become a lot more obscure.

Before O'Dowd returned from speaking to the DCI, Beth checked her emails in case anything had come in. There were a couple of missing persons' reports that piqued her interest.

The first was a fourteen-year-old girl who'd had a row with her parents about a party she'd wanted to go to, and had stormed out of the house last night when her parents had refused to let her attend. Beth figured the girl would have gone to the party and was now avoiding her parents so she didn't have to deal with the fallout. She'd either turn up at a friend's house or would go home with her tail between her legs.

The second was more concerning. Willow Brown had been on a night out in Maryport and hadn't come home. There wasn't anything unusual in that for a women in her late twenties. She was a grown-up and could do as she wanted. Her parents had only called the police because Willow was due to join them for a day in the Lakes and a lunchtime meal to celebrate her mother's birthday. Like the teenager's parents, they'd tried her mobile on numerous occasions. Unlike the teenager's phone, Willow's had gone straight to voicemail, which indicated it was switched off.

As probable as it was that Willow hadn't returned because she'd met a guy, something about the situation made Beth think that Willow had acted out of character. The photo the parents had given to the police showed a good-looking woman with tumbling auburn hair. Unlike the sullen and pudgy teenager, Willow would be deemed attractive by most men. While it was a fact that the Lakeland Ripper wasn't targeting a particular 'type' of woman, and his victims were getting younger, her instincts were telling her that his actions were fuelled by sexual desire, and of the two missing females, Willow was by far the more attractive of the two, which made Beth fear far more for Willow than the missing teen.

CHAPTER FIFTY-SIX

26 July

Dear Diary

I have done a terrible thing and I don't know what compelled me to do it.

You will of course remember that last night was the night when Derek threw his celebratory party.

We left the hotel and hailed a cab. He invited me back to his for one last drink.

Drunk as I was, I still knew he was trying to seduce me. I didn't want him and I did want him.

Instead of leaving I started to unbutton his shirt and then his hands were upon me. The sense of guilt and betrayal I felt when I made love to Derek sort of… heightened the experience though. I risked everything, and for a few earth-shattering seconds, when my insides exploded, it was worth it.

I felt sick with guilt as I dressed and then left without saying goodbye. I still feel sick now.

He knew how to charm me. And I let myself be charmed.

When I look in the mirror, I no longer see a faithful wife.

Howard must never find out. Learning I've cheated would kill him.

I'll be calling in sick on Monday. I'll use the day to start looking for another job.

Until tomorrow.

CHAPTER FIFTY-SEVEN

Andrew Cooper levered himself up from the table, popped a painkiller into his mouth and washed it down with a glass of water.

His nose still hurt from where Willow had butted him with her head. She'd complied with his instructions when he'd pressed the knife against her throat and told her to get into the rear compartment of his pickup, but when he'd been tying her to the bed she'd lashed out and tried to make a break for freedom. None of the others had shown such bravery. They'd all been craven in their cowardice.

It had pained him to take a hacksaw to a shotgun, but lopping eighteen inches off the barrel's length had made it even more menacing as well as much easier to hide under a coat. Each one had answered his call for help when he'd feigned looking for his two-year-old daughter. They'd all been stupid enough to follow him to his pickup so he could get his phone to show them a photo of his 'daughter'. He'd opened the pickup door to get his phone, reached under his jacket and produced the shortened shotgun. After that it had been easy to get the women to comply. Terror has been his ally.

He knew he'd been too cocky with Willow. Knew he should have been holding the shotgun instead of a knife when lashing her to the bed. He'd managed not to hit her back, but it had been a struggle. Willow had scratched at him, called him names and had even tried to bite him. The insults she hurled at him had stung him to the point where he'd felt the need to gag her.

He understood her terror; after all, he'd seen it on every occasion he'd tied a woman to that bed.

Their fear gave him a buzz like nothing he'd ever experienced.

Now that he had Willow to himself, he was looking forward to feeding off that fear, to drinking it in when he lay with her.

He knew the feelings he got from his victims' terror were rooted in a sense of control. He was used to being looked down upon, to being mocked and not taken seriously.

When she'd visited him to talk about his investments, Willow had taken him seriously, but he'd known it was an act, that she was just doing her job. She'd been polite and had listened to him, but he knew that he was just another customer who needed to be dealt with.

He was more than that now. He'd gone from genial customer to a dominant force.

Willow was now his to do with as he pleased.

He walked along the passage and took hold of the door handle to the bedroom where he'd imprisoned her. When he stepped into the room, the fear in her eyes filled him with anticipation of pleasures yet to come. He wasn't going to take her yet. He needed to build up to the moment, prepare himself and, most of all, he had to make her fear build. The more terrified his victims were, the more pleasure he took from sating his urges.

Willow writhed on the bed as he tore her clothes from her body. He could tell she was petrified.

To increase her fear even further he placed a hand on her bare, trembling thigh and looked into her eyes.

'I've a couple of jobs to do, but don't worry, it won't be long before I'm back.'

CHAPTER FIFTY-EIGHT

Beth took a right off Curzon Street and wound her way through the housing estate until she found herself outside a semi-detached house. She'd run the visit to Maryport past O'Dowd and had got the DI's agreement, if not full blessing. Tracking down Willow was a job she could do without, but she couldn't stop herself from worrying that she had been taken by the Lakeland Ripper.

According to Willow's parents, she had last been seen by her friends around 12.30 a.m. when they'd parted company when she had gone to get a taxi home. As Willow hadn't yet been missing for twenty-four hours and wasn't considered to be a vulnerable person, there was little the police could do officially, but a constable who'd gone to school with Willow had spoken to a few of the taxi drivers and one had recalled arranging to come back for Willow, but by the time he returned from dropping his fare off, she'd vanished.

It was still unknown if Willow had hooked up with someone while waiting for the taxi to return. Her friends had told Willow's parents she'd chatted to a couple of guys, but hadn't acted as if she was going to take things further.

So far as Beth could work out, Willow had gone missing around 12.45 a.m., which meant that she'd now been missing for a full eleven hours. That might not seem like a long time, but if Willow had been taken by the Lakeland Ripper, those eleven hours would seem like an eternity to her.

The Lakeland Ripper's selection of victims had got younger until Felicia Evans and something in her gut had convinced Beth that he hadn't satisfied his urges with the elderly lady. While only her mother would describe Joanne Armstrong as pretty, Harriet Quantrell was an attractive young woman. However, Willow was better-looking than Harriet, which further fuelled Beth's conviction that he had taken her to finish the job that had been started with Felicia Evans.

There was always an outside chance that Willow had been abducted by someone else or had taken off of her own accord, but Beth didn't waste time thinking about either of those scenarios.

CHAPTER FIFTY-NINE

Beth took in the area as she walked along the narrow concrete path to the Brown's front door. Everything was neat and the ages and models of the cars suggested a certain level of affluence. The people who lived in this street wouldn't be classed as wealthy, but neither would they have to scrimp and save just to survive.

Willow's father answered the door. He was a short man with a straight back and, while he was obviously worried about his daughter, there was a stoicism to him that boded well should Beth's fears prove correct. Beth had learned very soon in her career that people who fell apart emotionally were unreliable as witnesses; their recollections were vague, and that rather than give questions proper thought before answering, they blurted something out, rather than face harsh truths that may be uncovered by internal analysis. Mr Brown may not be a witness in the strictest sense of the word, but he was still giving them information and answering their questions.

Mrs Brown was a delicate woman who insisted on making Beth a cuppa. She fussed around, all of a twitter as she plumped a cushion, got a coaster and tossed looks towards the kitchen as she waited for the kettle to boil.

The TV in the corner was showing a cookery programme, but its volume was low and Beth was confident neither of the Browns had paid it any real attention.

When the woman was sitting in a chair, her legs crossed and uncrossed at the ankle as her worry manifested itself as nervous energy, Beth started to put her questions forward.

The clock on the mantelpiece ticked off seventeen minutes as Beth wrung every drop of information she could from Willow's parents.

Beth hadn't known Willow had walked out on her husband. For a moment she'd entertained hopes that the missing woman had called him when drunk and had gone back to him, but when she learned why Willow had returned to the family home, she'd given up on the idea.

Another possibility was that the husband had come back for her. That he'd persuaded Willow to get in his car and had taken her back to the marital home. It was unlikely if his tastes lay in another direction. Plus, when Willow sobered up, her mind would change, or she'd at least contact her parents.

Could her husband have kidnapped Willow? she wondered. But according to the parents, he'd not fought for his marriage. He'd been civil and cordial as Willow moved out and the only possession he'd argued over was the springer spaniel curled up by Mr Brown's feet.

At every mention of Willow's husband, Mr Brown's hands had clenched into white-knuckled fists then relaxed only to clench again.

Beth could understand his emotions; he'd have been furious that his daughter had been hurt. The primeval part of his DNA would compel him to seek vengeance for the daughter he'd failed to protect.

Her own father was the same way. Only once in her life had she seen him angry enough to fight. His usual calm and understanding manner eroded away by his desire to punish the men responsible for the broken bottle which had slammed into her cheek. Her mother had interrupted his rant by taking his arm and pulling him alongside the hospital bed until Beth could hold his hand. She'd never forget the words her mother had used to calm him. 'Beth needs you to be the dad you've always been. Be her dad. Leave it to the police to punish the men who did this.'

Beth's mother had been right about her needing him to be the dependable father she'd always known and loved, although she'd been wrong about the police catching the two fighters.

Mrs Brown brought out a laptop and showed her Willow's Facebook feed. The information available was only what Willow's mother could see as a friend, but it showed pictures of Willow laughing and dancing with friends the previous evening. The last update to her Facebook profile happened at 12.15 a.m. – it was a blurry picture of a tray of chips with cracked pavement as a backdrop. The accompanying words simply said 'Chips. Cheeeese. Gravy. #Delish'. It was a typical social-media update that showed the world she was having a good time.

What grabbed Beth's interest more than anything was the way Willow was dressed. The canary-yellow dress she wore clung to her body. Its hem was mid-thigh at best and in Beth's mind, it was a statement that screamed 'hey everyone, look at me'.

She knew it was a leap, and that she was making assumptions, but Willow's choice of dress suggested to her that she'd gone out with the intention of being noticed. That was fine by Beth, people could and should wear whatever they liked, however, to some twisted idiots, a dress like Willow's suggested an invitation the wearer had never sent.

With this thought came the fear that she was wasting her time; that Willow had gone off with an admirer and would turn up in time for work on Monday with a wide smile and a fistful of apologies to her parents.

One of the common ways to trace missing people was to track their mobiles. By triangulating signals from the masts, the phone and its whereabouts could be followed. If Willow had shacked up with someone for the weekend, her phone would reveal her location. Had something more sinister happened to Willow, the phone would either lead them to where she was – provided whomever had taken her hadn't disposed of it – or because the signal kept working even if the mobile itself was switched off, they'd be able to find the phone itself. If the phone had been smashed or dumped, they'd be able to assess whether Willow's disappearance was the result of foul play.

Beth got the phone numbers of Willow's friends from Mrs Brown. She planned to call them while she waited for Willow's mobile to be traced.

CHAPTER SIXTY

O'Dowd was outside Carleton Hall puffing on a cigarette when Beth killed the engine of her car. The DI's face was thunderous as she inhaled smoke into her lungs one scowl at a time.

'Tell me you've got something worthwhile.'

Beth outlined not just what she'd found, but her suspicions about the Lakeland Ripper having taken Willow as O'Dowd listened without interrupting. When Beth was finished the DI arced her cigarette butt in the general direction of the sand bucket that was the ashtray and pulled out another.

'That's all I have, ma'am. Have you got anything new?'

'Not a bloody thing. Although I did have the pleasure of being reminded what it's like to be eviscerated by Hilton.' A pause to rasp the wheel of her lighter and touch its flame to her cigarette. 'Bloody man has a cheek. First he halves my team and then he expects us to not only cover for them, but also to double our efforts.'

Beth winced in sympathy but kept her mouth shut as it was clear to her that O'Dowd was in a foul mood.

'To make matters worse, that preening bag of rotten offal, Mannequin, was there. Just when I thought I'd got myself off a hook, he'd point out some procedural point or other and then I'd have even more explaining to do. It's the first time I've known that bugger to be in on a Saturday morning. He's up to something and I for one would like to know what it is.'

There was no way she was going to say it just now, but the thoughts running around Beth's head were centred on the idea that the superiors, whose oversights had allowed the Lakeland Ripper to remain undetected for so long, were setting up O'Dowd and the FMIT as the scapegoats for their own failings.

'Have you had any word on replacements for Thompson and Unthank?'

'Yes.' The word came out as a hiss. 'Due to annual leave and everyone being up to their eyes in it, we're not getting anyone else until Monday at the soonest.'

'What, just you and me to investigate four murders? Jesus wept, don't they want us to catch this killer? Have they forgotten about all the media attention that's on us?'

'That's enough.' O'Dowd kept her voice low, but there was no mistaking the anger in her tone. 'Their hands are tied as much as ours are. Whether we like it or not, it's just the two of us until Monday. If you've got any sense about you, you'll accept what you cannot change and keep your trap shut. Lots of cops want to be on FMIT, and if you're overheard complaining about what the chief super has or hasn't done, you may just find yourself being transferred.'

Beth raised her hands in a gesture of surrender. 'Ma'am, you still haven't commented on what I've told you.'

'What do you want me to say? That you've done well? Is that the only reason you came back here tonight, to get a pat on the head?'

'No. I came back here to report to you. To let you know what I've learned, and to see if you can use your experience to find something I've missed. Another reason I came back is that I trust you to tell me if I'm barking up the wrong tree so I won't waste any more time on ideas you don't think will pan out.' O'Dowd's words had cut Beth deep enough that she couldn't keep the venom from her reply. 'So which is it, Detective Inspector? Am I on the right track, or do you have another direction you'd like to point me in?'

Beth knew from the twist of O'Dowd's face that using O'Dowd's rank the way she had was a mistake, but she couldn't take it back now. Instead she waited for the swearing that would undoubtedly come her way.

'Problem, ladies?' Mannequin's question made them both jump. 'You both seem somewhat animated.'

Beth hadn't heard the man's approach, but that didn't surprise her. *Rubber-heelers.*

'Why would there be?' Rather than let O'Dowd blow at him, Beth knew she had to rescue the situation. 'DI O'Dowd and I often have this kind of frank discussion. Both of us have found that a spot of verbal cut and thrust, where no quarter is either given or expected, stimulates our thought processes.' Beth tilted her head as she looked at Mannequin. 'You know what it's like when five minutes after having an argument you think of the point that would have given you a guaranteed win? Well this is the same thing; we come out here, have a go at each other on the understanding that nothing that's said is really meant, and we see what shakes loose.'

'I see.' Mannequin's tone was filled with doubt. 'Well, I shall be most interested in seeing what conclusions your tête-à-tête has brought forward. In future, though, I suggest that you have your, ahem, discussions, in a more respectful way. Should either of you be inclined to register a complaint against the other, I would be available if you'd like to have that conversation.'

As Mannequin strode away, O'Dowd shot an undecipherable look Beth's way, but when her mouth opened, there was no trace of the earlier anger. 'Not only are you a liar, but you're a very convincing one. Should I be worried about you ever lying to me?'

'Never. And, truth be told, I didn't lie to him either.' Beth gave a shrug. 'Okay, so we don't plan our arguments, but the principle stands all the same. I had a whinge at you this morning and you slapped me down. I was angry, but the anger got my brain working at ways to out-think you.'

'Did you think of anything?'

'You've heard it all.' Beth gave O'Dowd a soft grin as yet another cigarette was pushed in the DI's mouth. 'But you still haven't told me what you think.'

O'Dowd's arms flapped outwards from her sides like the wings of a penguin. 'There's not a lot to say. I think you're stretching things a bit with the Brown lass, but otherwise, I can't fault your thinking.'

'Thanks.' Beth turned and went towards the back door so she could enter the building.

'Where you going?'

'I've got reports to write up and there's no way I'm leaving them until tomorrow.' Beth set off towards the office, fully intent on spending a few hours with her spreadsheets as soon as she'd got her paperwork up to date. She also planned to chase up the detectives in Bolton and Newcastle who'd been tasked with speaking to Christine Peterson's and Joanne Armstrong's families.

It was 9.00 p.m. when Beth pushed back her chair and rose to her feet. Her spreadsheets were up to date and she'd gone over them a dozen times without finding a connection that made sense. She'd also looked for further evidence to back up the nasty suspicions she had about Felicia Evans's assault and murder.

Willow Brown still hadn't returned home or made contact with her parents, but at least the teenager who'd been reported missing had been found. Granted the lass had gone back to the family home with her neck covered in love bites and reeking of alcohol, but at least she was safe and sound.

She'd managed to get a hold of the Bolton and Newcastle detectives but neither family had anything to add to their original statements.

Perhaps the morning would produce some better ideas, but she knew that was more a case of wishful thinking than a likely probability.

CHAPTER SIXTY-ONE

As much as he fancied pouring himself a large cognac, Derek Forster reached for the carton of orange juice instead. This had been an interesting week and he still had work to do.

A lot of his duties as mayor might well be ceremonial, but he'd managed to use his position to do a lot of good as well. Whenever a win-win situation came up, he made sure that he took full advantage of it.

His goal was to become an MP, to gain a seat in the most powerful building in the country. With luck on his side, and a favourable electorate, it would happen within the next two years. After that, who knew what chances may come his way? A seat on the cabinet or shadow cabinet depending on which party was in power. Maybe even one of the plum jobs like home or foreign secretary.

So far as the top job went, he had no interest in that. He wanted power, great power, but he knew that he didn't want the poisoned chalice that was the premiership. That's why he'd sold SimpleBooker; it had grown too big for him: the next stage of its development would have required a large workforce, a call centre and layers of managers.

He didn't want to be a CEO; he'd enjoyed being on the ground floor with his team, had loved the challenges associated with creating a programme which meshed with so many other systems, but he'd recognised that running the business was losing its lustre for him the more the company grew. The company he'd sold SimpleBooker to had added all those other things at their main office, and they had promoted Inga to manager so that his old team had some structure.

Forster had found that his time as deputy mayor had given him a taste for politics. More than anything, it gave him a chance to acquire his biggest thrill on a regular basis.

Sex, alcohol or money may be drivers for other people, but for him, the bending of people to his will was the greatest high he could get. Whether he changed their opinions about a political issue or persuaded them to do something he knew they didn't want to, nothing came close to the feeling he got when he could manipulate others.

The women he dated were those he had to pursue. The easy conquests held no interest for him. He wanted to earn his reward, to fight for what he wanted. The brazen women who launched themselves forward repulsed him more than they attracted him. When a woman showed indifference to his charms, he found himself besotted by them. They became all he could think about until he bedded them.

Beth was the target of his current project. Even with the scarred cheek she was a beautiful young woman. She was strong, determined and tenacious to the point of being single-minded. Try as he might, he couldn't get her out of his mind.

As he flicked through his diary, he found an entry that made him smile. He was invited to a party tomorrow evening. Nothing too fancy, just a few drinks and a bite to eat in the garden of a plush hotel in Keswick.

The person throwing the party was an old friend Forster had run the odd welfare project with. He was top-drawer when it came to charitable funds. He was someone Forster had already planned on consulting, but it would make sense if Beth could join them.

Forster's plan was to get Beth as deeply involved in the charity as he could. Not only would her inner fire benefit the charity, it'd tie her to him. They'd meet on many occasions and he'd be able to worm his way into her affections, and then her bed.

He didn't believe that she'd want anything long-term or serious with him, but that wasn't important to Forster: what mattered was that he could get her into bed in the first place. To him that would represent victory. After that, repeat performances would be a bonus, but if there was to be no encore, he'd move on to someone else having already claimed his prize.

Forster tapped out a message inviting Beth to join him as his plus-one at the garden party. Some people didn't believe in mixing business with pleasure. Forster did. After all, why bother with a business if it didn't give you pleasure?

CHAPTER SIXTY-TWO

Beth powered up her computer and filled a glass with water as she waited for the machine to crank itself into life. As a rule she'd start her working day with a cup of tea, but the sun was already threatening to make today even hotter than yesterday.

The text she'd got from Forster last night had surprised her. She'd expected him to get in touch at some point, to suggest having another meeting over dinner, or to work at his office on setting up the charity. What she hadn't anticipated was him taking her to a party as his plus-one.

She wondered if that was how he thought of her; a woman to have hanging off his arm and every word as he bullshitted his friends and scattered his effortless charm on those who could benefit him. He'd have to think again if that's how he planned to treat her. Beth wasn't anyone's little woman and never had been. There was no way she planned to start now. On the other hand, if Forster was going to set up the charity, she wanted to do her bit.

She fired off a reply telling Forster that she'd be there if work allowed, but she couldn't see how she'd get a chance. Not with four murders to investigate along with Willow's disappearance.

The first thing Beth did after logging onto her PC was check her emails. Of the six that had appeared through the night, she ignored five and directed her cursor to the sixth. It was the trace on Willow's phone.

As she ran a search on the coordinates of the mobile's final location, Beth lifted the phone and put a call into the Brown household. It was early to be calling someone, but she didn't think that either of Willow's parents would have got much sleep.

After a brief conversation she hung up. It had been a forlorn hope that Willow had returned during the night, but she'd had to check.

The early-morning traffic was light as Beth sped along the A66 towards Maryport. For the majority of the journey she had the road to herself and could keep her foot close enough to the floor to ensure that she was travelling at an illegal pace.

Her iPod was again playing a playlist of power ballads as she felt it was too early in the morning to listen to anything more upbeat, or angry. For her, Aerosmith's 'Don't Want to Miss a Thing' was especially poignant as the song's title was how she felt about her job.

When she'd filled in O'Dowd on the contents of her emails, the DI had sent her across to Maryport so she was on the scene. O'Dowd had also called Workington Station and requested that an officer with local knowledge join Beth in Maryport. Beth figured the DI must have struck lucky because she was called by the officer twenty minutes after she'd left Carleton Hall.

As soon as Beth had got the results for the whereabouts of Willow's phone she'd overlaid them on a map and had seen how, on Friday night, Willow's phone had moved around Maryport in a manner that would have been expected of someone enjoying a night out. It would be static for an hour then travel a hundred or so yards as its owner went to a different venue.

It was at the end of the evening that things became interesting. Rather than move in the direction of home, Willow had gone to a small park bordering the River Ellen. A check on Google Street View had shown the park as being ornamental rather than activity based.

The only reason that Beth could think of for Willow going to the park was that she'd wanted to go somewhere private and – at that time of night – that probably meant she had hooked up with someone. However, the union must never have happened, as a mere six minutes after entering the park, Willow's phone indicated that she'd left.

The next time the triangulation signal kicked in, the phone's location was further along, near the point where Ellenborough Road bridged the river. If Willow and the guy she'd hooked up with had been disturbed and gone somewhere else it would have been understandable. However, the phone had never moved from its new location by the bridge.

This was a huge red flag to Beth. In her mind, circumstances had changed in the park, and the fact that Willow's phone was now residing in an area Street View had shown as an overgrown riverbank, jangled every one of Beth's professional nerves.

Beth didn't know what she might find if she could retrieve Willow's phone, but she knew it was something she'd have to do. There was no telling what evidence the phone may hold, and there was also the possibility that they might get a fingerprint, provided the mobile hadn't got soaked by the heavy dew that was in place when Beth had gone for her early-morning run.

Maryport was starting to wake up as Beth pulled off Ellenborough Road onto Selby Terrace and parked behind the liveried Astra. The officer who climbed out of the police car confounded all of Beth's expectations. From the voice on the phone, she'd expected to find the officer was at least forty-five, but the one who greeted her would be lucky if he was twenty.

Maybe it was the drawled West Cumbrian accent that had fooled her, or maybe she'd been preoccupied with her thoughts on the case. Either way, she had what looked to be an inexperienced officer to help her.

The officer tossed a self-important greeting her way when she introduced herself. She watched as his eyes swarmed over her and locked onto the scar decorating her left cheek. His mouth dropped open and he kept his gaze on her face a full five seconds. When he realised what he was doing, he turned to the river, the reddening of the back of his neck a sign of his embarrassment.

Beth joined the officer at the metal railings which edged the road. A series of allotments thirty-feet long stretched between the wall and the bushes and trees which lined the riverbank.

Beth made a point of keeping her voice level. The young officer had reacted badly to her scar, but she'd faced worse and he'd at least had the decency to be embarrassed by his actions. 'You never told me your name.'

'PC Russell, ma'am.'

The way he looked at her made Beth suspect that he thought she wanted his name so she could lodge a complaint.

'You don't need to ma'am me. I'm a DC. So, PC Russell, since we're probably going to be groping around here for a couple of hours looking for a mobile phone, why don't you tell me your real name?'

'It's Kieran.'

'Mine's Beth. Right then, Kieran, let's try and find that phone.' Beth pulled out the screenshot she'd printed and compared it to the area in front of her.

Once she'd fixed in her mind where the phone was likely to be, she found a small gate with squeaky hinges and made her way along the flagstones laid by the allotment's owner. To her left and right a variety of different vegetables were sending green shoots skywards in search of sunlight and rain.

A row of old doors lying on their sides marked the end of the allotment and there was a compost heap she had to skirt before she could step over the doors. If her reckoning was right, the mobile phone would be within ten feet of where she stood. The problem was, the area was overgrown with riverside shrubs, long grass, and there was no clear indication of where the ground ended and the river began. So dense was the shrubbery, it was only the tinkle of water tumbling over stones that confirmed the river's presence.

Beth turned to face Kieran who was still in the allotment, a look of worry on his face. 'Can you see a stick of some kind, something I can use to test the ground?'

Kieran walked off scanning the area and came back with a bamboo cane. It was the perfect tool for the job and Beth used it to probe the grasses to determine where the riverbank started.

Rather than join her search at close range, Kieran stayed on the allotment side of the doors. Beth would have chastised him to join her, but she didn't trust him not to do something stupid like knock Willow's mobile into the river.

A branch was right in front of her face so she pulled it to one side and moved forward another few inches, the cane in her hand alternating between sweeps through the grass and jabs at the ground to test its firmness and incline.

From what she'd glimpsed of the river when crossing the bridge, she didn't think it would be deep, but that didn't mean she wouldn't get a soaking if she fell in.

She probed and swept her way forward until the bamboo cane no longer connected with anything solid.

Beth straightened her back and looked both left and right along the riverbank.

Something in the tree to her left caught her eye.

It was a violet colour and looked out of place.

As she focussed on it, she realised that she was looking at something which may well be Willow's phone.

Beth backed out of where she was and crossed the five paces to where the tree curled its way out from the side of the riverbank. She lifted another branch out of her eyeline and used the cane to test the ground as she walked forward. Now she could see the violet object was indeed a mobile phone.

There was no doubt in her mind that it must be Willow's phone, as the odds of another phone being in the exact place that Willow's was at, were too long to contemplate.

In an ideal world, she'd be able to walk to the edge of the bank and reach out and lift the phone from where it had stuck in the 'V' between two branches. However, the point where the branches met was four feet away from the bank. The only way to get within reach of the phone would be to clamber down the bank until she could stand on the trunk of the tree and climb up the first few branches until she could reach the mobile.

It was a simple plan apart from one serious flaw: to reach sunlight, the tree had arced itself away from the bank. As Beth didn't know how secure the tree's grip of the bank was, she worried that attempts to retrieve the phone would see the tree fall into the river. Not only would she get a soaking, the phone would be ruined along with any evidence it potentially held.

Beth looked down at the river six feet below the riverbank. It wasn't calm, deep water that would cushion a fall, it was a patch of large rounded stones interspersed by lazy rivulets of water. A fall onto those rocks could quite easily break a bone or two.

Once again, she backed away from the riverbank. When she was free of the branches she turned to Kieran and told him what she'd found.

'Nice one. Who are you going to call to get it down from there?'

'I'm calling no one. There's two of us: we'll easily get it.' As she spoke, Beth was watching the emotions running across Kieran's face. Excitement had turned to uncertainty, which in turn became fear.

'How are we going to do that?'

'By climbing the tree.'

Beth couldn't believe what she was seeing. Kieran had retreated back until he was three feet inside the allotment. She'd expected him to offer to climb the tree for her. He had at least four inches in height on her, and the way his arms hung by his sides, suggested that he'd only have to climb one of the slim branches before he'd be able to pluck the phone from between the branches. A devilish part of her wanted to test his mettle. 'C'mon then, I'll hold your utility vest while you get the phone back.'

'Me?' His face blanched. 'I'm not climbing any tree. I can't do it.' His face brightened. 'I haven't been on the course.'

Beth knew the line about the course was him trying to hide his cowardice behind bureaucracy. 'Neither have I, but I'm not going to let that stop me.'

She peeled off her jacket, retrieved an evidence bag from its pocket and stuffed it into her waistband. Her next move was to pull a pair of nitrile gloves over her hands.

'Right, Kieran, it's decision time for you. I'm going to climb that tree. If you were on the bank you'd be able to help me. Are you willing to do that, or are you going to need to attend a course in helping colleagues first?'

Beth had to give Kieran his due: he stepped forward, although he didn't look happy and there was a shake to his hands as he went to move a branch for her.

She turned her back on him as she ducked under the branch and crept her way to the edge of the river, her feet tilting downwards as the bank curled away to nothingness. Her hands grasped a thin branch as she neared the edge. It wasn't strong enough to support her weight, but holding it gave her more confidence.

Her feet edged forward, heels dug into the bank as she neared the point where she'd have to take a step down so she was standing on the tree's trunk. It was only a foot below her, but as she was sending her left foot down towards it, the bank beneath her right foot gave way.

Beth pitched forward, her shoulder thumping against the tree even as her arms encircled it. Her feet scrabbled at the base of the trunk until they gained purchase and she could stop worrying she was going to land on the boulders below.

The tree had survived the sudden addition of her weight, but Beth's only thought was for the phone. When she looked up and saw it was still jammed between the branches she let out a relieved sigh.

Once she'd got her heart rate under control, Beth gripped the branches above her head and put her foot on a branch that was at knee height. Every time she progressed upwards, she moved further away from the bank.

After three successive movements, she had the phone in front of her face. It should have been easy to get the phone into the evidence bag, but the way the tree had flexed to a 45 degree angle not only unnerved her, but it made her want to grab the phone and toss it to Kieran before everything landed in the river.

She was also suffering from a lack of hands as she was using both of hers to cling to the tree's branches. Slowly, an inch at a time, she laid her body against the tree's narrow trunk until she could release the branches and balance herself.

Her left hand retrieved the evidence bag and moved it round so it was below the phone. She teased it open and then reached for the violet rectangle six inches from her nose.

As soon as her fingers touched it, the phone moved. In a panic that it would tumble into the river, she grabbed the mobile and got a firm grip of it.

She eased it out from its resting place and dropped it into the evidence bag.

With the bag safely wedged into her waistband, she moved her hands back to the branches and levered herself to a more vertical position.

The readjustment of her weight caused the tree to lean further towards the river. Its lower branches now trailed in the water and caressed the boulders in the riverbed. As quick as she could, Beth clambered back down until she was standing on the curve where the tree emerged from the bank.

Kieran held out the end of the bamboo cane to her, so Beth planted a foot on the bank and through a combination of her own strength, and his pulling, got herself back onto solid ground.

The first thing she did was retrieve the evidence bag and hold it up to take a look at the phone. It appeared to be switched off, but that didn't mean they couldn't get fingerprints from it which may well identify Willow's abductor.

Beth dusted herself down. There were stubborn green stains where some form of lichen or algae refused to be brushed off, but she wasn't too worried; the dark material of her trouser suit hid the worst of the staining.

'Well done.' Kieran's face and his voice held a measure of respect. 'There's no way I could have done that.'

'We all have our different strengths.' Beth didn't need his compliments or his admissions. Her mind was already on the next steps she had to take. 'Thanks for helping. You can get back to your station now. Do me a favour when you write up your report though, just say I shinned a couple of branches up a tree, there's nothing to be gained from overdramatising things.'

Now that she'd done what was needed, Beth was looking at it from Mannequin's point of view. He'd doubtless consider her climbing the tree to have been foolhardy and dangerous; therefore he'd deem it worthy of a reprimand she didn't have time to waste hearing.

'I'm not to go back to the station. My sarge says I've to help you until you go back to Carleton Hall.'

'Fair enough.'

As Beth led him back to where their cars were parked, she couldn't help but wonder if his sergeant wanted Kieran to be educated or babysat.

CHAPTER SIXTY-THREE

As she drove to the Brown household, Beth recalled her conversation with one of the friends Willow had been out with on Friday night. The woman had been chatty enough and Beth hadn't heard any hesitation or subterfuge in her voice when she questioned her about the night out.

Willow had been chatted up by one or two guys, but she'd not gone any further than a spot of flirting. She'd also talked with lots of people she knew from the town, but hadn't got drawn into any lengthy conversations.

The friend had admitted that the way Willow had dressed had drawn attention, but while she'd enjoyed the looks she was getting, she hadn't led anyone on in any way.

With every new piece of information she received, the greater was Beth's conviction that Willow had been deliberately taken by the Lakeland Ripper.

Her first knock on the Browns' door went unanswered, so she rattled her knuckles off the glass a second time with a little more force.

The door swung open to reveal an agitated Mrs Brown. Her hands flapped at nothing as she stepped back to allow Beth and Kieran into the house.

'I'm sorry to bother you, Mrs Brown, but I need to show something to either you or your husband.'

'What is it? Please, dear God no. Please don't show me a picture and ask if it's our Willow. I can't cope with that.'

'Don't you worry, lass, it's nowt like that.'

To some, Kieran calling Mrs Brown 'lass' when she was old enough to be his mother might seem odd, but Beth knew the addition of 'lad' or 'lass' to a sentence was a trait common to Cumbria, and the familiarity of the expression seemed to settle Mrs Brown.

Beth wondered if that's what his skill was, calming worried or hysterical relatives, because there was no way he could be classed as a man of action.

She got why Mrs Brown had reacted the way she had. The woman's greatest fear would be the police arriving to inform her of her daughter's death.

'What is it then?'

'We think we've found Willow's phone.' Beth opened her briefcase and lifted the evidence bag and held it where Mrs Brown could see the mobile. 'Do you recognise this?'

'Yes. That's our Willow's.' Mrs Brown lurched forward. 'Give it to me. That's my daughter's phone and I want it. You have no right to keep it.'

Kieran moved so he was between Beth and Mrs Brown. 'We're sorry, but now you've identified it as being your daughter's it's evidence. We'll need to keep it for a while, but only so we can use it to find Willow for you.'

Mrs Brown collapsed onto a chair. Her hands hid her face, but they couldn't conceal her whimpers.

Beth gave Kieran a mental gold star for the way he'd handled Mrs Brown. After his performance at the river, he was still in negative equity, but at least he'd prevented an ugly scene. She may have refrained from offering false hope, but once he'd received a tongue-lashing from an aggrieved relative when he failed to live up to his promises, he'd learn.

Beth eased herself down until she was crouched at Mrs Brown's eye level. 'I'm sorry, I know this is a tough time for you, but I have a couple of questions I'd like to ask you.'

'What is it? What do you want to know? I'll tell you anything if it helps you find my daughter.'

With as much consideration for Mrs Brown's sensibilities as she could inject into her words, Beth put her questions forward. When she asked if Willow had complained about any men who'd creeped her out, Mrs Brown had shaken her head so violently Beth could hear the woman's neck crack.

Having seen how fragile Mrs Brown could be, it didn't surprise Beth that Willow hadn't mentioned anything to her mother. The woman was the type of person to worry herself about things that would never happen, and such news would likely have triggered sleepless nights.

For a moment she wondered where Willow's father was, and then she thought of what her own father would do in the man's position. He'd drive round looking for her. He'd recruit all the friends and family members he could, and set up his own search parties.

Mr Brown had seemed to be cut from the same cloth as her own father and as such, he'd be unable to wait at home. He'd have to be out, doing something. Looking for Willow himself rather than sit at home feeling useless.

With her last question answered, Beth nodded to Kieran and then stood to leave. The next part of the trail had been mapped out, and all she could do was hope it wasn't a dead end.

CHAPTER SIXTY-FOUR

The woman who opened the door to them wasn't what Beth was expecting of Willow's closest work colleague. She'd anticipated the Natalie that Willow's mother had referred to would be of a similar age to Willow.

Natalie appeared to be retirement age, but regardless of the lines on her face and the grey in her hair, she dressed and styled herself as if thirty years younger. It was a hard thing to do, but she pulled it off. Her home was also furnished in a modern and stylish way.

Beth explained why they were troubling her as it was obvious from Kieran's uniform who they were.

'I'd heard she'd gone off. It's not like her, I have to say. She's dependable and not at all impulsive.'

'We'd like to know if she complained to you about anyone who made her feel uneasy. You know, creeped her out?'

Natalie rubbed at her chin as she thought. 'There's a few people who pissed her off, but that's part of the job. When you're giving financial advice to folk, there's always some who think they know best or have unrealistic expectations.'

'That's not what I'm looking for, unless they lost a fortune. She's a good-looking woman and I'm after anyone who may have been inappropriate to her. Can you think of any names she might have mentioned?'

Beth fell silent and shot a warning look at Kieran in case he spoke and interrupted Natalie's train of thought.

'There were a couple of people she asked me about. One is a right charmer, or at least he thinks he is; truth be told he's more of a lech than anything else. He's on his fourth or maybe fifth wife. Believe me, he chases anything in a skirt. One time I was there he openly ogled me when his wife was sitting beside him.'

Natalie scrunched her nose. 'I never liked him. I can't say he was ever anything but polite with me, but I always got the sense that he was undressing me in his mind. He never did anything about it, never flirted or asked me out, but he was the type to always be trying to sneak a look down your blouse if you know what I mean?'

'I do indeed.'

The way Kieran blushed made Beth like him that little bit less.

As much as Beth liked what she was hearing, the fact this man had been married a few times suggested that he didn't have a problem meeting and seducing women. This was at odds with every psychological profile she could think of for the Lakeland Ripper. All the same she jotted down his name and address.

'And the other guy?'

'If it's the guy I'm thinking of, he's a farmer, well he used to be. Now all he does is rent his fields and sheds out. Other than keeping the fences and hedges in good order, he doesn't do much at all. He tried to flirt with me every time I had to visit him, and I'm sure he'll have done the same with a bonny lass like Willow.'

'Did he have a wife, a girlfriend?'

'Not as far as I was ever aware.' Natalie's nose gave a rabbit wrinkle. 'Tell you the truth, he's not an attractive man. Don't get me wrong, he's not physically ugly, more that he tries too hard with his flirting and makes inappropriate comments all the time.'

Beth's pulse raced as she listened to Natalie's opinion of the farmer. Everything the woman was saying about him was making him a prime suspect.

'Do you have his name and address?'

'I can't remember his name. Sorry. But I do know that he has a farm that's about halfway to 'Spatri, it's something Scales. A compass point, but I can't remember if it's north, south, east or west. Sorry.'

Beth understood the abbreviated name for Aspatria. The Scales farm shouldn't be hard to find. There wouldn't be that many options, and a quick search of an electoral register would yield the right result if she couldn't google it on her phone.

One thing was for sure, once she found where the farm was, she'd be going there, and if Kieran was coming, he'd be riding in her car. As she'd followed him across Maryport to Natalie's house he'd been the most cautious driver she'd ever encountered. It was as though he was sitting his driving test or chauffeuring the queen.

CHAPTER SIXTY-FIVE

Willow's entire body ached as she fought against the ropes restraining her. Her wrists were chafed raw from the rough hemp, as were her ankles. The muscles of her arms and legs were numb from hours spent thrashing in vain efforts to free herself. Even her neck and back hurt from where she'd contorted herself in attempts to put all her strength behind one particular limb.

Yet by comparison to the shame that she felt at having been so careless as to have been captured by what she'd thought was a white knight, none of the sprains or chafes or aches could begin to compete with the dread in her heart.

It hadn't been a noble rescue. It had been a real frying pan to fire experience. She'd read the papers, watched the news. Willow knew all about the four women who'd been raped and murdered. She'd learned with horror of the fate which had befallen them.

Andrew Cooper had visited her three further times since he'd brought her here after saving her by the river on Friday night.

Each of his visits brought a new level of horror.

Once he'd tied her up, he'd talked to her for an hour. She'd been disgusted by the way he'd outlined his sexual fantasies in detail after lurid detail.

On his next visit, he'd ripped every shred of clothing from her body.

His third visit had creeped her out even further. He'd brought a camera with him and had taken hundreds of photos of her as she lay trussed to the bed. He had taken pictures from the other side of the room and he'd held the camera an inch away from the flesh he was making crawl with his actions.

Cooper's fourth visit gave her the most concern though. He'd brought a basin of water, a towel and a sponge. He'd washed her from head to toe in silence. The only saving grace was that, as much as his eyes caressed her body, all she felt touching her skin was the coarse sponge.

Willow knew in her bones that it was only a matter of time before he raped her. The cleansing was a sure sign that he was preparing her as a receptacle for his lusts.

The sound of footsteps clumping along wooden floorboards made Willow thrash against the ropes even harder, as she knew what would happen to her when her captor entered the room.

She knew she couldn't defend herself. And that if Cooper was the Lakeland Ripper he'd be planning to kill her once he'd enacted his fantasies with her.

Willow didn't want either to happen, but the only defence she could think to mount was to hold onto the full bladder she was struggling with until she could be sure he'd be within range. The cleansing of her body had shown hygiene was important to him, and while it might earn her a few punches, it may well also keep her alive a little longer while he cleaned them both up.

CHAPTER SIXTY-SIX

The farmhouse at North Scales was surrounded by whitewashed farm buildings. Somewhere in the distance Beth could hear the heavy diesel engine of a tractor, and her nose was assaulted by the pungent farmyard smells. The air hung with the mixed smells of freshly cut grass and the tangy, potent stench of manure.

Outside the front door a black pickup truck sat with its nose an inch from the wall. The vehicle was layered with dust, but its licence plate showed it as being only a year old.

She remembered the description of Andrew Cooper from Natalie and what she'd heard had strengthened her belief that he may be the Lakeland Ripper. She could imagine the teenage Cooper being rejected by the girls he'd fancied because of his cack-handed approach. This would continue into adulthood, all the while fostering the bitterness inside him. If he was the Lakeland Ripper and his penis was as small as Dr Hewson had speculated, then he'd have even less appeal to the opposite sex. If he was their killer though, nothing on earth could justify what he'd done.

'We should call for backup.'

'Do we have any hard facts to reinforce our suspicions?'

Kieran answered Beth's question with a shake of his head.

Beth pressed a finger against the doorbell. 'In that case, we check it out; if we get any kind of confirmation, we can get all the backup you want. If not, we keep looking for Willow.'

She couldn't hear the doorbell sound inside the house, but it was possible its buzzer sounded in a room at the other end of the building.

Nothing happened, so she held her finger against the button for the count of ten.

Nothing happened a second time.

She rapped her knuckles against the door, but still nobody came to answer it.

Beth tried the door handle. It was locked.

On the assumption that Cooper must be out and about, she decided to scout round the house. With Kieran trailing after her mumbling a series of protests, Beth walked along the house's wall. When she came to a corner she veered away from the wall in case Cooper was lying in wait.

She encountered a small wooden porch which had a couple of jackets on its ledges and a pair of wellies standing beside a sliding door.

Beth tried sliding the door open, but it wouldn't budge, so she resumed her circuit of the farmhouse's exterior.

The next corner she rounded brought her into an unkempt garden. She could see where flowerbeds had once bloomed before being neglected. A ranch fence had rotten timbers and peeling white paint.

As she walked along the front of the house, she could begin to hear a faint noise that got louder as she neared the far end of the building. It was music, but not the kind of music that she expected to hear at 10.00 a.m. on a Sunday morning.

It was possible that Cooper was having a Sunday morning roll-together with someone, but she knew that for a farmer, anything after 9.00 a.m. was considered to be the middle of the afternoon.

The music got louder as she approached a window where the curtains were drawn. Considering that the window overlooked nothing but fields, she thought it strange the curtains were closed, so she put her ear to the glass. She held the position for the count of ten, then wheeled away, grabbing at Kieran's arm as she went.

As soon as she was ten paces from the window she broke into a run.

The begging she'd heard wasn't part of any Sunday morning roll-together.

As she ran she explained to Kieran what she'd heard.

Beth saw his hand reach for his radio, but there was no way that she was going to wait for backup. If her suspicions were right, Cooper was in the throes of raping or murdering Willow and she had to save her.

A flick of her wrist brought her extendable baton to its full length.

The glass of the sliding door broke on the first strike. After a circular sweep of the baton to clear the glass, Beth snaked a hand in and slid the bolt free of the door.

Various outdoor clothing hung on a coatrack as she passed through a utility room that had cured meats hanging from hooks. She passed through the kitchen, hardly pausing to look at the Aga or the long table with timber benches at either side as she progressed towards the area of the house where the music was blaring out.

Beth slowed her pace as she neared the music's source. The music reduced the need for stealth, but she still didn't take silly risks.

She cast a look at Kieran: his face was pale, but his jaw was set in determination. He too had his baton extended.

Beth took her pepper spray from her pocket. She used the tip of the baton to indicate that Kieran should open the door. He took two swallows before he reached out his hand, but at least he was rising to the occasion.

Too much, in fact: he shouldered the door open as soon as he'd pressed the handle down and charged into the room.

Beth was at his heel as he tripped over something on the floor and went sprawling in a heap. She wasn't watching him though; she was conscious of the two figures on the bed: a naked woman and a man wearing a grubby shirt and black socks.

The man sprang off the woman and lashed a foot backwards at Kieran as the young PC was clambering back upright.

There was a crunching slap as Cooper's heel struck Kieran's jaw and sent him back to the ground. From the way he slumped, Beth knew she wouldn't get any help from him for a while.

Cooper raised himself to his full height. The top of his head may have been level with Beth's shoulder, but he was no less intimidating because he was short.

His eyes were the thing that scared Beth the most. They were sinkholes, lying dormant, until they chose to swallow something up.

Cooper pointed at the woman tied to the bed as he stepped towards Beth, his arms at his sides like a gunfighter about to draw his pistols. 'It looks like I'm getting me a two-for-one deal.'

CHAPTER SIXTY-SEVEN

Beth held her baton like a sword, but Cooper paid it no heed as he lurched forward full of menace.

He continued forward, his left arm rising to deflect the blow Beth was aiming at him.

The baton thudded against his bicep causing him to yelp, but he didn't slow down.

Beth stepped back, brought the baton into her body and tried a backhand slash.

It didn't work as Cooper had closed the gap enough that she couldn't get any real power into the blow.

She could smell his foul, kippery breath as he reached for her. The pepper spray in her left hand hissed as it shot into Cooper's face.

He yowled in pain, but he'd built up a momentum that caused him to crash into Beth.

His arms wound around her waist as he fell to the floor. Beth found herself being dragged down by him. He was thrashing about, swearing at the pain as he rubbed his face against her shirt.

Somehow Beth found herself beneath Cooper as they writhed on the floor. Her trying to escape him, and Cooper trying to alleviate the agony in his eyes.

Cooper's face was pressing against her stomach as he tried to use the material of her blouse as a cloth to wipe away the pepper spray. His head sawing back and forth moved up her body until his forehead was buffeting her breasts.

Beth jabbed the point of her baton into Cooper's kidneys, but all it achieved was a grunted oof as he continued to writhe above her. With Cooper showing no signs of calming down, she adjusted her aim and caught the back of his head.

Cooper slumped a little, but continued to fight against her.

She hit him again, harder.

His movements stopped apart from slight twitches of his head.

Beth took hold of Cooper's right arm and hauled him sideways. He moved six inches.

She had to repeat the action three times before she could wriggle out from under him; but as soon as she was free, she snapped her cuffs onto his wrists. She'd read him his rights when he came to.

The woman on the bed had taken to sobbing and when Beth looked at Kieran, she found him on his knees, shaking his head from side to side as he tried to deal with his brief concussion.

Beth whipped off her jacket and laid it over the woman's naked body. Her next move was to start untying the woman's wrists.

'Kieran. You okay?'

'Yeah.' He sounded groggy to Beth, but he could be checked out when an ambulance got here.

'Good. Go find me a sheet to wrap this lady in. A clean one if you can find such a thing in here.'

Beth released the first of the woman's wrists. 'My name is Beth. Are you Willow?'

The head turned her way and nodded.

As she looked into Willow's face and saw the emptiness in her eyes, Beth felt her anger start to grow.

She could see first-hand the damage that Cooper's actions had wrought. Gone was the woman she'd seen on Facebook who'd been joyfully partying with friends and eating cheesy chips. In her place was a woman who would remember this horror for the rest of her days. When Beth moved to untie Willow's ankles, she had to resist aiming a kick at Cooper's genitals. The idea of burying her foot a few times was appealing but she didn't want to do anything that may contaminate evidence or give him a legal loophole to exploit.

He was on his side and his shirt had ridden up onto his stomach.

As much as she didn't want to look at his crotch, she knew it could hold vital evidence.

She took a quick look.

A condom hung off a penis that was no longer than the first knuckle of her thumb.

The urge to assault Cooper vanished as she realised she had confirmation that Andrew Cooper was definitely the killer and rapist they called the Lakeland Ripper.

'Here.' Kieran handed her an orange sheet. Its colours were washed out, but it looked clean and didn't carry any nasty smells.

'Cheers.' Beth draped the sheet over Willow and bent to untie the final knots securing her to the bed. 'Go outside and call in for an ambulance and a CSI team. Tell them we'll need someone to do a rape examination when Willow gets to hospital.'

Willow's head slewed from side to side. 'No. No rape.' A shudder that shook Willow's whole body was followed by a stream of tears. 'Not yet. He was about to. He'd told me what he was going to do. How he was going to rape me.'

Kieran hovered, unwilling to leave, but not sure what to do.

Beth nodded at the door. 'Go on, out with you. It's ladies only in here from now on.'

With the sheet covering Willow, Beth tried to find the right words to soothe her. She kept her voice soft as she repeatedly told Willow that she was safe now, that Cooper would go to jail for a long time and that he'd never bother her again.

Even as she was speaking, she knew her words were trite, meaningless. She wasn't trained to deal with this kind of thing. Instinct made her want to rub Willow's back while giving her a great big reassuring hug, but something else inside her was telling her not to make any physical contact until Willow reached for her.

Beth knew that if Forster could get his charity set up in the right way it would be invaluable to people in Willow's position.

CHAPTER SIXTY-EIGHT

Beth fidgeted in her seat as she waited for O'Dowd to instigate the interview. The struggle with Cooper had torn three buttons from her blouse. She'd managed to borrow a T-shirt from a female PC when they'd got back to Workington police station, but the PC was a size smaller than her, which left her feeling suffocated by the tight top.

O'Dowd switched on the recording equipment and read out the charges after naming all those present.

'So, Mr Cooper. It would appear that you have, quite literally, been caught with your pants down. As we speak, an officer trained to deal with rape victims is taking a statement from the woman you abducted and attempted to rape. She's also been examined by a doctor who specialises in sexual trauma. Whether or not your victim testifies against you doesn't matter. You were caught in the act. End of. You're going to jail for what you did; the only real questions I have are: For how long? And for how many crimes?' O'Dowd fixed him with a stare.

'No comment.'

'I don't blame you for saying that. Let's face it, your lawyer has probably told you to say nothing until they've had a chance to study all the evidence against you. Trust me, that'll take a while because there's lots of it. Tell me, do you honestly think you're going to get away with what you've done?'

'No comment.'

The lawyer laid his pen on the table with a deliberate precision. 'I think you're on the point of crossing a line, DI O'Dowd. What

Mr Cooper has said is that he was making love to his… girlfriend when two of your officers broke into his home, assaulted him and then arrested him. He tells me he is innocent of the charges laid against him.'

Beth noticed the lawyer's particular turn of phrase, and also the way he'd physically positioned himself to put as much space between him and his client as possible. It was everyone's right to be defended and duty lawyers didn't get a choice on who they were representing, but they didn't have to like it.

'I'm sorry, Mr Irving, but I don't believe that's the case at all. And, I'm sad to say, I don't think even you believe that version of events.' Beth shot a look at the lawyer. 'I was there, I saw what your client was doing. I spent an hour comforting her. That wasn't going to be consensual sex, not even close to it. His victim was traumatised. When she finally stopped crying long enough to tell me what happened, she told me your client had told her several times over that he intended to rape her. Her wrists and ankles were chafed bloody from where she'd been struggling against the ropes binding her.' Beth held up a hand to stall Irving's protests. 'I know you have a job to do, but please, credit us with a little intelligence while you do it; otherwise you're going to end up making yourself look foolish when you peddle his lies for him. So, Mr Cooper, Mr Irving, you might want to have a think about your options, because from where I'm sitting, pleading guilty is the only thing that can lessen your sentence.'

'No comment.'

Irving looked at his client, who sat back in his chair and folded his arms, so Beth did the same until she felt a tap on her ankle from O'Dowd.

'Tell me, Mr Cooper, do the names Christine Peterson, Joanne Armstrong, Harriet Quantrell and Felicia Evans mean anything to you?'

'No comment.'

Beth put a puzzled expression on her face. 'That's odd. Either you're going to say no comment to everything we ask you, or you've just made a serious mistake. You see, those four women were all murdered after being raped. What you should have said instead of no comment, was no. But you didn't, did you? That makes me wonder if you said no comment because you don't want to comment on those women.'

Without waiting for an answer, Beth pulled open a folder and removed four pictures which she put on the table. As she laid each one down she named the victim, said a little bit about them and stated the date and location of where they were found.

O'Dowd's hand slapped onto the table. 'Cat got your tongue, Mr Cooper? Are you not going to say no comment again?'

'Please, DI O'Dowd. There's no need to be rude.' Beth laid a hand on O'Dowd's wrist as she gave the prearranged admonishment. It was one of the routines they'd developed. Sometimes Beth would play good cop, and at others, she'd ramp things up past O'Dowd's level. The inclusion of the word rude was a signal to O'Dowd that she was about to really turn the screw on Cooper and that O'Dowd should back off a little.

O'Dowd gave a curt nod and a mumbled apology.

'Those women were all sexually assaulted and strangled. One of them was assaulted further after she died and one was only assaulted after she'd been strangled.' Beth gave her head a tiny shake. 'That's the kind of monster we're looking for. A man who'd satisfy his lusts on a woman he'd just killed. Can you imagine what a criminal psychologist would make of such a man?'

'No comment.'

Beth was just getting started; she'd only tossed a question in so Cooper would become part of the conversation.

'My guess is they'd say the killer was a single man, between twenty-five and fifty-five, but then, they always say that. They'd also say the rapist and killer was someone who harboured a lot of resentment towards women. That he'd been repeatedly scorned or spurned by women. They might suggest that he was a virgin until he raped his first victim, or that the only success he'd had with the opposite sex had been with prostitutes. Does any of this sound familiar to you, Mr Cooper?'

'No comment.'

'I reckon the criminal psychologist would speak of the killer's anger, their resentment. He may purport to a sexual inadequacy, such as erectile dysfunction, as a major reason the killer has had to force himself on women and then kill them to ensure their silence. Another thing he may well suggest is that the killer was unattractive to the opposite sex, perhaps on a visual level and maybe on a personality basis. I'm not going to shy away from it, Mr Cooper. We have statements from Miss Brown and another lady that state that your personality was best described as predatory. But I need you to tell me if what I'm saying is true. Can you do that? Can you admit that you had to resort to rape because woman after woman spurned your advances?'

'No comment.'

Beth leaned forward and rested her elbows on the table. She wanted to close the gap between her and Cooper, both physically and psychologically. When she started speaking again, she made sure her tone was soft.

'You do know you're in a lot of trouble, right? I caught you, remember? You were caught by a woman. I bet that doesn't sit well with your opinion of women, does it? You probably see us all as bitches for rejecting you. You probably hate all women because of the ones who've spurned your advances.' Beth pointed to her cheek. 'I hated all men for a while after I picked this up. I get why you feel that way. I understand that you probably hate me as well. That goes with the job; I caught you, I'm the reason you're going to prison. It's natural for you to hate me. In a way I'm your nemesis. Tell me, Mr Cooper, how does it feel to have been caught by a woman? You couldn't beat me when you tried to escape, you're not going to beat me now. I have you, I have the evidence against you and I'm going to hand you over to the CPS in a gift-wrapped box tied up with a pretty pink ribbon. Would you like to know how I'm so sure you raped and murdered four women and were about to rape a fifth that you also planned to kill?'

Irving gave a dry cough. 'I would.'

'When we searched your client's home, we found clothes in his wardrobe. Nothing unusual in that. Clothes are supposed to be in a wardrobe. It's just that Mr Cooper lives alone.' Beth made sure she had eye contact with Cooper before she dropped the piece of evidence that would seal his conviction for murder. 'And the items of clothing were women's. Specifically, they were an exact match for the clothing worn by Christine, Joanne and Harriet. They are, of course, being tested for skin flakes, hairs, etcetera, so they can be verified as belonging to the victims, but let's face it, they were in a bag on the floor of the wardrobe, so trying to tell us they are his sister's or girlfriend's is a waste of everyone's time, as they were the only items of women's clothing in the house. Something else we found was a bag containing a digital camera and its accessories. The camera is a match for the make and model of the one Christine Peterson had with her when she was taken, and her husband has identified the bag as hers. Willow's dress and underwear were found in a corner of the room where she'd been tied to the bed.'

'Fuck.' Cooper's head tilted back so he was looking at the ceiling. Beside him, Irving's face was grey.

'Also, and perhaps this may seem spurious or circumstantial to you, Mr Irving, but when I caught your client about to rape his fifth victim, he was naked from the waist down and I couldn't help seeing his genitalia. Please understand me when I tell you this, I'm speaking objectively as a police officer. The pathologist's reports state that the first three women were raped by a man with a micropenis. My colleagues also found a number of devices, creams and pills that all purport to increase penis size.'

Irving's eyes closed in defeat. When they opened, he looked at O'Dowd. 'If it's agreeable with you, Inspector, I'd like to request that this interview is suspended so that I can consult with my client.'

O'Dowd gave a short nod and suspended the interview.

As Beth walked out of the interview suite she wanted to punch the air. The interview was done for the time being and they had more than enough to charge Cooper, which meant they didn't have to worry about releasing him when his twenty-four hours were up.

She also knew the real reason Irving had requested the interview be suspended. He'd want to point out the hopelessness of Cooper continuing to plead his innocence. They had him on five counts, plus the usual resisting arrest and assault of a police officer. When the interview resumed, it would be confession time.

'Ma'am, when are you planning to resume the interview?'

O'Dowd shrugged. 'Whenever his poor lawyer persuades him to sing. Why?'

'You know that the mayor and I have been looking at setting up a charity to help victims of serious sexual assault?' O'Dowd nodded. 'Well he's going to some party today and he's invited me along because the host is someone who's set up charities before. Do you think you could get someone else to finish off for me? After all, he's going to plead guilty, isn't he?'

'Jesus, Beth. Do you never stop trying to do good? You need a hobby, or better still, a man in your life! Not the mayor though, he's too old for you. Go on then, get yourself off.'

CHAPTER SIXTY-NINE

When Beth parked her car, she felt out of place before she even opened the door. The car park of the Lakes and Fells Hotel was littered with flash vehicles. There were Mercedes, BMWs and a couple of Bentleys.

The hotel itself was a tall building with three main storeys and dormer windows indicating a loft conversion at some point in the building's history. The gardens were manicured to the point where there wasn't so much as a blade of grass out of place and the bushes and shrubs were trimmed into perfect spheres.

A small marquee was visible to the left of the hotel, so rather than going directly inside when she got to the top of the steps leading to the entrance, Beth followed the path round towards the marquee.

The feelings of unworthiness she'd had when parking returned when she took in the guests at the garden party. There was an air of money and class emanating from every person her eyes landed on. The women were dressed in designer summer wear and the men wore either linen suits or corduroys topped with a striped blazer.

It was a different world than she was used to, and she had to battle the temptation to turn around and go home.

Beth quashed her nerves and stepped forward before she changed her mind. She'd been pleased with how she looked when she'd checked herself in the mirror. The calf-length pleated skirt she'd pulled from her wardrobe suited her. Its powder blue colour was a perfect contrast for her black strappy top. She was glad she'd chosen to wear heels rather than the ballet pumps she'd first chosen.

Not only were they a bit smarter, but she was happy to have a little extra height. Her entire outfit had cost less than fifty pounds and she doubted that any of the other women present had ever spent that little on any single item of their clothing.

Beth's eyes picked out the mayor as she accepted a glass of orange juice from a sweating waiter. Forster was holding court with a group of five men. Two had cigars in their hands and they were all laughing at something.

Beth hovered at the edge of the marquee; the evening sun was still strong and she was glad to find a little shade.

She waited until Forster's group splintered a little and walked over to him.

He greeted her with a hug, and flashed a smile at her that held traces of brandy and Cuban leaves. Try as Beth might, she couldn't stop the instinctive stiffening of her body when his hug got that little bit too tight.

The next hour passed her by in a blur as Forster introduced her to various people. The most interesting of these was the host. A rotund man, he had a sharp mind and a quick wit. She only had a brief conversation with him, but in less than five minutes, he imparted a lot of wisdom about establishing a charity.

Despite herself, Beth was enjoying the experience. Forster was bigging her up more than she cared for, but he was selling the concept of the charity to everyone he spoke to.

What amazed Beth more than anything, was the way people were offering patronage to the charity before it was even established. This was an element of society she neither knew nor understood. They had their reservations about her, she could see that and she didn't mind. It was natural for them to be wary.

The only downside to the day so far had been Forster's hands. They hadn't wandered or anything crass like that, it was just that every time he touched her back, either the tips of his fingers or the ball of his thumb landed on the clasp of her bra.

She was standing with Forster when a familiar face approached her. It took Beth a moment to place him because he was out of uniform, but there was no doubt it was the chief super.

Her first thought was panic. He was expecting her to be working not mingling in the same social group as him.

'I hear you had something of a result today.' Hilton's inscrutable face cracked into a tight smile. 'In fact, I do believe you deserve praise for your actions. Well done, DC Young.'

'Thank you, sir.'

'I also hear that you're working with Mayor Forster to set up a charity for rape victims. And that you're insistent on helping the victims to report their ordeal.' Hilton gave a sharp nod. 'That is something I can only applaud. Should you run into any issues dealing with members of Cumbria Constabulary, my door will always be open.'

'Thank you, sir, I appreciate your support and endorsement.'

A wry smile caressed Hilton's mouth. 'Careful now, you're starting to talk like a politician. Be yourself at all times. Show your determination and that fine mind of yours and you'll do well. Become another corporate drone and you'll end up being ignored.' Hilton gave her an exaggerated wink as he turned to leave. 'Oh, and well done again for catching "Justin".'

Beth felt her own smile widening as she realised the undertone to the conversation she'd just had. With Hilton, she now had a high-ranking ally, but his parting shot at the end had also been a warning. To the best of her knowledge, only the four members of FMIT knew about Thompson christening the killer with the derogatory name 'Justin', yet the chief super had heard about it. That meant he had spies in the camp.

Another pleasant hour passed and then the host stood on a chair to make a speech. He was a good orator who could work a crowd, but when he waxed lyrical about the rape charity and called

Beth and Forster to his side, Beth knew the perspiration covering her body had little to do with the evening sun.

As she posed for pictures with the host and Forster, Beth could feel the mayor's hand on her back. Unlike the host, who'd kept his arm at shoulder height, the mayor's hand was lower. So low she could feel his fingertips against the waistband of her skirt. When he lifted his hand away, he ran one finger upwards over the knuckles of her spine.

Had Ethan done the same thing, Beth would have shivered for a different reason. Forster's smile told her that he thought he'd had the effect she expected from Ethan.

As confusing as this was for Beth, due to the way she was beginning to feel about the mayor, she knew that so long as she was seeing Ethan, nothing would happen.

After another half hour, she made her excuses and left. Forster gave her a goodbye hug that saw his fingers again caress the fastening of her bra, and arranged for them to meet later in the week to start getting the charity established.

CHAPTER SEVENTY
2 AUGUST

Dear Diary

I let Derek seduce me and forsook every vow I said in God's house.

Howard must never learn of this secret.

I no longer feel that I can cuddle my husband because I fear he'll feel my betrayal against his skin.

My marriage lies broken around me and I do not have the strength to fix it.

If Howard learns of what I've done, he'll be destroyed. I cannot let that happen.

Goodbye, Dear Diary. You've been a good friend to me. A companion through my life. You've never judged me. I, however, have judged myself, and I'm broken by what I've become.

P.S. At least I'll soon see poor darling Harriet once again, and am safe knowing that whoever raped and killed her will be going to Hell.

CHAPTER SEVENTY-ONE

Beth raised her glass in a silent toast to the day's successes. Ethan chinked his pint against her wine glass and gave her a smile before he continued with his story.

Rather than dine somewhere in Penrith, they'd driven the five miles to Langwathby. It had been Ethan's suggestion and Beth liked the idea of having him to herself without any of their friends joining them at any point. They both knew a lot of people in Penrith, and by coming out to the Drover's Rest they'd reduced the chances of interruptions to their conversation. Being out here would also mean she could focus on Ethan rather than get distracted with her habit of scanning her surroundings looking for the man with kisses tattooed on his neck.

The Drover's Rest was a typical village hotel-cum-pub. There was a small dining room and a comfortable bar which had a beamed ceiling and an earthy, yet homely feel. It was the kind of place where strangers are a welcome distraction to the regulars. Pewter tankards hung from eyehooks screwed into the beams and there was more chance of getting a flight to the moon than a cocktail.

'So there we are, treating this woman for a broken wrist when her husband appears at the ambulance door. He's naked from the waist up and his jeans are hanging down low enough to show that he's wearing women's underwear.' Ethan took a drink of his pint. 'Next thing, this big bloke comes tearing out of the house, apologising to the woman. He's six three at least, built like the proverbial brick outhouse with a shaved head and a beard you could hide a badger in. Thing is, he's wearing a bright-red dress with a split in the side that's opening up enough to show his stocking tops.'

'So what did you do?'

'The only thing I could do. I leaned out the window and said, "I'm sorry, madam, but we're treating a patient" and left him for the husband to deal with.'

'Oh my god. What happened next?'

'We took her to hospital and she got her arm fixed. Turns out she knew her husband liked to wear women's clothing, but she didn't know her brother did as well.'

'So how did she break her wrist?' Beth lifted her drink and guided the straw to her mouth.

'She did that when she punched the brother.' Ethan fiddled with a beer mat. 'She wasn't very big, but by hell she was a wild woman. Even with her broken wrist she wanted to go back out and have another go at him.'

Beth scrunched round the table a little so she was close enough to lay her head on Ethan's shoulder for a moment. It was an act of intimacy, but she wanted him to know how she was feeling and she'd always believed actions spoke louder than words. As much as she found Ethan handsome, it was his caring nature that drew her to him more than anything. On their first date, he'd been passionate when telling her about his job and the various highs and lows it brought into his life.

She drained her glass and went to the bar to get some more drinks as Ethan stepped outside for a cigarette. He claimed not to be a heavy smoker, but his smoking was the one thing about him that she didn't like. To her, smoking was a smelly habit that shortened lives, but it was his life, and so far, he'd always made sure that he had mints to hide the smoke on his breath.

O'Dowd had called her earlier to let her know that Cooper had confessed in the hope of getting a lesser sentence when his case went to trial. The only victim he'd stood firm on not being responsible for was Felicia Evans.

As a rule Beth wasn't a big drinker, but tonight was a night for celebration. Not only had she caught a murderer and a rapist, but she'd also got the necessary evidence to guarantee a conviction. Ethan could leave his car in the car park; she'd run him through for it in the morning.

Beth suddenly realised the subtext behind her plan of having more drinks than usual. She was building her confidence up so she could take Ethan to bed.

They chatted for an hour, and as Ethan went to visit the bathroom, a man walked into the bar. As a reflex action borne of long habit, her eyes flicked to his neck.

Beth's mouth tightened when she saw the two lipstick kisses tattooed onto the side of the man's neck. One pink and the other scarlet.

The man asked the barman for his usual as Beth turned her face away from him.

Kisses. Tattoo. Pain. Justice. The four words were shouted in her head, but her mouth never uttered a sound.

She'd been looking for this man for four years.

He was one of the men who'd been fighting the night a broken bottle had slammed into her cheek.

He wasn't the one who'd held the bottle, but he was the one who'd deflected it into her face.

Ethan came over with a last drink for them while they waited for the taxi to arrive. All Beth wanted to do was go and confront the man, ask if he knew who she was, demand to know if he'd ever thought about the innocent woman who'd fared worse than either him or the man he was fighting.

She'd dreamed of this moment and what she'd do should it ever arrive.

All those plans went from her mind as she sat and pretended to listen to what Ethan was saying. Now that she was in this position, she was at a loss as to what to do. Her instincts told her to stay calm and to try to learn more about the man. To find out who he was, to discover who he'd been fighting, as his opponent had been the one to escalate the fight by smashing the bottle to use as a weapon.

It might have been the wine she'd drunk or the fact the man at the bar had never been punished for his part in her disfigurement, but something made Beth throw caution to the wind.

She rose to her feet, grabbed her purse and strode over to the bar, her heels pocking on the tiled floor.

When she got to the bar she made sure that she was at Neck Kisses' right-hand side so her scarred cheek would be on full view. He didn't look her way, wasn't bothered about anything except his mobile.

Beth made sure her voice was a little louder than it needed to be. 'Can I get two bags of cheese and onion crisps, please?' She added a little slur to her voice for effect, but she'd never felt more sober.

Neck Kisses turned and flicked his eyes over her. There was no spark of recognition. He took in the scar, but he didn't look at it any more or any less than most people. All he did was give her a polite nod and twist his head back to his mobile.

Now she knew he didn't recognise her, Beth felt a strong sense of elation. She'd be able to come back here another time. She'd engage him in conversation, find out who he was and then she'd be able to pounce. Get the justice she'd always been denied.

A double-beep from outside signalled the taxi had arrived.

As they travelled back to Penrith, Beth took Ethan's hand in hers. Today had been a good day and she didn't want it to end.

When Ethan leaned in for a kiss, Beth responded with a hunger she hadn't realised was inside her.

CHAPTER SEVENTY-TWO

Beth printed off the transcription of Cooper's interview and the subsequent confession and started inputting the details into her spreadsheet. The more she read, the more she felt that her theory about Cooper and Felicia Evans was correct.

Cooper had denied killing and sexually abusing Felicia Evans and despite seeing first-hand what a monster he was, she believed him on this point. When she'd shared her concerns with O'Dowd, the DI had been dismissive and had demanded proof, as she believed he wasn't coughing to that murder as he'd not actually been able to penetrate the dying woman himself.

Regardless of this, Beth had spent the day poring over her spreadsheet and every report she could find.

O'Dowd was preparing to leave when Beth called her over.

'What is it, Beth?' O'Dowd looked at her watch. 'It's the hubster's birthday today and we're going out for a meal. He'll also expect to come across to my side of the bed tonight, so I'm going to need time to shave my legs before we go out.'

It took all of Beth's self-control to blot out the mental images O'Dowd's words were painting.

'I have evidence that Cooper didn't kill Felicia Evans.'

'Show me.'

Beth turned her monitor round so O'Dowd could see the spreadsheet. 'The search of Cooper's house didn't unearth two vital things. Number one, Felicia's nightie. We know he kept the clothes of his other victims, so hers being missing is an anomaly.'

'It's little more than circumstantial. I need something better.'

'Please, let me finish what I'm saying, ma'am. They also failed to find any kind of sex toy that could have caused the internal injuries Felicia had. Most of all, the timings were wrong; the more I thought about it, the more I realised that he had to build himself up to the attacks. Even when he had Willow at his mercy, he took his time preparing both Willow and himself for the attack Kieran and I thwarted. There's another key fact, and that's that he was raping them because he needed to get his rocks off via penetration. Whomever it was who murdered Felicia didn't have penetrative sex with her. Instead they used a sex toy.'

'Are you sure of that? What if he did his thing and then used the sex toy to cover his tracks?'

Beth nodded. 'I thought of that too, but it still stands that there was no sex toy found at his house. If he was changing his methods then he would have had one to use on Willow Brown, wouldn't he?'

'Dammit, Beth. Are you certain there's another murderous rapist out there?'

'Yes and no. When I got as far as I've just explained to you, I checked what Digital Forensics got from Cooper's iPad. He was watching porn well into the early hours of last Monday morning. Right around the time Felicia was being killed and her corpse defiled.' Beth looked into O'Dowd's eyes. 'You know all the accusations against the mayor? Well I think that Felicia was killed and the mayor's credit card was dumped with her so the mayor would be tied to her murder. In effect, she was killed so her corpse could be used to frame the mayor. Also, Digital Forensics found a whole load of pictures of the other victims on Cooper's mobile, but none of Felicia.'

'Shit, shite and buggery.' Another look at the watch. 'He'll go spare if I have to call off tonight. Can you track down the mayor and tell him to stay in a hotel? He needs to be protected.'

'Of course, ma'am.'

*

Beth walked into the foyer of the Halston Hotel in Carlisle and asked for directions to the Lonsdale Suite. She'd remembered Forster had told her he was attending a function here, and when he hadn't answered his mobile, she'd travelled up to Carlisle to find him face to face.

She could have done without having to drive to Carlisle as she'd hoped to meet up with Ethan when his shift finished.

The receptionist gave her directions to the Lonsdale Suite and as she walked along the corridors, Beth flashed back to childhood memories of being brought to the cinema which had once stood on this site.

When she entered the room she had to cast her eyes around every table until she found Forster. As befitted his station, he was seated at a table next to the small stage where a well-dressed man was delivering a speech about affordable housing.

Beth was aware the eyes of the room were on her as she weaved between the various tables until she reached Forster. The tap she gave his shoulder startled him, but he recovered his composure in a flash.

'I need to talk to you. Urgently.'

A sharp nod. 'Two minutes.'

Beth left the mayor to make his apologies and made her way back to the corridor.

Forster was as good as his word and joined Beth as she was tapping out a message to Ethan.

'What is it?' His face was flushed and Beth caught traces of brandy on his breath.

'It's not good news, I'm afraid. I've spent today reviewing the case against the Lakeland Ripper.'

'Yes?'

Beth caught more than just inquisition in the single word. There was a trace of apprehension and possibly even a quiver of fear.

'Specifically I was looking at the murder of Felicia Evans. The Lakeland Ripper denied killing her and we found no evidence whatsoever to tie him to her murder.'

'I don't follow you.' A glance back at the Lonsdale Suite. 'Can you explain what you're getting at, please?'

'I'm sorry to have to tell you this, but we believe that Felicia Evans was killed for the sole purpose of framing you. When you put everything together it's a definite campaign. First the minor attacks, then the child abuse images were secreted onto your computer so they'd be there when your PC was taken in response to the anonymous letter sent to the chief constable. When the letter sat unopened for almost a fortnight, the person framing you escalated his campaign by stealing your credit card and then leaving it beside Felicia Evans's corpse. There was even an invitation to one of your Christmas balls to make it crystal clear which Derek Forster owned the credit card.'

Beth used a soft tone as she spoke, but there was no lessening the impact of her words. The colour drained from the mayor's face and he looked as if he was about to collapse.

'Are you sure? Please, tell me this is a sick joke.' There was no mistaking the beseeching tone or the look of desperation in Forster's eyes.

'I'm sorry, but while we can never be certain of anything without hard evidence, everything we've worked out suggests that what I'm telling you is correct.'

'Oh God. That poor woman. She died because of me. Because someone hates me. Surely ruining me isn't as precious as that lady's life?'

'If it helps, and I don't expect that it does, she had terminal cancer and only had a few weeks to live.'

The mayor shook his head then knuckled at both of his eyes. 'It doesn't help. She died because of me. Nothing you say, however well-meaning, will help. She died because of me and I have to find a way to live with that fact.'

Beth was full of sympathy for Forster, but she still hadn't got to the reason why she was here.

'You will. However, you've more pressing concerns at the moment. We believe the person who killed Felicia Evans will try and attack you again. Only now that everything else he's tried has failed, we're concerned that he'll try and attack you in person.' Beth locked eyes with Forster as she was unsure her words were sinking in. 'We'd like you to stay in a hotel tonight until we can organise some protection for you or catch the person who's trying to frame you.'

Forster gave a shake of his head as if he could toss out the bad thoughts and escape the fact his life may well be under threat.

'No. No way. I won't hear of it. I'm not staying in a hotel. If this… this despicable fiend is going to target me, then there's no way on earth I'm having anyone else's life put at risk.' Another shake of the head. 'I'll stay in my own home and take my chances.'

'Derek. That's not a good idea. You'll be safer in a hotel.'

'Maybe. But it's bad enough one person has died because of me. There's no way I'm prepared to gamble that the person after me won't kill a hotel worker or another guest to get at me. Not happening.'

Behind Forster, Beth saw the doors to the Lonsdale Suite open and a smartly attired woman approach them.

'Derek, is everything okay? You're due to say your piece in a couple of minutes.'

Forster gave his head another shake and took a deep breath. 'I'm fine.' His gaze shifted to Beth. 'I've a speech to give and then I've got the closing address to make. After that, I'm going home.'

The determination in Forster's expression told Beth that it would be a waste of time arguing with him. She made a snap decision and fired a question at Forster.

He looked at the ceiling before answering her. 'Around eleven I should imagine.'

'Fine. I'll pick you up then.'

CHAPTER SEVENTY-THREE

Beth settled herself into a chair and smiled at the message from Ethan. It was a welcome spot of light relief as Forster had been more than a little difficult. He'd taken the news about Felicia Evans's murder hard, and when she'd arrived back at Halston Hotel to pick him up he'd been on the verge of being drunk.

She'd debated going home to pick up a change of clothes and her toothbrush, but had decided against it. Instead she'd nipped to Asda after grabbing a McDonald's.

Forster had argued about the need for her to stay at his house, but having seen how much he'd drunk, there was no way Beth was going to back down.

He'd continued drinking when he'd got home and when he'd tottered off to bed, he was paralytic. When she'd heard the click of a lock being turned in the solid bedroom door, she'd retrieved a chair from a spare bedroom and had positioned herself where she could ambush anyone who came up the stairs.

Beth had called Control and requested another officer to stand guard with her, but she'd ended up getting a mouthful from an Inspector who'd come on the line and told her that without a direct order from the silver commander – the senior officer who was on call for major incidents – there weren't any officers to spare for an unspecified risk.

It had crossed Beth's mind to call O'Dowd so she could get her to put the request to the ACC, who was this week's silver commander, until a shudder-inducing memory of the DI's plans for the evening changed her mind.

The more she thought about it, the more she doubted that anything would happen tonight, but that didn't stop her from making sure her collapsible baton was fully extended and laid across her lap. Beside the chair she had placed a pair of ornate candlesticks. As makeshift weapons they were heavy and cumbersome, but their presence at her side reassured her.

She adjusted herself in the chair and prepared a reply to Ethan's message. Once that was sent, she bent her mind to the case and tried to work out who was framing the mayor.

Beth woke with a start. At first she was unsure where she was, but she soon realised she was in the mayor's house.

She wasn't sure what had woken her but there was a strange whooshing roar coming from downstairs.

It was decision time. She could either wait where she was and prepare for whoever came up the stairs or she could go down and investigate.

Beth chose to wait. She lifted one of the candlesticks and stood at a point of the landing where she could see who was coming up the stairs. If they were wearing a mask or carrying a weapon of any kind, the candlestick would be launched at their head.

Nobody came, but the whooshing roar increased.

Beth realised what the roar was and her blood turned to ice as the first wisps of smoke started to wind their way upwards.

Even so, she had to have confirmation.

Ten seconds later she had it when she saw the tendrils of smoke emanating from underneath the door of Forster's study.

'Shit. Derek.'

As she dashed back upstairs to wake the mayor, Beth was certain the fire was no accident and was the work of the person framing the mayor. She used one hand to dial treble nine on her mobile as the other reached for the handle of Forster's bedroom door.

The ancient handle turned, but the door didn't open.

'Hello, fire brigade please.'

As Beth gave the operator Forster's address, she remembered the clicking sound as Forster had closed the door. It was locked and there was little that she could do to change that fact.

Her eyes landed on the heavy candlestick that stood beside the chair she'd slept in.

'*I've got three appliances on their way to you now.*'

'Please, hurry. There's someone in the house with me and he's unconscious in a room that's locked.'

Beth lifted the candlestick with her free hand.

'*Do you have a key for the room?*'

'No. He locked it from the inside.'

'*We'll have someone with you in less than five minutes. Can you get out?*'

Beth drove the candlestick into the door. She was aiming where the lock was, but all that happened was the candlestick vibrating in her hand from the impact.

'Yes, but the mayor's in there. I need to save him.'

'*I hear what you're saying, but you need to get out. We're four minutes away.*'

'We're upstairs.'

Beth cut the call and picked up the candlestick with both hands. She picked her target as she drew the candlestick back and launched it forward with every bit of strength she could muster.

Once again the candlestick did nothing more than bounce off the door.

A splintering whoosh sounded from below and smoke came billowing up the stairs.

Beth stopped what she was doing and risked a look over the bannister. Through the peels of smoke she saw yellow flame tongues.

Five, six, seven times she slammed the candlestick into the door. All she achieved was a series of dents in the wood.

The smoke was now so thick that she was coughing and choking as she fell to her knees. For the first time since learning the fire was spreading, Beth realised she was trapped. She kept her nose to the carpet and crawled to the bathroom, where she soaked a bath towel and draped it over her shoulders.

Beth trembled with fear as she crawled back to the landing. Her attempts to break into Forster's bedroom and save him hadn't just failed, they'd put her life at risk. It galled her that she had to abandon him, but she knew there was no way she was going to get through that door without a fire axe. She just had to put her trust in the fire brigade and hope they'd arrive in time to save him.

Opposite the mayor's room was another bedroom and that's where Beth went. She closed the door behind her and, after a deep breath, stood and whipped the duvet off the bed then stuffed it against the bottom of the door to limit the amount of smoke coming into the room.

Back on her knees she crawled to the window. Her fear that the sliding sash had been painted closed proved unfounded when she tested it and found it lifted with ease.

She knew that opening the window was a bad idea as it would give the fire below more oxygen, but it was still a better idea than staying put and inhaling any more smoke. As it was she was coughing after every breath and her eyes were streaming.

Beth heaved the window up and put her head outside so she could get some of the clear air that was instantly being drawn into the room.

She looked down. There was a heavy window ledge she could use to hang down and drop the few feet to the ground.

As plans went it was a good one apart from a single fact.

Fire was pulsing out from a window directly below. If she dropped straight down, she'd pass through the flames. While they might not harm her, if she fell the wrong way, she'd land in the fire.

The roaring whoosh of the fire on the landing was growing louder as Beth endured another coughing fit.

She looked up. Two fire engines were barrelling across Eden Bridge towards the house. They were maybe a hundred yards away.

Beth did a quick calculation. Twenty seconds to arrive and draw to a halt. Ten to spot her and at least thirty more before a ladder could be put to the window.

A minute wasn't a long time, but it was too long for her to stay in a smoke-filled room.

She crawled out onto the window ledge and perched like a gargoyle.

Beth straightened her legs as powerfully as she could and aimed for the patch of grass at the other side of a gravel path that skirted the house.

As her feet neared the grass she let the tension go out of her legs and rolled as soon as she made contact.

The impact knocked what little air was in her lungs, but when she gasped for air, the air she got was sweet and pure.

As she pulled herself to her feet, Beth was urging the first of the firefighters to come her way to save the mayor.

The next thing she knew a firefighter was pulling her back to a place of safety as hoses were run out and the house fell under siege to torrents of water.

CHAPTER SEVENTY-FOUR

There was nothing quite like the smell from a house fire. It held elements of woodsmoke from burnt timber, traces of charred fabrics and the unmistakable stench of electrical components that had been caught in the blaze.

The house's roof was intact, but all of the windows had blown out and the raging flames had left soot stains on the walls above each opening. Old houses like this one with their lath and plaster walls burned quickly due to the amount of tinder-dry timber within the construction.

Firefighters moved through the wreckage of the house and there were several different agencies represented. The police were there, as was a fire investigator, and tragically, also one of the vans used to transport bodies to the mortuary.

The fire investigator had a dog sitting patiently at his side. Beth surmised it would be an Accelerant Dog, trained to identify the use of substances such as petrol or kerosene in cases where arson was suspected.

A TV news crew were present, as was a crowd of onlookers.

Beth stood with O'Dowd and looked at the house as two firemen carried out a stretcher bearing a body bag. She knew it was more her imagination than anything else, but Beth would have sworn she could smell the roasted pork scent of charred human flesh.

There would have to be a formal identification, but Beth knew it was Derek Forster's body which was being loaded into the back of the plain white van. A firefighter had told Beth and O'Dowd the body had been found in the remains of a four-poster bed.

That Forster had stayed in his bed suggested to Beth that he died from smoke inhalation rather than being burnt alive. It was a small mercy in the circumstances.

The overriding feeling that Beth had was one of guilt. She'd failed to save Forster. Had fallen asleep when she was guarding him. She'd failed to awaken him or even get through the door and drag him out.

There was also disappointment. She believed in, and wanted, Forster's charity to be established, but she knew that with him dead, the charity would never be founded without its main driving force and principal benefactor. She could have a stab at it herself, but without Forster and his connections, she'd be fighting a battle she was never going to win.

The fire investigator beckoned them over, his head shaking with an unvoiced fury.

'I'm sorry to have to tell you this, but you're looking at murder. There's a brick in the middle of the floor in what I'm guessing was a study. There were also remnants of a broken bottle there and an intense burning that's synonymous with an accelerant.' He pulled a face as he ruffled the back of the Accelerant Dog's neck. 'Nige here barked his head off when I took him near the bottle. There's no doubt in my mind this was arson.'

Beth got the picture at once. Someone had lobbed a brick through Forster's window and had followed it up with a petrol bomb.

It was a simple way to start a fire, and what it lacked in subtlety, it made up for in effectiveness.

Another wave of guilt hit Beth. If she'd not abandoned her job to attend the party, Forster may still be alive. The same applied to her date with Ethan. Had she been working on her theory about the mayor being targeted by someone other than the Lakeland Ripper, she may have been able to prevent a murder. There was also the feeling that she should have realised sooner that the mayor himself may come under threat and taken measures to protect him. With everything the framer had tried having failed, she should have anticipated his next move.

Beth knew that it was a leap to assume it was the framer who'd torched the mayor's house, but considering everything else the framer had done, it made logical sense to think he was behind the mayor's murder.

The weight of her guilt became suffocating as Beth revisited her idea that her life was currently on a good day, bad day cycle. She should have been aware that bad would follow the good and put her own agendas aside.

As she walked back to where her car was parked, Beth found herself plagued with doubts about her ability to focus on the job at hand. She'd been swayed by thoughts of doing some good for society and had abandoned her post when there was still a murderer to catch. That couldn't happen again, if she was to retain her place in FMIT; she had to put the case first, second and third.

The theory she'd had about Felicia Evans's killer seemed like their best lead, but she wasn't sure about it.

Beth took a deep breath. 'Ma'am, I've had an idea about something, but I'm not sure I'm on the right track.'

'I don't care. You're going home. You've been through enough.'

'With all due respect, ma'am, I'm not going home. I've a killer to catch. He killed a man who intended to help a lot of victims of sexual assault. Without Derek, that charity will never happen, it's not just Derek I've failed, it's all the people who could and would have been helped by the charity. Please, ma'am, don't send me home. Not now. I feel bad enough about not saving Derek as it is. I *have* to catch his killer.'

Beth felt the look O'Dowd gave her was burrowing into her soul, but she stood her ground and made her face as determined as she could.

'What are you thinking?'

'Felicia Evans only had a couple of weeks to live, right? Yet she was killed and sexually violated, but Dr Hewson suggested that she was assaulted with an object rather than raped.'

'I do know all of this.' O'Dowd scowled as she pulled her cigarettes from a pocket. 'Get to your point.'

Beth needed to track it all out so O'Dowd could follow her thinking. 'Hear me out, please.'

The DI gave a roll of her hand for Beth to continue.

'We think Felicia Evans was killed to set up the mayor. The sexual assault was done post-mortem to make it appear as if she was killed by the same person as killed the other three women.'

'Hang on, how did he link the three other murders when the investigating officers didn't?'

'He didn't have to link them. One of them was from Carlisle. Harriet Quantrell's murder would be on the news and in the papers. I know we have no proof, but if he'd heard about her murder, there's no saying he didn't take inspiration from it when trying to frame the mayor. That's why the mayor's credit card was left by her body; to incriminate him.'

'And your point is?'

'Felicia was murdered a few weeks before cancer would have killed her. The odds of someone being murdered in Cumbria are very low, that's a given. But, it happened to her. I told you earlier that I think she was deliberately chosen as a victim because she had terminal cancer, because she lived alone, because she wasn't a social person. The person trying to get the mayor into trouble probably rationalised to him or herself that killing someone who was dying was less of a crime. They may even have told themselves they were doing Felicia a favour euthanising her the way a vet puts animals to sleep.'

O'Dowd nodded and flicked ash from her cigarette.

'Felicia Evans wasn't a friendly woman; she'd didn't engage in any of the gossip that's a normal part of rural life. None of her neighbours knew anything about her. They didn't know about her family, her interests or her likes. None of the people I spoke to knew of anyone who'd exchanged a more personal comment than "good morning" or "nice day" with her.'

O'Dowd dropped her cigarette butt down a road drain. 'What are you getting at, Beth?'

'Not many people would know she was close to death. But if we work on the theory her killer selected her because they knew she was dying, we should be looking at the people who knew about her cancer.' Beth pointed at Forster's house. 'Look at the progression, ma'am. First the chief constable received an anonymous letter, but when that wasn't opened for almost a fortnight, then someone killed a dying woman and tried to frame the mayor again, by somehow stealing his credit card and leaving it beside Felicia's body.'

'Then when we arrested Forster and found all that child abuse on his computer, it didn't stack up because the guys at Digital Forensics worked out it had been planted, but someone had put it there for a reason. When that didn't work, he tossed a brick and then a petrol bomb through the mayor's window to kill him.'

Beth was pleased O'Dowd had taken control of the conversation as it meant they were passengers on the same train.

Beth had a thought and she wasn't pleased with it. 'You know what? I think that now the mayor is dead, whoever is behind it will go back to their normal life. They've achieved their aims. Maybe they wanted to ruin the mayor rather than kill him, but they were swept up by events and ended up killing him. Whichever it is, they've no reason to continue now that Forster's dead. I think that if we trace everyone who knew about Felicia having cancer we'll be able to find the person who killed her and the mayor.'

'I'd like to think you're right. However, we don't know the killer's motive. Forster may have just been the first person on his shit list. Find out everyone who might have known about her cancer and check them out.'

CHAPTER SEVENTY-FIVE

Beth was in the Oncology ward of Cumberland Infirmary waiting for Felicia's doctor and the head of the Administration department. As it was only a mile or so away from the mayor's house, it was the logical place to start.

In the absence of friends and family who'd know about Felicia's cancer, she'd come to the hospital. While patient files were confidential, there would always be some leakage of information and it wasn't beyond the bounds of possibility that the killer was someone who worked at the hospital.

Beth recognised the doctor when he came into the room. He was a genial enough fellow for someone who dealt with death on a regular basis. The same could not be said for the head of administration.

She was mid-fifties and wore her job title as if it was a crown. Her spectacles rested on the tip of her nose and she had her head tilted back to see through them. Everything about the woman told Beth that she'd have a tough job getting any kind of help from her.

'Hello again.' The doctor offered a hand which Beth shook. 'This is Ms Chisholm.'

Ms Chisholm folded her arms when Beth put out her hand.

'I'm sorry to trouble you again.' Beth was doing her best to be placatory, but Ms Chisholm's attitude was making her want to threaten the woman with an Obstruction of Justice charge. 'I'm afraid that I need to talk to you about Felicia Evans again.' She looked around the ward. 'Is there somewhere we can talk in private?'

When they'd each taken a seat in the small chapel at the end of the Oncology ward, Beth explained why she was there.

'That is a ridiculous accusation.' Ms Chisholm's mouth puckered into a tight knot that reminded Beth of a cat's backside. 'I can assure you that not one of my staff would ever do such a thing. To even suggest it is deplorable.'

Beth took care to keep her anger out of her voice. She'd been expecting that kind of response from the older woman. 'I hear what you're saying, Ms Chisholm. But I have to ask you a few questions. How many staff do you have on the Oncology team? Are they all permanent, or are some of them temps? How many of them have money worries? Do you know who their friends are? Their enemies? We may well be wrong in our assumption, but to honour the victim, you understand that, don't you, we have to pursue every line of enquiry, however unlikely it may seem?'

Ms Chisholm leaned back into her chair. Her expression didn't give much away, but Beth could tell her words had had the desired effect. The head of the admin department was now deep in thought and a little cowed.

Beth turned to the doctor. 'I'll need a full list of the nurses and doctors who would have had access to Felicia Evans's file. I'd also be grateful if you could include the information for any cleaning and janitorial staff who might have had contact with Ms Evans.' She had a thought. 'If you could get me the names of the staff who were on duty throughout last Sunday night and Monday morning, that would be very useful.'

'That's when she was murdered, wasn't it? You want to know who was working so you can rule them out of your investigation, do you?'

'You're very perceptive.' Beth's attempt at flattery bounced off Ms Chisholm without having any effect. 'I'm guessing that the admin team you oversee are pretty much nine-to-fivers. I'll need to have the names of everyone who could have accessed Ms

Evans's file, regardless of whether or not they're connected to the Oncology department.'

'I'll get you what you need.' A vicious twinkle filled Ms Chisholm's eyes. 'You'll have your work cut out though. There are more than two hundred administration staff across the hospital and any of them can log into the computer and look up a patient. None of them should access a patient's confidential medical records unless it's to do with their job, but that doesn't mean it can't happen.'

'Really?' Beth couldn't hide the dismay in her voice. She had expected that there may be up to a dozen admin staff involved in Oncology; two hundred was a hell of a lot of people to run checks on and possibly interview.

'I'm afraid that there'll be at least two or three dozen medical staff to add to your list as well, plus the same again for cleaning, welfare and janitorial who may have met Mrs Evans as they went about their jobs.'

Beth tried not to let her frustration at this turn of events show in her face. Looking into the best part of three hundred people would take for ever. The supposed help they were promised had never arrived and now they were after someone who was getting more direct with their methods. If O'Dowd was right and the person who'd killed Forster had other scores to settle, there might be other people in the killer's sights.

A thought jolted her from her doldrums. It was one she felt she should have had earlier, but she'd been distracted by the idea of investigating hundreds of people.

Beth turned to Ms Chisholm. 'The software that you use to manage patient files, does it show who has accessed particular files?'

'Yes, it can.'

The curtness of the woman's reply informed Beth that Ms Chisholm had thought of this herself but had deigned to hold the information back.

'Good, I'd like you to get me the names, addresses and national insurance numbers of everyone who accessed Ms Evans's records before she was brutally murdered.'

Ms Chisholm didn't move until the doctor asked her to go and bring the information. Her reluctance made Beth wonder if she'd find the woman's name in the log. It wouldn't be a surprise to her to learn Ms Chisholm made random checks of files to see if details were being fed in properly.

As much as she disliked Ms Chisholm, Beth felt the woman would favour acerbic put-downs to murder when she was crossed.

'I take it that I'm on your list of suspects as well?' The doctor's genial tone suggested he wasn't in the least bit worried about being a murder suspect.

'Everyone is a suspect until we can rule them out.'

'Fair enough.' The doctor gave a nonchalant shrug. 'I was working last Sunday night. You probably won't take my word for it, but the staff rotas will show I was here from three on Sunday afternoon until three on Monday morning. One of my patients had a bad turn after surgery and I had to oversee their care.'

Beth chatted with the doctor until Ms Chisholm came back and handed over a collection of printouts. 'Here you go. This is the full list of all those who accessed Ms Evans's file and their details. We have had some IT issues of late, but I think they're accurate.'

'Thanks.' Beth flicked through a couple of the printouts as an idea came to her. 'You say you've had IT issues, who looks after your IT systems? Is it a local company, or is there a national one which looks after lots of hospitals?'

'We have our own experts. The hospital trust felt it was more economical to hire our own rather than outsource the work.'

'Okay. Do you think you can get me their details as well, please?'

Ms Chisholm tapped the printouts. 'Already done.'

CHAPTER SEVENTY-SIX

Beth's fingers danced across the keyboard without missing a step. After leaving the hospital she'd got the same type of information from the company who managed the community care and had come back to Carleton Hall so she could check out everyone.

The first thing she'd done was write the name 'Doug' beneath Unthank's scrawled 'what do you call a man holding a spade?' on the whiteboard.

Despite there being more than a hundred names on her list, she'd chopped the list down to thirty by – at least initially – excluding the women. While it was possible the killer was a woman, statistics showed that women rarely killed in cold blood. The murders they committed were in self-defence, or maybe they'd stab their husband with a carving knife after enduring years of abuse.

Had it not been for the sexual element of the attack on Felicia, Beth wouldn't have excluded the women at all. No matter how she tried to imagine a woman debasing the corpse of another woman in such a way, she couldn't conjure up the mental image.

Only a small percentage of the admin staff were male, which meant she was mostly looking at doctors, male nurses and a janitor as well as two carers. When she was almost done she got to the names of the two IT specialists employed by the hospital trust. As soon as she saw the names she realised she'd gone about the process the wrong way.

The IT specialists should have been her first suspects. The child abuse images planted onto Forster's computer had shown that the person targeting the mayor had considerable IT skills.

She checked out the first name. The details that came back to her held nothing of note. They hadn't been arrested for anything, and when she ran the national insurance number she saw the person was two years younger than she was.

While it was wrong to assume anything to do with a suspect that wasn't backed up by hard evidence, Beth felt that the killer was an older person.

The second IT specialist she looked at was a different matter. He had two arrests for assault on his record and three for threatening behaviour. The fact he had a temper put him in the frame for being the killer, but when Beth thought about him, she realised she'd heard his name before.

She pulled up the spreadsheet she'd created for the Lakeland Ripper and searched it for 'Howard Stanton'. She found it against the details of Harriet Quantrell's family. He was the uncle who'd overreacted through grief. As Harriet was his niece, he'd have known all the details about what had happened to her. That explained how he'd known to violate his victim anally as well as vaginally. Maybe he believed the mayor was responsible and, in his own twisted way, was trying to bring him to justice.

The next thing Beth looked at was Stanton's marital status and when she saw he was bereaved, she couldn't help but wonder if there was a connection between this fact and his anger. If there was, the question would be which had come first: his wife's death, or his anger?

She checked the dates and saw that while Howard Stanton's wife had died a year ago, his arrests had been spread over a number of years, which indicated that his temper was something he'd had before losing his niece and then his wife, although the two deaths may well have tipped him towards a murderous level of grief.

The counterpoint to this was that Stanton's arrests had never been followed through. Not once had there been enough evidence to charge him.

Out of curiosity, Beth took a quick look at Stanton's wife. A police report showed she had committed suicide.

Beth's first thought was that Karen Stanton had escaped her abuser by slitting her wrists in the bath after downing a bottle of Prosecco. Her second thought was that Karen had been Howard Stanton's first victim. Her murder made to look like suicide.

As she scanned the details of Karen's death, Beth saw an entry that made her blood run cold and boil at the same time.

A rapid google search got her the telephone number she needed.

Two minutes after dialling the number, she was heading along the corridor to DCI Phinn's office. She knew that's where O'Dowd was and that Phinn would want to know her news as well.

She winced at the knock she'd given the oak door of Phinn's office. Rather than a respectful rat-a-tat, she'd given the purposeful machine gun of a knock that she used when going to a suspect's house to enforce an arrest.

'Come in.' Phinn's instruction wasn't a bellow, but neither was it a whisper. The volume and tone the DCI used suggested that the reason for his being interrupted had better be a good one.

Beth strode into the room, her excitement at identifying a solid suspect overriding her worry about any reprimand she might get for disturbing them.

'I know who was trying to set up the mayor, and who probably killed him.'

'Who?' O'Dowd and Phinn asked the question at the same time.

'Howard Stanton. He works as an IT specialist at Cumberland Infirmary, which means he would have been able to access Felicia Evans's medical records. His wife used to work as a PA for the mayor, his niece was the Lakeland Killer's third victim and he's got form. He's twice been arrested for assault, and three times for threatening behaviour. He'd even interviewed for a job with the mayor's company, SimpleBooker, before the mayor sold it, which means Stanton missed out on a quarter million bonus when the company was sold.

Beth had got this last piece of information by calling the SimpleBooker office and asking Inga if Howard Stanton's name was familiar to her.

Phinn reached for the phone on his desk. 'Do you have an address for him?'

Beth gave him the Post-it note she'd used to jot Stanton's address on.

'Well done, lass.' Phinn looked at his watch. 'I'll have a team lift Stanton and take him to Durranhill Station for you.'

'Tell them not to go in until we get there.' O'Dowd rose from her chair. 'C'mon, Beth. This is one collar you're not going to have to make alone.'

CHAPTER SEVENTY-SEVEN

Wetheral was one of Carlisle's satellite villages. Where once it had housed a mixture of families, rising property prices meant Wetheral had become the home of many of Carlisle's professionals. The large detached houses with spacious gardens were owned by doctors, teachers, lawyers and accountants. The house listed as Howard Stanton's address was one of only a few semi-detached properties in the village.

Behind Beth and O'Dowd, a van emptied six PCs who'd been sent along to make the arrest. The largest PC carried an Enforcer.

Known unofficially as the Big Red Key, the Enforcer was a simple battering ram with two handles. In the right hands, the Big Red Key could apply more than three tonnes of impact force to whatever it struck.

O'Dowd directed three of the PCs to watch the rear.

Beth walked up the gravel path behind O'Dowd and watched as the DI banged on the door.

Four times O'Dowd knocked and hollered for Stanton, but there wasn't a sound, and when Beth glanced through the windows, the house looked to be deserted.

O'Dowd turned and pointed at the PC holding the Big Red Key. 'Hey, Ali Baba, time for open sesame.'

With a grin on his face, Ali Baba stepped forward. One grunted swing later and the door was open. The PCs swarmed into the house and shouts of 'clear' reverberated outwards as they checked every room.

Beth and O'Dowd followed them in, but Beth wasn't expecting Stanton to be at home. The lack of a car on the drive suggested he was out, and after what he'd done last night, it would have been either foolish or egotistical of him to not expect the police would be coming for him soon.

If he'd gone on the run, he may well be tough to find, but she knew that unless he left the country, he'd make a mistake at some point and then they'd catch him.

While O'Dowd searched the living room, Beth entered the kitchen to see what she could find. The room was neat and tidy, but it had a lived-in feel to it. There were no unwashed dishes by the sink and when she opened the fridge the food looked to be fresh.

A laptop sat on the table beside a diary and when Beth lifted its lid, she saw a Post-it note with a jumbled series of letters and numbers on it that could only be a password.

She switched the laptop on and flipped through the diary as it powered up. When she came to the last entry she read it through twice and then closed her eyes in silent grief as she understood the whole picture.

Karen Stanton had slept with the mayor and, unable to handle the guilt she felt at cheating on her husband, had taken her own life. Her husband had been left widowed and at some point when he'd cleared out her things, he'd found the diary.

With a target to blame for his wife's and niece's deaths, he'd waged his campaign against the mayor, escalating as each step failed to get Forster into serious trouble.

What would have started out as a tragedy, had become a quest for vengeance in the form of an increasingly illegal campaign to smear the mayor's character and, when that didn't work, the mayor's murder.

In Beth's mind, Karen Stanton hadn't been avenged by her husband's actions, she'd been betrayed by his refusal to accept and understand what had happened.

As she lay down the diary and keyed the password into the laptop, Beth knew that a combination of Howard's anger and Karen's and Forster's mistake in sleeping together had set off a whole chain of events that had so far cost three people their lives.

The police being made aware of Cooper's actions, the prevention of Willow's rape and her life being saved were the only positives that had come out of the whole sorry mess.

Beth waited until the laptop had done its thing and had woken to show a picture of Harriet Quantrell with an older woman, she presumed was Karen Stanton, on the home screen.

A single tab was open on the taskbar, and when Beth clicked on it, she saw that it was a webpage for DFDS Seaways. The page showed a booking confirmation for a ferry leaving Newcastle at 8.00 p.m. that day.

Instinct made Beth look at her watch even though she knew that it was after four when they arrived at the house.

CHAPTER SEVENTY-EIGHT

As O'Dowd charged through the house spitting orders to the uniformed officers, Beth stood alone in the kitchen. Her fingers drummed against her stomach as thoughts whirled through her mind.

Stanton had known they would be coming. He'd left the laptop and diary where they'd be easy to find. He'd even left the password for his laptop. He was playing his end game, preparing for the next step.

Whether the ferry booking was a red herring to throw them off the scent or a genuine trip to begin a new life, there was no way of knowing. That would be O'Dowd's call to make not hers, although if she had her way, Stanton would be allowed the chance to board the ferry and then once aboard, he'd be easily picked up as he'd have nowhere to run.

A thought entered her head. It was strong enough to make her fingers pause mid-drum.

The laptop had been warm when she'd opened it. Warmer than the room's temperature warranted. Therefore it had been in use shortly before they had arrived.

Which meant that Stanton wasn't too far ahead of them.

The question was, where was he going: the ferry or elsewhere?

Something clicked inside Beth's mind. Stanton was in his end game. He was leaving; therefore he'd want to say goodbye.

'O'Dowd. Search. Papers.' Beth hadn't meant to shout, but she knew where Stanton was going. At least she knew the theory, if not the specific destination.

O'Dowd's head poked round the door frame.

'What the hell are you shouting about?'

'Stanton, ma'am. He's leaving. We've only just missed him but we have a chance to catch him if we can find it out.'

'Find what out?'

Beth looked up from the drawer she was rummaging through. 'Where his wife is buried. He's leaving. He still loved her. He'll have gone to say goodbye. Now please, stop asking questions and help me find something which will tell us where she was buried.'

CHAPTER SEVENTY-NINE

Beth whipped the wheel over and slid her car to a halt beside a large council van with a low trailer attached to its tow bar. O'Dowd was out the door before Beth had even pulled on the handbrake.

The cemetery was quiet save for the low hum of a mini digger excavating a new grave. When she took a look around the village's cemetery Beth saw seven people: two council workers, an elderly couple and three people standing by themselves. One of the three was a woman: that left the two men.

Both men were of a similar build to the file description of Stanton and, as both had their backs turned, they didn't know which one to approach first.

O'Dowd pointed at herself and then Beth as she assigned them each one of the men.

As she walked along the gravel path, Beth was watching O'Dowd's approach as well as keeping her eye on her own quarry. The closer she got, the more she was preparing herself for action. Should Stanton take flight, as had been proven with the pursuit of Gracie, she'd have to be the one to catch him.

O'Dowd's roar broke the serenity of the graveyard. 'Hoy! Come back here you bugger.'

Beth's body snapped into action by the time her head had twisted to look O'Dowd's way. Within two seconds, she'd wheeled round and was haring back towards the cemetery's gate. She knew she ought to take a direct route rather than follow the dog-leg of the gravel path, but she knew that any time she saved going straight at her quarry, would be lost by dodging the heavy headstones and avoiding standing on graves.

O'Dowd chased after Stanton, exhortations for him to stop spilling from her lips as she lumbered along.

When Beth got to the path's 90-degree corner she made the mistake of not slowing her pace. The gravel crunched beneath her pumping feet, but while it provided plenty of vertical support, it offered up no lateral strength to give her traction.

Her right leg was on the inside of the turn she was making and it was this foot which lost traction first.

She went down hard, rolled over twice and sprang back to her feet ignoring the rip to the knee of her trousers or the gravel rash her hands had picked up as she'd tried to break her fall.

The gate was only twenty yards away and she saw Stanton dash through it a clear ten yards ahead of O'Dowd.

Beth pumped her arms and legs as hard as she'd ever done and got to the gateway at the same time as she heard a car door slam.

Rather than waste time trying to prevent Stanton driving off, she dashed towards her own car.

CHAPTER EIGHTY

Beth slammed the car down two gears and stood on the brake with all her weight. Beside her O'Dowd was using one hand to hold her phone to her ear and the other to brace herself as Beth threw the car into the corner.

Stanton's BMW was far more powerful than Beth's little VW, but on these narrow country roads, its rear-wheel drive was proving a liability on the corners as its tyres struggled for traction under Stanton's liberal use of its immense power.

It was all Beth could do to keep up with the car ahead, but that was all she had to do. O'Dowd was directing reinforcements to their location, and Stanton would soon find himself hemmed in.

Beth rounded the corner and exited onto a long straight. Ahead of her she could see Stanton's car bouncing along the uneven road. The corner was strewn with tiny stones where rainwater had crossed from a natural gully at one side to one on the other.

She controlled the understeer and buried her foot to the floor at the earliest moment.

Stanton's car disappeared round a blind corner.

Beth's entire focus was on driving. Her thoughts were staccato instructions of what she was doing and what she needed to do.

Change up a gear. Bury her right foot again.

Dodge the pothole.

Scan the hedgerows looking for emerging animals or farm machinery.

Up another gear. Stand on the throttle.

Blind corner approaching. O'Dowd barking requests into her phone for support.

Down two gears.

Brake pedal kicking back. Thank God for ABS. Swing the wheel right, crest the corner as fast as the car can maintain traction.

Disaster. A huge pothole on the inside of the corner. Deep. A wheel wrecker.

No time to stop. Go round or smash a wheel.

Tease the steering wheel left a little. Put two wheels on the grass and aim to miss the edge of the pothole by as little as possible.

Don't look at where the outside of the corner falls away down to the bottom of a wooded glade.

Success. Eyes ahead again. Feed in the power again.

Assess everything .

See the inevitable crash before it happens.

Stand on the brakes and aim for the gap that's too small.

Stanton's BMW was straddling the road. Its front end all smashed in from its collision with a stone wall. As she tried to steer round the back of the stationary car, Beth realised there wasn't enough room. That her little car would tumble down the glade until stopped by a tree.

She did the only thing she could do and aimed for the back of Stanton's car. It was the lightest part of the car and therefore would be the softest part to hit.

Even as she braced herself for the impact, she noticed the BMW's front wheel was smashed. Most likely from a hard impact with the cavernous pothole.

The two cars collided with a thudding crump.

It wasn't a straight head-on collision for the VW. More a glancing blow. The BMW slowed them but the VW was rebounded away in the direction of the slope.

The roadside grass offered no traction to her brakes.

Beth tried to steer a path back onto the road.

Failed.

The car was almost stopped when its front wheel crossed the edge of the slope.

'Shiiiit.' O'Dowd's screamed curse was one Beth agreed with.

For a moment it balanced on two diagonal wheels until the weight of the engine pulled the car off balance.

As the little VW went into its first roll, Beth realised that instead of trying to fight the inevitable, she should have turned the car so it was facing down the slope after colliding with Stanton's BMW.

CHAPTER EIGHTY-ONE

When Beth came to, she found the inside of the car was filled with the talcum powder used to pack airbags. She had to bat down the airbag from the centre of the steering wheel. The next thing she saw was Stanton looming over the windscreen. He had something in his hand and was swinging it downwards. A determined, desperate look on his face.

Something was off about the scene. It took a moment, but Beth realised the car was on its side. Down and to her left, O'Dowd was moaning.

The already broken windscreen caved under Stanton's onslaught.

Beth fumbled into her pocket for something she could use to defend herself against Stanton.

Trussed by the seatbelt and hanging sideways, it was a struggle for her to even get her hands into her pockets let alone mount any kind of defence. The lower part of her right arm was a ball of agony and she presumed she'd either broken or sprained it during the crash.

She moved her feet to assess the condition of her legs. While they protested the movement, the pains she felt were minor compared to her right arm.

As her left hand felt for the pepper spray Beth realised she'd not yet replaced the one she'd emptied into Cooper's face.

Stanton's fingers grasped the edge of the now-shattered windscreen and hauled it from its rubber mounting. 'Quick.' He thrust a hand inside. 'I can smell petrol, you have to get out.'

As soon as he mentioned the petrol, it was all Beth could smell.

The urge to thrash her way free was overwhelming, but Beth knew that she'd fall on top of O'Dowd as soon as she released the seatbelt.

She reached a hand downwards and craned her neck over so she could guide her hand.

O'Dowd's seatbelt sprang free with an audible snap.

The DI gave a series of grumbled curses as Stanton helped her climb through the windscreen.

As soon as O'Dowd was clear, Beth got herself ready for the impact when she released her own seatbelt.

With her right hand out of action and her left needed to unclip the seatbelt, there was no way she could prevent herself falling across the car and slamming into the door. Sure she could brace her legs to try and slow her descent, but that would only have limited effect.

There was one last thing to do before she reached for the seatbelt clasp. Using her left hand to give her right arm extra support, she tucked her right arm below the seatbelt so it wouldn't snag when she fell.

By the time her fingers found the clasp, she was bathed in sweat from the effort, the agony in her arm and the fear that the car would explode into a fireball at any moment.

Beth pressed the catch and tucked her head into her shoulder as she felt gravity pull her downwards.

There was a thump to her head and her vision blurred, but she didn't pass out this time.

Stanton was back at the windscreen. 'Come on. Quick.' His hands reached through the opening and grasped her right arm.

Beth screamed. She hadn't experienced pain like that since the bottle was plunged into her cheek.

'Sorry. Quick, give me your other arm.'

With Stanton's help, Beth managed to clamber free. Her legs were unsteady as he led her over to where he'd left O'Dowd.

The DI was sitting in an untidy heap with blood pouring from a cut on her head. 'What happened?'

'We crashed.' Beth let Stanton lower her to the ground then looked up at him. 'Why did you come back for us?'

Stanton's head shook as sadness overcame his face. 'Too many people have died because of me. I couldn't let there be any more deaths.'

Beth levered her way to her feet. Reached for her handcuffs. 'You know I'm going to have to arrest you, don't you?' When Stanton didn't answer, she pressed on. 'Howard Stanton, I'm arresting—'

'No, you're not.'

Stanton trotted away from Beth, his course leading him back towards the little VW.

Beth lurched after him, but her myriad injuries meant she couldn't begin to match his pace.

Rather that skirt the VW, as she'd expected him to, he climbed inside and sat on the window of the passenger door.

'Stay back.' He lifted his right hand while fishing in his shirt pocket with his left.

Beth kept going until she saw what was in his left hand.

'No. Howard, listen to me. Don't do it. There's always another way.'

The faint wail of an approaching siren sounded in the distance.

Stanton's head shook as he retrieved a cigarette from the packet and put it to his lips.

'I'm going to see Karen, Detective.' A wistful look filled his face. 'Please, walk away now. I'm going to light this cigarette at the count of three and I don't want you hurt.'

'No! Don't do it. Yes, you'll go to jail for what you've done, but that's got to be better than dying.' Despite her words and the horror of what Stanton was about to do, Beth started walking backwards away from her car.

Stanton lifted the lighter so it was in front of his face. 'One.'

Beth could do nothing but watch, powerless to help. A part of her was saying that having saved her, there was little chance that Stanton would blow himself up when she would get caught by the blast. However, his whole demeanour had changed once he'd got her and O'Dowd free. He'd morphed from being a desperate rescuer into a fatalist.

'Two.' Stanton's thumb rested on the lighter's wheel.

The approaching sirens were getting louder.

A smile appeared on Stanton's face. 'Just you wait there, Karen. I'm coming to join you. Three.'

The lighter sparked and a fireball engulfed Beth's little VW.

Beth felt a whoosh of warm air and heard Stanton's agonised screams as he burned.

Blue lights strobed across the leaves of the trees as Beth sank down and put her good arm around her DI.

The gesture wasn't to give comfort. It was to receive it.

CHAPTER EIGHTY-TWO

Beth lay down her fork then took a sip of her fresh orange juice. Today had been a trying one and if she had a glass of wine she'd only want to drink the whole bottle. Across the table, Ethan smiled at her and she returned the smile. Being around him felt natural to Beth and while she didn't want to make plans for the future, she was comfortable with the way the relationship was developing.

Her day had started out by attending Derek Forster's funeral and had progressed through a meeting with Mannequin and a pile of paperwork. To add a further level of sorrow to the day, O'Dowd had informed her and Unthank that Julie Thompson had died peacefully in her sleep.

As tragic as her death was, Thompson would be able to get a level of finality from it.

The case against Stanton had been made with ease. A letter had been tucked into the pouch with his ferry tickets and it had laid everything out for them.

Now the whole sorry affair was over she felt nothing but sadness for all the victims and their families. The victims' families would get some closure, but Stanton's family had still lost a loved one, even if he'd been driven to murder.

She'd never forget Stanton's final letter. It was haunting in its honesty as he bared his soul and admitted his guilt. His handwriting grew erratic as he neared the end and there were splotches on the paper which Beth attributed to teardrops.

To whom it may concern,

I do not blame my wife. I never have. I never will. She was taken in by the seducer Derek Forster. If she'd told me that she'd chosen to sleep with him, I could have found a way to have forgiven her. Could have found a way to get past the hurt and the betrayal.

She didn't choose though. He chose for her. I don't believe she was seduced. I believe she was raped. That Derek Forster forced himself on my sweet, gentle Karen against her will.

After what had happened with Harriet, my Karen took her own life rather than hurt me by telling me what he did. That was the cruellest hurt of all. She hid her diary at the back of a drawer. She must have known I'd find it one day.

It was almost a year after her death that I found her diary. I'd thought I was coming to terms with her death. Reading Karen's diary broke my heart, and if I'm honest with myself, my brain. All I could think of was getting even with the rapist whose seductions had destroyed my wife; my life.

I believed he was responsible for Harriet's death until my sister called this morning and told me that the Lakeland Ripper had confessed to raping and murdering Harriet.

I wanted Derek Forster to suffer for his actions.

I sent the letter to the chief constable warning that the mayor had killed and raped. I admit that I was the one who planted child pornography on his PC. It shames me to admit to this, but I was the one who killed Felicia Evans and planted evidence with the intention of framing Derek Forster. At the time I killed her, I told myself she was dying and I was easing her suffering. I was a fool. Last night I set Derek Forster's house on fire. I checked the news. He died in the fire. It was then that I realised what a monster I had become.

I am far worse than Derek Forster. His seduction or rape of my Karen, whichever is the truth, was unforgivable. But I killed the mayor and Felicia Evans through a desire to seek a primal revenge. That is even worse.

I knew what I had to do, so I booked a ticket on the earliest ferry I could, and got ready to reunite myself with Karen. They say that drowning is an easy way to go. I will know in a few minutes. Wait for me my beautiful darling. I will be with you soon.

To the world, I am sorry. I have done things that were unforgivable and rather than cost the state a fortune to try, and then imprison me, I am going to be with my wife.

The first time she read the letter, Beth had been unable to think of anything but Stanton's last moments. He'd more than likely saved her and O'Dowd's lives. Then rather than face imprisonment, he'd gone back to his original plan and had chosen to take his own life.

Instead of the peaceful drowning he'd planned, Stanton had died screaming in agony. It was a terrible death and, along with the sleepless nights Beth had had about the fire at Forster's house, she'd also had nightmares about what happened on that slope.

Despite all this, she knew she had to push those events from her mind and concentrate on the future.

Ethan took a glug of his beer and leaned out of the way as the waitress removed their empty plates. He rested his hands on his stomach and gave Beth another one of his heart-melting smiles.

The chefs at the Drover's Rest would never win any culinary prizes, but they were very good at traditional pub grub. Beth's lasagne had been excellent, and the way Ethan had wolfed down his mixed grill spoke of the quality of the cooking.

Beth had been pleased when Ethan had suggested they dine here again. If he hadn't, she would have.

As nice as the meal was, she knew she'd never bring Ethan back here though. Neck Kisses had just walked in and had ordered, 'the usual'.

Now Beth had confirmation her one-time attacker was a regular, she'd be back. Alone and prepared to give off the impression she was single. She'd be friendly with Neck Kisses, have a joke or two and then, when she knew more about him, she'd cash in on the justice that was due to her.

A LETTER FROM GRAHAM

Thank you so much for choosing to join Beth and me for her second outing. I do hope that you enjoyed the story and that you'll want to keep yourself up-to-date with all my latest releases. If you do there's a link below and don't worry, your email address will never be shared and you can unsubscribe at any time.

www.bookouture.com/graham-smith/

As for *A Body in the Lakes*, I feel it was a really interesting story to write as it gave me the chance to explore the idea of someone being framed for a crime they didn't commit, while also having Beth investigate some cold cases. Both these threads were of course intertwined and, again, I got to take us all on a journey around the beautiful place that is Cumbria and the Lake District.

One of the things I love most about writing Beth is that she's pretty much at the start of her police career and has now just embarked on a relationship with Ethan. This gives me so much scope to put her under the microscope so we can all see just what makes her tick. And that's before we even mention that after years of looking for him, she's finally found the man she called 'Neck Kisses'.

I'm not going to give you any spoilers, but I will say, I have some really great ideas about where that storyline is going and I'm looking forward to sharing it with you all in the next DC Beth Young novel.

If you've loved *A Body in the Lakes* and are kind enough to leave a review, I'd be delighted to read it.

I love to hear from my readers and you can get in touch via my Facebook page, through Twitter, Goodreads or my website. We've even got some handy links below.

Thanks,
Graham

grahamnsmithauthor

@grahamsmith1972

www.grahamsmithauthor.com

ACKNOWLEDGEMENTS

As always, there are a whole host of people who deserve thanks. Those family members and friends who are closest to me deserve the first mention as without their support and encouragement I would never have had the confidence to pursue my writing ambitions.

Second of all I'd like to extend a massive thanks to the team at Bookouture. My editor, Isobel Akenhead, improves my writing with every comment, suggestion or critique. The publicity team of Noelle Holten and Kim Nash create a publicity storm for me at every stage with cover reveals and NetGalley releases, and their amazing work on blog tours and blitzes is unparalleled. As for the others, well they just begin at awesome and get better and better.

I'm fortunate to have a fantastic network of fellow authors, from established stars to those with a head full of aspirations and a blank page. Each of them has encouraged, cajoled and supported me and all deserve my grateful thanks.

Special thanks go to Nigel Adams for his advice on all things fire related, Col Bury for the late-night chats thrashing out plot ideas and all the others who've been peppered with questions by an author looking for authenticity.

The blogging community is filled with superstars who support me with blog tours, articles, features and great friendship. Every one of them is valued far beyond their knowledge or my ability to put into words.

Finally, the largest and best group of all is you, dear reader, knowing that people are reading my books and hopefully enjoying them is what makes it all worthwhile for me; after all, without readers, I'm nothing more than a stenographer for the voices in my head.

Thank you all.

Printed in Great Britain
by Amazon